Anne Baker

NANCY'S WAR

headline

First published in 2010
by HEADLINE PUBLISHING GROUP

First published in paperback in 2011
by HEADLINE PUBLISHING GROUP

1

Cataloguing in Publication Data is available from the British Library

ISBN 978 0 7553 5667 6

Typeset in Baskerville by Avon DataSet Ltd,
Bidford on Avon, Warwickshire

Printed in the UK by Clays Ltd, St Ives plc

Headline's policy is to use papers that are natural, renewable and
recyclable products and made from wood grown in sustainable forests.
The logging and manufacturing processes are expected to conform
to the environmental regulations of the country of origin.

HEADLINE PUBLISHING GROUP
An Hachette UK Company
338 Euston Road
London NW1 3BH

www.headline.co.uk
www.hachette.co.uk

NANCY'S WAR

BOOK ONE

Book One

CHAPTER ONE

April 1939

As she sauntered down the lane to Hawthorn Cottage, Nancy Seymour's head was full of service wives' chatter. She'd just had lunch with her friends Helen and Jean at the Copper Kettle, enjoyed a laugh with them and made plans for a big get-together in the mess on Saturday night. They'd admired her cream sleeveless dress and her new shorter hairstyle. Charlie, her husband, was trying to persuade her to have her fairish curls brightened to golden blonde, but she felt she was an ordinary wife and mother and not cut out to be a glamour girl.

Nancy stopped and looked up. The sky was azure blue and empty. Usually, on a clear day like this, it buzzed with small yellow Tiger Moths and Masters on training flights from the flying school up at the airfield, and she wondered why they were absent today.

Moving on, she turned the corner in the lane and saw

the dark green MG Midget parked outside her gate. With a little smile, she quickened her step. She hadn't expected Charlie to come home until this evening. But why was he sitting in the driving seat instead of going inside?

It wasn't Charlie. A taller, slimmer figure in RAF uniform got out and turned towards her, and she recognised Charlie's friend Gavin Freeman. She knew him well, having seen a lot of him over the last year or so, but today his usual roguish smile was missing.

'Hello, Gavin. What brings you here in the middle of the afternoon?' She noticed how sombre and withdrawn he looked, his face unnaturally grey against his dark hair.

'Can we go inside?' He took the key from her hand and opened the front door, then led the way to her living room. This wasn't like Gavin. Normally he'd have stood back and let her go ahead of him. Something about him was making her shiver with foreboding.

'Is something the matter? Where's Charlie?'

'You'd better sit down, Nancy.' He led her to the sofa.

'Has he had an accident?' It wouldn't be the first time, but so far Charlie had walked away virtually unhurt. Always at the back of her mind was the possibility that he could have a major crash, but he was an excellent pilot, experienced enough to teach others to fly, and usually she managed to suppress the fear.

'Yes, I'm afraid he has.'

'What? An accident? Is he badly hurt?'

4

'I'm sorry.' Gavin looked devastated. She could see now that he was still in shock.

'Come on, Gavin, tell me. What's happened?' Gavin was shaking his head, distraught dark eyes looking into hers. 'Is he all right?'

'I'm sorry, Nancy, I wish I could make this easier for you. He didn't survive the crash.'

'No!' She was stunned and collapsed on to the sofa. 'No, surely not Charlie!' She covered her face with her hands. 'No!'

She felt the springs give as Gavin sat beside her. Felt his arm go round her shoulders and knew he was trying to comfort her, but nothing could. Not if Charlie was . . . She jerked to her feet again.

He groaned. 'It's an awful thing to have to tell you. I'm so sorry. I'll miss him desperately too.'

She shivered, a numbness creeping over her. She felt half dead. Without Charlie, she would be.

Gavin's voice went on, low and full of sympathy. 'There's something else I have to tell you.'

Nancy choked on a sob. She could guess what that meant. 'Surely Charlie wasn't fooling about? Not again?'

'I'm afraid he was. You know what Charlie's like.'

Yes, she knew. For him, life had always been a bubble of fun and thrills. Enjoyment was what he sought. According to Nancy's father, Charlie had been spoiled rotten by his parents. They'd given him everything he wanted and allowed him to do pretty much what he pleased. He'd grown up feeling he had that right, but the Royal Air Force didn't share his view and he had been told off about it repeatedly.

He'd lived for flying. He'd loved every minute he spent in the air. He'd even loved the small training biplanes with open cockpits, saying they were more fun than the spanking new Spitfires.

He loved to loop the loop and fly upside down and hedgehop within yards of the ground. Nothing scared him; recently he'd flown under the Clifton suspension bridge and Tower Bridge on the Thames and reckoned he could manage lower obstacles than that. The wing commander had heard him saying in the mess that he'd like to try the Severn railway bridge.

Charlie had told Nancy that the wingco had marched him straight to his office and told him he should have joined a flying circus. He was irresponsible, misusing valuable government equipment and unnecessarily endangering his own life and that of others. He'd told Charlie he could expect to be court-martialled if he did anything like that again.

Gavin was trying to explain what had happened. 'We were hanging about. Neither his pupil nor mine had turned up when they were supposed to. Charlie suggested we go up without them, for a warm-up and a bit of fun.'

'Gavin! You too?'

He nodded ruefully. 'We were trying to outdo each other. Showing off, I suppose; belly rolls, that sort of thing. Charlie would do something and then I'd copy him. We were enjoying ourselves, but Charlie was way too low. He let his wingtip brush against a power cable. He had no time to pull out of the spin.'

Nancy felt the tears rush to her eyes. 'You shouldn't have let him fool around like that.'

'I know.' His voice was thick with guilt. Gavin was two years older than Charlie, more responsible and more serious; she'd always thought he had a restraining influence on her husband. 'I suppose the truth is, Nancy, that as always we egged each other on. But would I have been able to persuade him not to do it?'

'No.' How many times had she told Charlie that flying like that was dangerous? How many times had he told her he could handle it?

She turned to Gavin and buried her face on his shoulder. His arms tightened round her in a hug.

'I feel so guilty,' he said. 'We none of us could say no to Charlie. What was worse, our trainee pilots were late because they'd been caught up in a traffic accident and had taken two elderly ladies to hospital.'

Nancy swallowed hard. 'No point in blaming yourself, Gavin. It was an accident, I just wish . . .'

'. . . that it hadn't happened like that,' Gavin said with feeling.

She felt a searing loss. 'How am I going to manage without him?' He'd been everything to her these last eight years.

He sighed. 'There's more to tell you. It seems everybody on the airfield was watching us, including the wing commander. He was furious. Said Charlie had been asking for it for years and that we were playing about like irresponsible schoolboys. He's told me I can expect to be court-martialled.'

'Oh, no!' Nancy could see herself in the mirror over the fireplace. She looked a parody of the girl who had set out this morning to meet Helen and Jean. Her eyes were red and her cheeks white and tear-stained. 'But at least you're still alive.'

He said angrily, 'Why did it have to be Charlie who bought it, a married man with responsibilities? If it had been me, there'd have been nobody to worry about it.'

Nancy could see he was very upset too. 'That isn't true, Gavin.'

Gavin's wife Colleen had died of TB fifteen months before after a long drawn out illness. That was why Charlie had brought him home so often. He'd not wanted his friend to be left on his own too much.

Gavin said, 'What am I thinking of? I should be making you some tea.' He went to the kitchen and began to fill the kettle.

Nancy leaned against the doorframe watching him. 'The caddy's on the shelf there.'

'Nancy, you need to let your family know. Your mother . . .'

'I have no mother,' she reminded him. 'She died having me.'

'Yes, I'd forgotten. I'm sorry.'

'I'll ring my father later.' When she was more in control. They had a phone in the cottage, put in so there'd be no delay in contacting Charlie when he was needed.

'Do you want me to tell Charlie's family, or will you? We should let them know as soon as possible.' Gavin was spooning sugar into both teacups.

'I don't take that.'

'Today you do. It's good for shock. It'll make you feel better. About Charlie's mother . . .'

'I'll ring his father at the factory, then he can break it to her.'

'Yes, probably better that way.'

Gavin knew Nancy didn't get on with her mother-in-law. Charlie hadn't got on with her either; he'd said that was the main reason he'd left home at the first possible opportunity, but this was no time for bearing grudges.

'You need somebody with you, Nancy, and I can't stay. I'm on duty. Shall I ask your friend Helen to come down?'

She shook her head. 'No, I'd rather be on my own. I'll have to tell Caro. She'll be coming out of school soon and I usually walk up to meet her.'

'Poor kid, she's going to miss Charlie too.' His sigh was heavy. 'Everything's looking bleak at the moment, isn't it?

Few doubt that war is on the way – everyone thinks that appeasement's dead in the water.'

'Charlie said he was preparing for it. Now he's gone.'

'He'd want me to help you with this. Is there anything else I can do?'

'You could give me a lift up to Caro's school. It's getting late for me to walk up.'

'Of course. Anyway, the MG will belong to you now, won't it?'

'I suppose so, but I can't drive.'

'Come on, let's go and fetch her.'

As Gavin drew up at the school gates, the children were streaming out into the yard. Caroline had recognised the car and was running towards them waving her school panama and several sheets of drawing paper. She was a sturdily built child of seven years with a mop of bouncing curls, much tighter than Nancy's own and of the shade Charlie had admired, a brighter, lighter blonde. Nancy opened the passenger door and the child flopped in to sit on her knee.

'Hello, Mummy.' She smiled at Gavin. 'I thought you were Daddy. Look, I've drawn pictures of both of you up in your aeroplanes.'

Nancy hugged her daughter. 'They're lovely pictures.'

'This plane is Daddy's and this one is yours, Uncle Gav. They're good drawings, aren't they?'

Nancy was fighting to control her tears.

'Very good,' Gavin choked. 'I'd like to keep that one, if I may.'

'Of course. I'll give it to you. You must put it up on the wall in your room.' She turned to Nancy. 'Where's Daddy? Is he on duty?'

Nancy's arms tightened round the small firm body. 'I'll tell you about Daddy when we get home.' She was struggling with her tears again, but at least she still had a little bit of Charlie left in his daughter.

'About his car . . .' Gavin said in a low voice as they got out at the gate of the cottage. Caro was already skipping down to the door.

Nancy shook her head. 'I can't think about it now. You carry on using it, Gavin. You've more or less shared it.'

'Are you sure?'

'Of course.'

'Thank you. For the time being then. Will you be all right? I hate leaving you like this.'

'I need to be alone with Caro, to tell her.'

'Yes, of course. You know where I am if there's anything I can do for you.'

For Nancy, telling Caro about her father's accident was one of the hardest things she'd ever done. She watched the light go out of their daughter's face and wept with her.

'Does that mean Daddy's gone to heaven?'

'Yes, love.'

'He won't be coming back?'

'I'm afraid not.'

'He didn't say goodbye.' The child gave an almighty sigh. 'Why has he left us?'

'He didn't want to. He'd rather be here with you and me, but he had this crash in his aeroplane. He had no choice.'

Caro was quiet for a long time trying to take that on board, then she said slowly, 'Mummy, you might have an accident too. If you did, who would look after me?'

'Nothing like that will happen to me.'

'Daddy didn't think it would happen to him either.'

'No, but I don't spend every day flying round the sky in an aeroplane. I'll always be here to look after you.'

Innocent blue eyes gazed into hers. Caro looked worried. 'But if something horrible did happen to you, like being hit by a car, and you were hurt so much you had to go to heaven too, I'd be left all by myself, wouldn't I?'

'No,' Nancy said firmly. 'There's Grandpops, isn't there? He took care of me when I was small.'

He'd been both father and mother to her and she'd always felt close to him. She wanted to hear his voice and have the comfort of his concern now. 'I must ring him and let him know what's happened.'

He was in Birkenhead, where his name, Miles Milton, appeared over the door of the Lord Nelson public house as licensee. The phone rang and rang but nobody picked it up. Dad lived in the flat above the pub, but his only phone was behind the bar which would be closed now in the middle of the afternoon.

'Grandpops isn't there?' Caro's eyes were filling with tears again. 'He must have gone out.'

'It isn't easy to hear the phone ring from upstairs, love.' Nancy thought it more likely that her father had dozed off. This was his rest time and he hadn't been well recently. She asked the operator to try the number again but he still didn't answer.

Caro looked worried. 'Grandpops isn't so sick that he'll have to go to heaven soon, is he?'

'No, of course not,' Nancy said, without conviction. She'd been pleading with him for some time to see his doctor about his shortness of breath.

'Grandma and Grandpa would look after me if you weren't here, wouldn't they? And Uncle Toby too?'

'Of course. They'd all want to take care of you. Particularly Grandma.' Nancy sighed. She'd never found Charlie's mother easy to get on with.

'Yes. Grandma always gives me presents when I see her.'

'So do Grandpa and Uncle Toby.'

It was some time before Nancy felt able to do anything about telling Charlie's family, but when she saw it was nearly five o'clock she realised she should ring his father straight away if she wanted to catch him before he left his sausage factory.

When she was put through to him there was a hearty welcome in his voice. 'Nancy, to what do I owe the pleasure?'

'It's no pleasure,' she said, forcing the words out, and told him.

There was a moment's silence, then Jago Seymour flashed out in anger, 'The silly fool! Just when I thought he was growing up at last.' But she could hear the anguish in his voice. 'It's the sort of prank a sixteen year old would get up to. And to lose his life like that!'

Charlie had been closer to his father and his Uncle Toby, Jago's twin brother, than he had been to his mother.

'I don't know what to say, Nancy. You must be feeling terrible. Devastated. I know Henrietta will be.'

When Nancy had answered all his questions about the accident, her father-in-law went on to ask about the funeral and about her plans for the future. Nancy couldn't tell him anything on either score. She put the phone down and busied herself getting tea ready for Caro. The last thing she wanted was food, but routine was everything at a time like this and a child has to be fed.

She had to force herself to swallow the fried fish as a good example to her daughter. Then, telling herself she felt better, she went back to the phone to ring her father. He would be downstairs, ready to open up at six o'clock, and she wanted to catch him before the bar filled up with customers. He'd been fond of Charlie. The news would upset him too.

'Oh, my goodness! Oh, Nancy, how awful for you! Poor Charlie! Well, poor you and Caro really. Look, I'll ask Alma to stand in for me tonight and come straight over.'

'No, Dad.'

'I can help you. You'll have a lot to do, a lot to sort out.'

'Yes, but I can't think straight now. I can't do another thing. Why don't you come tomorrow morning? I'm shattered, Dad. This has knocked the stuffing out of me. I'll see Caro into bed and crawl into my own straight afterwards.'

'Yes, perhaps that would be best.'

'I only hope my head will be clearer tomorrow.'

'It will be, love, if you can get a good night's sleep. I'll come round in the morning, then.'

But before Nancy could get to bed the wing commander in charge of the airfield arrived to offer his condolences. He'd put his anger behind him and spoke kindly of Charlie.

'I understand you know the circumstances of your husband's accident, Mrs Seymour?'

She nodded, fearful of what was coming.

'Nevertheless, the squadron will want to provide a military funeral.'

'Thank you.'

15

'We are all shocked and upset at his untimely death. Flying Officer Seymour was well liked,' he told her. 'The padre can arrange the funeral if that is your wish.'

'Thank you.' Nancy had been wondering how to go about it.

'I'll get him to come and talk to you tomorrow.'

Chapter Two

M ILES MILTON HAD not been able to sleep. He'd tossed and turned for hours after Nancy had told him of Charlie's death.

He feared his daughter's life was mirroring his own. He'd lost a much loved wife unexpectedly in childbirth and had never found anybody to take her place. He'd been full of guilt, knowing she wouldn't have died if he hadn't made her pregnant, and the awareness had made him determined to do his best for her child. He and Nancy had always been very close. Even after her marriage to Charlie, she'd come home often, bringing her husband and daughter. He'd taken all his holidays with them and had truly felt he'd gained a son rather than losing a daughter.

When he'd begun to feel unwell a year or two ago, he'd been very glad she was at Hawarden on the border of Cheshire, with North Wales not very far away. His doctor thought the problem was a touch of bronchitis and had given him a tonic. Miles hadn't thought it was serious and hadn't told Nancy.

But he had told Alma Banks, a longtime friend who'd been his second in command for the last four years and had noticed he had a nasty cough and less strength and energy than before. She'd nagged at him until he'd gone back to the doctor and been given another bottle of tonic.

Last night, he'd arranged with her to look after the pub on her own today. He was up and dressed very early, eager to drive to Hawarden to offer what comfort he could. He arrived before he was expected. Nancy had to get out of bed to let him in, and after much hugging Caro was sent back upstairs to get dressed. It made him feel he was being more of a trouble than a comfort.

Nancy was drifting aimlessly round in an old pink dressing gown which made her cheeks look putty-coloured. Miles had always thought her a good-looking girl, but today she looked red-eyed and listless. He felt a rush of sympathy and gave her another hug.

She also looked vulnerable, and younger than her age. Having been the indulged wife of a free-spending officer, she was now alone in the world apart from him, with a child to bring up.

'I want you to come back and live with me,' he told her. 'You don't want to stay here on your own, do you?' She looked at him blankly, as though she hadn't thought about what she'd do next. 'I gave it a lot of thought last night. There's plenty of space on the top floor of the pub; you can make a little flat up there for yourself and Caro. You'd be near me but still have a home you could call your own.'

'Thanks, Dad,' she said, but she looked dazed and he doubted she was taking in what he said.

'What about breakfast? You must eat, and so must Caro.'

'Yes, eggs. Boiled eggs and soldiers.' But as Nancy continued to stare out of the window and made no effort to cook, Miles set about it.

'You'll be sending her to school this morning?'

That got her attention. 'Should I?'

'I think so. It'll be more upsetting for her to see you like this, and she won't understand about all the changes that are coming. Better if you try to keep her life as normal as possible.'

Caro came downstairs in her school uniform a few moments later. She was unusually quiet and subdued, although at seven she probably couldn't appreciate the terrible finality of death. She was a very pretty child. Miles felt a frisson of pride that she'd inherited the Milton curly hair and fair colouring. Playfully, he pulled a strand and straightened it out, then let it spring back.

He let her time the eggs, but both she and Nancy toyed with their food. Mostly Caro walked to school, but the time was drifting on and eventually Miles ran her there in his car.

When he got back Nancy was still sipping her tea. 'What am I going to do?' she asked. 'I can't manage without Charlie.'

Miles knew a lifetime without a spouse was no fun. 'You've been my mainstay and prop since your mother died,' he said. 'Now I want to be the same for you.'

The trouble was he didn't know where to begin.

'You want me to give up this cottage and move back in with you?' Nancy asked. She'd had a bath and got dressed. She looked better, more alert.

'It makes sense, doesn't it? Would it be difficult to give up the tenancy?'

'No, a month's notice.'

'You don't want to stay on here, do you? Just you and Caro?'

'There's her school. She likes it there.'

'It's you I'm thinking about.'

'Dad, I don't really know what I want.'

'I know, love, but I think you'd be better off with me, at least in the short term. You'll need time to come to terms with what's happened and think through how best to deal with it. Anyway, I'd like to have you back with me.'

Through the window, Miles saw a young man in RAF uniform striding down the path holding a large bunch of flowers. 'You have a visitor,' he said.

'It's Gavin Freeman, Charlie's friend.' Nancy went to

open the front door. As they stood talking in the hall, Miles couldn't help but hear every word.

'Hello, Nancy,' the newcomer said. 'I hope I'm not intruding? I see from the car outside that you have someone with you.'

'Yes. My father's here.'

'We had a whip-round in the mess and I bought you some flowers. They're from all of us.'

'Thank you. They're lovely. Come in for a moment.'

'Are you sure?'

'Yes.' Nancy brought Gavin into the sitting room. 'You've met Dad, haven't you?'

'I have. How are you, Mr Milton? A terrible thing to happen to Charlie. It's knocked us all sideways. Especially with all the other trouble as well.'

'What trouble?' Nancy asked.

'You know, I told you. Charlie and I were fooling round when it happened. Doing belly rolls, sky diving, that sort of thing.'

Miles stiffened. Would this be a further problem for Nancy? 'Are they saying it's not a genuine accident?'

'I'm afraid they are,' Gavin said. 'I'm to be court-martialled, charged with irresponsible behaviour leading to loss of life and damage to air ministry property.'

'Oh, dear! So he's got you into trouble too?'

'Well, Mr Milton, we all have to be accountable for what we do.'

Miles couldn't help but admire Gavin's stiff upper lip.

21

He had liked Charlie's friendly manner and knew he'd been a good husband to Nancy, a good father to Caro too, but he admitted to himself now that his son-in-law had been a bit too fond of enjoying himself and having fun.

Moments after Gavin had driven away, the padre arrived to talk about Charlie's funeral.

'It can be arranged in any way you like,' he said. Miles could see that his daughter was at a loss. 'The whole point of the funeral,' the padre explained gently, 'is to honour the achievements of the deceased, and to give those who loved him the opportunity to reflect on all he gave them. To give thanks for his life and to say goodbye. Flying Officer Seymour was a very popular man. He will be given full military honours, of course. I've had offers from his friends to read a lesson. Shall I arrange that with them? And do you want him buried in the churchyard here or do you want his body taken home?'

Nancy was covering her face with her hands. 'Here,' she decided. 'It's quiet and peaceful here and Charlie didn't have strong ties with his home.'

The padre went on to fix the date and the time and to suggest the hymns. 'I'll see to everything,' he finished, to Nancy's relief. She was on the brink of tears again as she closed the door behind him.

'All these decisions,' she said as she arranged Gavin's flowers in a vase. 'It's not like real life at all.'

'We're making progress,' her father comforted her.

*

They'd started to box up some of Nancy's belongings ready for the move when a chauffeur-driven car drew up at the gate. Moments later Henrietta Carrington Seymour was rapping imperiously on the front door.

'Oh, dear,' Nancy said. 'I don't feel strong enough to deal with Lady Henrietta this morning.'

'You'll be fine,' Miles whispered. 'Don't worry about her. She'll have come to offer comfort and she'll be upset too.'

He opened the door. 'Hello. Good morning,' he said.

Henrietta was her usual well-groomed self, though dressed from head to foot in deepest mourning. Rocking back on her heels, she looked him in the eye and demanded, 'Who are you?'

He was taken aback, but said, 'I'm Miles Milton, Nancy's father. Don't you recognise me?'

She was pushing herself in. 'I take it Caroline and Nancy are here?'

Nancy had come to the living room door. 'Hello, Mother-in-law. Come in and make yourself comfortable. Would you like a cup of tea?'

'Do you have Earl Grey?'

'No, sorry, only ordinary tea.'

'I don't care much for that.' Henrietta took off her hat and gave it to Miles. He laid it on the table in front of her while she peered in a mirror, patting and pulling at her hair. Cut in the latest fashion, it showed recent and

23

perhaps too frequent attention from her hairdresser. She threw herself down on the sofa.

'I'm quite out of my mind with grief,' she announced. 'What a terrible thing to happen to Charles. There must have been a fault with the plane's engine. I think we must make sure that is fully investigated. It's so wrong to blame the pilot.'

Nancy was staring at her. 'Charlie was playing around, having fun. You know what he was like.'

'If you had any sense, Nancy, you'd refute that. It's not only Charles's reputation at stake, you know – it could affect your future finances.'

That caught Miles's attention. He was concerned about Nancy's financial situation, half afraid she'd be left with no home and little money. The Seymour family had a more sophisticated grasp on finances than he and Nancy.

'Poor Charles. Not yet thirty-two, with all his life in front of him. You don't realise, Nancy, what it means to a mother to have her child die before she does. It goes against the natural order of things.'

Miles went to the kitchen and put the kettle on; he and Nancy were going to need tea even if she didn't. Henrietta's eyes were darting round the room like a bird's. 'Where's Caroline?'

'We sent her to school,' Miles said.

'To school! But I want to see her. I've come all this way to comfort her. Her daddy is dead, and she'll need me. She shouldn't be in school on a day like this.'

'We wanted to keep things as normal as possible for her,' Miles said. 'We thought it might upset her to hear us talking about the funeral.'

'Ah yes, the funeral. I'll arrange to have Charles's body taken to Grindley. He'd want to be buried in the family vault there.'

Miles froze. He could see panic on Nancy's face. 'Oh, dear,' he said. 'Henrietta, I'm sorry, but that's already been decided. The air force is to give Charlie a service here with full military honours.'

She was indignant. 'But I should have been consulted! I'm his mother. I've made a list of the hymns I want and I've written a eulogy which his father will read.'

'I'm sorry,' Nancy said. 'I was pleased about the military honours . . . The squadron band will play, as well. I thought you'd be pleased too.'

'Yes, well . . .'

'I'm sure if you went to see the padre now,' Miles said hurriedly, 'he'd be happy to accommodate your wishes.'

'I will. The RAF can provide its military service here, and then we'll take him home. My family have been buried in the family vault at Grindley parish church for generations and I fully intend to join them when my time is up. I want Charles to be there with us. I take it you have no objection to his being buried there?'

'No,' Nancy said faintly.

'You and your family are welcome to join us for the service, of course.'

Nancy's mouth dropped open.

Henrietta sat back in her chair and appeared to relax. 'Now, Nancy, what are your plans for the future?'

'I haven't had time to think . . . We'll be moving in with Dad for the time being.'

'Not to that public house?' Henrietta's face showed disgust. 'I don't think it's a suitable place for Caroline to be brought up. By law, children are not allowed on licensed premises, you must know that?'

'I was brought up there,' Nancy said with a calm she was far from feeling. 'There's a side door leading up to the flat above. I didn't go near the bar and Caro needn't either.'

'The idea of my granddaughter living there horrifies me. A child needs fresh air and a garden. It wouldn't do for Caroline to be brought up in poverty.' She was gasping with distress. 'No, you mustn't worry about Caroline. As her grandmother I feel I should prevent that. I'll take over all responsibility for her upbringing, give her a comfortable home and take good care of her.'

Miles could see that she had taken Nancy's breath away. His daughter's cheeks were scarlet.

'Anyway, you won't be able to bring her up on your own.'

'Why ever not?' Nancy was outraged.

'Without Charles's income, you won't have the money.'

Nancy was making a big effort to stay calm. 'No,

thank you, Mother-in-law. I intend to bring my daughter up myself.'

'Won't you need to work?'

'I'll be all right. Charlie took out a life assurance policy in case something like this happened.'

Miles's relief on hearing about the life assurance policy lasted less than a minute. By all accounts Charlie had been dicing with death. It hadn't been a straight-forward accident. Would they pay up on it? It might depend on the wording of the policy.

The kettle was boiling hard and filling the kitchen with steam. Nancy went to make a pot of tea.

In the silence that followed, Miles had time to think. He wanted to help Nancy get a clear picture of her financial situation. 'Charlie told me he drew an income from a family trust fund?' he said.

'He did.' Henrietta was frosty. 'From my family.'

'Can't that be used to support his wife and child? Surely that's what Charlie would want?'

'No,' Henrietta said firmly. 'The terms of the trust are quite clear. It was set up by my father to support our family. Charles's share reverts to the trust on his death.'

'But they are your family. Caroline is the direct blood line.'

'Yes, and when she was born I added her name to the beneficiaries of the trust. She will draw an income from it from the age of twenty-five, as the rest of us have.'

Nancy had returned with the tea. 'It has already been paying her school fees,' she pointed out.

'Yes, and it will continue to do so, and meet any other immediate needs she may have.'

Miles was angry. 'But what about Nancy?'

Henrietta's gaze swept haughtily over Nancy. 'What about her?'

Nancy was pouring out tea and looked ready to give up.

Miles took a deep breath. 'Surely the trustees of the fund would not want to cut Charlie's widow off without a penny?'

'As the main trustee, it's up to me, and I feel Nancy is young enough to make her own way in the world. She can't expect to be kept for the rest of her life because she was once married to Charles.'

Miles was furious. Nancy handed Henrietta a cup of tea, and he watched her lift it and take a sip. 'Oh!' She crashed it back on the saucer, pulling a face in disgust. 'Terrible tea. I can't drink that.' She mopped at her mouth with a white lace-edged handkerchief. 'You were brought up to earn your own living, weren't you, Nancy? As a barmaid?'

Another hot flush ran up Nancy's cheeks. 'I had a job as an accounts clerk.'

'Then you'll have no difficulty getting another one.'

Miles could see horror spreading across his daughter's face. He wasn't ready to give up yet. He told himself he must keep calm.

'Caroline's standard of living is very much tied to Nancy's,' he pointed out. 'It would make sense to allow the trust to make her a small allowance.'

'This has nothing to do with you,' Henrietta said in her lordly fashion. She got up to leave. 'I have decided otherwise.'

As the door closed behind her, Nancy dissolved in tears on her father's shoulder. 'I'll never let her take Caro from me. Never!'

CHAPTER THREE

LATER ON THAT afternoon, Nancy asked her father if he would drive her to Caro's school a few minutes before home time.

'I want to see the headmistress,' she said. 'I suppose she'll have heard about Charlie, but I need to tell her Caro will be leaving.' She consulted the calendar on the kitchen wall. 'There's three and a half more weeks to half term. That'll give me plenty of time to pack up here.'

Nancy had to steel herself to talk to the headmistress. She found it difficult to keep her tears at bay when speaking about Charlie. It was hard to take sympathy, however well meant, but she managed it. She heard the bell ring as she was getting up to leave. The corridors were suddenly full of chattering children.

Once outside, she saw her friend Helen, a raven-haired beauty, waiting to collect her four-year-old son. She'd been a fashion model in London before she was married and still did a little work when she could. She came to wrap her arms round Nancy in a comforting hug.

'I'm so sorry,' she murmured, and Nancy could see tears welling in her dark eyes. 'We're all devastated about Charlie. I walked down to tell you, but I saw you had visitors.'

'I still have,' Nancy said. 'Come tomorrow. I'll be on my own then.'

She looked up to see her father standing at the school gates with his arms open, and Caro rushing towards him. He swung her up in his arms and Nancy was comforted by the love she could see each had for the other. Nobody could take Charlie's place, but Dad would try.

She was walking quickly towards them when she saw her mother-in-law's car parked further down the road. As the chauffeur had the back door open, Henrietta descended like a queen, clutching a gift-wrapped parcel, and Nancy's heart sank. She'd hoped not to see her again today.

'Caroline,' Henrietta called.

'Grandma!' With a gurgle of pleasure, the child left her grandfather to throw herself at Henrietta.

With a pang, Nancy realised there was love on both sides there too. Charlie had encouraged it. 'Caro may need support from the wider family as she grows up,' he'd said, and at the time it had seemed reasonable. Now, Nancy was trying to choke back her resentment.

Henrietta was keeping her arm round Caro. 'Darling,' she said. 'How sad about your daddy. We're both going to miss him terribly.'

Other children were weaving between them. Nancy went closer, aware that her father was following. 'You've not gone yet, Mother-in-law?' she said.

'I couldn't go home without seeing my little grand-daughter.' She gave Caro another hug. 'How you've grown. And what lovely rosy cheeks you have. What shall we do now, my pet? Shall we go and find a tea shop? Perhaps we can get an ice cream for you.'

'Yes please, Grandma. That would be lovely.' Caro was pushing her hand into Henrietta's and dancing around with excitement.

'That's a nice idea,' Miles said brightly. 'Mummy and I will come too. I won't be able to stay much longer, and I don't suppose Grandma will either. Then Mummy can take you home.'

Henrietta billed and cooed. 'Isn't she lovely? You'll be a real beauty when you grow up, pet. Give Grandma a kiss.'

'The Copper Kettle in the high street is the best place for teas and ice cream,' Nancy said, trying to keep control of the situation. 'Do you want to follow us, Mother-in-law?'

'Yes, I suppose we'd better. Bennett doesn't know his way round here very well.' She gave Caro's hand a squeeze. 'You come and have a ride in Grandma's car, pet.'

Nancy wasn't prepared to let Henrietta separate her from Caro. 'Parking isn't that easy in the high street,' she said. 'Why don't you leave your car here and come with us? Bennett can have a rest and we can bring you back later.'

Henrietta gave Miles's Morris Eight a disdainful look. 'Will that be big enough?'

It was Caro who solved the dilemma. 'Let's all go in your car, Grandma,' she said. 'You'll like it, Grandpops. It's really nice inside, and you can stretch your feet right out.'

'Darling, I've bought you a little present.'

'Oh, thank you, Grandma, thank you. Can I open it now?'

'In a minute, love,' Miles said. 'At least wait until you're in the car.' He got into the front beside the chauffeur.

Nancy slid on to the back seat feeling she'd won that round until she saw Henrietta pull her grandchild on to her knee. Usually, Caro let people know she was too old for that, but she was concentrating on her gift, ripping the paper off. 'Books, Mummy.'

'Yes, Nancy, books on how to teach a child to draw.'

'Caro loves drawing. She's better at it than most children of her age.'

'Use the books properly and she'll be better still. They give the basic rules; one's for drawing portraits and one's for landscapes.'

Caro was already flicking through the pages of one. 'I love them, Grandma. Thank you.'

Nancy was a little disconcerted to see there was room to park a couple of buses outside the Copper Kettle. She had no appetite, and felt ill at ease as she sipped a cup of tea. She wished Henrietta would go home and leave them in peace.

That night Nancy found it a relief to get into bed and lie down in the dark, but she couldn't get to sleep. Charlie was gone. Why oh why did it have to end like this? They'd been very happy together for nearly eight years and she'd expected it to go on for the rest of her life. She couldn't manage without him. But Charlie had never been sad and would not have wanted her to be now. He'd loved life.

Her mind went back to the time she'd first seen Charlie across the bar of the Lord Nelson. It was a busy place in the centre of town with a lounge, a snug and a large public bar; close to the Argyle Music Hall, cinemas, cafés and dance halls, it was popular with young bachelors looking for a night on the town.

She worked in an office during the week, but really enjoyed serving behind the bar on Friday and Saturday nights to help her father. Few women came into the pub alone, so Nancy had received plenty of attention.

She'd thought Charlie, handsome in his RAF uniform, a sophisticated man of the world. He'd come in with a group, but once he'd set eyes on her he'd ignored the others and perched on a bar stool chatting to her whenever she could break off from serving. He told her he was twenty-four, and a pilot stationed at Hawarden on the Wirral. He was of athletic build and just a little taller than Nancy. Nobody forgot his face, with its strong, even features and a smile that seemed to hover permanently on his lips. He was full of fun.

He began coming in regularly and soon got round to asking her father if he could take her out so he could have her undivided attention. Nancy was in love well before her father started referring to him as 'your boyfriend', and she had every reason to believe Charlie loved her.

He'd been a real extrovert and when Nancy was busy he'd found others to chat to; he'd encouraged the party atmosphere and then become the life and soul of it. Her father, who was a man with high moral values and a pillar of the church, was also very sociable, and he'd taken to Charlie immediately. He said he was a laugh a minute, good company and very good for business. Nobody could be bored in his presence.

Soon Charlie was wanting more of her company. When he had a day off, he'd come in the morning and take her out for a quick snack in her lunch hour, and he'd be waiting at the office door at five o'clock when she finished. When he was given a forty-eight-hour pass, he'd book into a nearby hotel and be around all the time. It hadn't taken Dad long to suggest he might prefer to stay in their guest room.

The floor above the pub provided enough living space for the two of them, and the top floor of the three-storey building was hardly used. They stored a bit of stock there and one room was furnished for visitors. It wasn't much of a guest room and only rarely did they have anyone staying, but Nancy spring-cleaned it, bought a blue satin eiderdown and a new bedside rug to smarten it up, and after that Charlie came to stay as often as he could. He'd asked her more than once if he might come down to her bedroom after her father had gone to sleep.

'It would be marvellous, wouldn't it?' he'd whispered. 'If we could spend a few hours entirely alone and I could really show you how much I love you? I'll take good care not to get you into trouble.'

Nancy was not so daring. She knew her father would be horrified; he trusted everybody and expected them to share his high standards of behaviour. What was more, he slept in the next room to hers; she knew she'd find that inhibiting, especially as sometimes she could hear him snore. She knew it would be safer to creep upstairs to Charlie's room, but it was months before she could bring herself to do it. When she did, for Nancy there'd been no greater thrill than to lie in Charlie's arms under the blue satin eiderdown.

Six months had passed before she first began to suspect she could be pregnant. It terrified her, particularly as Charlie had been sent on a training course at a large RAF station near Lincoln and she wouldn't be able to see him for two weeks. Even worse, he'd told her he was expecting to be posted to another airfield before much longer.

He telephoned her from time to time, but the phone in the pub was within hearing of others. She asked Charlie to ring at times when the bar wouldn't be open, but in the mornings it was being cleaned and in the evenings her father could go down early to stock-check, or the new lad who helped with the cellar work might be hanging about. Nancy didn't dare hint at anything that might alert them to her problem. Dad mustn't suspect until she knew what her future would be.

When Charlie told her he'd received his posting to Cherry Hinton in Cambridgeshire she was really cast down, particularly as every day he was away was confirming her fears.

When he rang to say he was coming to Merseyside on Wednesday, and would be there in time to take her for a proper lunch if she got time off from her insurance office, Nancy asked for a day's holiday; she was worried stiff and had to find out what Charlie meant to do. What she wanted was marriage, but he'd never mentioned that. His mind was always on the next ruse, the next fun thing he could arrange for them to do.

The pub was open when he arrived. Nancy was dressed in her best ready to go out but was helping her father behind the bar because Polly, the part-time barmaid, had not yet arrived. She found Charlie's broad smile and happy chatter somewhat reassuring, but she was still quaking in her shoes about what she would do if he didn't offer marriage.

Dad sent them off, saying he could manage, and once outside they met Polly scorching up the pavement explaining she'd missed her bus. Still, Nancy was on edge, and when Charlie threaded her arm through his she was tempted to get the bad news off her chest straight away.

She made herself wait until they were in the restaurant and the drinks came to the table. Charlie raised his glass and said, 'Cheerio, here's to us and all that.'

Clutching her wine glass, Nancy blurted out, 'I think I'm having a baby, Charlie.'

His smile disappeared and he stared silently at his beer. She saw his fingers tighten round the glass. Her spirits plummeted; she felt cold and empty. She was ready to close her eyes and count everything lost. Then his hand snaked across the table and felt for her fingers.

'I didn't take enough care,' he said. 'I'm sorry, Nancy. I've put you in a hell of a spot. How d'you feel about marrying me?'

Tears of relief sprang to her eyes. 'Really?'

He squeezed her hand. 'Best thing for us, under the circs. You're sure about this baby?'

She nodded, biting her lip. 'I haven't been to the doctor but I'm pretty sure.'

He passed her a large white handkerchief with his other hand. 'Do you know when it'll be?'

'I'm nearly three months gone. Charlie, you do want us to get married, don't you?'

'Of course I do. I love you, Nancy. I've told you lots of times.'

She was flooding with gratitude, unutterably relieved that Charlie had no intention of leaving her to face motherhood alone.

'Nancy, I'm head over heels in love with you. The only reason I haven't mentioned marriage before is my present lack of funds. I wanted to put it off for a year. If I was twenty-five, I'd have another source of income and in addition I could claim marriage allowance from the RAF on top of my salary. They might also give me a house to live in. The trouble is, I'm only just twenty-four. We could be in for a hard year.'

She tried to smile. 'Money doesn't matter.'

'There are more important things now,' he agreed. 'We need a quick wedding, within the next few weeks if possible. If I can't raise some funds, it'll mean no frills, I'm afraid.'

'I don't care about the frills.' That sort of thing didn't matter to her, but she knew Charlie liked the luxuries of life and was prepared to spend on them. 'I just want . . .'

'Yes, I know.' He squeezed her hand again. 'You want a husband before you're a mother. I'm sorry it had to happen this way. I've messed things up. I should never have talked you into coming up to my bed. I'm sorry.'

'But everything's going to be all right now.'

She'd not seen Charlie as serious as this before. He said, 'If things hadn't happened this way, would you have wanted to marry me?'

'Oh, Charlie! Yes, of course. There's nothing I want more.'

'Then let's have a celebratory lunch and make our plans. The sooner everybody knows and the arrangements are in place, the better.'

'First things first,' Charlie had said as they'd left the restaurant. 'We must tell your father. You're only nineteen; you'll need his permission to get married.'

Nancy had cringed. 'I'm not looking forward to this. He'll guess I crept upstairs to you. I went behind his back.'

'It's human nature, love.'

'I feel guilty. Dad thinks I never do anything wrong.'

'Leave it to me.'

The pub had closed at half past two and her father was eating his lunch of bread and cheese in the kitchen. Miles Milton was tall, well built and without an ounce of surplus flesh on his body. He was wearing the sleeveless Fair Isle pullover Nancy had given him for his forty-seventh birthday with his shirt sleeves rolled up showing strong muscular arms, a man at the height of his physical strength. His brown hair was thinning and losing its gloss, but his eyes were bright periwinkle blue and his expression was kindly.

Charlie sat down at the table facing him, so Nancy did the same. He took her hand in his and said, 'Milo, Nancy and I want to get married and she needs your permission.'

'Married, eh?' Dad had smiled at her and gone on spreading Branston Pickle on his bread. He'd had a very relaxed attitude to bringing up a daughter and she felt her childhood had been a happy one. 'Tradition has it, Charlie, that I should ask you about your prospects and if you can afford to keep a wife.'

'Oh, dear, I'm afraid the answer to that is no. I can't afford much of anything. I'll try and do something about it, but our first year is likely to be spent in poverty. The reason we want to get married now is that I've jumped the gun.'

Nancy was gripping his hand so hard that her fingers went white while Charlie told her father every embarrassing detail.

Dad was looking from her to Charlie. 'Oh, dear! What a surprise. Well, that alters things. What are your plans?'

'To get married as soon as possible.'

'Everything costs money, Charlie. Weddings certainly do.'

'Then we'll have to do it on the cheap. You know I've

got my posting to Cherry Hinton? It would have parted
us, but now I'll be able to take Nancy with me, so in a
way I'm not sorry things have happened like this. I'll rent
somewhere for us to live.'

Her father was frowning and shaking his head. 'You're
very young, Nancy. Are you really sure you want to
marry Charlie? This is not because . . .'

'I'm sure, Dad, quite sure.'

'Then of course you have my permission.'

'Thank you, Dad.' She leapt to her feet and ran round
the table to kiss his cheek, boiling over with relief and
gratitude. She was going to have her dearest wish. 'I've
never known anyone like Charlie.'

Dad was eyeing him. 'He's a wild and reckless young
man.'

'I have been, sir,' Charlie assured him. 'But once we're
married, Nancy will calm me down. Thank you for
taking it like this. I know I've done wrong, but I love her
very much and I'll do my level best to make her happy.
I'll take good care of her.'

'Then you have my blessing.' Miles beamed from
Charlie to her. Nancy was overflowing with affection for
him.

'You've been a great dad to me,' she told him.

'Thank you,' Charlie said. 'We'd better get on with it
then.' He pulled Nancy to her feet. 'We need to fix the
place and the date. Register office or church?'

'Church,' Miles said firmly. 'St Bede's. Nancy, you

could walk round there now. If you like I'll ring the vicar and tell him you're on your way.'

'Yes please, Dad.'

'Nancy has known St Bede's and Reverend Hetherington since she was a child,' Miles explained to Charlie. 'He'll fit you in, I'm sure.'

'After that,' Charlie said, 'I must take Nancy to meet my family.'

'Is that far?' Miles asked. 'Where do they live?'

'Liverpool. Well, in the suburbs. Gateacre.'

'Gracious! I didn't know they were that close.'

'I don't get on all that well with my mother.' For once Charlie looked ill at ease.

Nancy was surprised too. Charlie had hardly mentioned his parents and she knew he didn't go home very often. To her amazement, there was actually a tremor in his voice when he said, 'Well, I'd better bite the bullet, I suppose. Can I go down and use your phone to let them know we're coming?'

CHAPTER FOUR

ONCE THE DATE of the ceremony has been organised with the vicar and they were on their way to Gateacre to see his parents, Nancy asked, 'Why don't you get on with your mother? Never having known my own, I might take to yours. A mother-in-law is the next best thing, isn't it?'

'No.' He paused, sucking on his lip. 'I doubt you'll like mine.'

'Charlie, that makes her sound awful!'

'I know. It's just that she can be difficult at times.'

'In what way?'

'She's a bit of a snob – thinks she's a cut above everybody else. She was born Henrietta Carrington, daughter of Sir Henry Carrington of Grindley Manor, a Lancashire landowner. My father's family started calling her Lady Henrietta as a joke, though they knew very well she should really have been plain Miss Carrington.

'But Mother is very ladylike; so very formal with everybody and she so obviously looked down on the

Seymours as her social inferiors that it stuck. She didn't realise Dad was poking fun at her and didn't correct him, though she's the first to correct any other social error. She liked being called Lady Henrietta and still does.'

Nancy giggled. 'I'm to call her Lady Henrietta?'

'No, not to her face. Mother feels she's come down in the world now she's Mrs Seymour of Lexington Avenue, wife of Jago Seymour who earns his living making sausages.'

'But you said he owned the sausage factory.'

'He does. Seymour's Succulent Sizzlers. Sausages at their best. Their neighbours refer to him as the Sausage King and that really annoys her.'

'But why? Doesn't it lend status to be thought a king?'

'Not of a sausage empire. That's trade and she's landed gentry. I think Mother was expected to marry up the social scale and repair the family fortune that way, but the right proposals didn't come.'

'Why not? Did she spend all her time in the depths of the country at Grindley Manor?'

'No. Her family had a place in London too when she was young and she did the season. Judging by her photographs she was pretty, and she can really shine socially when she's with those she thinks of as her social equal or higher, but I think she's always been a bit difficult. Anyway, no one asked her to marry them until Dad fell under her spell. Henrietta was thirty-three by then and she probably decided it would be her one and only chance of marriage.'

'If he owns a factory he must have been rich.'

Charlie beamed at her. 'When he first met her the family business was stockbroking. He and his twin brother, my Uncle Toby, were working in the company offices in Liverpool. Mother found that reasonably acceptable. He's nine years younger than her and possibly he didn't have much experience of women.'

Nancy smiled. 'It isn't a happy marriage? Is that what you're saying?'

'I think they both try to make the best of it.'

'Oh, dear!'

'It might have been happy to start with, of course.'

'Then what went wrong?'

Charlie shrugged. 'I think it was money.'

'Surely they weren't short of money?'

'Not in the way you mean, but they liked to live well – extravagantly. Especially Mother. I understand she gave everybody the impression she was heiress to a great fortune while the family money was dwindling. At the same time she and her family believed stockbroking was a means of minting the stuff while really Dad's firm had to work hard to attract its clients.'

Nancy pulled a face. 'She isn't going to like my dad running a pub.'

'You mustn't let her upset you. She's inclined to be outspoken and she'll have no regard for your feelings.

Mother can't see anybody's point of view but her own.'

Nancy glimpsed the name on the gatepost as Charlie turned the car into a short drive. 'The house is called Carrington Place?'

'Yes, Mum insisted on it. Carrington was her name before she was married. She likes to double-barrel it with Seymour, and she called me Carrington too. When I'm asked for my home address, I give it as number eight Lexington Avenue.'

Nancy gasped when she saw the house. It was enormous; a fashionable up-to-the-moment design with lots of big windows, which were all open to the pretty garden on this sunny day.

'I can't imagine why you preferred to stay in our spare room,' she said.

'Yes you can. I wanted to be with you.'

'But before that, you stayed in a hotel instead of coming here.'

'Yes, and you'll see why in a moment. I spoke to Dad when I rang, and he said he'd wait to meet you. Uncle Toby is with them today, so you'll see all the family.'

A uniformed parlourmaid who looked well past retirement age opened the door to them. A starched and pleated cap was pulled down on her forehead and hid most of her grey hair, but she was all smiles when she saw Charlie.

'Gertie, how are you?' He bounded inside and whirled her round, kissing her cheek. 'Well, I hope?'

'Yes sir, thank you. Nice to see you home again.'

47

'Gertie has been looking after the family for as long as I can remember,' he told Nancy. 'And this, Gertie, is Nancy. She's just agreed to marry me. Is Mother in a good mood?'

'Yes, she is.' Gertie smiled shyly at Nancy before turning back to him. 'I'm so pleased for you, sir. The family's out in the garden. Lovely afternoon, isn't it?'

'Were you brought up here?' Nancy whispered as they followed Gertie through the house.

'Yes. Dad had it built to please Mother.'

The maid opened a glass door for them and asked, 'Shall I bring you some fresh tea?'

Nancy would have liked some, since trepidation was making her mouth dry, but Charlie said, 'Better not, Gertie.'

As she stepped out on to the lawn, Nancy had a glimpse of the family in three basket chairs pulled up to a tea table under the trees: two men, Charlie's father and uncle, who were identical twins, and Charlie's mother.

Nancy immediately felt the frigid gaze assessing her. Henrietta was of matronly build and wore a tea gown of kingfisher-blue silk with a wide-brimmed matching straw hat. She looked as though she was dressed for a royal garden party. The men rose to their feet with welcoming smiles.

Charlie strode forward, pulling Nancy with him. 'This is my father. Hello, Dad, how are you?' He was swept into a bear hug. The second man gave him another hearty hug. 'Uncle Toby, lovely to catch you here like this.'

Nancy found the twins spectacularly alike. She looked from one to the other and was unable to see the slightest difference apart from their clothes. Both had alert blue eyes that seemed to miss nothing. She studied Uncle Toby. Much about him seemed almost boyish, but his clear fresh complexion, large nose and strong broad shoulders were belied by a thick thatch of snowy white hair. Charlie's father looked exactly the same. They both beamed with friendliness and had the polish and sophistication that a lifetime of rich living gives.

Henrietta remained seated. 'How are you, Mother?' Charlie bent to give her a dutiful peck on the cheek. 'I've brought someone special to say hello. This is Nancy Milton.'

'Hello,' Nancy said, putting out her hand. 'I'm very pleased to meet you.'

Charlie's mother's gaze was stony. She ignored the outstretched hand, but his father gave Nancy no time to dwell on that because he came over to clasp it firmly.

'Hello, Nancy. I'm Jago. We don't often get a chance to meet Charlie's friends.'

His mother's voice cut coldly across them. 'Charles, why are we being honoured with this introduction?'

Nancy felt Charlie's arm slip round her waist to pull her closer to him.

'Nancy and I are about to be married. On August the

49

twenty-ninth at two o'clock at St Bede's church in Birkenhead. You're all invited. I've brought her to meet you first.'

'Married in August? This August?' Henrietta's eyebrows had risen. 'What nonsense! I was afraid it might be something like that.' Her face had gone scarlet. 'Charles, you need to think carefully about marriage. It's an important step. You mustn't rush headlong into it.'

Nancy froze. Charlie's mother was trying to persuade him not to get married!

Henrietta leapt to her feet and went on, 'Perhaps we'd better go inside; it's getting cooler now. What did you say your name was?'

'Nancy.'

'Our cook's name is Nancy.'

Nancy cringed. This was awful. 'It was my mother's name. I was named after her.'

'Well, you'd better tell us about yourself.'

Nancy found herself in an oversized armchair in a huge drawing room. She refused the glass of sherry that was offered to her. Henrietta Carrington Seymour was radiating superiority. It was evident in the tilt of her head and even more in the angle of her nose.

'Come along, girl. Tell us where Charlie found you.'

Nancy was sure Henrietta would not consider her a suitable wife for her son. She felt tongue-tied and wondered if she dared say, 'In the bar of the Lord Nelson.'

Charlie said the words for her. They brought a gasp of horror from his mother. 'The Lord Nelson?'

'My father is the licensee,' Nancy said quietly, knowing she mustn't hide the fact. 'I work for him sometimes.'

'As a barmaid?'

'Yes, amongst other things.'

Nancy knew that had settled it. Henrietta's face said it all. She was totally unacceptable as a wife for Charlie.

Charlie's father and Uncle Toby were trying to gloss over the ill feeling Henrietta had generated. Nancy was doing her best to hide the fact that she was upset.

'I take it your pub is named after Admiral Lord Nelson?' Toby asked.

'Well, no, not really.' Nancy had recounted the story many times. 'The tale goes that a sailor called George Nelson jumped ship in Australia at the time of the gold rush. He went panning for gold and found a large enough nugget to cause his fellow gold seekers to start calling him Lord Nelson, because he was throwing his money about. He bought himself a passage home on a liner and travelled under that name. It got him a seat on the captain's table.

'He'd found enough gold to change his life, and by the time he landed in Liverpool he'd decided he'd like to run a pub. So he bought one.'

'And he called it the Lord Nelson!' Toby laughed. His face shone with friendliness. Nancy was glad to find him on her side.

'Yes, and ran it for thirty years. The Birkenhead Brewery bought it when he died. It needed a bit of refurbishment by then and it was decided that it would be more correct to call it the Admiral Lord Nelson. That's when the inn sign showing a picture of the Admiral was first hung outside. But it didn't catch on as a name, and it's still known as the Lord Nelson today.'

Toby smiled. 'So you help to run it?'

'I work for an insurance company. I'm a book-keeper and shorthand typist, but I help Dad too. With the accounts and the ordering, and I write his business letters for him as well. My mother died giving birth to me and my father brought me up, so you see, it was easier for him to run a pub than go out to work.'

Charlie's father said, 'It sounds as though you have a very busy life.'

'It doesn't feel like work to be in the bar.' Nancy smiled. 'It's fun. I couldn't wait to turn eighteen so I could. As a child I used to listen to the sounds of jollity . . .'

Henrietta cut across her. 'Charles, I do beg of you not to rush into marriage. When I wanted you to meet Margaret Lacey, you said you weren't going to think of it for years.'

'I hadn't met Nancy then, Mother. What I was trying to say, diplomatically, was that I wouldn't need help to choose a wife.'

'No, but let's be practical. What do you propose to live on?'

'That's a bit of a problem. I was wondering if . . .' Charlie smiled at her. 'Mother, this family trust fund that Grandfather set up for us, the Carrington Trust. Would it be possible for me to have a little from it now?'

'No!' She straightened her back, looking every inch the aristocratic Lady Henrietta. 'Certainly not. That's quite impossible.'

Charlie's voice had a pleading note. 'Isn't it written into the trust that family members too young to draw a regular income can be given cash to meet certain expenses? School fees, for instance? So why not marriage?'

'School fees yes. As the main trustee, I won't agree to anything else.'

'Next year I'll be twenty-five and entitled to my share. It doesn't seem unreasonable to ask for a few hundred now to help me support a wife. I realise of course that it will reduce your share, and I'm sorry . . .'

'Charles, that is not the point at all. I understand my father's intention was to help the weaker members of the family, but I see absolutely no need for you to get married now. You've plenty of time. You're very young.'

'Sorry, Mother, the one thing we haven't got is time.' Charlie winked at Nancy. 'I'm about to make you a grandmother.'

'A grandmother? Good God!'

Nancy felt sick. Henrietta's dark eyes were boring ferociously into hers. 'I might have known. What a disgrace to bring on the family!'

Charlie remained unruffled, beaming round them all. 'If Nancy and I get married, it'll be transformed into a happy event, won't it? So as a trustee, why not authorise a release of a couple of hundred to me now? Just as an advance. It would make all the difference to us.'

'Certainly not.'

'Next year I'll be entitled to a marriage allowance from the RAF so I could manage without anything from the trust then. It's now I need it.'

'Charles, when I say no, I mean no. You're acting like a spoilt child. I don't think you should get married yet. You may be physically twenty-four but your mental age is barely fourteen. In my opinion, it makes more sense to raise the age at which you receive this money. Twenty-eight might be more appropriate. I'll look into that tomorrow morning. Now, I hope you'll excuse me. I need to lie down after such bad news. You make outrageous demands, Charles. You've given me a headache.'

There was a stunned silence as she marched out of the room. Nancy wanted to sink back and hide under the cushions of her chair.

Charlie's father got up to pour himself another whisky. 'Don't worry, Charlie. A trust fund is a legal document and the terms set out cannot be altered at this stage, not even by your mother.'

Toby signalled that he wanted more whisky too. 'You'll get your share when you're twenty-five, but as your mother seems to be set against giving you an advance, I'm afraid you'll have to wait until then.'

'It would be politic to let her have her way,' Jago said.

'Absolutely.' Uncle Toby was getting out his cheque book. 'But she needn't know what I give my only nephew as a wedding present. Would five hundred do the job?'

Nancy watched him write out the cheque and couldn't believe what she was hearing. Five hundred pounds was an enormous sum.

Charlie was almost overcome with gratitude. 'Thank you. That's marvellous. Thank you, Uncle Toby. Thank you.' He was hugging his uncle and pulling Nancy forward to be hugged too.

His father kissed her cheek and said, 'I hope you'll be happy with Charlie. I know you won't be bored – he's always up to some caper.'

To Nancy, the tide of relief flooding through her felt like balm. She was thrilled and happy that Charlie was as keen as she was to be married.

'And the baby will be very much welcomed when it comes,' Toby said. 'You can be sure of that.'

He poured more whisky for himself and his twin while the latter was seeing Charlie and Nancy out. 'Trust Charlie to give us a shock,' he said when Jago came back.

Charlie's father sighed heavily. 'I don't think his mother took it well.'

'Badly enough to upset the girl. Did you see her face fall?'

'Henrietta meant to choose Charlie's wife for him. She

was never going to like anybody he picked out.' Jago sighed again. 'Our father chose a wife for me, so I shouldn't be surprised. But Nancy's father's a pub licensee, she's a barmaid and she's already pregnant. She didn't stand a chance with Henrietta.'

'No, Charlie's plea for funds was dead in the water before he started.'

'What did you think of her?'

'A pretty girl, very young and innocent.' Jago was frowning. 'Charlie's got her pregnant, so he's got to do the decent thing and marry her.'

'Yes, and better that he does it straight away,' Toby said. 'I had to give him the means. Anyway, no point in keeping them on the breadline. She might even suit him. Marriage might settle him down.'

'Yes, thanks for stepping in with the five hundred. You think more quickly than I do. Better if we keep Henrietta in ignorance about that, though.'

'Absolutely. I wish she'd think before she opens her mouth. She hasn't started off on a very good footing with her daughter-in-law.'

'Henrietta won't care about that. She's written Nancy off as unsuitable. As far as she's concerned, she doesn't want to know her.'

'She's got to know her. She'll be her daughter-in-law.'

CHAPTER FIVE

WHILE JAGO WAS seeing her and Charlie off, Henrietta was upstairs lying on her bed, seething with fury. Both Jago and Toby were in favour of letting Charlie marry that girl. They meant to go against her express wishes. Charlie deserved better; he needed to be protected from girls like that. Having her in the family would lower the status of them all.

Nancy was from the bottom of society. It wouldn't hurt her if Charlie did walk away. A girl like that didn't have to worry about her reputation; she'd have no future to look forward to anyway. Now, everything was going to be made easy for her. She was having a life of middle-class comfort handed to her on a plate. It made Henrietta burn with resentment.

Henrietta had had to fight for what she wanted, and even then she frequently hadn't managed to get it. Nancy was only nineteen years old and already she was pregnant. She'd have no trouble breeding like a rabbit. Henrietta had gone through years of longing and trying

57

for a baby before she achieved it. And there'd been only one when she'd wanted a proper family. No wonder she felt this overwhelming envy, when fate was kinder and life itself was proving so much easier for Nancy than it had been for her.

At her age, Henrietta had been head over heels in love with Justin Cooper and he with her. He'd asked her to marry him and she'd been thrilled. He'd then approached her father for his permission and his blessing.

Justin had been a twenty-five-year-old lieutenant in the army. His prospects had been good – in fact he'd been promoted to captain a few months later – but her father had immediately refused his consent and for-bidden them ever to meet again. Justin was sent away with a flea in his ear.

Her father reminded Henrietta that she was an attractive girl of good breeding and he expected her to marry up the social scale not down, preferably into a family with a fortune to cushion her.

Justin's father was a major in some minor regiment, and his salary was his only income. The Coopers' social position simply didn't equate to that of the Carringtons. As a dependent daughter of nineteen, Henrietta had had little choice in the matter. She'd done as her father had ordered, but she'd had a fiery relationship with him from then on.

*

Nancy's wedding present from her father had been money to buy herself a new outfit. She threw herself into the preparations and chose a dress of filmy apricot-coloured georgette with a hat to match. They invited six guests. Nancy wanted only her father and her friend Polly, who helped in the pub on busy nights. Charlie asked only one friend with his family. He apologised to Nancy for a wedding that was going to be no fuss and no frills, but she laughed and said she was sure it would be a very happy day for them both.

Henrietta came to the church dressed to the nines, but she kept a car and chauffeur standing by, to take her home as soon as the ceremony was over and the photographs had been taken.

The wedding party then returned to the bar of the Lord Nelson, which was then open, and Dad provided a couple of bottles of champagne to drink to the couple's future. After that they went upstairs for the buffet lunch Nancy and Alma had set out on their dining table that morning. Everybody was in high spirits and the jollity and fun carried Nancy along until it was time for her and Charlie to drive off for their week's honeymoon on Anglesey.

She was curious about Charlie's family, and couldn't stop asking questions about them.

'I've never known a family that had money like yours,' she said on the first morning, while they were sunbathing on the beach.

'We didn't have all that much. Grandfather's stockbroking business almost dried up once the Great War started. Half his employees volunteered to fight and a lot more were called up, including Dad and Uncle Toby. It was 1917 by then and they were thirty-two, so they were given desk jobs in this country.'

'And the business?'

'Grandfather hung on by his fingernails, but we were all hard up when the war ended. The firm had to cut down on costs to survive and Dad and Uncle Toby had to find other jobs, but with family connections they managed to get employment in a London clearing bank. By the mid-twenties the family's finances were recovering.'

'Your father and Uncle Toby were lucky their father had taught them about stockbroking,' Nancy told him. 'I don't think you realise what a difference a skill like that makes when you start looking for a job. My dad would be envious.'

'He taught them a bit too much, Nancy. Grandfather went to prison for selling stock he didn't own and forging stock certificates to make it appear that he did. He never really recovered from that and his business went to the wall. He died a broken man. That's why we don't talk about him or the old firm. Your father would probably be too honest to do anything like that.'

'Forgery?' Nancy was horrified. 'My dad would be shocked if he knew. He's as honest as the day is long.'

'My mother's family were shocked too. To the core. They won't talk about it either.'

The weather changed, and during a boat trip round the island to see puffins and seals it started to rain heavily until nothing could be seen through the murk. When the boat turned for home and they had to huddle together under mackintoshes, Nancy said, 'Tell me what happened to your family after their business went bust.'

Charlie did his best. 'It's not that easy to remember back that far. Let me see. Dad and Uncle Toby were already working for the bank, and in 1925 Uncle Toby went to work in their head office in New York. The stock market there was booming and he started speculating, trying to build up a personal portfolio. He'd learned a few things from Grandfather about giving himself an advantage over other investors, and in New York he learned many more.

'He pulled strings to wangle Dad a job there. They're both very clever with money and over the years that followed they built up their portfolios. They could see that many investors were gambling with borrowed money and that the market was heating up.

'Mother wouldn't live in America. She went for visits, but she didn't like it. Dad and Uncle Toby had always meant to return to this country, and they were lucky enough to have the move in hand, and to have most of their funds out of the market when it crashed in 1929.'

'Was that good luck or good management?'

'I don't know, but they got out with a lot of money. Uncle Toby bought the Hattongrove estate, and set himself up as a gentleman farmer. He's got a fine house with a large farm and several cottages.'

'And your dad?'

'He went back to his job in the London bank. It was considered respectable and what Mother wanted, but by then the Depression was on us. Things were pretty flat and have been ever since.'

'But your dad came back from America with plenty of money too?'

'Yes, but Mother was going through it rapidly and he couldn't stand being apart from Toby. So eventually he came back to Liverpool.'

Once their honeymoon was over, Charlie had to go down to his new posting at Cherry Hinton. He took Nancy with him, and found them temporary lodgings while Nancy looked round for something more permanent to rent. Visits to estate agents and looking at their lists made her ask Charlie about his parents' lovely house.

'Oh, dear, that's a bone of contention. Mother had big ideas about the house she wanted, and after Grindley Manor nothing they looked at was good enough.'

'What happened to her old home?'

'William, her older brother, inherited it. He meant to farm the land and look after the estate as their father had, but he was killed on the Somme in 1916. Unfortunately for Mother, only eight months earlier he'd married Julia Lockhart. She was the daughter of William's history professor at Oxford. So Aunt Julia inherited Grindley. You can imagine what Mother thought of that.'

'Oh, dear!'

'I understand Mother made herself quite ill, thinking of Aunt Julia living in her childhood home as lady of the manor after such a short marriage. Particularly as on William's death, had he not been married, it would have gone to George, her younger brother. Then, when he was killed too, Mother would have inherited it. She would have had her dearest wish. I don't think she ever got over her disappointment.'

'Is your Aunt Julia still living there?'

'No, she couldn't afford the upkeep. She sold it and it was turned into a hotel, otherwise Mother would have insisted on buying it back. When it came to choosing another home, Dad and Uncle Toby had to make up her mind for her. She says she hates Carrington Place.'

'How could anybody hate it? It's her frame of mind. I bet she hates the sausage factory more.'

'You're right there. She stays well away from that. Toby has an interest in it too. His farm supplies the meat for Dad's sausages and they both hope they'll earn a lot from it, but the factory was only set up a few years ago and it's not in full production yet.

'As you probably know, most butcher's shops make and sell their own sausages, and some are good and some are not. Dad's idea is to make premium grade beef and pork sausages and sell them ready packed through grocer's shops. He thinks that'll be the way in the future. The Co-op has already agreed to stock them.'

'That's good, isn't it?'

'Very good. He's also supplying some big hotels, but in the present economic climate he isn't making rapid progress.'

'Then why do it now?'

'Dad needs more money. Mother thinks she has a right to be kept in comfort and her upkeep doesn't come cheap. She's a lot more extravagant than the rest of us, but she thinks she's being thrifty, because she runs that house with just a cook and a parlourmaid.'

'Charlie! She has a car standing ready all the time and a chauffeur to drive it.'

'That's what I mean. She doesn't want to learn to drive so Dad has to provide a driver for when he's out doing something else. Actually, Bennett works in the garden too. Mother doesn't hold house parties or big dinner parties any more, and no longer buys her clothes in Paris and London. She thinks her standard of living is slipping. To please her, Dad needs to earn more.'

'But doesn't she have money of her own? If her father was a landowner?'

'I'm afraid he too liked to live well. Grindley Manor was two hundred years old and cost a lot to keep up. He had to sell much of his land at the wrong time to pay for repairs to the roof and provide for his family. Like many traditional landowning families, their fortune was declining from the turn of the century. Times have just got harder. Not that she's penniless – her father put money into a trust fund for her so that she'd always have something, but like everything else it isn't producing much of an income.'

Nancy felt she understood his family circumstances better after that.

Within two weeks they were moving into a small flat close to the airfield. It was their first home together and only partly furnished, so they had all the fun and excitement of tracking down pieces of furniture they really liked.

She felt settled in by the time their daughter Caroline was born, and it was the happy event that Charlie had predicted. She was a beautiful baby, with silvery blonde curls, big blue eyes and perfectly formed tiny limbs. Nancy loved her from the moment she saw her and Charlie doted on them both.

Charlie's parents came down to see the new arrival and Nancy was surprised to see how moved Henrietta was when she held the baby.

'She's lovely, absolutely lovely, and she's just like you were, Charlie, at this age. I wanted another child, you know. I'd have loved to have a little girl myself.'

'Well, you've got a granddaughter now,' Nancy said, thinking that, now she was Caroline's mother, Henrietta would come to accept her in time.

She saw more of her mother-in-law after that.

Henrietta came bringing expensive presents for the baby and billed and cooed over her cot. As Caro grew older and more responsive, Henrietta came more often, wanting to take her out. Over the little girl's childhood years, Charlie said his mother established a closer relationship with his daughter than she'd ever had with him. Nancy went out of her way to be as pleasant and friendly as she could towards Henrietta, but Henrietta's hostility remained like a wall between them.

These days, Henrietta's entertaining was virtually no more than inviting Toby to Sunday lunch. Today he'd arrived early and was in Jago's study enjoying a glass of whisky with him while Henrietta got herself ready to receive her guest.

Jago was complaining that Henrietta had seen a sable coat in a Bold Street shop window, and though she already owned two fur coats, she expected him to buy it for her.

'We always knew Henrietta would be an expensive burden,' Toby said.

'You did? Dad told me marriage to her would make my fortune.'

'And you believed him?'

'We both believed Dad knew it all, didn't we? We're going back donkey's years now and he certainly knew more than we did.'

Toby said, 'We were still wet behind the ears. How long is it since you first met Henrietta?'

'It must have been 1903.'

'A different era.'

'Yes. Nineteenth-century wealth and privilege still existed then.'

Jago sat back, musing about those long gone days when he and Toby had been allowed to join their father's stockbroking firm.

Dad considered them mere apprentices and rarely let them loose on a client by themselves; certainly not on Henrietta's father, Sir Henry Carrington of Grindley Manor in Lancashire. He was a sufficiently important client for Dad to visit him at home or even at his London address in Egerton Gardens should he be asked to do so.

On one occasion when Sir Henry had summoned Dad to London, he'd taken Jago with him to help carry the documents and act as his clerk. To allow time for the journey down from Liverpool, they had a mid-afternoon appointment. Jago had never been in so grand a house before and was impressed. Lady Carrington was preparing to hold some sort of soiree that evening and was directing her staff as to where and how she wanted the flowers arranged. She ignored them as the butler showed them to Sir Henry's study.

Sir Henry was portly, with a skimming of silver hair round the back of his head fringing a pink and shiny scalp. He was not happy with the return his shares were giving him. He wanted to sell some to release cash, in order to buy into more profitable companies. While his father talked Sir Henry through his portfolio and they pondered over which of his securities he should sell, Jago recorded their decisions and listened carefully to what they said, as Dad insisted he must.

Sir Henry had strong opinions and voiced them firmly. He was convinced shares in Caledonian Steel would prove satisfyingly profitable, but Dad didn't agree and suggested he bought, instead, shares in his current recommendation, the Liverpool and Manchester Bank.

The meeting went on longer than expected. Jago could hear Lady Carrington's guests beginning to arrive. When the butler was sent in to remind Sir Henry that he was expected to come and act as host, he said to his father, 'Sorry I've kept you so long. Why don't you both come and have a drink? I expect Lord Elkington will soon be here; he's a director of Caledonian Steel. I'll introduce you. He believes the company will shortly be taken over and the share price will double.'

Jago could see his father was more than eager, and he himself was keen to see more of this house. They talked at some length to Lord Elkington, who convinced them that it would be an excellent idea to buy shares in Caledonian Steel.

Sir Henry introduced them to his wife and his daughter Henrietta, both of whom sparkled in that atmosphere. Jago didn't quite know what to make of Henrietta. She seemed a lot older than him, more sophisticated and very much at ease in that society. She was a good-looking woman, proud and elegantly turned out, but unaccountably she seemed to unbend towards him as though she liked him. He thought her and her family formidable and at first found them intimidating.

It was Henrietta who introduced them to the other leaders of trade and industry who were present. Jago heard several discussing their business and its prospects. He could see his father was in his element: being sociable, enjoying himself but staying alert and concentrating hard. Jago knew the conversation would give his father an inside view of those businesses; an informed base from which to decide whether to recommend other clients to buy shares in them or not.

They caught the night train back to Liverpool, and though they had sleepers booked his father kept him awake for much of the night making lists of securities they must buy and others they must sell, not only on Sir Henry's behalf but also for his father's personal portfolio.

Jago remembered staggering off the train in the early hours of the morning still half asleep, eating a large breakfast in an overnight café and going via their office to the Liverpool Stock Exchange as soon as it opened, where they spent an exceedingly profitable morning.

'They have old money,' Mr Seymour had explained to his sons the following day. 'They live in a different world. Jago, I want you to make a friend of Henrietta and accept any invitations she might offer.'

In order to return Sir Henry's hospitality and encourage more invitations from him, once the Carringtons returned to Grindley Manor Mr Seymour invited them to have lunch with him and his sons at the Adelphi Hotel. At that time, almost everybody entertained at home, but Dad's excuse was that he'd been a widower for many years and had no hostess to help him.

Afterwards, Toby and Jago had laughed about that. They knew their father was anxious that their modest house in Waterloo should not be compared with Grindley Manor, and he was not a widower. His wife had abandoned her two-year-old twins when she was twenty-three and run off with another man. By all accounts she meant to have a good time in life, and her husband and babies were not providing it. Charlie was said to take after her.

Sir Henry told Mr Seymour they'd all enjoyed the lunch at the Adelphi and a few weeks later Jago heard from Henrietta that he was taking guests of his own there. The Seymours were invited to parties at Grindley Manor as well as Egerton Gardens, where they soon learned to draw out their fellow guests. Mr Seymour thought of other places the Carringtons might enjoy and proceeded to invite them there, insisting his sons came too. He said he was pleased to see Henrietta taking a fancy to Jago.

'What an advantage it would give us to have Henrietta as our hostess,' he enthused. 'If she were to invite them, the local captains of industry would flock to our house. It would be an enormous help to us.'

'She's a snob,' Toby said.

His father had been serious when he said, 'Jago, it would do you no harm to be seen with an elegant lady like Henrietta on your arm. She's interested in everything, a very superior companion.'

'She's looking for a husband,' Toby had pointed out.

'You could do worse,' his father had insisted to Jago. 'She could be the making of the business, and of you too.'

At that time, Jago felt no need for a wife, and didn't think seriously about marrying Henrietta for several years. Henrietta, on the other hand, with her thirtieth birthday on the horizon had no other suitor in view and seemed to attach herself to him. Father thought every man was in need of a wife and expected to persuade Jago into it eventually. He made a friend of Henrietta and continued to bring them together as often as he could.

She had two brothers, and Sir Henry was happy to socialise with the Seymours because he thought they could help him maximise his income, and that stockbroking might make a suitable career for his younger son. The Seymour family came to know the Carringtons well and assumed a social front for their benefit.

Jago knew the relationship between Henrietta and her father was turbulent. As he got to know her better, she began to confide in him, giving him blow by blow accounts of the rows they had and a deeper understanding of the life she led.

Jago was nine years younger than she was, and had not made sufficient progress in his own career to be considered a good match for her. But Henrietta had other ideas, and though theirs was a long, slow courtship, her family was eventually persuaded to accept him and Jago was persuaded to propose.

Everything changed for the Carrington family one Sunday morning early in the summer of 1908. That afternoon, a distraught Henrietta sent for Jago, saying a disaster had overtaken her and her family.

Jago set off for Grindley Manor early the next morning, as his father thought it would be inconsiderate to arrive during the evening. He found the household in a state of unrest; Henrietta was red-eyed, tearful and almost out of her mind.

The drawing room had not been tidied. Jago sat her down on the sofa, took both her hands in his and did his best to comfort her. She kept breaking down in torrents of anguish. It took her a long time to get her story out.

The previous morning, she'd got up to go riding with her father. 'The groom had our horses fed, watered and saddled up by half past six. Usually, Father rides Beulah, a gentle old mare, but she'd gone lame the day before so the groom had saddled up Hero. He's much more spirited and highly strung. Fencing work was being done on the far boundary of the estate, some two miles from the house, so we rode out that way to see what progress had been made.'

Henrietta dabbed at her eyes with a damp handkerchief, then went on to tell Jago that Sir Henry had been leaning out of his saddle to take a closer look at the work when something had startled Hero. She said it sounded like a gunshot. The horse had bolted in fright, taking her father by surprise and making him lose his balance and slide out of the saddle. Worse, one of his boots caught in its stirrup and he'd been dragged all the way back to the stables.

Henrietta said, 'I was paralysed with horror but I did my best to catch and stop Hero. He was absolutely terrified and galloping wildly so I wasn't able to. Father was dragged for two miles along stony paths.'

Jago was beginning to feel sick. He'd heard of accidents like this before and knew the likely outcome. 'How is he?'

'He was badly cut and grazed, particularly the back of his head and shoulders. He never recovered consciousness and died from his injuries last night.'

Jago was shocked and saddened. He was sympathetic and did his best to support and comfort her.

CHAPTER SIX

FOR HENRIETTA THAT was the worst Sunday morning of her life. The account she'd given the world of her father's accident had been a varnished version. Every time she thought about it, she shook. The truth was totally harrowing.

Ever since Father had forbidden her to marry Justin Cooper she'd resented the power he had to control her life. Over the years, her feelings for him had hardened from indifference to hate and loathing. She'd tried many times, but found it impossible to get away from him.

To think of ways in which she could started as a sort of game. She would imagine ways to get even with him, ways to hurt him, ruin him, or make him ill. Her imagination seemed to provide the only comfort she could hope for.

She worked out all sorts of plans to defeat him and they'd got wilder and wilder over the years until she was actually planning to kill him. She'd thought of a dozen different ways to end his life, and the one that seemed foolproof was set to take place on one of those mornings when he insisted on getting her out of bed to go riding with him. Every time he offended her or forced her to do something she didn't want to, she'd think through her plan and make little refinements.

She wished he'd simply die, but Sir Henry was fit and strong and continued to lord it over her. She was not allowed the freedom her brothers enjoyed. Her mother didn't understand; Father treated her with more respect and she seemed content with her lot.

For years, Henrietta found satisfaction only in her imagination. She fantasised about other things, too. One of her most beguiling dreams was that Jago would ask her to marry him and take her out of her father's clutches.

When he actually proposed, it seemed to Henrietta that all her other fantasies could just as easily become reality. She was overjoyed and so was her mother, and together they began planning the wedding. By then she was thirty-two and even her father had had to accept that her prospects of marrying into the aristocracy had receded to vanishing point.

She knew he was reluctant to give his blessing even though her mind had been set on Jago for years. She was determined that this time he would not stop her. If anybody could be blamed for the troubles that followed, it was he. He brought it on himself.

When he was at Grindley, Sir Henry used to ride

almost every morning. He kept a stable of six horses, two for his own use and four for his wife and children. Henrietta had been taught to ride as a child but she didn't care for it, even though she had a horse of her own called Dido. Sir Henry was a strict and controlling father. He said she needed fresh air and exercise and forced her on many occasions to get out of bed and ride with him.

On that Sunday morning, almost as soon as they'd headed their horses out of the stable Sir Henry had sealed his fate. In his usual autocratic manner, he'd delivered his ultimatum. 'Better if you send Jago Seymour packing,' he'd told her. 'Break it off now. He won't make you happy, he can't. You'll find him quite impossible as a husband.'

Henrietta felt the blood scorching into her cheeks. She was ablaze with fury. It seemed a vicious trick to keep her in servitude. She'd fired angry questions at him.

'What on earth makes you say that? I thought you approved of stockbroking as a career. You've made a friend of his father . . .'

Sir Henry was dismissive. 'It's not his career I object to, it's other things.'

'What other things?' she'd demanded, aware that her voice had risen an octave.

Father had hummed and hawed and it had sparked another row. While she fulminated against him he remarked several times on what a beautiful summer morning it was and directed her to look down the valley where the mist was just burning off. That had infuriated her even more.

When they reached the edge of the estate and the newly erected fence, her father tossed Hero's reins to her to hold and dismounted to inspect the work more closely.

To Henrietta, it seemed the most natural thing in the world to hook both sets of reins over a branch and slide down from Dido. Silently she'd followed her father across the grass. Rage was half blinding her. She lifted one of the fencing posts lying ready for use. Its weight surprised her and made her stagger, but she swung it at the back of his balding head with as much force as she could muster. The sound of wood crunching against flesh and bone went through her. It still came back to haunt her and make her shudder.

Father had fallen forward on his face. She could hardly bring herself to glance at the awful wound she'd inflicted on the back of his head, where blood and flesh were leaking into the fringe of thin silvery hair. He wasn't moving or making any sound. She thought he was dead and for a few moments she was filled with quiet triumph. Never again would he lay down the law to her. At last she'd got her own back for all the times he'd humiliated her and made her feel a fool.

But she'd never seen a dead body before and suddenly what she'd done filled her with terror. She took several big breaths to steady her nerves. She told herself she had her plan ready; all she had to do was carry it out.

She rolled him over and found dust, grit and splinters of wood sticking to his face; blood was oozing from his nose. In her imagination it hadn't occurred to her that she'd cause damage to his face. She took out her handkerchief and tried to brush the dirt from it, but she mustn't waste time.

She backed Hero up as close to the body as she could get him, meaning to lift Father's left boot and thread it through the left stirrup. That proved harder than she'd thought it would. He was a large man, his right leg was very much in the way, and the weight of his limbs was almost too heavy for her. She was hot and sticky by the time she'd succeeded.

She thought she'd done the hard part and all that remained was to whack the horse on his rump to make him drag the body along the stony path. She'd expected Hero to bolt: that's what he'd done when she'd imagined this scene. Father had said he was an edgy horse living on his nerves, but he seemed puzzled by the weight he pulled behind him and kept turning his head to look at it. Worse, the horse's back leg kept kicking against the body. Hero walked slowly and carefully as though trying not to hurt his master.

During the journey back, Henrietta had to whack Hero several times to keep him moving. She was in a fever of anxiety to make what she'd done look like an accident. By the time they were getting close to the stables she could feel tears of desperation running down her cheeks, but that was all right, it would seem a normal reaction. A gardener saw the horse coming and went running to fetch help. Joseph Digby, the groom, came to meet them. Henrietta had timed it well. She caught up with Hero at just the right moment, and Digby helped her release her father's foot from the stirrup.

Henrietta went rushing then to the house to get help for her father and give a breathless and tearful account of what had happened. She'd known she'd have to do that and she had it all prepared. When she blurted out the news, her mother slid under the table in a dead faint that terrified her and almost ended her pretence.

Over the following days, it seemed she'd been forced to tell her story a hundred times over; to her mother, the doctor, Jago, Sergeant Bloomfield the local policeman, and later on her brothers. They'd all seemed to accept it without question.

All except Joseph Digby. She'd watched him run his hands over Hero's coat while his dark eyes searched her face. 'Bolted, you say? He's as quiet as a lamb and he's not been sweating.'

That made her shake. She was afraid he was telling her he didn't believe her story. When she'd planned this end for Father, she'd rehearsed in her mind what she must do and what she must say, but she hadn't given enough thought to the part the horse must play.

And she'd given no thought at all to the fencing post she'd used to bludgeon Father. He'd ordered them from the saw mill, branches of uniform thickness cut to the required length and then split in half. It was only during the first sleepless night that followed, when the wound she'd inflicted had played on her mind, that Henrietta had realised she ought to check that there were no incriminating bloodstains, fragments of flesh or hairs on it.

She'd got up very early before the housemaids were stirring. Shivering in the cool moist air and unable to face Joseph Digby's accusing eyes, she'd walked to the edge of the estate where it was being refenced. The post was where she'd flung it and yes, on the white cut surface there were what appeared to be bloodstains. She was glad she'd come.

There'd been a shower in the night and the grass was wet. She rubbed the cut surface of the post up and down on the ground. That partly removed the original stains and partly covered what remained with green stains from the grass.

It would have to do. She carried the stake to the pile lying ready for the fencers to use and tossed it on top. It clattered down, and she pulled a few more posts down on top of it.

She was turning to go when she saw Joseph Digby watching her. His head was thrown back, his legs wide apart in a triumphant stance. His brooding eyes were challenging hers. 'What would you be doing that for, Miss Henrietta?' he asked.

*

Henrietta had known Joseph Digby almost all her life. He'd taught her to ride when she was ten years old, but she'd been slow to learn and he'd made her feel inadequate. She'd disliked him. Now her flesh crept and her heart was in her mouth.

She'd killed her father and thought she'd got away with it; what she wanted desperately was to push it out of her mind. She wanted things to be as normal as they could as soon as they could.

The groom came closer, mocking her. 'Poor Sir Henry. Not exactly what a loving daughter should do, was it?'

She turned without a word, wanting to get away from him, but he caught her wrist and swung her back.

'I've asked around. Nobody was out hunting yesterday morning. Nobody else heard gunshots.'

'Let me go,' she screamed, trying to shake him off.

He hung on to her grimly, putting his face close to hers. 'You caused that so-called accident, I know you did.' His voice was a threatening whisper. 'You wouldn't want me to have a word with Sergeant Bloomfield, would you?' The hairs on the back of Henrietta's neck were standing up in terror. Digby's mouth twisted with spite. 'I'll keep silent but you'll have to pay me.' The sum he mentioned seemed outrageous.

Henrietta was panicking. She couldn't think properly. 'If I do pay, how do I know you'll keep your mouth shut?'

'I promise.'

'I don't have money like that.'

'But you can get it.'

'It'll take me time.'

'Three days,' he said. 'Bring it to me. I'll see Sergeant Bloomfield on Thursday if you don't.'

'I'll have to think about it,' she choked.

'You do that.'

He let go of her and she stumbled away as fast as she could.

She'd paid up on Wednesday. She'd given him what he asked for. Really, she'd had to. She couldn't have coped without his silence. Facing people was agonising, and so many offered their condolences. The accident was on everybody's tongue and was kept there by the coming inquest. Henrietta had to keep her mind clear and stay alert. She hoped and prayed that the present turmoil in her life would settle down.

But Sir Henry's death had thrown everything into flux. Her elder brother William had inherited the Grindley Manor estate and returned from Oxford to run it. Knowing he'd have to reduce the running costs, he began selling off some of the horses and reducing both the inside and outside staff. It scared her to find that Digby survived that cull.

Both Henrietta and her younger brother George had been left enough money to bring in a small income. He intended to pursue his medical training and eventually make his career as an army doctor.

Then other disasters overtook them and added to her suffering. Two months later poor Lady Carrington had a heart attack and collapsed. Nobody had known she had anything wrong with her heart until it happened. Henrietta sent for the doctor, and finding her dangerously ill he arranged for a nurse to look after her.

The doctor blamed it on the shock of Sir Henry's sudden death. Henrietta had been closer to her mother than anyone else in her family so it lay heavily on her conscience. Lady Carrington hovered between life and death for three months, and when she died Henrietta was devastated. But she could now see herself as mistress of her beloved Grindley Manor. She took over her mother's role and set about acting as William's hostess and running the house.

'It'll give you something to do to get you through these first painful months,' he told her. 'But later on you'll marry Jago, and I'll have to look for a wife.'

Henrietta was desolate. She loved Grindley Manor; it was her childhood home. It was a large house and she tried to persuade William to allow her to make a home for herself and Jago in one wing, but he wouldn't hear of it. She was overwhelmed by the changes that resulted from what she'd done. Her life had altered for the worse in many ways, some of which she should have foreseen.

The Seymour family attended the funerals of both Sir Henry and Lady Carrington and sent generous wreaths to show their respect. Jago was particularly attentive and did his best to console Henrietta, but there was much she couldn't tell him and it played on her mind.

The weeks passed and Henrietta told herself she must put the past out of her mind. One day she was walking round the rose garden, admiring the blooms, when suddenly she found herself face to face with Joseph Digby's slight, skinny figure. His foxy face showed no mercy for her.

'You must have found the post-mortem report on your father upsetting,' he gloated, his gaze full on her face. 'His right leg fractured in several places.' Henrietta was petrified.

'It was assumed the horse kicked him or tripped over his body. I could explain exactly how it came about.'

'No,' she cried, 'no.'

'Another hundred pounds,' he demanded. 'Otherwise I will.'

'I don't have money like that. I can't!'

'You can, you'll have to. I'll give you one week to get it. By next Saturday, or I'll go to Sergeant Bloomfield.'

CHAPTER SEVEN

HENRIETTA WENT TO her room and threw herself on her bed. She was furious. She'd made it perfectly clear when she'd handed over the first hundred pounds to Digby that she only intended to pay once. She hated the thought of parting with more money because she was going to marry Jago and would need it herself. Also, it appeared that Digby would go on and on demanding more, if she didn't put a stop to it.

As the months since her father's accident had passed without her part in it being suspected by anyone but Digby, she'd begun to feel she was safe, but this ultimatum from him was undermining her. The threat played havoc with her peace of mind, and she was afraid she'd be reduced to a bundle of nerves again. She had to put a stop to his blackmail once and for all.

Henrietta had no intention of handing over more money. Instead, she would use this week to plan how she'd get rid of Digby. She couldn't hope to make a second death look like an accident, but she didn't mean to allow any suspicion to fall on her. She stayed in bed late in the mornings with the curtains closed, thinking through her options.

Henrietta had access to her father's sporting guns, but firearms left a traceable identity and she wasn't a good shot. He'd also owned some sharp knives and those would not be so readily traceable. But she was afraid Digby's greater strength would allow him to wrest a knife from her grasp and use it against her. She knew her attack would have to surprise him and the first strike must kill him.

George was training to be a doctor and had in his room a collection of books on anatomy and physiology. In order to learn where a cut was most likely to prove fatal, she studied them.

She'd had in mind to aim for the heart, but learned it was encased in a bony ribcage. She might be able to thrust the knife between Digby's ribs and into his heart, but it could just as easily strike a rib and do him little damage. She looked for another site. His throat had seemed likely: she'd heard of people who'd had their throats cut. But no, it seemed she might only nick his windpipe, which could be repaired. Much better, it seemed, to aim for one or other side of his neck, where the main arteries took blood to the brain. A cut there and he'd almost certainly bleed to death.

On the day Digby had stipulated she must pay him,

George was to receive his medical degree in London, and she and William planned to attend the ceremony. Henrietta knew it would be late when they returned to Grindley and went to the stables to ask Digby to wait until the following day.

Digby was adamant. 'You can pay me the day before if you like, but I must have the money by midnight on Saturday.' He added, 'I usually see Sergeant Bloomfield in church on Sunday mornings.'

William liked to ride after his lunch on days when he could be reasonably sure the weather would be fine. On Wednesday Henrietta said she would like to go with him and a maid was sent to the stables to tell Digby to saddle up Dido and Beulah and bring them to the front door by two o'clock.

Henrietta had made her plans by then. She changed into her riding habit and was outside waiting for Digby five minutes before the set time. When he came, leading both mounts, William had still not appeared.

She took Dido's bridle from Digby and said, 'I'll meet you at midnight on Saturday in the church porch.'

'You could give the money to me now,' he said.

'I don't have it yet.'

'Just bring it to the stables when you do,' he sounded irritable.

Henrietta wanted him well away from the Grindley estate. 'I'm not coming to the stables again,' she told him. 'The other day, two maids and a gardener saw me going to talk to you. That's no good for either of us. The church porch at midnight.'

She had by then inherited Irene, her mother's ladies' maid, but she told her she expected to be late home on Saturday and she was not to wait up for her. They travelled down to London on Friday and booked into the Savoy, where George joined them for dinner. The following day, William and Henrietta attended the ceremony and said goodbye, because George wanted to celebrate with his friends that evening.

They had dinner on the train coming home and Digby met them at the station with the carriage. Henrietta had spent the time preparing herself to do what was needed. She couldn't meet his gaze, though he stood deliberately close to her.

'You could hand it over now,' he hissed while William was tipping the porter who carried their bags.

'I haven't got it all with me,' she told him. She felt horribly apprehensive, and to see her beloved Grindley a black mass on that dark night, with lights only in the hall and on the stairs, made her more so. But William was tired, and after locking up he went straight to bed.

Henrietta followed him upstairs and listened for the click of his bedroom door before going into her own room and throwing off her London clothes of deep mourning. Earlier in the week, she'd taken some of George's clothes from his wardrobe and hidden them in her room, things he'd long outgrown and probably forgotten. She'd cut out the maker's name, that of a school outfitter, from dark grey flannel trousers and a white shirt, and chosen a plain dark jacket to keep her warm.

George had been keen on penknives as a boy and she came across his collection while she was in his room. She picked out a plain one with a sharp blade. She dressed herself in the clothes now, checked that the chosen penknife was in the pocket of the jacket, and pushed her hair inside one of George's old caps.

She left the house through the garden room, locked the door behind her and slipped the key into her pocket. It was a darkish night with racing clouds; there was a sliver of a moon and a few stars which gave barely enough light to see her way. All the better, she told herself. Digby wouldn't see who came at him.

The village church was ten minutes' walk away. She used the grass verge of the lane to deaden her footsteps, listening all the time. She heard an owl hoot in the distance but nothing else. She'd easily hear an approaching horse, but if Digby was on foot she didn't want him to get close without her knowing.

There was no light at all in the church. Against the dark sky the bulk of the Norman tower seemed black and threatening. She went silently through the lych gate to the churchyard. It was a creepy place at midnight.

She'd come early because she wanted to be here first, but she crept forward slowly in the heaviest shadows until she'd made sure Digby hadn't beaten her to it. Then she hid herself in the shadows cast by the big open stone porch, took the penknife from her pocket and opened the blade in readiness.

When far above her head the church clock began to strike midnight, it bounced her heart almost into her mouth. Then, within moments, she knew Digby was approaching, although she couldn't yet see him. He was making no attempt to be quiet, his boots scraping on the ancient flagstones. She pushed herself further back and waited, pressing her white face against the cold stone wall so he wouldn't see her.

She heard him strike a match, and peeping between the fingers of her black gloves saw him light a cigarette. He was nervous, she knew; his breathing was heavy and he couldn't stand still. Henrietta pushed her gloves into the pockets of her jacket and shrugged it off her shoulders, gently laying it on the ground. If she cut him in the right place the blood would spurt out. She didn't want it on her if it could be avoided.

She'd planned to have no drama, she'd just do the job and get it over. Also, if she remained unseen he wouldn't be able to identify her if he managed to survive.

She waited, poised. Her eyes were used to the dark now; she could make out his neck and he wasn't wearing a scarf. He turned his back to her and she leapt, slashing as hard as she could with the knife, dragging it through as much of his flesh as she could.

He gave a scream of pain. His arms were flailing madly, and one hit her painfully on the head, making her bounce back out of reach. His blood felt warm on her hand; she could smell it. He made a horrible gurgling sound and sank slowly to the ground.

She'd schooled herself not to rush away in panic, knowing she could not afford to be seen. She slipped back for a moment into the deep shadow beside the porch to take off the shirt. She could see shining wet stains on it and it felt heavy. She wiped the blade of the knife, closed it and wiped her hand and wrist on the dry part at the back. Then she put the jacket on again and buttoned it up.

Check, she told herself. Yes, her gloves were in the pockets and so was the knife, she had the rolled-up shirt in her hand; she was leaving nothing behind. There was nobody about, nobody had seen her. Digby was still making noises but they were getting fainter. She hoped they were his death throes.

She set off across the churchyard and then across a field towards the river, to a place where a well-trodden path took anglers and children down to the edge. It wasn't much more than a bubbling stream a few yards wide, but there were deeper pools here and there. The water was numbingly cold as she pushed the shirt into it and rubbed hard at the black stains. She thought the blood was coming out but it was impossible to see.

She found the two large stones she'd placed here

earlier in the week, having brought them from further up the bank. Wrapping them in the shirt, she flung the bundle into one of the pools a little way upstream. It fell with the clunk that indicated deep water. If it spent several days there with the river swilling over it, there could surely be no blood left on it.

She shivered and pulled her gloves on to her still damp hands. It was all done now and time she went home. If she could get to bed unseen all would be well. She felt exhausted, and it was a struggle uphill back to the church.

The church clock told her it was twenty minutes past twelve. She was amazed to find she'd accomplished so much in such a short time. She had to pass by the porch. Digby was a crumpled mass on the flagstones. She started to run then, she couldn't help it, but she stayed on the verge and nothing passed her in either direction.

It was a blessed relief to be back at Grindley, back in her familiar bedroom. The candle that had lit her way upstairs an hour or so before had almost burned away, but she had another ready to replace it. She held it up in front of her mirror to see herself. She hardly recognised her frightened face and windblown hair. She could see no sign of blood on her but she stripped off George's clothes, rolled them up and hid them under her bed. She'd deal with them first thing in the morning.

Another wash then to make sure and into her nightdress. She'd done it; it was over. But once in bed she found it impossible to sleep. Her mind was racing and so was her heart. The hours dragged by.

But this time she thought she'd committed the perfect murder. Everything had gone exactly as she'd planned, but there was one risk she'd had to take. She knew Digby had a wife and baby who lived with him over the stables.

It was possible he'd told his wife he was blackmailing her; it was possible she knew why he'd gone to the church. Henrietta had never spoken to the woman, a plain little thing even smaller than Digby. She had to hope that if Digby had had to explain away the money he'd received from her, he'd said it was a gift or a legacy from her father. Apart from his wife, nobody could possibly know she had any reason to kill him.

Towards morning, Henrietta slept heavily. She was woken by a maid bringing her breakfast tray. The clock on her bedside table told her it was nine o'clock, and she knew Digby's body must have been found by now. Just to think of it made her heart flip over. Hardly daring to breathe, she closed her eyes, sank back against her pillows and waited.

Soon, she heard a commotion in the hall below and William's agitated voice. The front door slammed; silence then and another wait, with every minute dragging out as long as ten. It seemed hours before she heard William return and come up to her room.

His face was red and running with perspiration. 'Wake

up, Ettie. For God's sake, wake up. Digby's been murdered.'

She dragged herself up the bed, feigning bewilderment. 'What?'

'Knifed. He's had his head half cut off.'

'Who? Digby?'

'What's the matter with you, Ettie?'

She yawned. 'I'm still half asleep. We had a busy day in London yesterday. Digby's been murdered, you say?'

'Yes, in the church porch. The curate found him when he arrived to prepare for Holy Communion. The next thing the communicants were flooding into the porch too.'

Henrietta yawned again. 'How awful.'

'Oh, for heaven's sake.' William was exasperated. 'But why would anybody want to kill Digby?'

The story got into the newspapers and caused endless gossip in the neighbourhood. It provided a riddle the police couldn't solve.

The Seymour family were alarmed. Henrietta was grief-stricken after her father died. Jago tried to comfort her, but it seemed she didn't want him near her. Her mind was no longer on getting married.

'We must postpone it,' she told him, wringing her hands in anguish. 'This isn't the right time.'

Jago was both puzzled and surprised at the depth of her grief. Henrietta had frequently complained about her father's heavy-handed treatment and it was no secret that their relationship was frosty.

When her mother died too, she grew worse. He would not have said she was close to her mother, but to see her so ill for so long must have been a harrowing experience for her. Although Lady Carrington had a nurse, he knew Henrietta had kept vigil by her bedside for long periods.

Troubles are said to come in threes, and after that extraordinary occurrence, the murder of the Grindley groom, Henrietta took to her bed. The doctor was in attendance for some months, and her brothers too became concerned for her.

She seemed troubled by all manner of anxieties and physical illnesses and only began to feel better when public interest in that inexplicable murder died down. Her illness surprised Jago, because he had thought her strong in mind and body.

All her family were relieved when after the best part of a year, Henrietta began to recover. 'It was the shock,' she said, 'of being orphaned so suddenly.'

In the late summer of 1906 Henrietta married Jago and posed for photographs in her wedding finery in the same church porch. She told him she'd had a terrible bout of depression when her parents died, but she'd now recovered and as his wife she felt she could look forward to a happy future.

In the weeks following Digby's death she'd held her

breath every time William went near the stables or a stranger came to the house. She was mortally afraid his wife would know enough to speak up and throw suspicion on her.

When at last William told her, without her having to ask, that he'd given Mrs Digby money and she was going home to live with her parents, Henrietta breathed a sigh of relief. But her freedom had come at a price. She'd never been able to shake off the horror of what might have happened to her. She'd had terrible visions of being charged, found guilty and hanged. That had frightened her rigid and still gave her nightmares from which she'd wake up hot and sweaty.

She'd decided she'd never kill again, however much others provoked her. Instead, she'd use other people, get them to provide her with every comfort. That was not against the law. She'd be able to sleep well at night and still have the pleasure of seeing her inferiors slave away on her behalf. The more people got on her nerves, the harder she'd make them work. It would be tit for tat.

CHAPTER EIGHT

NANCY FELT LOST without Charlie. No longer was he on hand to drive her into town, or take Caro to school. Gavin knew this and kept ringing her up and offering to run her about.

'I'd like you to take me shopping, please,' she told him on the phone one day. 'I need to get more food.'

She was ready and watching for him from the window and saw him pull up at her gate, exactly at the time he'd said he would.

'It's kind of you to do this,' she told him as she settled into the familiar bucket seat of Charlie's car.

'Nancy, I feel I'm taking advantage of you. This car really belongs to you now. Wouldn't you like to learn to drive? I could give you a few lessons before you go.'

'I know I should, but I don't have the energy these days. It seems a big effort to get anything done.'

She saw him glance at her. 'You'll feel better in a few

weeks, I'm sure. It must be very hard for you. How is Caro taking it?'

'She isn't sleeping as well as she used to. She's crawling into my bed waking me up in the middle of the night. Wanting to cuddle up to me.'

'She's missing her dad.'

'Yes, so I can't send her back to her own room. She used to be such an easy child to manage, but not any longer. She can be quite naughty sometimes.'

'Poor kid. Would you like me to come on Saturday and take you both to the zoo at Chester?'

'Would you, Gavin? She'd love that, and so would I. It's not easy to get out any more.'

'Of course. I'll pick you up straight after lunch. Look, about this car. I've always fancied it. I'll buy it off you, if you want to be rid of it.'

'I think I would.'

'Shall I ask round the mess and find out what would be a fair price?'

Nancy swallowed hard. It would be like cutting a cord that bound her to Charlie. 'Please, if you would. It would be one less thing for me to cope with.'

In the days before the funeral, her father came quite often to help her to do all the things connected to Charlie's death that had to be done. She was making a salad for their lunch the day Gavin came round again, and she invited him to join them.

'I can't today, Nancy, thank you. I just popped in to tell you about Charlie's car,' Gavin said. 'I'd like to buy it, if you're sure you don't want to keep it.'

'It's no use to me.'

'We had a discussion in the mess. They thought two hundred and fifty pounds would be a fair price. What do you think?'

Nancy shook her head. 'I've no idea. What d'you think, Dad?'

'It sounds about right to me,' Miles said slowly.

'You are sure, Nancy?' Gavin took out his cheque book.

She was looking at him helplessly.

Her father said, 'You can't drive, and living at the Lord Nelson you wouldn't have much use for a car anyway. All the shops and cinemas are close at hand. Besides, I've got one I hardly use. I can run you about.'

Nancy was near to tears. 'Charlie loved that car. It's hard for me to part with his things. But to you . . . He'd probably want you to have it, Gavin. I'd better be sensible and take the money.'

'Thank you. I miss him too, Nancy.'

'We all do,' Miles echoed.

Nancy knew everybody was trying to be supportive and was grateful. Her friend Helen came round almost daily.

'I need an outfit for the funeral,' Nancy told her on

one visit. 'Come and help me choose something that doesn't make me look like a crow. I've nothing much in black; I find it depressing.'

'Then don't wear it,' Helen said. 'Think back. Do you remember two years ago Queen Elizabeth was in mourning for a family member when she had to make an official visit to France with the King? She chose to wear all white, because in some societies that is worn for mourning. It made her look very glamorous.'

'White?' Nancy felt cheered. 'That's a good idea. But it's one thing for the Queen to do it – would it be all right for me?'

'Of course it would. Charlie would approve, wouldn't he? It's spring, and getting warmer.'

With Helen's help, Nancy bought herself a white floaty dress and wide-brimmed hat. She bought a white outfit for Caro too.

'White suits both of you,' Helen told them. 'You look very summery.'

'It's very early in the year. What if the weather turns cold and wet?'

'The forecast is for a warm spell,' Helen said. 'Look on the bright side.'

Charlie was rarely out of Nancy's mind. 'How am I going to get through the funeral? There'll be lots of air force ceremonial, it'll take for ever.'

'You must think of it as Charlie's passing out parade. Just concentrate on saying goodbye to him.'

'I will.' She wouldn't let herself think about going through it again the following day.

The country was in the grip of a heat wave, and both funeral days were hot and sunny. Nancy kept her mind firmly on the fun and the good times she and Charlie had had, and took strength from her father standing beside her. She kept Caro's hand clasped tightly in her own.

Henrietta, in deepest black, was disapproving of their outfits, but at the reception she complained of feeling faint from the heat. Nancy had to find her a seat near a fan and help her to remove her jacket and heavy black veiling.

Uncle Toby told her she and Caro looked absolutely charming in white. He and Jago offered to help in any way they could.

'You'll need a van to move your belongings to the Lord Nelson,' Jago said. 'Let me know when you want it and I'll send you a van and driver.' Nancy felt very grateful.

She took Caro back to Hawarden to pack up the house and was very glad Helen kept coming round. She longed for Charlie but at the same time was furious with him for risking his life in the way he had. Having lunch at the Copper Kettle with Helen and another friend or two had been a weekly event and Helen insisted she carry on.

One morning, Charlie's wing commander telephoned

Nancy and asked her to come up and see him. She was nervous, knowing this could be about compensation and that in financial terms her fate hung in the balance. He was kindly, but told her that as Charlie had been fooling about and had in effect caused his own death, the Air Ministry did not feel compensation was due. However, a small pension would be paid to her on compassionate grounds.

Nancy walked out holding her head high, but had a little weep when she returned home. This was a bitter blow. She was grateful she'd have a widow's pension; at least that was something. Thank goodness Dad wanted them to live with him, because she wouldn't be able to afford another home for herself and Caro. But she didn't want to be a burden on him either.

She was glad of the books Henrietta had given Caro because there was nothing her daughter liked better than drawing and painting. They read through each chapter together and when Nancy was sure she understood the point of it, she organised Caro to work through the suggested exercises listed at the back. The child's talent was being stretched.

Nancy knew she must organise a school for her in Birkenhead, and rang the primary school she'd gone to to give Caro's details to the school secretary. A few hours later the headmistress rang her back to say they'd be on their half-term break on the date Nancy had said Caro would be able to start. She suggested Nancy bring the child in to see her the following Wednesday morning when the school re-opened.

'We have a place for a child of Caroline's age. You'll be able to leave her with us, if that is what you want. I look forward to meeting you, Mrs Seymour.'

Nancy felt better once that was arranged. In the week before they left, Helen put on a farewell meal at her home one evening and invited Gavin Freeman and Jean round too. Caro played with Helen's young son and tried to draw portraits of them all so she'd remember them.

It was a pleasant evening and for the first time nobody mentioned Charlie's name. Afterwards, Gavin drove Nancy and Caro home in the MG and she asked him in for a cup of coffee. He made it while she saw Caro into bed. It was past the child's bedtime and she was tired, falling asleep almost as soon as her head touched the pillow.

Gavin was yawning and Nancy felt tired too when she sat down with him to drink the coffee. Although Charlie had been bringing Gavin home regularly for the last year or so, he and Nancy had become much closer friends since Charlie had died. Nancy hadn't forgotten that he had problems too.

'I've been taken off all flying duties and put to work in the supplies office. Everything's awful at the moment,' he said. 'I hate clerical work.'

'What about your court martial?'

'I'm dreading that. I've been given a date for it: two months to wait.'

Nancy sighed. 'What will they do to you? I mean what punishment will you get?'

'Nobody seems to know for sure. The worst possibility is that I'll be dismissed the service. Or I could just be kept on clerical duties – possibly for a year, but maybe for ever.'

'War seems close now. They'll need you, Gavin. You'll be flying again.'

He said soberly, 'Whatever happens, I still have my life.'

They reminisced about how the three of them, Nancy, Gavin and Charlie, had planted a vegetable patch in the cottage garden.

'I'm eating the lettuces now . . .' Nancy caught her breath and stopped. She'd expected Charlie to be eating them with her.

She and Gavin always talked of Charlie. What else was there for them to talk about? Charlie's company was what they'd had in common.

'He was the best friend I ever had,' Gavin told her. 'When I knew Colleen was dying, it was Charlie who kept me sane. He helped me through it. It was his friendship, and yours of course, that brought me back to normal life. I'd like to do the same for you. I feel I owe you that, but I can't. I have to stay here and you and Caro have to go.'

Nancy's heart turned over and she found she was fighting back tears.

He patted the back of her hand. 'You need your family more than you need me.'

'I need my friends too, but I can't have them.'

'No. I ought to go, it's getting late.'

'It's the end of an era, isn't it?' Nancy said.

'That's what makes it so hard to say goodbye.'

She pulled herself together. 'It doesn't have to be a permanent goodbye, Gavin.'

'No.' He stood staring down at her.

'I'd like to know how you fare at the court martial. Do you ever come to Merseyside?'

He shook his head. 'Not very often these days.'

'Come and have a drink at the Lord Nelson, any time you're near.'

'I will,' he said, giving her a quick hug at the door. A moment later she heard the MG pull away up the lane.

The weather changed on the day Nancy moved back to Birkenhead. It was unseasonably cool, with heavy grey cloud. She travelled the short distance from Hawarden in the front seat of the van Jago had sent, with Caro sitting on her knee. It wasn't easy turning her back on the home where she'd been so happy. She kept giving Caro little hugs; her daughter was her most precious possession now.

The Lord Nelson occupied the corner plot between

Argyle Street and Market Street. The driver slowed down in front of the main entrance in Argyle Street, a wide doorway embellished on both sides with advertisements for Birkenhead Brewery's Pale Ales. Over the door was a board with a painting of Admiral Nelson in full uniform.

'Would you please go round the next corner into Market Street?' Nancy asked. 'There's a door there to our flat.'

She turned her key in the lock. It was all so familiar, even the smell of ale that wafted out. A narrow hall with a door into the bar, and stairs leading up to their living quarters. The pub was open and sounded quite busy, but her dad came hurrying out.

'Welcome home, Nancy.' He tried to lift Caro up, but found her too heavy, and instead bent to kiss her. 'You too, love.'

'You don't look well this morning, Dad. Are you all right?'

'Yes, but I've been a bit off colour recently.'

'What's the matter?' Nancy was alarmed.

'I'm a bit chesty, that's all.'

'You've got a cough?'

'Yes, a bit of one.'

The van driver had opened up the van and was starting to carry her things upstairs, but it was beginning to rain.

'I'll send somebody out to help,' her father said. 'You

'don't want your stuff to get wet. You tell them where you want things to go.'

'Thanks, Dad. You go in. You mustn't stand about in this drizzle.'

Nancy loaded Caro's arms up with toys and encouraged her to scamper up and downstairs with the lighter things while she herself lugged suitcases indoors.

She was very surprised when the door to the bar opened and she saw Kevin Cochran beaming at her. 'Hello, Nancy. Sorry to hear about Charlie. Awful. How are you?'

'Kev! You're back working for Dad?'

'Yep, cellarman, barman and anything I can turn my hand to. I've come to help you right now.'

Nancy had counted Kevin a friend for years and was cheered to find him here. He looked younger than he was, a rather pale and skinny lad who even now had a waif-like look about him. His grin was cheerful and his brown straight hair much in need of a trim.

'It's nice to see a friend at a time like this,' she said. 'But I didn't expect . . .'

'Your father's been very good to me,' he said. 'A real gent. You're lucky to have a dad like that behind you.'

'I know,' she said. Kevin was Nancy's age and they'd been in the same class at primary school. At eleven they'd both done well in the tests and been given places in the Higher Elementary School in Conway Street, but while she'd stayed until she was sixteen, Kevin had left at fourteen to work as a delivery boy in a butcher's shop in Rock Ferry.

Three years later, he'd been found guilty of short-changing the customers and stealing meat. He'd been sent to a youth detention centre to mend his ways and had been out of work for some time after he'd come out.

Nancy's father was a regular churchgoer and the vicar had asked him to employ Kevin on compassionate grounds. Kevin was the eldest in a fatherless family of five children and his mother needed help. When Kevin turned eighteen, her dad had taken him on and she'd heard him say, 'I'm giving you a second chance, Kevin, but if I catch you doing anything wrong, there won't be a third.'

She'd heard him promise not to short-change the customers, to pay for any alcohol he took from the bar and to drink only in moderation. He must never get drunk.

'Better if you don't make a friend of him,' Dad had warned her.

'We've been friends for years.' She'd been indignant. 'We always got on well together at school. I can't just ignore him now he's working for you.'

'No, you mustn't ignore him, that wouldn't be kind, but be aware he might get into trouble again. You must help him to avoid that.'

Nancy knew her father thought of her as a little angel who could do no wrong, but she'd never been like that.

She was afraid that however hard she tried, she could never achieve his standards.

Nancy had enjoyed Kevin's company behind the bar, and had spent many hours chatting to him in the back yard or down in the cellar.

'I'm ambitious,' he'd told her. 'I want a job I'll really enjoy. Like driving a rich man round in his Rolls Royce. I'm going to learn to drive.'

She understood that Kevin's life was very different from her own, and knew that for months he'd saved part of his weekly wage to pay for driving lessons. He told her about his girlfriends, Gladys Hopkins and Nora Smith, whom she remembered from school. He also told her about risks he took that she found thrilling, but these she kept to herself. Innocent though many of them were, they were things that would have made her father shudder.

Dad had not always approved of her friends. Nancy had wanted the things Kevin wanted: lots of money to buy nice clothes and to go to theatres and expensive restaurants. She wanted to have a good time.

When she'd started to work for the insurance company she'd mixed with office girls who felt themselves a cut above barmaids. They lived out in the leafier suburbs and they wanted the good life too. They saw that as buying their clothes in posh department stores like Bunney's, and being taken to the Bear's Paw or the Bowler Hat Club for a night out.

They knew she lived at the Lord Nelson; it was just a short walk from the office and most of them passed it on their way to work. They saw it as a pub for working men. Nancy didn't tell them she worked there as a barmaid on Friday and Saturday nights. They wouldn't have understood that, as she worked full time with them. She soon learned that no office girl would go into a pub unless escorted by a man, and no man worth their attention would go into the Lord Nelson.

Kevin had been working at the Lord Nelson for her father for a year when he was caught breaking into the butcher's shop that had previously employed him. Stock and money had gone missing over previous months. Nancy knew before it came out in court that he'd had keys copied while he worked there so he could get into the storerooms.

When the butcher's shop was closed, the door was locked and bolted top and bottom, but Kevin had climbed over the back yard wall and got in through a small washroom window. Nancy knew he'd been doing this for some time and selling some of the meat he stole. He'd tried to rope her in as an accomplice, but she'd been too scared. He'd sworn her to secrecy so she'd said nothing to her father. Now she was worried stiff her father would find out she'd known about it and done nothing to stop Kevin before he was caught. To her relief, he didn't question her; in fact he surprised her by taking Kevin's side. 'He kept his promise not to take liberties with pub customers,' he said. 'Nobody has complained about him to me.'

When Kevin's case came up in court, Dad acted as a character witness, but Kevin was sent to jail for three months and she'd seen little of him after that.

It was about the time Charlie first came to the pub. Nancy felt so bad about not helping to keep Kevin out of trouble that she eventually told him about it.

He laughed it off. 'You can't snitch on your friends, Nancy. You've nothing to feel guilty about. You stayed out of trouble, didn't you? Your dad should be proud of you.'

'No, he'd expect more of me than that,' she sighed. She and Kevin had exchanged confidences and talked many times about how they were going to achieve the good things in life, but once she was married to Charlie Nancy had all the luxury she'd wanted and Kevin was gone. As Charlie's wife, she felt she'd had a social lift-up. She'd never had another job. Charlie had wanted her to enjoy the good times he arranged and he'd encouraged her to buy expensive clothes.

She twisted the diamond ring on her finger. It was a big one and much admired, and Charlie had given it to her to mark Caro's birth. She wore it over her wedding band, so it appeared they'd been engaged in the traditional way before they'd been married. Nancy felt she'd fallen on her feet. Charlie complained his mess bill was sky high and it took him all his time to pay for basic necessities, but he could find money for any amount of high living.

It made her shiver to think of that now. Charlie had gone and so had all the fun in her life. She was afraid she'd no longer be able to afford the luxuries she'd enjoyed with him. She was hoping Charlie's insurance policy would pay out, but if not, all she'd have to live on was a small pension.

Kevin had been asking the van driver about his job all the time they'd been emptying the van.

'Did you ever get your driving licence?' Nancy asked.

'Yes.' He grinned at her. 'I did, but I never found a driving job. I've been saving up to buy a car for years and I haven't got that either.'

With the van emptied and everything taken upstairs, Kevin said to the driver, 'Come and have a drink before you go. You deserve it after carrying all Nancy's clobber up.' They disappeared in the direction of the bar, while Nancy went upstairs to survey all the worldly goods she had to show for nearly eight years of marriage.

CHAPTER NINE

CARO WAS AS restless as Nancy was herself. 'I want to go on the ferry boat on the river,' she said.

'Not now, love, we haven't time.'

'Please, Mummy. Let's go out.'

'Let's put our macs on, then, and take a little walk.'

The rain had stopped and Nancy took her daughter to the end of the road and through the gardens of Hamilton Square. She stood surveying the handsome Georgian terraces, and in particular the building that housed the insurance company where she'd once worked.

It was good to be home, but the whole world seemed darker than it used to be. They could hear the clangour of heavy hammers from Cammell Laird's shipyard, and the ships hooting in the fog on the Mersey. After the fresh country air of Hawarden, the atmosphere smelled of the sulphur and coal smoke put out by heavy industry, which left a haze of black dust everywhere, indoors and out.

'I liked the fields and Hawthorn Cottage better, Mummy.' Caro swung on her hand.

'You'll like it here when you get used to it,' Nancy said. But although Argyle Street was still familiar, it no longer seemed as attractive to her as it once had, and neither did the other busy streets in the centre of town. It started to rain again and they turned back. Seen from a distance, Nancy thought there was something reassuring about the Lord Nelson pub. Smoke-blackened it might be, but it had an air of faded jollity. Built in 1867, it was only a few doors away from the famous Argyle Theatre where many stars of the music hall had made their names. There were cinemas and cafés all round.

'Can I see inside the pub?' Caro asked. Nancy held open the door of the public bar so she could. It was quite dark inside because the glass in the windows was decorated with vine leaves and bunches of grapes, making much of it opaque. The electric lights were on most of the time and glinted on the bottles behind the bar, most of which were rarely broached. Nancy had been back many times for short visits. Nothing in the pub had changed in years.

The air was blue with cigarette smoke and carried a strong whiff of beer. The child held her nose. 'It stinks. I don't like it.'

Alma Banks was pulling pints and gave them a wave. Nancy knew she'd taken her place as Dad's right hand. Alma was grey-haired and in her fifties but she had a cheery manner and always joined in any fun. She was very fat, and had a belly laugh that sounded like a man's and could make every ounce of her surplus flesh ripple. She was popular with the customers.

Upstairs, the living room seemed bleak. When her father came up for lunch, she said, 'I was very surprised to see Kevin back working for you.'

'I felt sorry for him,' he said. 'Nobody else would give him a job. He's been in and out of prison these last years and so has the rest of his family. His problem is that if he can't get a job, he's almost forced to steal to eat.'

'Is he still keeping his promise to you not to short-change the customers?'

'He is. I've always found him to be honest. Kevin and his family have never had enough money to make ends meet. To steal must be a terrible temptation to lads like that.'

Nancy realised her father was very forgiving. It made her ache with affection for him.

While the pub was open and Dad couldn't be with her, Nancy unpacked her possessions. Her bedroom seemed cramped now space had had to be made for Caro's camp bed. The child had settled down at the kitchen table with her colouring book. All was quiet and familiar.

Nancy was filled with nostalgia for those happy days when Dad had looked after her. He was not one to be fussy about housework; he'd let her do pretty much what she wanted. Mildred, who cleaned the pub, came upstairs three mornings a week to tidy up.

Dad used to cook their breakfast and walk her to school afterwards. At dinner time, the pub would be open and she'd walk home alone. When she rang the side door bell, either Dad or Alma would hurry from the bar to open it.

Often, if business was slack, Dad would come upstairs with her. Always she'd hear their dog Gyp barking a welcome. When she opened the living-room door, Gyp would jump up at her and she'd have to fuss and pat him. He kept her company when Dad couldn't be with her.

'Come and wash your hands,' Dad would say. Her lunch was always ready on the kitchen table: a glass of milk, and a sandwich waiting between two plates. 'This is your lunch, not Gyp's,' he'd often add. 'Make sure you eat it, love.'

He had to go back to work in the bar, but Gyp would come and sit near her, his tail thumping on the lino. Nancy gave him the crusts to make him sit up and beg. Dad would come to remind her when it was time to go back to school, and he'd wave her off.

For Nancy, the best part of the day was when afternoon school was over. The pub would be closed then and Dad and Gyp would be waiting at the school gates for her to come out. This was their time together. Sometimes they'd go for a walk, or on cold wet days he'd play snakes and ladders or Ludo with her. What Nancy enjoyed most was for Dad to take her to the market and let her choose what she wanted to eat for dinner. Then they'd go home and cook it together. Dad was a good cook, and he'd taught her to cook too.

They'd eat their dinner, but far too soon afterwards she'd hear the living-room clock chime six, which meant the pub had to open again. Dad would switch on the wireless so she could listen to that and she would curl up on the sofa with Gyp.

He was a medium-sized brown mongrel with a lot of terrier in him. Dad had taken her to the local dogs' home and let her choose which one she wanted. Gyp had looked at her with beseeching brown eyes.

'Children aren't allowed in the pub, but I have to earn a living there for both of us,' Dad had said. 'You must be a good girl and stay here with Gyp. He'll look after you and keep you safe when I can't be with you.'

Dad had taught her to tell the time when she was very young, because everything had to be done by the clock.

'I'll come back and see you into bed at nine o'clock. If you need me before then, and I mean really need me, send Gyp down the stairs into the pub to let me know.'

Gyp loved that. She'd only to open the door and tell him to find Dad and he'd go pattering down. It had been some time before she found out that Dad kept a bowl under the bar and filled it with beer dregs for him. Alma eventually told her that Dad would make a great charade of drawing half a pint for him. The customers loved seeing Gyp eagerly lap it up, and made a great fuss of him.

It was Caro who brought her back from her nostalgic meandering, waving a pack of cards and wanting her to play a game of snap. Caro was not yet at ease here. Nancy hoped she'd settle once she started at school, but there were a few more days to wait until the half-term break was over.

Nancy had planned to take her daughter out and do the things she'd enjoyed as a child, such as take the ferry down to New Brighton and swim in the big open-air pool. Caro would love the miles of golden sands and Nancy would treat her to a donkey ride and an ice cream.

But today the rain was hurtling against the windows and rushing in the gutters. The sands would be empty and forlorn and the donkeys wouldn't be out. The place would feel dismal and depressing.

After a day indoors, Nancy would have liked to spend the evening helping out behind the bar. Occasional shouts and bursts of laughter and song drifted temptingly up, but she didn't want to leave Caro on her own in a strange place, even after she'd put her to bed.

If only they were still at Hawarden with Charlie. It was at times like this that she really missed him.

That same Wednesday evening, Henrietta was getting changed for dinner. Toby had suggested she and Jago meet him at the Bell Inn but she'd been before and didn't care for it. She'd have preferred a quiet meal at home.

'We have to go,' Jago said. 'We told Toby we would; he'll have booked a table.'

'I've told you I feel dismally low,' she said. 'The death of my son has affected me badly. You're Charles's father, but even you don't understand. You're able to go to your sausage factory and occupy yourself there. You're very unfeeling, Jago.'

'Henrietta, it does you no good to drape yourself in black crepe and spend your days sobbing on the sofa. Nancy is back at the Lord Nelson. You'd feel better if you tried to help her.'

'Help Nancy! I need help myself. You don't seem to realise it's quite impossible for me to do anything but grieve.'

Of course, she'd always known she was more sensitive than Jago. Troubles affected her more. So, as usual, she had to fall in with their plans and go to the Bell Inn. Goodness knows why they liked the place.

Jago gave most of his attention to Toby. They talked endlessly about factory matters and farm animals, which they knew bored her to death. They had no idea how to include her in pleasant conversation.

'Everything is making me feel a little under the weather,' she said to Toby. 'I don't think I can cope with you coming for lunch on Sunday. It's too much for me.'

'But I always come to lunch on Sundays,' he said, affronted, as though it was his right.

'You'll feel better by Sunday, darling,' Jago said in his

rallying voice. 'And we'd both feel sorry to be eating on our own.'

When she'd married Jago, she hadn't realised what being married to a twin would entail. Toby was always about the place; she could hardly call her home her own. Dropping hints to him didn't stop him coming, neither did complaining to Jago about his twin's almost permanent presence.

When ill health or frailty forced her to beg for a little peace, as she had for next Sunday, it usually meant Jago deserted her and went somewhere else with his brother. Her marriage had never been easy. It had called for continual adjustment on her side to placate the twins.

She'd been sorely tempted many times to deal more heavily with them. But not with Jago; she was still fond of him, and he provided the cash she needed to live on. Toby was another matter, he drew Jago's attention away from her and always would. But just when she felt she could stand no more from Toby, he'd arrive with a great bunch of hothouse blooms and some delicacies from his farm.

'I've been thinking a lot about Caroline,' she told them, 'and the great love we have for each other. She's a sensitive soul too and must be missing her father.'

'I'm sure she is,' Jago said. 'We all are.'

'I think I could be a great comfort to the child, and to be with her would comfort me too. She'll carry on our family line, after all. I've just had a thought. If you are coming to lunch on Sunday, Toby, we could invite Caroline too.'

'Certainly,' Jago and Toby chorused in the irritating way they had. 'We could ask her with Nancy and Miles. It might cheer us all up.'

Henrietta felt they were being particularly infuriating. 'Are you trying to upset me?' she demanded. 'Caroline yes, but not that publican and his daughter. I draw the line at them.'

'Henrietta, darling,' Jago murmured in the sugary tone he used when he was trying to soften her up. 'It's very difficult to invite a seven year old to lunch on her own.'

'Not at all. You could go over and fetch her, Toby. I'm sure they'd be glad of a restful Sunday knowing Caroline was safe with us.'

'Nancy is our daughter-in-law,' Jago said. 'I think we have to ask her, even if we don't ask Miles.'

'Charles was so misguided. Not at all the sort of girl . . .'

'You'll make her feel slighted,' Toby pointed out. 'I'm sure she told me that Caro is her only comfort now. She might not want her to come to lunch at our place. She could turn you down, saying she has something else planned. If you're serious about seeing Caro, I think her mother has to be invited too.'

'If you honestly think . . .'

'We do.'

Henrietta sighed. She knew that however much she was suffering, she had to pull herself together if she was to help little Caroline. 'The pub people will have no idea how to bring her up. She'll be dragged up, if it's left to them.' Caroline should be living with her in decent surroundings. She could give her a happy childhood, bring her up to be a young lady. 'As Caroline's grandmother it's my duty to help the poor child.'

Jago smiled at her. 'You could best help her by making a friend of her mother.'

Henrietta wasn't pleased. 'Fine. Ask the mother on Sunday too, but not the publican. We have to draw the line somewhere.' She was finding the Bell Inn's dining room hot and noisy and overcrowded. The service was slow and the food indifferent; she was glad when the meal was over.

'Of course Toby must continue to come on Sundays,' Jago said as soon as they were alone in the car going home. 'You know his housekeeper has the day off. In return, he takes us out to dinner every Wednesday night when our cook is off.'

'Exactly. I don't want to complain, but he never asks me to his house.'

Jago was full of excuses for his twin, as usual. 'He's a bit embarrassed because our cook is so much better than his, and he knows he doesn't run his home as efficiently as you do.'

Henrietta groaned. It was a charade they still played,

though they knew very well she understood the real reason for Toby's embarrassment. Even now neither twin could say the word homosexual.

'Toby's domestic arrangements don't bother me in the least,' she told him. 'He has a lovely old house and should entertain more.'

'His cook . . .'

'If his cook is useless, he should sack her. I could try to find him a better one, though it's hard to get good servants these days.'

Jago said, 'Toby is an old bachelor and set in his ways. He's in a rut, and without a hostess to help him he can't cope with entertaining at home.'

'All right,' she'd conceded as she always had to. 'If Toby has to be fed on Sundays, then I must make him welcome at lunch. You're lucky you have me to help you, Jago.'

'I know, love, and I do appreciate it,' he said.

Thursday morning was wet again but by afternoon the rain had eased to a drizzle. Nancy took Caro shopping for food in the market. It was a huge place and very close, almost anything could be bought there. It cheered her to be out and about with something definite to do.

When they returned to the Lord Nelson, Nancy found that a letter had come from Charlie's life assurance company. She feared the worst and left it unopened while she put the shopping away.

When she steeled herself to open it, she found it confirmed her worst fears. It said that at the time of Charlie's death he was behaving in a way that endangered his life. It drew her attention to the exclusions, namely item 5 in section 3 of the policy.

Tears were stinging her eyes and blurring her vision. It took a moment before she could read on:

This makes it clear that though the terms of the policy covered your husband's normal flying duties it did not provide cover for aerial acrobatics. We understand he was engaged in such manoeuvres at the time of the fatal accident, and therefore we regret that we are unable to pay out on this policy.

Nancy had half expected it, but even so it made her feel sick. She knew this would severely reduce her options in the years ahead. She'd have to work to support herself and her daughter.

She took a deep breath. It was no good feeling sorry for herself, and the sooner she picked herself up and got on with things, the better. She ran down to tell her father and give him the letter to read.

When he came up to have lunch with them, he said, 'I'm so sorry. I know you were hoping they'd pay out. I'm afraid it means you have some big decisions to make.'

Nancy was struggling to swallow the scrambled eggs she'd prepared. Caro was bolting hers.

Miles said, 'It's hard to look after a child as well as

earn a living, Nancy. I know coming here was meant to be a temporary measure, but I can't help thinking your best plan is to stay with me. You can make a flat for yourself and Caro on the top floor and I could pay you to work in the bar. There's a sort of phone we could have put in.'

'An intercom?'

'Yes, so we could be in contact . . .'

'Would I be allowed to talk to you on that?' Caro was bubbling with joy at the thought.

'Of course. It would be specially for you, so we'd know what you were up to.'

'You're very generous, Dad,' Nancy choked. 'I'm grateful.'

'Come and have a look at the rooms on the top floor,' he said when they'd finished eating. Halfway up the stairs he had to stop to get his breath.

'Are you all right, Dad?'

He was coughing and wheezing. 'I haven't been too good recently.'

'You should go to see the doctor.'

'I have, love. Twice.'

'What does he say?'

'It's a touch of bronchitis. The cold damp Mersey air isn't good for me.'

'Does he give you any medicine?'

'Yes, cough syrup.'

'It doesn't sound as though it's doing you much good.'

'It must be. Some days I feel fine. I thought this room could be made into a living room for you. And you'd be able to have a bedroom each.'

'Yes, I've been up for a look round more than once, Dad. It wouldn't take too much to make the place habitable.'

'That's right. Anyway, I like having you here and there'd be two of us to keep an eye on Caro.'

'Thanks, Dad.' She smiled. 'At least you've helped me to see there is a way forward.'

CHAPTER TEN

THAT SAME EVENING, when Nancy was settling Caro into the camp bed Dad had set up as a temporary arrangement, Alma came puffing up to tell her that two men had come into the bar.

'They said to tell you Jago and Uncle Toby had come to see you.'

'Oh, that's kind of them.' Nancy kissed Caro good night and told her she was going downstairs for five minutes. She saw them sitting at a table in the lounge with her father pushing a pint of bitter in front of each of them. Two gentlemen, each with a head of thick silvery hair, stood up as one as she went in.

'Nancy!' She was pulled into warm hugs.

'How are you? Lovely to see you both.'

Dad came back with a glass of lemonade for her. 'You'll have to excuse me,' he told the twins. 'We're quite busy tonight.'

'How is Caro?' Jago asked.

'She's fine most of the time, but she misses her dad.'

'Henrietta is quite anxious about her. She wants you

to bring her to lunch on Sunday. Can I tell her you will?'

Nancy wasn't keen on seeing more of Henrietta, but Charlie would want her to keep in touch, and for Caro's sake she must.

'I'll come and pick you up,' Toby offered.

She nodded, unable to refuse. Two sets of astute dark eyes probed into hers. 'Are you managing all right?' Jago demanded.

She was feeling low, and knew they could probably see it. Her fingers brushed the letter she'd pushed into her pocket. She drew it out and handed it to Jago. 'You've caught me at a low moment.'

'We want to help,' Uncle Toby told her as he took the letter from Jago to read.

'You must let us,' Jago added.

'Come upstairs to Dad's flat,' Nancy stood up. 'I don't like leaving Caro alone up there. Bring your drinks with you.'

They followed her up the shabby stairs. Dad had done nothing to the place since she'd left home. Before they reached the landing, she could hear Caro calling out, sounding quite hysterical.

'Mummy, Mummy! There's a bogeyman here! He's going to get me!'

Nancy went straight to the bedroom they shared and snapped the light on. The child was sitting up in bed, her face scarlet and wet with tears. Nancy sank down beside her and put an arm round her.

'No, love, there's nobody here. Nothing to be frightened of.'

Small arms sprang round her neck and tightened like wire. 'I saw him moving. He's there! Behind the door!'

Nancy lifted her up and took her to the bottom of her bed and moved the door. 'Open your eyes. Look, you can see for yourself, there's nobody here.' She gave her a handkerchief. 'That's better. Grandpa and Uncle Toby have come to see you, so why don't you give them a smile?'

'My poor pet.' Jago took Caro from Nancy's arms. 'There's nothing here to be frightened of.'

'I saw something move.' She was rubbing her eyes. 'I did, Grandpa.'

'Perhaps this is what you saw move?' Uncle Toby removed her dressing gown from its hook on the door and tossed it on a chair.

'It's quite breezy in here,' Nancy said. 'It might have been moving in the draught from the window.' She slammed it shut. 'Was that it?'

'It looked like a bogeyman,' Caro sniffed, but she was quietening down.

Jago set her down on her bed. 'You get under your blankets,' he said, 'and I'll read you a story. I used to read stories to your father.'

'I can read,' Caro said. 'I'm a good reader.'

'We know you are, love,' Nancy said, 'but you like

being read to, don't you? Uncle Toby and I will say good night,' she dropped a kiss on her forehead, 'and leave you with Grandpa.'

She gave the open book to Jago. 'She's loving Arthur Ransome. We're up to chapter eight.'

'Yes, *Swallows and Amazons*,' Caro said, snuggling down against her pillows. Nancy led Toby to the living room, picking up her glass of lemonade from the chest of drawers on the landing as she passed.

'Poor Caro,' he said. 'Sad to see that.'

'She used to go out like a light the moment her head touched the pillow and we never heard another sound from her until morning. It's losing her dad and all the upset of leaving Hawthorn Cottage.'

'You both need time to get over Charlie. You're happy to stay here for the moment?'

'I don't think I'd be happy anywhere right now.' Nancy was blinking hard again. She was wondering what Toby thought of her father's shabby living quarters. Hawthorn Cottage had been a cut above this.

'Sorry. It's a difficult time for you. I don't want you to be short of money, Nancy. Now I know what the situation is, I'll arrange something for you.'

The tears started rolling down her cheeks. 'You're very kind. I didn't expect that. I wasn't asking . . .'

He patted her arm. 'I know, but Charlie wouldn't want you to be hard up. He'd expect his family to do something about it.'

'My dad suggested I make a home for myself and Caro on the floor above. I really don't know . . .'

'You've done the right thing coming back here.'

'Henrietta doesn't think so.'

'You need your father right now. Do what he suggests, make yourself comfortable here. Give yourself a year or so to find out what you really want. You're still young, Nancy. You've got a future in front of you. See how things pan out.'

Jago came in. 'Caro's eyelids are going down. She's on the point of sleep. She'll be all right now.'

A little later there was a tap on the sitting-room door and Kevin came in. 'I've come to ask if you'd like more drinks.' He came in and put their empty glasses on his tray.

'That's kind of you,' Jago said.

Kevin brushed the hair off his forehead. 'The boss sent me.' He beamed at the visitors. 'He's dead pleased that Nancy's in-laws have come to look her up.'

Nancy smiled. 'This is Kevin,' she said. 'We've been friends for years.'

'That means you've been working here for a long time?' Jago asked.

'Off and on.' He winked at Nancy. 'So what's it to be? Another pint for each of you gentlemen?'

'Better make it a half,' Toby said.

'Nancy?'

'I don't want anything, thanks.'

'There's a new brand of orangeade just in, it's smashing. Wouldn't you like to try it?'

'Oh, go on then.'

When he'd gone, she said, 'Kevin and I were at school together. He stood up for me if I was ever in trouble.'

'Looks as though he still does.'

'My dad looks after him now,' she said, but she didn't mention why he needed to. When Kevin came back with the drinks, they chatted to him about his family.

Half an hour later, when the twins prepared to leave, Nancy said, 'Thank you both. You've made me feel much better about things.'

Toby said, 'I'll come and collect you and Caro for lunch on Sunday, about twelve.' He pecked her cheek like a real uncle.

Later, when the pub closed, her father came up and she told him what had happened.

'Charlie loved them both,' she said. 'And they've always been friendly towards me. But even so, I didn't expect Toby to be so understanding. They're both very kind.'

'So they should be,' Miles said. 'I like them too, but I've never seen two men so much alike. They were very pleasant when they came in; Alma was quite bowled over. They must know that none of us can tell them apart because Jago introduced himself to me, but by the time I'd taken them to the lounge and got them a drink I wasn't sure which was which again. I almost called one of them Toby, but had second thoughts and got confused, and then I lost the thread of what I was saying.'

'I'm sure they're used to that.'

'I've noticed Toby has a little scar on his chin,' Miles said. 'I was looking for that, but it's so small it isn't easy to see.'

'I wouldn't worry. They think it's a bit of a joke. Sometimes they try to confuse Caro, but they can't.'

'She always knows which is which?'

'Charlie taught us both how to do it.' Nancy was smiling. 'Look at them carefully and you'll see they're mirror images of each other.'

'Are they?'

'Yes. Jago is left-handed while Toby uses his right. When Caro wants to make sure, she watches to see which hand they use. They try to tease her sometimes, but she knows the same is true of the whole side of their bodies. She'll kick a ball towards them, or get them to put her spy glass to their eyes. That always betrays who they really are.'

'Glory be, I've never noticed! Why is that?'

Toby did no work on Sunday mornings. He liked nothing better than to hang over his farm gates watching his pigs. Today, a heavy shower blew up but Toby enjoyed being out in all weathers.

He reminded himself that he'd promised to fetch Nancy and Caro to have lunch with Henrietta today and must cut short his morning walk. Before going indoors, he went to his glasshouse to pick two bunches of flowers, one for Henrietta, and the other for Nancy.

He took a quick bath and changed into new fawn slacks, a clean cream shirt and a brown striped tie. At the last minute he added a sports jacket; clothes of the minimum formality Henrietta would consider acceptable for a guest coming to one of her Sunday lunches.

Then he drove through the tunnel to Birkenhead to pick up Nancy and Caro. He rang the bell at the side door and a minute or two later Nancy opened it. She seemed pleased and surprised to be presented with the large bunch of multicoloured dahlias. He watched her bury her face in them.

'Thank you, Toby, they're lovely. Did you grow them? Can you hang on a minute? I'd like to run them up to the kitchen and put them in water.'

As usual, Caro chatted nineteen to the dozen until her mother came back. They were both wearing the white dresses they'd worn for Charlie's funeral under their macs. Toby couldn't help but notice that Nancy was pale and had grey shadows under her eyes. He felt sorry for her. Poor girl, being reduced to widowhood at such a young age. Sighing quietly, he led them to his elegant Jaguar sports saloon.

CHAPTER ELEVEN

CARO WAS EXCITED about going to her grandma's house for lunch, but Nancy was dreading it. When the car turned into Lexington Avenue she pulled herself up in the car seat to see the wide and leafy suburban road. She'd not been to Charlie's childhood home very often, but it always impressed her when she did.

Soon they were crunching over the short gravel drive and then the big modern house came into view. Such an unusual design; even in the rain it looked gorgeous. Charlie, and the rest of the Seymours, said they preferred Toby's house, but Nancy had only seen pictures of his. Caro hardly seemed to notice how greatly these houses differed from the succession of flats and cottages near airfields that had been homes to her.

Toby rang the front door bell as he inserted his key to let them in.

'Hello, Gertie,' he said when the parlourmaid appeared. Nancy had thought her elderly the first time Charlie had brought her here, but she didn't look any older now. 'We just need you to take our coats.'

Even on this dark day, Nancy thought the hall full of light. She'd never been here without Charlie to stand between her and his mother. She was missing him more than ever.

Jago pushed a glass of sherry into her hand and came to sit beside her. 'You both look very pretty in your white dresses.'

She saw Henrietta assessing her coldly over Caro's head. Nancy had found white cardigans for them on this cool day but hers spoiled the line of her dress. She no longer felt smart.

'I think white suits a child very well,' Henrietta said, 'but it's hardly suitable mourning for a woman who's just lost her husband.'

Nancy found that hurtful. 'Charlie will understand,' she said, wanting to give as good as she got. 'He didn't like me wearing black.'

'At a time like this, mourning shows grief and respect for the departed.'

Nancy felt overwhelmed by grief and was trying to hide it. She could think of nothing to say.

Henrietta asked frigidly, 'Are you enjoying being back in the pub?'

Nancy took a gulp of sherry. 'I don't know that I'm enjoying much of anything just now, Mother-in-law.'

'No, and I'm sure you must be finding that place particularly hard. What's it called?'

'The Lord Nelson.'

'Hm. It might be named after an aristocratic hero but I'm sure you find it a bit downmarket after Hawthorn Cottage.'

All Nancy's previous dislike of her mother-in-law came thundering back. She didn't mean to take this lying down.

'The Lord Nelson is home to me,' she said, 'and my father is very supportive. I think at the moment it's the best place for me and Caro.'

Toby came to her aid. 'Now, Henrietta,' he murmured. 'You said you wanted to make friends with Nancy.'

She ignored him. 'It might be the right place for you, Nancy. I'm a bit worried as to whether Caroline will fit in.'

'I do, Grandma,' Caro piped up. 'Grandpops is very kind. He brings me bottles of lemonade from the pub and plays draughts with me.'

'Not that fizzy stuff?'

'Yes. I like it, Grandma.'

'It isn't good for your health. She is looking a little pale, don't you think, Nancy?'

'She looks the picture of health to me,' Toby said quickly.

'You aren't the most perceptive of men, Toby. I was thinking I should take Caroline to the seaside for a little holiday. It would do her good. You'd like that, wouldn't you, pet?'

'Oh, yes, Grandma. Daddy took us to Cornwall last summer, and we had a lovely time on the sands. When can we go?'

'As soon as the weather improves. In a few days.'

'No,' Nancy protested. 'It's not holiday time yet.'

Caroline was tugging at her dress. 'When will it be holiday time, Mummy?'

'Soon,' her grandmother said. 'Though I see no reason why we shouldn't go early in the season.'

Caro's blue eyes were pleading. 'You will take us, won't you, Grandma?'

'I promise, pet.'

Nancy was finding this scary. It sounded as though Henrietta wanted to take Caro away on her own. Nancy didn't mean to be parted from her daughter. 'Caro needs to go to school,' she said. 'It's not good for her to miss lessons.'

'Yes indeed. We must choose a good school for you, pet. Education is very important, if you're to do well in life.'

Caro giggled. 'Mummy's already chosen it. I can start next Wednesday.'

'What?' An outraged Henrietta swung round on Nancy. 'What school is this?'

'It's the one I went to.'

'Quite unsuitable for Caroline!' Henrietta barked indignantly. 'Charles would never agree to such a thing. We decided she should go to a nice little school in Hawarden. Wasn't it called Summertrees?'

'Yes.' Nancy could feel the heat running up her cheeks. 'Charlie called it a dame school but said it would do her no harm to start in a gentle environment with small classes.'

'Exactly, and she's learned her very nice manners there. My family trust paid the fees and would be more than willing to carry on doing so.'

Nancy felt manipulated. 'That's kind of you.' She took another gulp of the sherry. 'But Charlie thought that later on it would be good for Caro to get used to the rough and tumble of an ordinary school.'

'Well, I don't. She'll pick up the most dreadful accent and all sorts of swear words. Probably she'll get nits in her hair. She won't get proper lessons there and she'll fall behind. I do think you should have consulted me about her schooling.'

'I didn't think you'd feel so strongly . . .'

'Caroline!' Her grandmother swung back to her. 'You don't want to go to there, do you? Have you seen this place and the horde of ruffians you'll have to mix with? It isn't very nice.'

Caro was looking troubled. 'I've only seen the outside.'

'This is a matter for Nancy to decide,' Toby began, but Henrietta had already swung furiously back to Nancy. 'You mean you haven't even vetted this council school?'

Nancy told herself not to let Henrietta steamroller her into changing her mind.

'It's closed for half term, Mother-in-law. There's a

new headmistress since I left and I'm taking Caro to meet her on Wednesday morning. As I said, I was at that school for six years and it did me no harm.'

Her voice was icy. 'That is a matter of opinion.'

'Now, Henrietta,' Jago said. 'You're being rude, and very unkind to Nancy.'

'I do apologise, Nancy, if you feel that,' she said loftily. 'But I do want you to think again about finding a better school for Caroline. There's no desperate urgency to get her started next week. It would be wiser to give yourself time to consider all the available options. Surely, private education is available in Birkenhead?'

'It is. I've thought hard about this, Mother-in-law,' Nancy said quietly, 'and discussed it with Dad.' There was a cluck of impatience at that, but Nancy ignored it. 'This school is within easy walking distance and the private schools tend to be in the suburbs, too far for Caro to walk. My father does have a car but I don't want him to have the daily task of taking and fetching Caro. He already has a good deal to see to.'

'A taxi could be arranged,' Henrietta retorted. 'There's always a way round everything.'

Nancy dug in her heels. 'I've already made up my mind, Mother-in-law. Caro will go to Wilbraham Street School. I will walk with her for a while, until she learns the way, but at her age I used to go by myself and soon she'll be able to. I enjoyed that school and I hope she will.'

Henrietta looked shocked. At that moment, there was a tap on the door. Gertie the parlourmaid opened it and announced, 'Lunch is ready, ma'am. Shall I take the soup in?'

There was a moment's silence, then Jago jerked to his feet and said, 'Yes please, Gertie. We're all ready for our lunch.'

'No.' Henrietta overruled him imperiously. 'Wait ten minutes, Gertie, if you don't mind. We ladies need to wash our hands first. Come along, Caroline. I'll take you up to my bedroom.'

Caro bounded for the stairs. Nancy, realising she was included, followed reluctantly. The bedroom was enormous, with white satin coverings on the bed. The only time she'd seen anything remotely like it was in a Hollywood film. In the adjoining marble bathroom, Henrietta supervised Caroline, and wiped her hands on a fluffy towel.

'Now you go back to Grandpa,' she told her. 'Mummy and I will be down in a minute.'

Nancy went into the bathroom and shut the door. She was scared. Henrietta wanted to talk to her alone and she didn't like the idea one bit.

When she came out, Henrietta was at her dressing table powdering her nose.

'Nancy,' she said. 'There are a lot of advantages I can give Caroline that you can't. A first-class education, for one. I don't think it's safe for her to go running round the corner to this council school you spoke of. Think of the traffic.'

Nancy tried to speak but Henrietta wouldn't let her.

'I know you've made up your mind, but I ask you to think again. You surely don't want her to leave school at fourteen knowing next to nothing?'

Nancy was acutely uncomfortable. 'It's by way of being a stopgap for Caro.'

'These are valuable years in Caroline's schooling. You should be thinking of her. I spent my early years at home with a governess and when I went to boarding school at thirteen I found it quite hard to catch up with my school work. Caroline will have the same problem.'

'I'm sure she'll manage. She's very bright.' Nancy was heading for the door. She wanted to escape.

'I have only Caroline's well-being in mind. I feel as her grandmother I have a duty to do my best for her. You've no objections to her having a short holiday with me when this so-called school breaks up in the summer?'

Nancy had, but was past being able to voice her objections.

Henrietta fulminated all week. Nancy was being very silly, refusing every offer of help she made. She couldn't make her see sense, but what else could she expect from a barmaid?

'Jago,' she said, 'I think we should have a talk.' He was sipping a pre-dinner whisky in the armchair opposite her.

He smiled. 'I was just thinking the same myself. It's our wedding anniversary soon and it falls on a Sunday.'

'Not about that.' She held up her hand. 'I think we should make a stand against Nancy, otherwise Caroline will grow up an ignorant guttersnipe.'

Jago stifled a groan. 'Give over, dear. Nancy doesn't know whether she's coming or going yet. Give her time. At the moment she wants to look after the child in her own way. Shall we have a special lunch on our wedding anniversary? Ask more people?'

'Not all Nancy's relatives, I hope. Our wedding anniversary is not a day to fill the house with every Tom, Dick and Harry. Why would I want the extra work that involves?'

'It's a day to celebrate.'

'You're forgetting, I have nothing to celebrate.'

Silently, he got up and helped himself to more whisky.

On the following Saturday morning at Hattongrove House, Toby's alarm went off at six o'clock as usual. He was already half awake, listening to the rain hurtling against his bedroom window. In the semi-darkness he felt the mattress lift slightly as Colin Osman slid out of bed, and heard him begin to pull on his clothes, ready to go out and start the milking. Toby smiled fondly. Colin was a handsome young man of twenty-six with a lot of brown hair that flopped over his forehead.

Jago had spent the night here too. A door banged in a

distant part of the house, indicating that Leslie Gibson was up too, so the farm work would start on time. They were good workers, both of them, but all this talk of war was making Leslie restless. Last night he'd told them he wanted to volunteer for the Navy, which had upset Jago. He didn't want Leslie to leave and nobody wanted the war. They'd all tried to persuade him to stay.

For the last few years, Toby and Jago had been considering how best to protect their own interests should another world war break out. In the last one their father had sat back and waited for peace to return, expecting his clients to come back and earn him the profit they had before. He couldn't have been more wrong; the Great War had changed the world for ever. Toby meant to prevent the next war from ruining him and Jago if he could.

Toby liked getting up early as he had the house to himself then. His housekeeper arrived on her bike at nine o'clock and worked until five, which suited him well. He rolled out of bed, pulled on his old clothes and went down to the kitchen. As he'd expected, Jago was already there.

'Terrible weather,' Jago greeted him. 'Listen to that wind.' It was howling in the chimneys.

'I'm pleased to see the rain,' Toby said. At this time of the year his three hundred acres of market garden needed rain. His farm was well placed to sell the potatoes, fruit and vegetables he was growing into the markets which fed the urban population of Liverpool.

Jago had set the coffee pot to percolate and was making toast. Toby put the butter dish and the marmalade on the kitchen table and looked for the pot of honey. At fifty-six, he was content with his life and satisfied with what he'd achieved, though he knew Jago was not so happy. As the years went on, his brother was finding Henrietta more of a burden than he'd expected.

He switched on the wireless so they could listen to the news broadcast while they ate. In clipped accents, the announcer told them, *Over recent years, Britain has been importing over fifty million tons of food annually, and should war come that cannot continue. The government wants to encourage farmers to increase food production. Help and advice from representatives of the Ministry of Agriculture, Fisheries and Food is being made available to them.*

Toby laughed. 'I'm getting my visit from a Mr Bellamy this morning at half past ten. The letter said he'll help me assess my annual food production, which will enable me to fill in forms to entitle me to an allocation of animal feed. I don't like the sound of that. I don't need help to assess what I'm producing. I know that minutely.'

'Shh. He's saying they'll allocate fertiliser to you too. You'll need that.'

New committees are being set up to consider how best to ration the food available and prices will be controlled.

'I don't like the sound of that either. Controlled prices

will be low prices and won't allow much profit for the farmer.'

'We need to put our heads together before this man comes,' Jago said. 'Decide what we should say to him and exactly how we'll manage the farm and the sausage factory.'

'Yes,' Toby said, switching off the wireless. 'Let's get down to work.' Still munching on his toast, he led the way to his study. His file for future planning was already open on his desk.

'This war could last for years. Our first aim must be to see that our family and friends have all the food they need. We don't want to go short. The second is to grow more stuff for general sale, but of the sort that ensures we're not short-changed by their controlled prices.'

'This fellow who's coming to see you,' Jago said. 'If he asks you to put a figure on what you expect to produce . . .'

'Don't worry, I'll reduce all my figures by twenty-five per cent.'

'That should help. It'll keep as much as possible away from government markets.'

'I'm going to get rid of my milking herd,' Toby said. 'It's work intensive, and once milk is rationed there'll be little profit. Two cows only to provide us with fresh milk. Perhaps a small suckler herd to raise calves for beef.'

'Beef will be rationed too.'

'It will, but it'll be impossible to keep count of how

many calves are born, or check how many are brought on to slaughter weight. We'll be able to keep a few on the side.'

'True. And you'll keep more pigs?'

'A lot more.' Toby liked pigs. He already had a big number of large white and landrace sows. 'I might try a few saddlebacks too.'

He sold the pigs he bred into the fresh meat market, or in the warm months of summer to a bacon curing company. The remainder of the flesh went to Jago's sausage factory.

'You can't go wrong expanding pig production, because I use all the offal and any offcuts,' Jago agreed. 'Especially if you can grow all their feed.'

'This spring I planted a couple of extra acres of mangels and I've sown extra barley and oats. That should feed them over the winter. I'll definitely increase my chicken flock, and rear ducks and turkeys for the Christmas market.'

'Eggs are bound to be rationed.'

'They are, but it'll be easy to juggle those numbers.'

For some time the brothers worked on the figures, arguing occasionally and breaking off for coffee when Toby's housekeeper arrived at nine o'clock. At last, Toby sat back with a sigh. 'Wouldn't it make it easier if we knew what was going to be rationed and what wasn't?'

'It certainly would. I'd give a lot to know what they intend to do about sausages.'

'We can ask this man today, but I doubt he'll know any more than we do.'

'If rationing comes, there'll be a huge demand for food of every sort.'

'Food prices went sky high in the last war.'

'It'll be the same this time. They won't be able to control everything.'

'The truth is, Jago, the war will make us a fortune if we play it right. And we're putting our plans—'

Toby broke off as he saw a figure flash past the window and throw open the back door. It was Colin, and he looked panic-stricken. 'Toby, come quick!'

Both Toby and Jago jerked to their feet in alarm. 'What's the matter?'

Colin was breathless. 'Leslie's hit somebody, a man. He's collapsed.'

'What man?'

'We don't know him. Some guy who was prowling round.'

Toby's heart had begun to race. He was pulling on his gum boots. 'A prowler, you say?'

'Yes.'

'Where is he?'

'Behind the cowsheds. Come on, I'll show you. I think Leslie's killed him.'

CHAPTER TWELVE

TOBY COULD HEAR Jago pounding along behind him as he raced after Colin. 'Leslie can't have killed anybody. What did he do?'

Dash, his border collie, bounded along with them, thinking it was some sort of a game. A terrified Leslie met them at the garden gate. Tears of anguish were mixing with raindrops on his cheeks.

'I'm sorry, Toby. I didn't mean to kill him, just frighten him off. He was trespassing and I know we don't want strangers here.'

Toby grunted in distress and raced past him. If Leslie really had killed a man on his property, all hell would be let loose. What he'd successfully kept hidden all these years would come out in a murder inquiry. Everything would be raked up. It would be disastrous for him and Jago, and all their plans would come to naught. Half blinded by the rain, he skidded on the wet grass.

When he reached the yard behind the cowshed he

could see the figure sprawled face down in the mud and manure. 'Oh, my God!' He was fighting panic.

The stable door was open and Dobbin, his fine shire horse, was standing completely unrestrained, his huge hooves only a couple of paces from the prostrate body. Leslie caught up with Toby and stood wringing his hands in the heavy downpour.

'He was snooping round. I had to do something. You keep telling us not to bring our friends here and how important it is to keep the public away.'

Toby was struggling to get his breath back. 'Get hold of Dobbin's halter,' he puffed. 'He could step on this fellow and finish him off.'

It was Jago who turned the body over and used his handkerchief to wipe the muck from the face.

'He's still breathing,' he gasped. 'Thank God, at least he's still alive. We've got to get him to hospital as soon as we can. The last thing we need is to have him die here.'

Toby was functioning again. 'Colin, fetch the van down from the house. Who is he?' The man was wearing city shoes and a city mackintosh covering a grey suit. 'And what is he doing here on my property?' Toby felt in the pockets of the stranger's suit and brought out a wallet; tucked inside he found several visiting cards. 'He's an adviser employed by the Ministry of Agriculture, Fisheries and Food,' he said, feeling shocked to the core. 'His name's Robert Bellamy.'

Jago's mouth had dropped open. 'Isn't this the man you were expecting?'

'Bellamy?' Toby told himself he had to calm down. He couldn't think straight. 'Yes, of course, Bellamy. He said he'd come at half past ten.' He looked at his watch. It was only twenty past now.

'He came early,' Jago said.

'To snoop round,' Leslie added. 'I had to stop him, didn't I?'

'Leslie, what exactly did you do to him?'

'As soon as he turned away I hit him with a spade. The mucking out spade.' The lad was a quivering wreck. 'I saw him peeping through the stable window. I was going to put Dobbin in the cart shafts.' A shaking hand indicated the figure. 'He'll be all right, won't he?'

'Let's hope so.' Toby turned the man's head so they could see the back. 'I thought I saw a cut.'

'Not a big one,' Jago said, 'but it has bled.'

'If we take him to hospital,' Toby said, 'we'll have to give some explanation of what's happened to him. We can't say he was coming by appointment and when he was passing the cowsheds you hit him with a spade.'

'He was snooping round.' Leslie was even more agitated now. 'You could say you found him like that on the lane, hit by a car perhaps. You picked him up, Good Samaritan and all that.'

'No,' Jago said. 'He's covered in cow manure. He slipped in the muck and banged the back of his head on a stone, knocked himself out. Can anyone do better than that?'

Toby felt he was wobbling on the brink of a precipice. 'How did he get here? He can't have walked.'

The van was bumping over the rough ground. Colin edged it as close as he could before jumping out.

'There's a car in the lane,' he said. 'Parked well out of sight. He didn't mean any of us to see him.'

'Was there anybody in it?' Toby asked, as panic rose in his throat again. 'What if he had somebody with him?'

That made Colin pull up. 'I'm not sure. I couldn't see properly, the hedge . . .'

'We've got to get him to hospital,' Jago insisted, yanking the back of the vehicle open. 'Help me lift him in.' It took all their strength; he was a middle-aged man running to fat and they were slithering in the mud and puddles.

Jago said, 'Colin, you drive and I'll come with you. Leslie, don't talk to anybody. You're in no fit state now. If this fellow doesn't survive . . . You said you wanted to join up last night.'

'I still do,' he moaned.

'Then the safest thing is for you to leave now and do it straight away.' Jago took some money from his wallet and pushed it into Leslie's hand. 'I'm sorry it had to end like this, but if anybody ever asks you about this, you don't know what they're talking about. Are you listening, Colin? That goes for you too.' He climbed into the passenger seat. 'Toby and I found him; there was nobody else about at the time. Make sure you leave any talking to us.'

Colin grunted, 'That suits me.'

'I'll be back as soon as I can,' Jago said to Toby.

'Good job you've kept your head.'

'It's not my farm. Go back to the house till you get over this. You're still shaking.'

Toby watched the van bump across the grass in the pouring rain. Then he caught hold of Dobbin and led him off to a field. He pushed the gate open, took off his halter and reached up to give his huge rump a firm pat. The horse moved in, nibbling at the grass; he preferred to be out rather than in, and he didn't mind the weather. He'd be happy here until somebody had a job for him to do.

Toby went to take a closer look at the car parked in the lane. It was empty and locked. He told himself he could relax, it was over. He went slowly back to the house. The thin jacket he'd hurriedly pulled on was wet through. He'd had a nasty fright and he felt absolutely shattered.

He worried about Leslie. What a stupid thing to do. In the past, he'd been in trouble with the law, charged with grievous bodily harm and theft. Toby had never taken to him. Thank goodness Colin had proved to be an upright and serious young man. As far as he was concerned, Leslie was a headstrong and foolish teenager. The farm would be a safer place without him.

*

Toby changed into dry clothes, but when Jago and Colin returned he felt he still hadn't quite pulled himself together. He made them hot tea.

'Bellamy was stirring by the time we got him to hospital,' Colin said. 'It looks as though he'll recover.'

'But does he know what really happened?' That was Toby's fear now.

'I don't know. He was saying a few words but not making much sense,' Jago said. 'The nurse said he was confused. We gave them the story about him falling and banging his head and they seemed to accept it.'

'His car's still parked near our gate,' Colin said. 'Shouldn't you do something about that?'

'Yes,' Toby said. 'We can't just let it stay there.'

'The police?' Colin suggested.

'No, not them.' Toby wanted to keep the police as far away as possible. His way of life made that imperative.

'The best thing,' Jago said, 'is to ring the Ministry of Agriculture.' He took out Bellamy's visiting card and put it on the table. 'You were expecting this man; he'd made an appointment to come. Then we took him to hospital saying he had an accident here. If that was exactly the truth, we'd ring and let them know, wouldn't we? And you'd say his car is still in your lane.'

'Yes. You do it, Jago.' Toby was reaching for the teapot. 'The sooner the better.'

Jago took the card and went out to the hall. Toby

listened. He'd always known Jago could stay cool and think on his feet in a tight corner.

'Bellamy,' he heard him say. 'Robert Bellamy. No, we were waiting for him in the house and don't understand why he didn't just drive up and present himself. We found him unconscious in the farm yard; we think he must have slipped and fallen, knocking himself out. But what he was doing there we've no idea. We took him to hospital.'

There was a pause. 'He needed urgent attention; we didn't have much choice. There's a car, a Morris Eight, parked in our lane some five minutes' walk from the house which we think must belong to him. Could you arrange for it to be removed? Yes, it's locked and perfectly safe for the time being. No, of course I don't have the keys. I can only assume that if the car belongs to Mr Bellamy, they're in his pocket. Neither am I very clear about the purpose of his visit. I'm intrigued now. Could you enlighten me?' Another longer pause, and then Jago brought the call to an end and came back. Toby poured more tea for him.

'The purpose of the visit,' Jago said, 'was exactly what the letter said – to help you make plans in the event of war.'

Toby felt unutterably grateful. 'You struck just the right note. Bellamy mishandled his visit, and now he's beholden to us.'

'He was snooping round,' Colin said. 'I can't see

that city folks like that would be much help to any farmer.'

On Sunday, Toby got up at his usual time. It was his housekeeper's day off and he liked having his house to himself, but he still felt shaken by what had happened the day before.

He rang the hospital to ask after Mr Bellamy and was told he'd recovered consciousness. It was a huge relief to know there'd be no murder inquiry, and with luck nobody would come round asking questions about the accident. But it left him wondering if Mr Bellamy could remember what had happened to him and whether or not he accepted the story Jago had concocted.

On Sunday mornings he liked to walk round his farm and check on what was happening. The heavy rain had passed on but it was still showery and there were puddles everywhere. His dog Dash heard him coming and was bouncing with excitement as he unchained him from his kennel. They headed for his cowsheds, Dash bounding ahead through the small copse that hid the working farm from the main house.

To his left was Hattongrove Farm, with the curtains in the upstairs windows still drawn. Roy Williams, his farm manager, his wife and brood of seven children were enjoying a day off. The farm had been built sufficiently far from Hattongrove House to ensure that the smell of cows and pigs couldn't reach it, but Toby actually liked honest country smells. He was a country man at heart.

Splashing through the puddles in the yard behind the cowsheds, he kept his eyes averted from the spot where Bellamy's body had fallen. Colin was just releasing his herd of Hereford shorthorns and sending them out to the meadow. Toby employed six young men to work on his land and provided bachelor accommodation for them in two estate cottages. They did the essential Sunday work. Colin was officially one of them, though he spent much of his time up at the main house with Toby. He was the most sensible of them all. To replace Leslie, he'd taken one of the others away from work in the market garden.

Toby stopped for a word with them. 'How are you liking the change of job, Gareth?'

'I do. I'm right fond of cows.'

'Is everything all right, Colin?'

'Everything's fine, sir.' He always called Toby 'sir' if there was anyone listening. 'Forty-three gallons of milk we got this morning, even though we have three cows about to calve.'

Toby exchanged a smile with him. 'We'll sell those at market as soon as they have calves at foot. I'd like to go through the herd with you after evening milking tonight.' They'd decide which few to sell right away. Mustn't put too many on the market at once, or they'd never make their price. Another knowing smile from Colin, and Toby said, 'I'll see you about six then.'

He felt better when it was time to go and collect Nancy and Caro, and have another of Henrietta's lunches. Before leaving the house Jago rang the hospital again.

When he got through to the ward he was told that Mr Bellamy would be seen again by a doctor and it was probable he'd be discharged. That afternoon the car disappeared from the lane, though nobody saw it go. Toby decided he'd waste no more time worrying. It could have been much worse.

With Caro attending the school she'd chosen for her, Nancy was able to help behind the bar in the session that lasted from eleven till two. Once Dad realised that she enjoyed the work and could manage without him, he took that time off and was able to rest upstairs. She was beginning to worry that he was more seriously ill than he admitted. Nancy was getting to know the staff and in slack moments she chatted to Kevin.

She felt settled with her father at the Lord Nelson but saw Henrietta as a problem. She felt threatened by her, and was afraid she meant to take Caro from her.

Caro had not found it easy to settle in her new school. To start with, she'd said some of the boys were rough. They chased her and pulled her hair.

'You've got to stand up to them,' Miles had told her. 'Show them you're as tough as they are.'

It seemed to be working, and Caro was happier. One

afternoon, when Nancy met her coming out of school, there was a boy with her.

'This is Billy,' she said. 'He's my friend. Can he come home and have tea with us?'

'Now?' Nancy asked. 'Won't your mother be expecting you home, Billy?'

'Nah, Mam's at work. She doesn't come home till five o'clock.'

'Well, you could come for an hour and have a glass of milk,' she said.

Caro took hold of her hand. 'Billy's good at drawing. He thinks I'm good too.'

'She's bloody marvellous at it,' the lad said. 'I wish I could draw like her.'

'I want to show him those books Grandma gave me. They'll tell him how to do it too.'

Nancy knew Grandma wouldn't approve of Billy. His jersey was none too clean and had holes at both elbows; he had no socks and his dirty toes could be seen through holes cut in the top of his plimsolls because he'd grown out of them. He was hungry, and ate a thick slice of bread and jam as well as cake and milk.

At the kitchen table, they pored over Caro's books, used up all her drawing paper and never stopped talking. Nancy felt Caro got as much from the session as Billy. Rather reluctantly, she sent him home at five o'clock.

'I didn't like him at first,' Caro said as the door closed behind him. 'But he's nice when you get to know him.'

Nancy was back in her old routine of preparing a dinner they could eat together at half past five before her father went down to open the pub at six. He was slicing the green beans when Nancy came back and picked up the potato peeler.

'There you are,' he said. 'I told you to stand up to those rough boys, Caro, and now you have everything is all right. I told your mother the same thing when she was small. If you think you see aggression, you must show you aren't prepared to take it lying down.'

Nancy was thinking of her mother-in-law. When Caro went to her bedroom she said to her father, 'Henrietta is aggressive towards me, but I can't stand up to her.'

'You are standing up to her. Caro's going to Wilbraham Street School. You're bringing her up in your own way.'

'Henrietta thinks it's a terrible place. She says Caro's losing out because of my obstinacy.'

'She doesn't like the school because the children look scruffy, but they're as bright as buttons. A lot of their fathers come in here. Some are out of work and make half a pint last all night, but they're decent fellows.'

'Henrietta scares me. She's determined to get her own way, and I don't trust her. She hasn't given up the idea of taking Caro and bringing her up herself.'

'All you have to do is keep on saying no to that. Are you getting neurotic about Henrietta?'

'Probably, Dad.'

'Look, she loves Caro, and Caro loves her grand-
parents. Nancy, you need to relax, take Henrietta in
your stride. What are we going to eat with these
vegetables?'

'I've bought some Seymour's sausages. I thought you
ought to try them.' Her father had always done his food
shopping in the local market, where the butchers' stalls
made their own sausages. He picked up the packet, and
read: *Seymour's succulent sausages, premium quality pork.* They
were wrapped in greaseproof paper banded in red and
gold with a picture of them sizzling in a frying pan,
browned and ready to eat.

'A good idea. I should know what they taste like.'

Nancy opened the packet and pricked the skins while
Miles turned on the wireless in the living room. She came
to the door to listen. The news was depressing; nobody
doubted that war was coming and it was creeping closer
all the time. Everybody felt anxious. Nancy feared for
Gavin and Charlie's old friends at Hawarden. They were
likely to feel the brunt of it.

The sausages were delicious. 'Excellent,' Miles said.
'They should make a fortune for Jago.'

'I like the sausages Grandpa makes,' Caro said. 'He's
very clever. I must tell him next Sunday.'

Nancy felt they were seeing too much of Henrietta. As
soon as one Sunday lunch was over she and Caro were
invited again for the following week. She would have
liked to make some excuse to stay with her father, but

Miles thought she should go. 'Caro should get to know the other side of the family,' he said.

This Sunday, Henrietta showed them a new Leica camera she'd bought. 'I have so few photographs of Caroline, and she's growing so quickly. I have to have more.'

She posed Caro in the garden amongst the shrubs, then with the house as a background. She kept Nancy beside her, repeatedly asking her to straighten Caro's dress, or comb her hair because the breeze was blowing it out of place.

'I want you to look perfect on your pictures,' she told her granddaughter.

Then she positioned her against the bare white wall outside the house. 'I'd like a real portrait of you, darling.'

She turned to Nancy. 'When she's serious, she has such ethereal beauty, doesn't she? Let me take another like that.'

Once indoors again, Henrietta shivered. 'Jago dear, would you mind going upstairs to get my stole?' She simpered up at him. 'I shouldn't have gone out without my coat. It's quite chilly today.' However, when Jago returned with a crimson stole her affability deserted her abruptly.

'Not that one!' she said disparagingly. 'I can't wear crimson! Whatever are you thinking of? You haven't forgotten I'm in mourning for Charles? I must have a black one. Do use your head, Jago.'

'Sorry,' he murmured and went back upstairs.

To Nancy the silence that followed seemed heavy. It helped to find she was not the only one to feel the cut of Henrietta's tongue, but at the same time it shocked her to hear her mother-in-law talk like that to her husband. She was showing a lack of affection.

Jago returned with a black stole. 'Is this what you want, Ettie?'

'It will do.' She flung it round her shoulders. 'I'd like a picture of Caro with you and Toby now.'

Caro sighed noisily. 'Can't I do some crayoning?'

'In a moment, darling.'

'She's getting tired of being photographed,' Toby pointed out.

'Come and sit here by me then,' her grandmother cajoled. 'I must have some pictures of us together.'

Jago was then pressed into taking several of Henrietta with her granddaughter. 'Let's smile on this one, darling. Go on, finish up the film,' she said to Jago, and he did it to please her. Then he turned and saw Nancy.

'We haven't taken even one picture of you,' he said. 'You bought half a dozen films, Henrietta. I'll go and put another in.'

Nancy was getting used to this sort of treatment from Henrietta and tried to tell him not to bother.

'We must have one of mother and daughter together,' he insisted, and then took several of Nancy alone. Gertie was summoned to take one of the whole family, while they were all round the dining table tucking into their meal.

The following week, Nancy was shown some of the results. Jago had had the best ones of Caro enlarged, and gave her three. Henrietta was beaming with pleasure, and for once even Nancy enjoyed her lunch.

CHAPTER THIRTEEN

HENRIETTA FELT VERY put out when Jago came home from work and announced he'd invited his factory manager and his wife to lunch on their wedding anniversary. 'And I've asked Toby to bring his farm manager and his wife too.'

'What? You've already invited them? I thought we'd decided to have just our normal Sunday lunch.'

'We can't let our anniversary pass without marking it in some way.'

'Jago, we can't hold parties while we're in mourning.'

'It's not a party, just a few people round for lunch.'

'It's only three months since poor Charles died, and with Caroline and Nancy here, it's a family lunch. They won't mix with your factory friends.'

'I don't suppose Nancy will mind if she and Caro don't come for one Sunday.'

Henrietta felt a surge of irritation. 'I'm not prepared to cancel Caroline's visit. I even put up with Nancy so I can see the child.'

'Nancy's a charming girl. It's hardly a question of putting up with her.'

Henrietta was displeased. 'You take no account of my wishes,' she stormed. 'You do exactly what you want.' Yet again she was having to give in. 'You and Toby pay Nancy more attention than you do me.'

Henrietta really resented the way everybody found Nancy attractive. She had to admit it, the girl had blossomed in the years she'd been married to Charlie. She was now quietly beautiful, with a tall slim figure and a small waist. Her face was flawlessly symmetrical and her blue eyes set wide apart. There was nothing showy about Nancy, nothing brash; everything was in excellent taste, even her clothes. No barmaid had the right to look as she did.

It wouldn't last, of course. It couldn't. Even raving beauties lost their looks, but while Henrietta knew hers had gone, Nancy's were still bewitching Jago and Toby.

Henrietta had never had to worry that she'd be displaced by another woman. She knew they saw Nancy as their daughter-in-law. Their attitude was fatherly, but the girl was putting her nose out of joint all the same. Nancy's good-humoured way was to smile sweetly and treat everybody as a friend.

What Henrietta really envied was the way Caroline threw her arms round her mother and Nancy pulled her close. She'd never had a relationship like that and she craved it. When they did that wearing their white dresses, they looked like love personified. She ached to have Caroline love her like that, and she knew she would if only they could spend time together without her mother pushing in.

Jago had picked up the newspaper and was ignoring her. She said, 'Nine people is too many. A normal Sunday lunch would be impossible.' Henrietta gave a sniff of disdain. At Grindley Manor they could easily seat twelve round the dining table. 'And it would take you half an hour to carve enough off a roast to feed them. The rest of the food would be cold.'

Jago smiled. 'So it would. We'll have a buffet meal for a change.'

It was Jago's turn to drive through the tunnel to Birkenhead to pick up Nancy and Caro. Today was his wedding anniversary lunch party. He rang the side door bell and Caro ran down to open it. As usual, she threw herself into his arms. He swung her into a hug and told her she was a beautiful little girl. 'You'll be a real stunner when you grow up.'

'Like a film star, you said last time, Grandpa.'

'Yes, like a film star. A little present for you.' The day before, he'd bought a book of drawing paper and some crayons and left them on the back seat. Now she scrambled happily in to open the paper bags. Jago was fond of drawing too and understood Caro's obsession with it.

'I shall do a portrait of you while you drive,' she told him. 'Your back view, and what I can see through the front window.'

'You do that,' he said. 'And put your mummy in the picture too.'

He ushered Nancy into the front seat. 'We need to talk,' he said softly, 'and this is a good moment before we join the others.' He got in beside her and put the car in gear. 'I told you I'd see you didn't starve. Henrietta will make sure Caro wants for nothing, but . . .'

'I know she doesn't feel she has to do that for me,' Nancy said. 'But I'll be all right, Jago. Dad's paying me for the hours I work for him. I'm managing fine.'

'I don't want you to have to work unless you want to. What I've done is set up a trust fund. The money will be invested in the stock market and the interest on the shares paid to you.'

Nancy hesitated. 'That's more than generous, but I'll be all right. As I understood it, you were talking about making me an allowance.'

'I was, but having talked it over, Toby and I decided this way would have advantages for us all. You do understand that once we've signed the document, we won't be able to take the money back so you'll always have it invested in your name. Nobody will be able to take it from you. Toby and I will oversee the investments for the foreseeable future. It should produce about a thousand pounds a year, give or take a bit.'

'A thousand pounds! Year after year!' Nancy was almost overcome with gratitude.

'Yes. You'll never be left high and dry without funds to live on.'

'I don't know how to thank you. That's a fortune.'

'You don't have to. If you wanted to have your own home, you'd find it quite a modest amount. Charlie would want us to take care of you and Caro. His arrangements didn't work out, so we're taking over.'

He glanced at her. Nancy was turning away so he wouldn't see her mopping at her eyes. He felt sorry for her. Henrietta had gone out of her way to be nasty to her.

'I'm very grateful to you, Jago. You must be very rich.'

'It's not just from me. Toby and I provided the capital between us. We were brought up to understand money and we've found that knowledge very useful. We've always earned it when we can and we look after it. What we want you to do is to open a bank account into which the dividends can be paid. Or do you have one already?'

'No. Charlie had one, of course, but I can't touch the money in that until I get probate.'

'I was afraid that might be the case.'

'Fortunately, I have a Post Office savings account in my own name. Will that do?'

'No. It would be better if you opened an account in a nearby bank.'

As the car slowed down in Lexington Avenue, ready to turn into the drive of Carrington Place, Jago said, 'That's right, give Henrietta a little smile. Let her see she hasn't got you down.'

Just as Henrietta had expected, there was chaos in her kitchen that Sunday morning. Their staff of two was too set in its ways. They could cope with a sit-down meal but not a buffet for nine. It didn't make things any better that Jago said he was going to pick up Nancy and Caroline because Toby wanted to bring his friends with him.

'Just see you're back before the factory people get here then,' she retorted, which was not unreasonable as she hardly knew them.

Henrietta didn't mind doing the flowers, but this morning Gertie was too fraught in the kitchen to tidy up the drawing room. Jago had left his briefcase there, as well as the lovely cuff links she'd given him as an anniversary gift.

She scooped his belongings up, including the wrapping paper, went to his study and dumped them on his desk. The top drawer was slightly open and inside she could see letters and documents from his solicitor. This was where he usually kept documents relating to his financial affairs. She eased the drawer further open.

Occasionally, Henrietta checked Jago's portfolio and his bank accounts. He rarely talked about money and a wife needed to understand how her husband was placed. Now she thought about it, there'd been considerable correspondence from his solicitor in recent weeks.

As she'd have time to bring herself up to date with his affairs now, Henrietta went to get her spectacles from the drawing room. When she returned the first thing she picked up was his solicitor's bill for setting up a trust fund for Nancy Milton Seymour. The amount he'd paid in made her gasp.

She felt the heat run up her cheeks and couldn't get her breath. A trust fund set up for Nancy! All that money given to her! Wasted on her. She'd love to scratch her eyes out and ruin her looks. She spent the next ten minutes pacing round Jago's study engulfed in fury. They were ridiculously generous towards the girl. It was quite uncalled for. If only there were some way she could get rid of her.

It was only when she heard Gertie and Mrs Trott setting out the food on the dining-room table that Henrietta remembered she was expecting guests. She rushed upstairs to get ready.

Jago returned with Nancy and Caroline before anyone else arrived. Henrietta felt so angry she could hardly bring herself to speak to Nancy. Fortunately, Caroline wanted to tell her what she'd done during the week.

The Regans turned up promptly. Jago was all kindness and charm to them. Tom his factory manager was fat and bald and Doreen was a very plain woman, plainer than Henrietta remembered. She wore black too, a fussy frilly frock, and with her grey hair and pale cheeks it made her look washed out.

'I often wear black,' she said. 'Like you, I've found it has a slimming effect for those of us piling on the pounds.' Outraged, Henrietta didn't reply.

Toby was late, and when he arrived she could almost smell the cow dung on his farm manager and his wife, Roy and Maud Williams. She'd heard they had a brood of seven children but fortunately Toby hadn't brought them.

Jago made a great show of opening the champagne, 'To celebrate our day,' he announced, holding up his glass to Henrietta.

Our day indeed! Henrietta bristled with anger. Giving all that money away to Nancy and never mentioning it to her! Jago knew very well that marriage to him had been a big mistake for her. These were not her sort of people; she didn't like them. Caroline was cuddling up to Nancy and had her arms round her. This mother and daughter act was getting on Henrietta's nerves.

Maud Williams was twittering on about a concert she'd been to.

'Nancy,' Henrietta said, 'you don't realise how important it is for a child to experience the finer things in life. You should take Caroline out and about. She's just told me the only time she's been to a theatre was to see *Jack and the Beanstalk*. She's never been to a ballet . . .'

'Ballet companies don't often bring their productions

to Liverpool,' Doreen Regan said. 'Some things will have to wait.'

Henrietta snorted with rage. 'And Caroline knows nothing of music. It's essential that she experiences these things or she won't grow up to appreciate them.'

'Mummy does take me out, Grandma. We went to the pictures on Wednesday.'

'The pictures! There are not many I'd consider suitable for a child like you.'

'Oh, there are. We saw *Snow White and the Seven Dwarfs*, it was lovely. I want to see it again.'

'That's a cartoon, dear, not a proper film.'

'I've seen two Shirley Temple films. They're proper.'

'Shirley Temple indeed!'

'I loved them. I'd like to see lots more.'

'That's what I mean, Nancy. She'd love *Swan Lake* if you took her to see that.'

'Shirley Temple will do her no harm,' Toby said.

'I used to believe every mother wanted the best for her child, but not you, Nancy.'

'Give over,' Jago said. 'No need to pressurise the poor girl. When this war's over, Caro will have plenty of time to go to music recitals and the ballet.'

'Jago, you've never given me any support. Every wife should be able to rely on that from her husband.'

He tried to laugh it off. 'I do my best, love.'

Henrietta despised him. It had long been her fear that he'd only married her to provide himself with a wife and son so he could appear to be living a normal life. She was his protection.

She swung towards Jago, hissing under her breath, 'Should I make all these allowances because you're queer? Is that why you can't act like a normal husband?'

There was a sudden silence. Nancy was near enough to overhear. She smiled at Jago. 'We all have our queer moments, Mother-in-law,' she said, draining her glass. 'I know I do. I do all sorts of silly things.'

For a moment Henrietta wondered whether she'd gone too far and that Jago would say she'd let him down. She was not sorry to hear Nancy try to take the heat out of what she'd said.

'Even Grandpops does,' Caro sang out. 'D'you know what he did this morning? He cut up some bits of bread for the birds then opened the kitchen window. He meant to put the crumbs out on the sill for the sparrows, but he put the loaf out and took the crumbs to the breadbin.'

Everybody laughed. Toby lifted her up and told her she was a clever girl while Jago refilled glasses and said it was time to eat. Henrietta could see he was furious with her. His eyes kept flashing warning signals. She didn't care. He needed to know she was still capable of cutting him down. But perhaps it was just as well Nancy had stopped what she'd said from striking home. She wouldn't have believed the girl could be so quick-witted as to turn her meaning round. But being dragged up in the slums as she had been, of course she'd know all there was to know about such things.

What Jago and Toby were doing was against the law. They invited their boyfriends to Toby's house, and he did without the convenience of live-in staff in order to hide what they were up to from prying eyes.

Henrietta had been nicely brought up and had never heard of such behaviour. She hadn't even known such things existed when she'd walked up the aisle. Once she'd accused Jago of deliberately keeping her in ignorance until they were married.

That had made him see red. He said he'd tried to explain to her before they got engaged and that he'd thought she understood. But she had a good memory and she certainly didn't remember him saying anything about that. All he'd done was to give her a book in a brown paper cover.

'Don't let anybody see it, especially not your father,' he'd said. He'd been edgy and made it sound exciting, but the book had been about the life of Oscar Wilde. She hadn't read it all because she'd found it dull, and for years she hadn't realised the significance he was giving to it. That was Jago all over; he couldn't say anything outright. He was too frightened of being found out.

He always made a big fuss of their wedding anniversary. For him, it was the moment he had his safety net in position. It hid what was more important to him and Toby. Queers must never be found out. Henrietta felt he barely thought of her. This year he'd given her an umbrella, a smart one yes, but quite heavy and it wasn't as though she didn't already have six.

On earlier occasions when she'd found Jago particularly trying, she'd threatened to speak out about it. Nothing put the wind up him more.

'Please don't,' he'd pleaded more than once. 'It could bring all hell down on us. A public trial, all recounted in the newspapers. Then we could be sent to prison.'

She'd stayed loyal to him and never spoken of it to anyone, but he hadn't thanked her for it.

Recently he'd said, 'I don't think you'll do it. By now you must feel you can't. You wouldn't want people to know that Henrietta Carrington Seymour has been married to a queer for thirty-four years, would you? They'd pity you.'

She'd long since written Jago off as a husband. She couldn't expect any affection from him, and that was why she needed Caroline so badly; she was a granddaughter she could honestly love who would love her in return.

Henrietta was determined to take her to the seaside for a little holiday. Just the two of them, on their own. If Jago could override her wishes so easily about having this party, there was no reason why she couldn't override Nancy's objections about taking the child on holiday. Fresh air and sun would be good for Caroline's health and Henrietta would broaden the child's mind at the same time. It was her duty to make sure she was brought up as a little lady.

CHAPTER FOURTEEN

JAGO HAD TO rein in his fury with Henrietta until their guests had gone. He saw the flash of horror on Toby's face and knew he'd heard her outburst. It had ruined the lunch party for him too. Furthermore, she was barely polite to anybody after that. He was glad when the visitors stood up to go. Henrietta said a hasty goodbye and shot up to her bedroom, where they all heard the door slam.

Jago wanted to follow her and take her to task but he'd arranged to drive Nancy and Caro home. Perhaps that was a good thing, because it gave Mrs Trott and Gertie time to clear up. They had the rest of the day off and usually left as soon as they could. He wouldn't want them to hear what he had to say to Henrietta.

He wasn't at ease with the fact that Nancy might know his secret. He wondered whether he should thank her for her cover-up but didn't know how to. Fortunately, Caro chose to sit on her mother's knee and chattered away to them both throughout the journey.

He hadn't thought Nancy knew about them but it seemed she did. He and Toby had never discussed it with Charlie; it wasn't something one spoke about to one's son. Between themselves, they'd wondered if he'd guessed, because he'd been brought up knowing that his parents had separate bedrooms. Now it seemed he must have read the signs and that he must have told Nancy.

Jago had been delighted and relieved to see Charlie chasing the girls as he grew up. Theirs was a terrible problem Charlie had not had to grapple with. They'd welcomed Nancy with open arms, quite sure she'd make his life simpler and pleasanter than theirs had been.

But it had come as a shock to find Nancy knew their secret. It meant it was not so well hidden as they'd believed.

He drove fast on the return journey, turning over in his mind what he meant to say to Henrietta. The house was quiet when he let himself in. He went up to her bedroom expecting to find her resting but the room was empty and the bed unruffled. He found her in the now cleared kitchen. She'd taken flowers from some of the vases and was wrapping them in paper.

'I want to talk to you, Henrietta. That was a terrible thing you did.'

'Not now,' she said. 'I'm going to get Bennett to drive me up to Grindley. The house is like a florist's shop. I'm going to put some of these on Charlie's grave. I'll need to freshen up and get my hat.'

He knew she was trying to avoid him. 'What's the hurry?' He heard her bedroom door slam, but he didn't mean to let her get away with this. He rarely went to her bedroom but today he flung the door open.

Henrietta looked up indignantly. 'You might have knocked.' She was changing. He'd caught her in a pink silk slip; she held her dress in front of her as though embarrassed.

Jago was livid. 'You promised you'd never say anything like that in front of other people,' he burst out. He could feel himself shaking. 'If they've grasped what it was you were saying it could be round the country in no time.'

'None of them noticed. The barmaid covered up for you very quickly. So did Caroline. She copies her mother even now.'

'We don't know they didn't notice, do we? They may have done.'

'It went over their heads. Your friends aren't all that bright.'

'Tom Regan is a lot brighter than you are. Don't underrate him. Anyway, you and I made an agreement. You were never to say anything like that in public. In exchange for your silence Toby and I agreed to indulge every whim you have. I don't understand why you suddenly—'

'You've given Nancy a private income. I don't like you

179

going behind my back to do things like that for her.'

'Behind your back? You've been sneaking round my study, looking through my private papers.'

'What if I have? You never tell me anything.'

'I don't tell you because I know it will upset you.'

'You're right about that.'

'What I do with my money has nothing to do with you. I earn it and I spend it as I wish. You can be quite sure you won't go short. I've kept my side of the bargain, and you . . .'

'You're scared.'

'Of course I'm scared. Don't you realise what the law could do to me and Toby? It would rebound on your own head. If you stopped to think for one moment, you'd know that. There'd be less comfort for you here if I were sent to prison.'

'I didn't want those people here. You filled the house on a whim. And I don't want Nancy here either.'

'You worry me, the way you come out with things. People will remember, you know.'

'Give over, Jago, I've had enough. Fortunately Nancy covered it up.'

'You're doing risky things. I can't trust you . . .'

'Jago, that's it exactly, in a nutshell. I can't trust you either.' She picked up the two big bunches of flowers and headed for the door. 'I'm going to Grindley.'

He was afraid she'd won that round. He said weakly, 'For God's sake don't say anything like that again.'

*

Later in the week, at that time in the evening when the jollity in the bar of the Lord Nelson was getting louder, Nancy heard footsteps coming upstairs to her. It was Alma. 'There's a handsome air force officer in the bar asking for you,' she said.

For a moment, Nancy's head swam. This is what used to happen if she was upstairs when Charlie came. Don't be silly, she told herself firmly. You know it can't be.

'He said his name was Gavin.'

'Oh, yes.' Her heart was still thudding. 'Tell him I'll be down in a minute, will you?'

Nancy had just said good night to Caro. She opened the bedroom door quietly; if she was still awake she'd tell her she was going downstairs for a few minutes. Caro was asleep, her breathing deep and regular. Nancy went to the bathroom to powder her nose and comb her hair. She didn't want Gavin to see her as an untidy housewife.

The number of men in uniform among the bar's customers was increasing all the time, but she had no problem picking Gavin out. He was sitting by himself in the corner and looked quite woebegone.

She whirled up to him, 'Hello! I'm glad you've come. I've been wondering how you were getting on.'

He jerked to his feet and smiled. It transformed his face. 'How are you, Nancy? Feeling better about things, I hope?'

She forced a smile in response. 'I'm getting used to managing without Charlie.'

'So am I. Can I get you a drink?'

'No, thank you. Would you bring yours up to our living room? I've just put Caro to bed, and if she calls out for me I wouldn't hear her down here. That happened once, and she was dreadfully scared.'

'Of course. How is she?' He followed her out of the bar and up the stairs.

'She's fine. Coping better than I am, I think.'

'Is she still drawing? I've brought her some more paper.' He put a paper bag on the kitchen table.

'Thank you. Yes, and she can't get enough of that. How are you, Gavin? I couldn't stop worrying about the court martial, but I see you've still got wings on your uniform.'

His smile was broader. 'A bit of a damp squib, really. All I got was a reprimand. I think Hitler's saved me. Britain's gearing up to fight him, so I'm needed to train more pilots.'

'I'm delighted for you, I really am.'

'The worst part was the waiting. I was scared stiff. Things are better now, though I still have nightmares about Charlie's crash.'

'I didn't realise you were the sort to worry.'

'Yes, well, I feel partly to blame that you have no husband and Caro no father.'

Nancy was touched. 'You mustn't,' she said. 'It wasn't your fault.'

'Well, there's the war to worry about now. What have you been doing?'

Nancy told him she was thinking of converting the top floor of the building into a flat for herself and Caro.

'I haven't done much about it yet; I don't seem to have much energy. Come up and take a look. I could do with some ideas.'

He clattered up the bare stairs behind her. She put on the lights and threw open the doors. 'This is quite a small room but it'll make a bedroom for Caro. It would be better for both of us if she had a room of her own. I'll make this into my bedroom.'

'They only need redecorating.'

'And here is the biggest room. This will be our living room.'

'That's a beautiful old Victorian grate, but it's a bit small to heat this space. You'll need a bigger one if you're going to stay warm.'

'Yes, I've been thinking about that. But I'd have to carry the coals all the way up here and the ashes down.'

'What about a gas fire?'

'I haven't decided one way or the other. Then this will make a biggish kitchen. The water is already piped up to this floor.'

She showed him an enormous Victorian lavatory and a washbowl in another room. Gavin pointed out that if they were taken out, there'd be plenty of room for a modern bathroom suite.

'So there would, and it would be nicer than the one we're using now. Yes, I'd like to do that.'

Nancy usually made sandwiches for her father to eat after he'd closed the pub. Tonight, Gavin helped her cut the bread and they made more sandwiches than usual. They sat for another hour with a pot of tea, while Gavin brought her up to date with news of the friends she'd had at Hawarden. When he stood up to leave, she went down to see him out.

'Good to see you again, Nancy,' he said, as he pecked her cheek goodbye.

'Come again when you can. It's been lovely talking over old times.'

It gave her a pang to see he'd parked Charlie's MG at their side door. She watched him get in and drive off into the darkness.

That night, in the privacy of her own bed, she thought of Charlie and wept a little for what she'd lost. Gradually, she fell into a deep sleep and all was well with her world again. Charlie was lying beside her; she could hear him breathing. She put an arm round his waist and pulled herself closer.

She woke up to find she was cradling one of her pillows against her, realising that Charlie being with her had been nothing but a dream. It left her numb with grief again.

One night, Nancy was woken by the sound of her father coughing. When she heard him get up and go to the kitchen, she pulled on her dressing gown and followed him in.

He was struggling to get his breath, 'Did I wake you? I'm sorry.'

'I was awake, Dad. I heard you coughing.' She put the kettle on to make him a cup of tea. 'No ifs and buts. I want you to see the doctor again tomorrow morning. I'm worried that you're not getting any better.'

'I'm all right.'

'You can tell him I'm worried, then. You haven't seemed well since I came home. I'd like you to have an X-ray.'

She sat with him at the kitchen table for a while, drinking tea. 'I'm going to start work on the flat upstairs,' she told him. She and Caro were settling down here and they couldn't leave him if he wasn't well.

Her father sighed. 'I've been thinking about it. On second thoughts I don't think you should spend too much on doing it up. After all, it belongs to the Birkenhead Brewery, not to us. A kitchen sink, yes, but you've got a toilet and washbowl already and you could come down here for your baths. I wouldn't spend on getting the gas up there either, or a bigger grate. You could get an electric fire and the latest electric stove, which you could take with you if you decide to move.'

'I've got plenty of money now, Dad.'

'Yes, well, hang on to it until you've decided what you want to do. Just give the walls a lick of paint to freshen them up. If you did it yourself it wouldn't cost much at all.'

'It would be a big job painting all those walls.'

'I could send Kevin up to help you. In quiet moments of course. It would do you good to work on a big project like that.'

'Right, I'll go out and get the paint in the morning.'

The next morning at breakfast, they listened to the latest news on the wireless. Nancy had the feeling that war was closing in on them. She sent her father off to see the doctor, took Caro to school and went on to buy two large tins of cream paint.

She knew Kevin would have to finish his morning work in the cellar before he could help her. He had the empty barrels to move out of the way and full ones to set up so the beer could be pumped up to the bar. Nancy spent the time sweeping the dust off the walls and washing the woodwork in what was to be her new bedroom.

She found the work more fun once Kevin came up. He told her what he and his family had been doing over the weekend. She told him about the money she'd been promised.

'You jammy thing! A thousand a year! From those men who came to see you the other week?'

Nancy nodded. 'Yes, the twins. I'm very lucky, I know.'

'They must be stinking rich to part with money like that.'

She'd known Kevin so long she felt totally at ease with

him and went on to tell him that she'd been acutely aware of the tension between the twins and Henrietta, and that lunch had not been at all enjoyable.

'Henrietta was really rude to Jago. Not for the first time either.'

'What did she say?'

'Something about him being queer and not acting like a normal husband.'

'What? Straight out like that?' Kevin had stopped painting and was staring at her.

'Poor Jago looked really flummoxed.'

'I bet he did.'

'I had to stand up for him, didn't I? I said we all had moments when we were queer.'

Kevin was grinning at her. 'Do we, Nancy?' he said teasingly. 'What d'you mean by being queer?'

'Well, strange, out of the ordinary. We all do odd things when our mind's on something else.'

Kevin's grin was getting wider. He giggled. 'How come you've never heard of it? Queer, poof, pansy, it means a homosexual. Is that what you're talking about?'

'What?' That pulled Nancy up sharply. 'I don't know. Is that what you think she meant? But surely Henrietta wouldn't have called Jago that. He's her husband. And Charlie's father.'

'Are you sure he's . . . straight? You know, normal?'

'He must be, mustn't he? I don't know. Charlie never

said anything to me. Or did he?' She tried to think. 'Well, certainly not about his dad or Uncle Toby, but . . .'

'Did you notice the way Jago looked at me, that time you had them up in the flat and I brought drinks up?'

'No! How did he?'

'The same way fellers gawp at you. Some men can't help it.'

'Heavens, Kev. Oh, my! Are you sure?'

'Dead certain. You've led a very sheltered life, Nancy, even if you have been brought up in a pub.'

CHAPTER FIFTEEN

THE SCHOOLS WOULD soon break up for the summer holidays, but with war looming ever closer few people were thinking of going to the seaside. It was only twenty years since the Great War had ended and many older people had not forgotten the horror of the trenches. The possibility of another war was now the topic most talked about in the bar of the Lord Nelson.

Nancy was in the kitchen preparing lunch and she'd left the living-room door open so she could listen to the news on the wireless. She was shocked to hear doom-laden talk of the possibility of imminent gas attacks should war break out. The public was instructed that free gas masks were being handed out at local centres. Everyone was urged to collect one as soon as possible, and carry it with them at all times.

She ran down to the bar to tell her father, and he caused momentary panic amongst the customers by sending his staff off one at a time to do it. Nancy decided she'd collect Caro from school and go then. Caro thought everybody else looked funny in them when they were being fitted.

'They've all got snouts like pigs,' she giggled. 'Black pigs.' But when her turn came she hated it. 'I can't breathe and it stinks of rubber,' she howled.

'Just breathe deeply, dear,' she was told, as the straps were adjusted to get a tight fit. She couldn't get it off quickly enough.

The following afternoon she brought a letter home from school. It said that should war break out the government was planning to evacuate all schoolchildren from the area. Parents were invited to a meeting in the school to hear more details.

Nancy went along and heard that gas attacks and bombing raids must be expected in the city. Liverpool was a major port and there were several miles of docks on both sides of the Mersey, as well as ship building and repair yards, gas and oil installations and many factories. Nancy was scared out of her mind. It sounded too dangerous for Caro to stay. She signed a form, giving permission for the school to take Caro to a place of safety. She addressed an envelope to herself and was told she would be notified by post if and when it was decided to proceed. Each day seemed to bring the war closer and made her more anxious.

The following Saturday, Nancy and Caro met Billy and his mother in the market. She was heavily pregnant and pushing a pram holding two children.

'Are you letting Caro go?' she asked. 'They want to send me and all the kids to the country. I wish I knew what was the best thing to do.'

'I'm not going anywhere,' Billy said mutinously, kicking at a stone. 'I want to stay here and fight.'

When they moved on, Caro said, 'I'd never heard of Herr Hitler until last week. He must be a very bad man to frighten everybody like this.'

'He is.'

'A bogeyman?'

'A sort of bogeyman.'

'But Mummy, you said you weren't frightened of bogeymen and I mustn't be either.'

Nancy shuddered. 'Hitler is a real person. He's different.'

'Grandpops is frightened of him too, isn't he? So is my teacher. He must be awful.'

July was coming to an end and the school was due to break up after the morning session. Nancy had been out with Alma to look at kitchen sinks. Alma's husband was a plumber and though he worked for someone else, he would come and fit it for her in his spare time.

They had to pass Caro's school on the way back to the Lord Nelson and, as parents were gathering outside, Nancy said, 'I'll wait for Caro. You go on, Alma, Dad'll want you in the bar.'

She saw Billy's mother waiting, with just her youngest asleep in the pram.

'The teachers here are very good,' she said. 'They took our Frankie in at the beginning of term so I could get more rest, though he's only just four. I don't know how I'm going to manage through the next few weeks with all of them at home.'

The children were streaming across the yard to the gates. Billy came to swing on his sister's pram. 'Caro's gone,' he said, looking up at Nancy.

'No, she can't have, I've been waiting here for the last five minutes. I've seen everybody come out.'

'She went at playtime. She gave me her milk to finish. Her granny came for her.'

Nancy couldn't get her breath. She felt as if she'd been kicked in the stomach. 'Are you sure?'

'Yes, she went off in a car. We saw her get in. A posh car.'

'Oh my God!' Nancy shot into the school, fighting against the tide of children coming out, and found Caro's teacher.

'Caroline Seymour,' she gasped. 'Where is she? Billy says her grandmother took her away.'

'Yes, at morning break. She said you'd sent her.'

'I didn't.' Nancy sank against a small desk, folding up in horror.

'I'm so sorry. Shouldn't I have let her go?' The woman looked as stricken as Nancy felt. She shook her head.

'How could you have known? What time would that have been?'

'About half past ten.'

Nancy felt a wave of panic wash over her. She must stay calm, she must think. 'Did her grandmother say where she was taking her?'

'To the seaside for a holiday. She had a car waiting. I understood the whole family was going.'

'Did she say exactly where? A nearby seaside?'

'Just the seaside . . . I am sorry.' The woman was wringing her hands. She'd have been no match for Henrietta. 'I do hope she'll be all right.'

Nancy swallowed hard. She'd always feared Henrietta would do something like this. 'I expect her grandmother will look after her,' she said. 'Please don't worry. It's not your fault.'

She raced back to the Lord Nelson. She had a stitch in her side and was out of breath when she reached the bar. Her father was polishing glasses and regardless of the customers within hearing she blurted out, 'Dad, Henrietta's taken Caro. She's got her.'

'What? Where's she taken her?'

'To the seaside.' She could feel herself shaking. 'I've got to ring Jago, I've got to find out exactly where that would be.'

Miles put his arms round her. 'Calm down, love.' He stopped her from lifting the phone. 'Get your breath back first. Come on, tell me what's happened.'

It was Miles who picked up the phone a few minutes later and got the operator to put them through. Nancy repeated her story to Jago.

'What does she mean by the seaside? Where will she be taking Caro?'

'I don't know.' Jago sounded worried. 'She didn't tell me she was going away. Perhaps she's just taken her home.'

'No, she'd know I'd go straight there and bring her back. She talked of taking her to the seaside for a holiday, didn't she?'

'Yes, but I didn't think . . .'

'Does Henrietta ever go away by herself?'

'She often goes to London. To the shops and theatres.'

'But to the seaside?' Nancy couldn't imagine Henrietta wanting sea and sand.

'Well, she went to Le Touquet last year. She said she enjoyed it.'

'But that's France, isn't it? Is that a suitable place to take a child?'

'She won't go to France, Nancy. Not now, when the German troops could be marching across the French border at any moment. It wouldn't be safe.'

'Where, then?'

'I'll ring Gertie. If Henrietta's gone away, she'll have packed for her. Perhaps she'll know where she's gone. Nancy, I'll see what I can find out and ring you back.'

'Thank you. I'd be glad if you would.'

She put the receiver down and didn't know what to do with herself. She was furious with Henrietta, and although she'd told the teacher that her grandmother would look after her she was fearful for Caro. She'd surely be upset about being snatched away so suddenly without her mother.

Miles put his arm round her again. 'Caro will be all right, don't you worry. Henrietta will take good care of her. Riding round in the back of that limousine, she's unlikely to come to any harm.'

'She'll turn her against me. She'll not want me to have her back.'

'She has to, Nancy. Caro's your daughter. There's no question of her keeping her without your say-so.'

Nancy was exasperated. 'Dad, there should be no question of her taking Caro on holiday without my say-so, but she has.'

Kevin said, 'What did you do with that letter I gave you, boss? It was addressed to you, Nancy. It was stuck in the door when I opened up at twelve.'

Her father took it out of his pocket and turned it over. 'Could it be from Henrietta?'

Nancy almost snatched it. 'Expensive paper. It must be.' She had it open in seconds, but could hardly read the copperplate writing for the anxious tears that sprang to her eyes. 'Yes. Oh, Lord! Dad, she's taking her to Le Touquet. She thinks it will do her good.'

'Hell!'

In the appalled silence that followed, it was Kevin who voiced their anxiety. 'What if the Germans invade?'

Nancy felt demented with worry. At that moment Jago rang back. 'I know already,' she told him. 'Henrietta left me a note to say she's taking Caro to Le Touquet.'

'She left me one too. I got Gertie to read it to me. What a stupid thing to do! Everybody believes war is imminent.'

Nancy had a sudden thought. 'But no, she can't take her to France. Caro doesn't have a passport.'

'I thought of that too,' Jago said. 'But I think Henrietta could have got one for her. She took photographs of Caro, didn't she? She'd know somebody she could bamboozle into countersigning her application.'

In a burst of rage, Nancy said, 'Then she must have been planning this for weeks.' Her spirits plummeted. 'How can I find them? How can I get Caro back?'

Nancy worried herself sick. Everybody at the Lord Nelson offered sympathy. Jago telephoned her several times, but it was another forty-eight hours before he had any real news.

'Henrietta's rung me,' he said. 'Caro's safe. They're in a hotel near Folkestone, a place called St Margaret's Bay.'

'So she changed her mind about going to France?' Nancy could feel relief flooding through her veins, relaxing her.

'I understand she had it changed for her. She asked Bennett to take her across the Channel and he refused. It seemed she could get tickets for them from Dover to Le

Havre but the ferries were fully booked coming back. The British are flocking home from the Continent, but Henrietta still seemed sure she'd be able to get a boat back when she wanted it.'

'Thank goodness for Bennett.'

'Yes, but she sacked him, and that's left her high and dry because she can't drive. That's the only reason she rang me. Henrietta can't cope with inconvenience. She must have a car ready and waiting at her command.'

'How will they get home, then?'

'I've arranged for one of the factory drivers to go down by train and bring them back. He's catching the two o'clock to London.'

'That's a real weight off my mind, Jago. I didn't doubt Henrietta would get to Le Touquet if that was what she intended.'

'Neither did I. I'll ring her now and tell her to book an overnight bed for the driver and start back tomorrow morning. And I've told the driver to come through Birkenhead and drop Caro off at the Lord Nelson before bringing Henrietta home. It'll probably be late afternoon before he gets to you, because Henrietta won't be likely to make an early start.'

'I can't thank you enough, Jago. That's a weight off my mind.'

'I think we've both got Bennett to thank. Thank goodness he had the sense not to take them across the Channel.'

*

In the middle of the night, Henrietta woke up trembling, feeling as though she'd been visiting hell. She'd had her terrible nightmare again and the horror of it was with her still.

It took her a few moments to realise she was in the Carillon Hotel at St Margaret's Bay. Her plans had gone wildly wrong again. She'd trusted Bennett. He'd been her chauffeur for five years and she'd found him satisfactory, had even praised him. But now he'd foul-mouthed her and left her down. 'You stupid old woman,' he'd shouted, his face scarlet. 'Just be bloody grateful I haven't left you stranded on the wrong side of the Channel.' It wasn't as if it was her fault. Like everybody else she'd believed Chamberlain when he'd promised 'peace for our time'.

Henrietta climbed out of bed and went to the bathroom. So that she could have Caroline near her and they could be comfortable, she'd taken a two-bedroom suite with a small sitting room. She peeped into the second bedroom. In the half-light she could see the child was deeply asleep. 'Don't worry, Grandma,' she'd said yesterday. 'There's a beach here; it'll be just as good.' But Caroline didn't have to worry about how they were going to get back to Liverpool.

Henrietta told herself she mustn't panic, but she felt light-headed and unsteady on her feet, as she had when the plans she'd made for her father had gone so badly wrong. She needed to lie down before she fell. A setback to her plans always made her feel ill. She needed sleep, but she was afraid of being drawn back into that nightmare. Joseph Digby's accusing eyes on her. Digby in the church porch with blood spurting out all round him, and Father with that terrible wound on the back of his head.

'No,' she screamed out loud. 'No! I loved my father. How could I possibly hurt him?'

But she knew deep down that wasn't true; that she'd been turning her plan over and over in her mind for months, fantasising about how it could be done.

But it wasn't all her fault. If he hadn't threatened to stop her marrying Jago while they'd been out on their early morning ride, it might have remained mere fantasy. He'd been viciously cruel to her for years.

But she could see again Father's broken, twisted leg, which had got in the way of the horse's hooves. She could hear the agonising scream going on and on until someone came to shake her.

'Grandma! Grandma, wake up.' It was Caroline. 'What's the matter?'

Only then did Henrietta realise it had been she who was screaming. It was morning, and she was hot and sweaty and worn out.

The sweet child put her arms round her and gave her more sympathy than she would have received from anyone else. She quietened the child's fear by telling her she wasn't well, and Caro settled down in the little sitting room to draw pictures and allow Henrietta to rest.

But her nightmare was not over. She dozed off again and saw the evil features of that terrible man leering at her still.

That had been the worst time of her life. Her father's death had changed her life for the worse in a way she should have foreseen. She'd been gravely disappointed in her brother William. To see his wife Julia installed as mistress of Grindley Manor had been very painful. But to find she'd inherited it on his death had been the absolute end.

Chapter Sixteen

Later that same morning, Nancy was telling Alma that Caro was still safely in England when the phone rang. Alma picked it up. 'It's for you,' she said.

'Hello, Nancy.' It was Gavin Freeman. 'I've got a forty-eight-hour pass and I was wondering if you'd take pity on a lonely man and come out for dinner with me?'

She was pleased. 'I'd love to,' she told him. 'Tonight, you mean?'

'Yes. Not much notice, I'm afraid, but I've got a new posting, so it's now or never.'

'You couldn't have chosen a better time. Caro isn't with me and I need something to take my mind off that.'

'It sounds as though it'll do us both good to have a night out. We've come through some hard times, haven't we? Do you know a good place to go?'

Nancy asked in the bar and got plenty of advice. She walked down the road and bought tickets for the first house at the Argyle Music Hall, then booked a table for supper afterwards at the Queen's Hotel.

She chose a bright multicoloured dress that had been her favourite in the old days and spent a lot of time getting ready. She was down in the bar waiting for Gavin before he arrived. The bar staff were watching him, but he didn't seem to notice.

'You're looking more your old self,' he greeted her. 'More like the girl who used to dance half the night away in the mess.'

'With Charlie.' She smiled. She could talk about him again without feeling weepy. 'Would you like a drink here first? We've got plenty of time. I've got tickets for the first house at the Argyle and it's only just down the road. Flanagan and Allen are the star turn tonight.'

He smiled. 'Excellent. I've been once or twice with the lads.'

Nancy took him to a corner of the lounge and Alma brought their drinks. 'What's this about another posting? Are you going far?'

'Yes, the other end of the country. I'm driving down to Hawkinge on Thursday.'

'That's Kent, isn't it?'

'Yes. I asked to be sent on active service. It seemed a good idea at the time.'

Nancy's heart plummeted. 'Gavin! With all this talk of war? You had a safe job training others for that.'

'I was getting bored with all those training flights. I'll be flying Spitfires from now on.'

'Hawkinge is very near the coast. It'll be a front line

airfield if there's a war.' She shivered, afraid he might be killed.

'There'll be a war all right. It's just a question of when it'll start, now.'

They both agreed that the show at the Argyle was top notch. Nancy hadn't laughed so much for months. They walked down to the Queen's Hotel. She was leading the way through the foyer to the restaurant when Gavin said. 'Hang on a moment, I want to see if they've got a bed here for tonight.'

Nancy stopped, wondering whether she should take Gavin home with her. She'd never invited anybody but Charlie to stay in their guest room, though her dad had his cousins there occasionally. He'd attracted the attention of the man on the desk by the time she joined him and pulled at his arm.

'No, Gavin, you can stay with us. I've just finished painting the main bedroom on the second floor and putting the furniture back. Why don't you use it tonight? Stay with us?'

'Nancy, that's very kind of you. I'd love to, if it won't be too much trouble for you.'

'Of course it won't. Well, the bed needs making up, but that'll only take five minutes. I should have thought of it as soon as you said you had a forty-eight-hour pass, then I could have got things ready.'

'What about your father? Will he mind?'

'No, he'll make you welcome.'

203

'Right, then, thank you. I'd love to stay with you.'

'That and Caro's bedroom are the only rooms that are finished. The rest of the place is a mess, but I'm getting on with it now. Kevin and I have started painting the living room and the kitchen is almost finished. I've bought a lot of stuff for it, a sink and a cooker, and an electric fire for the living room. I'm looking forward to spreading out all the things I had at Hawthorn Cottage.'

He took her arm and led her towards the restaurant. 'Let's go and get something to eat.'

They had a very good rump steak. Nancy found Gavin easy to talk to and he could make her laugh. Somehow the invitation to spend the night had shifted their relationship up a gear. Gavin had always been her friend as well as Charlie's, but now he seemed more than a friend. Afterwards, they strolled back to the Lord Nelson and Gavin collected his overnight bag from his car. It was just on closing time for the pub, and Nancy took him through the bar so she could tell her father they had a visitor. Then she collected sheets and towels from the airing cupboard and led the way up to the second floor.

'It looks very nice,' he told her. 'You've done an excellent job. Here, let me help you make the bed up.'

Afterwards they spent half an hour with her father in the kitchen, and when Nancy went to bed she couldn't sleep. She was thinking of Gavin – were they falling in love? She couldn't remember when she'd last enjoyed an evening so much. She'd caught his dark eyes watching her several times during the evening and they'd seemed full of affection. Now she felt drawn to him as she never had before. But what would Charlie think? Restlessly she pummelled her pillow. If he couldn't be here, he'd be all for it. He'd want both her and Gavin to have another chance of happiness. That was his way.

The next morning she was late getting up. Dad had already had his breakfast and was down working in the pub.

She made scrambled eggs for herself and Gavin, and then, as it was a sunny day, they took the ferry down to New Brighton and had a paddle, a walk along the beach and a look round the old fort that had once protected the mouth of the Mersey. The donkeys were being led backwards and forwards with children laughing and shouting as they clung to their backs.

'You're missing Caro,' Gavin said. 'I can see from your face.'

'Yes, she'd love this. I think losing Charlie makes me cling more closely to her.'

'It's bound to. All that's left of Charlie lives on in her, doesn't it?'

Gavin was very understanding. She felt closer to him too. There was a fresh breeze off the Irish Sea and the sun was glinting on the waters of the Mersey and making it appear blue. They sat on a bench on the promenade to eat fish and chips before taking the ferry back to

Woodside. Walking home to the Lord Nelson, Gavin took her arm and twisted his fingers round hers. She was very conscious of his touch.

'I'll have to be on my way now. Caro will be back with you soon and the boys have arranged a farewell thrash for me tonight in the Red Lion at Hawarden.'

The Lord Nelson was closed for the afternoon and her father asked Gavin if he'd like tea and a piece of cake before he left.

Nancy was reaching for the teapot when she felt Gavin's arm accidentally brush against hers. It sent a thrill running through her body. Both his hands came to steady her and she thought from the look in his dark eyes that he too had felt that spark of something stronger than friendship.

But her father was with them slicing up cake. 'Nancy made this fruit cake before she knew you were coming,' he said. The moment passed before either could acknowledge it.

Gavin collected his overnight bag from upstairs and as he was going Miles stood up too, saying he wanted another packet of cigarettes from the bar and would see him off. Nancy went out to the MG with them, and Gavin patted the bonnet.

'I could have been flown down to Hawkinge on Friday, but I wasn't prepared to leave this behind.'

'I wish you hadn't asked to go there. You'd have been safer training others in Hawarden.'

'I felt I had to.'

She shivered. He'd be on the front line when the fighting started. She was afraid now she might never see him again. 'It's oppressive, isn't it, the way the war looms over everything, colouring everything. We're making decisions because of it.'

'What choice do we have? Thanks for everything, Nancy, you've cheered me up. I've had a lovely leave. You'll keep writing to me, won't you?'

'Yes, of course. Goodbye.'

He kissed her quickly on the lips and leapt into his car.

In the weeks since his disastrous visit to Hattongrove, Robert Bellamy felt he'd recovered, but it bothered him that he didn't have a clear picture of what had happened to him there.

Bob Bellamy believed himself to be a man with his wits about him who thought things through. He liked to think of himself as a 'go-getter', a man who'd had to make his own way in life and been successful. He'd been able to set himself up for retirement by buying this newly built semi-detached with a large back garden where he could grow all the vegetables he'd need. It was also more convenient for his present job.

His only son Johnny had lived with him until recently. Bob had encouraged him to follow in his footsteps and make his career with the police, so once he'd married Nora he'd been entitled to a police house and he'd moved out. Bob's gaze went to the photograph on the mantelpiece. Alas, Celia was no longer with him, having died in hospital years ago after an operation for a burst appendix. Bob now lived alone and was proud of doing everything for himself.

He shifted his bulk in the chair and glared across his living room at his son, who said, 'What d'you reckon, Dad?'

'Johnny, I've told you ten times, I really don't know.' He felt irritable. Johnny was a police constable and had developed the art of asking the same question in ten different ways. 'You don't have to keep probing to get the truth from me. I do it to myself. Don't forget I spent twenty-five years in the force and made the rank of sergeant. I want to know exactly what happened to me as much as you do. Probably more.'

'OK, Dad, don't get mad at me.'

Because Bob Bellamy's family had its roots in agriculture, he had been able to change his career.

During the Great War, food had become very scarce. The government had set up a Board of Agriculture and farmers were compelled to plough up more land and change their crops. In return, they received guaranteed prices, and seeds and fertilisers were made available at controlled prices. This led to a big increase in food production but, like many other things, agriculture found itself in the doldrums in the hard times that followed.

The government was determined not to be found

lacking in the coming war and marketing schemes were introduced and prices for pigs, bacon, milk and potatoes were regulated. Bob Bellamy had been hired to help farmers become more productive again. He was finding most of them suspicious and rather hostile to his advice, but he was determined they would heed it.

Johnny lit a cigarette with fingers stained with nicotine. 'Just tell me again what happened.'

'I remember getting there early to have a look round before going to the house. I saw the cows coming out after milking. I didn't see anybody and I didn't think anybody had seen me. The next thing I knew I was in hospital with a sore head. The nurses told me I'd been brought in by the brother of this farmer you wanted me to see.'

'Toby Seymour.'

'Yes. He'd told them they'd found me unconscious in the yard, and that I must have slipped and cracked my head on a stone.'

Johnny sighed. 'The doctor told me it's quite common for people to lose consciousness after a bump on the head, and though it's not so common to lose your memory, it's not unknown. He said it might come back.'

'Then I wish it would hurry up.'

'You don't think you slipped?'

'I've no recollection of losing my balance. That must have happened before the bump on my head, so surely if

I can remember walking round, I'd remember slipping too?'

Johnny tossed the butt of his cigarette into the fire. 'You had a nasty gash on your head.'

'Seven stitches, and I don't remember seeing anything on which I could give myself a crack like that.'

'OK, so we suspect foul play?'

'Well, I have an uneasy feeling that all was not as I was led to believe.'

'Dad, you made an appointment to discuss the preparations farmers should make to get through the coming war. That's government policy. He'd see nothing suspicious about that because you're going round other farms in the area doing the same thing. He couldn't know that I'd asked you to look out for any evidence of homosexual practices being carried on there.'

Bob gave a derisory laugh. 'For that sort of evidence, I think you'd have to catch them in the act. And as I was there by appointment, there was no possibility of that.'

'I knew that. I was more hopeful that you might be able to help in the search for Leslie Gibson.'

'Ah, yes, the lad who stole the takings and beat up the owner of that garage at Melling.'

'Yes, and was fool enough to leave us a good set of fingerprints before he disappeared.'

'I know you heard rumours that he was employed at Hattongrove, but he has a record and comes from the back streets. It isn't his sort of work.'

'Accommodation is provided as well as work, and he's queer, so I thought it quite likely.'

'I didn't catch so much as a glimpse of any employee, nor have the chance to ask about Leslie Gibson. But don't worry, I know how important it is for your career to get as many convictions as possible. You can trust me to keep an eye on Toby Seymour and Hattongrove.'

CHAPTER SEVENTEEN

SPENDING TIME WITH Gavin had soothed Nancy's hurt and anger with Henrietta, driven it back to a dull ache, but now he'd gone too.

She'd said goodbye to him and come upstairs in a whirl of energy to tidy up the flat, feeling she had to have it looking its best. Henrietta would bring Caro to the door and she couldn't not ask her up.

Nancy was very much looking forward to having Caro back home. Jago had told her it would probably be late afternoon when she arrived and it was half past four now, so not much longer to wait. She went to the living-room window to look down into the street. They might be back early.

Her father was reading in his armchair. He said he felt better on some days than he did on others and today was a good day.

She felt restless and time was passing very slowly. 'I hope Caro will be back in time for us all to eat dinner together,' she said.

'It's hard to know how long it'll take coming all the way from Folkestone.'

Nancy started to cook but kept going back to the living-room window, half expecting to see Henrietta's limousine drawing up underneath. At half past five she dished up her father's meal.

'I'm not hungry, Dad,' she said. 'I've eaten big meals today. I'll wait until Caro's here and eat with her.' She sat with him at the kitchen table drinking tea.

At five to six her father went down to open the pub. 'She'll be here soon,' he said.

Nancy was beginning to worry that Henrietta might have insisted on taking Caro home with her. She watched the clock, growing more and more anxious. At half past she heard a commotion down below and rushed to the window. There was no sign of the big grey limousine at the side door. But there were heavy footsteps on the stairs, and she ran out on to the landing to see Kevin striding up carrying a heavy bundle trailing swaths of dark green cloth.

'Where d'you want her?' he asked. It was only then she realised he was carrying a sleep-sodden Caro and that she was wearing a voluminous new dress she hadn't seen before. He'd lowered her on to the sofa in the living room before Nancy had time to answer.

'The driver says she's been asleep for more than an hour. He lifted her up and brought her to the door of the bar.'

'Where's Henrietta?'

'He said she didn't want to get out. He's gone back to fetch Caro's case.'

Nancy's anger had been building over the last hour or so, and now it boiled over. 'Caro didn't have a case,' she said through clenched teeth. 'Stay with her, Kev. I'm not going to let Henrietta sneak her back like this and get away with it.'

There were more footsteps on the stairs. A young man reached the landing. He wore a navy drill jacket with the words *Seymour's Sausages* embroidered in red on the chest.

'Have I picked up the right case? Does this belong to the little girl? Mrs Seymour is asleep now.'

Nancy felt ready to explode. 'Then I'll wake her up. I want a word with her,' she said. 'Wait here, I won't be long.'

She tore downstairs, shot through the pub and ran out on to the pavement. She thought at first the luxurious car was empty, but then Nancy saw Henrietta stretched out on the back seat, made comfortable with cushions and a light rug over her legs.

She snatched the back door open. 'Mother-in-law, you had no right to take Caro from school like that without saying a word to me.'

The heavy eyelids remained down but Nancy saw the thin lips twitch. She felt another rush of rage.

'It's no good pretending to be asleep. I want to talk to you.' She snatched the rug from her legs. Henrietta had slipped off her shoes, and now she drew her plump feet closer.

'Sit up and listen to me,' Nancy ordered furiously, and was surprised when her mother-in-law obeyed. 'I've been nearly out of my mind. I went to collect Caro from school only to find she'd gone. You'd already taken her away.'

'I did leave a note to let you know she was with me.' Henrietta sounded quite timid.

'How could you be so stupid? Did you think it would settle my mind to know you meant to take her to Le Touquet? You said, for God's sake, that you thought it would do her good!'

'We didn't get abroad.' She was cringing back in the seat.

'No, thank goodness your driver had more sense. What if the Germans had overrun France and you were both caught on the wrong side of the Channel?'

'I didn't think about the war. I didn't think it was all that close.'

'Then you're the only person in England not to have it on her mind.' Once started, Nancy couldn't stop. All the antipathy she had felt for her mother-in-law over the years wouldn't be stemmed. 'You always do exactly what you want. You think you're entitled to, that the world owes it to you. You've never liked me, and never stopped to consider my feelings. Or anybody else's for that matter. You've always given me a hard time, but this was way over the top.

I've had enough. I hate you, and I don't want you anywhere near Caro from now on. Stay away from us.'

Frightened eyes stared numbly back at her.

'Do you understand? Stay away from us.' Nancy whirled round and raced back upstairs to Caro, angry tears burning her eyes. She almost bumped into the driver, who'd come out on to the landing, and pushed past him to see her daughter. Caro was still only half awake. Nancy threw her arms round her and hugged her.

Kevin had stayed with her. 'She's all right,' he said. 'All in one piece. I'd better get back to the bar now you're back.'

'We looked in the case,' the driver told her. It had been lifted on to the table, and he opened the lid. 'It's full of childen's clothes so it must be the right one.'

Nancy stared at it. Spanking new, it was of tan pigskin with gilt locks. She'd never seen it before. She'd not seen the clothes before either. The driver was staring at her. 'You're her mother?'

'Yes.'

'Mr Seymour said I must be sure to bring the little girl straight to you.'

'Thank you very much. I've been worried about her.'

'Mrs Seymour wanted me to take them both back to Carrington Place.' He bent lower and said confidentially, 'Is she Mr Seymour's mother or his wife?'

'His wife,' Nancy said, and he whistled through his teeth.

Turning to leave, he said, 'I wouldn't want to work for her.'

Nancy kissed her daughter's cheek. 'Hello,' she said. 'You're home again.' Caro's blue eyes flickered and looked up into hers. Nancy knew her daughter had woken up when she smiled and opened her arms to her. She gathered up the child in a hug of utter relief. 'I'm so glad you're back, Caro. I've missed you.'

'I wanted you with us, Mummy. I missed you. I didn't want to go on my own with Grandma. I didn't like it. Except for the shopping trips. She let me have everything I wanted.'

Henrietta was boiling with rage as she lay back against the soft leather seat of her limousine. Bennett had made her ill. She hadn't felt right for the last few days. It was a good job she wouldn't have to put up with him any more.

It had been humiliating that her plans to treat her granddaughter to a nice holiday had come to naught, and that she'd had to ask for Jago's help to get them home. But to have Nancy fly at her like that had been the end. The girl showed neither gratitude nor respect for all she'd given her.

Henrietta closed her eyes in agony as the words replayed in her mind. *You've always given me a hard time, but this was way over the top. I've had enough. I hate you, and I don't want you anywhere near Caro from now on. Stay away from us. Do you understand? Stay away from us.*

Never had anyone dared to speak to her like that before, but what else could she expect from a hussy from the back streets of Birkenhead? A damned barmaid who'd entrapped her son, to worm her way into a decent family.

She'd never forgive Nancy. She'd make her pay in the way she'd made her father pay, and that fool Joseph Digby. Oh yes, Nancy, I'll get you sooner or later. You'll not get away with saying things like that to me.

Jago pulled his chair closer to the window that overlooked the front drive. He'd spent the last hour sitting here in his study, waiting for Henrietta to come home. He was too angry with her to be able to work, though there were papers on his desk he should be attending to.

He counted himself a mild man with plenty of patience. He'd done his best to treat her fairly and give her what she wanted over the years, though it had become obvious to him quite soon that they had little in common.

From time to time, his conscience had troubled him about what he'd done. He'd married her knowing they'd not have a normal married life. He'd tried to tell her what she was letting herself in for, and only found out several years later that his explanation had gone completely over her head.

He'd done his best in the early years of their marriage

to be the husband she'd expected, and had been thrilled when he'd achieved fatherhood. Poor Charlie. His mother might be easier to cope with now if he were still here.

Perhaps he'd treated Henrietta too gently; given her everything she wanted without question, pressed luxuries on her as compensation for what he could not give. Perhaps that had led her to believe she need consider nobody else's wishes and had made her what she was: a woman who believed that having been born into the upper middle class, she could always expect to have everything the world had to offer. She need never pay for anything nor work to get it.

He'd never dared to admit that his father had wanted him to marry her because she was a good hostess to the leaders of trade and industry. In the right drawing rooms and amongst the right people, Henrietta had shone. Undoubtedly, that had helped his father's firm to pick out the best investments for his family and for their clients. She thought now that it was to hide what she called his perverted sexuality, and of course his father had had that in mind too.

He wondered if ordinary married couples ended up feeling so disillusioned about each other. Perhaps not, if they still shared a sex life. But he understood many couples had given that up by the time they reached the thirty-fourth year of marriage as he and Henrietta had. Anyway, she'd never seemed very keen on sex.

Of course, there were the advantages of having a well-organised home kept clean and warm, but he wondered sometimes whether Gertie didn't do most of the organisation. Certainly Toby had managed almost as well without a wife, and he seemed to have a more carefree time of it. More fun, too.

At mid-morning the next day, Kevin ran up to tell Nancy that her father-in-law was on the phone and wanted a word with her.

'How is Caro?' Jago asked.

'None the worse for her so-called holiday.'

'And you?'

'Angry. I'm afraid I gave Henrietta a piece of my mind last night.'

'So I gathered. I can't blame you; she deserved it. She's distraught, Nancy.'

'Good.'

'You haven't calmed down yet?'

'No, I don't suppose I have. Caro's all I've got left, Jago. I was afraid for her safety.'

'Henrietta says you intend to keep Caro away from her in future.'

'I was blazing. Such a wicked thing to take her away like that.'

'She wants to apologise. She knows what she did was wrong. Please keep bringing Caro to Sunday lunch, Nancy. We need to keep in touch.'

That it was Jago who asked it of her made it difficult for Nancy to refuse. 'I don't know whether I can face her after what I said.'

'I don't know what you said, but it was probably justified. You've got Henrietta on the back foot. It will be harder for her to face you than the other way round. Can I ask Toby to come for you as usual on Sunday?'

'Are you fighting her corner, Jago?'

'No, what I'm trying to do is stop war breaking out in the family. Toby and I have been laying down the law to her about Caro. Please say you'll come and hear her apology.'

Nancy sighed. 'You and Toby have been so good to me, I can't say no.'

'Good girl. We'll all get over it, and the sooner the better. This is the best way.'

'Was Grandma naughty to take me away?' Caro asked Toby when he came to collect her and Nancy for Sunday lunch.

'Grandma didn't tell any of us that she was going to,' Toby explained. 'We were all worried because we didn't know where you were.'

He whisked her off, leaving Nancy to go alone into the drawing room. Henrietta stood up as soon as she went in, looking contrite.

'I'm very sorry I took Caro away,' she said. 'I won't do it again.'

Nancy felt she'd suffered for too long at Henrietta's hands, and was in no hurry to be all sweetness and light again. She couldn't resist saying, 'You must have known I'd be worried stiff.'

'Yes.'

So she'd meant to make her suffer. But Henrietta was biting her lip and was not at all her usual bombastic self. 'Please forgive me,' she whispered.

Jago was right, of course. Nancy knew she ought to put the episode behind her instead of letting it fester. She made a big effort.

'We need to make a fresh start, you and I,' she said. 'We got off on the wrong foot, didn't we? There are things I should apologise for too. I lost my temper and said some hurtful things to you. I'm sorry.'

'So we've made up our differences? All is well?'

Nancy almost said, 'Up to a point,' but she bit the words back and said instead, 'Yes, of course. But you gave me a bad fright. I can hardly bear to let Caro out of my sight now. I hope it's understood that in future she stays with me.'

'Yes. I do apologise, Nancy, for what I did.'

'I've told Caro she must thank you for all the pretty clothes you bought her, but you've been over-generous. She'll grow out of them before she'll get much wear from them.'

Nancy felt that because Henrietta's plans had ended in disaster, she'd lost some of her power. She'd never known her mother-in-law apologise for anything before. But although they'd both agreed that all was forgiven and must be forgotten, she could see from the way Henrietta glanced at her with eyes full of raw hate that it wasn't. To Nancy, it felt as though she really wanted to harm her. That Henrietta would not be content until she had Caro to herself. She just couldn't rid herself of the fear and distrust she had of Henrietta.

On Tuesday the following week, Nancy got up as usual and made sure Caro was up and dressing before going to the kitchen. Most days she found her father already there, preparing breakfast, but this morning the flat was quiet and there was no sign of him. She set the kettle to boil and knocked on his bedroom door. 'Dad,' she called, 'have you overslept?'

Hearing no answer, she pushed the door and peeped in. The curtains hadn't been opened and the room was in semi-darkness. Her father was still curled up under the blankets. 'Dad, are you all right?'

With a grunt, he stirred and turned over.

'What's the matter?'

'Haven't had a good night. I don't feel too good.'

She put a hand on his forehead. It felt hot and sweaty. She opened the curtains, and saw that he looked ill.

'Is it late?' he asked. 'I was awake in the night, must have gone off again at daybreak. I'll get up now.'

'It won't hurt if you have a lie-in for once. Stay where you are, and I'll bring you a cup of tea.'

'No, I'll be fine.'

Caro came in, fully dressed. 'Are you sick, Grand-pops?'

'Not very well,' Nancy answered for him. 'Do as I say, Dad. I'm going to start breakfast.'

That morning, Caro ran to school on her own while Nancy set out her father's boiled egg and toast on a tray.

'I'm bothered about you, Dad,' she told him. 'You feel as though you have a temperature and you haven't been really well for ages. I want you to stay where you are and I'll send for the doctor.'

'I'll be all right.'

'Dad, this has dragged on too long. It's time we got to the bottom of it. I'm going down to the bar to ring the doctor now.'

'There's no need,' he told her. But he couldn't finish his breakfast, and when he tried to get up he fell back on his pillows, coughing. He was fussing about the pub work and when they came in, Nancy ushered Kevin and Alma up to his bedroom so he could tell them what he wanted them to do.

'I'll take care of everything,' Alma assured him. 'Don't you worry about a thing.'

The doctor came after his morning surgery to listen to his chest and talk about Miles's breathing difficulties.

'Stay where you are for a few days, Mr Milton,' he

advised. 'I'll arrange for you to have another X-ray too, though the one you had a few months ago showed nothing definite.'

As she showed the doctor out, Nancy said, 'Dad hasn't felt well for weeks now. What's the matter with him? Sometimes he's fighting to get his breath.'

'He's had bronchitis for some years, but I'm wondering now if he has some additional problem. I'll know better when we have the result of this X-ray.'

He handed her a prescription for some pills and suggested she get some Friar's Balsam from the chemist and give him inhalations three times a day. She did as he suggested and followed the instructions on the bottle, measuring it into a bowl and pouring boiling water on top. Then she made her father sit over it under a tent of towels for twenty minutes, breathing in the steam. He said it helped and made him feel better.

Despite Nancy's protests, he insisted on getting dressed that afternoon and going down to the pub for the evening. Kevin said he didn't do much except sit talking to the customers, but he seemed happy enough there. Over the following days, he got back into his usual routine.

Nancy took him on the bus to the General Hospital for his X-ray, and a week later the doctor called again looking quite grave. He came to their side door and Nancy fetched her father from the bar and took them both upstairs. In the living room the doctor told them the

X-ray had shown that Miles had a small growth in his right lung. 'I'm going to refer you to a specialist.'

'I thought I was recovering,' he said. 'I feel a lot better.'

'Good,' the doctor said. 'Carry on with the tablets and the Friar's Balsam. Come and see me again in a month.'

When the doctor had gone, her father said, 'I thought he was going to tell me I'd got TB. It could be worse, couldn't it?'

Nancy thought it sounded pretty dire. She'd have to take more care of her father.

The weeks of August passed slowly, the feeling of imminent war pressing down on them all. One morning, Nancy picked up the post that had been put through the side door and cringed at the sight of an envelope addressed to herself in her own handwriting. She'd written it at Caro's school on the afternoon they'd outlined the government's plans to evacuate the children.

She took a deep breath before she opened it and learned that the planned evacuation would take place on Thursday 31 August. There were more forms to fill in and lists of instructions. Nancy felt sick at the thought of sending Caro away and not knowing exactly where she was going.

Thanks to Henrietta she knew exactly what that would be like. And Nancy couldn't see her daughter being content to stay with complete strangers when she'd not enjoyed going away with the grandmother she loved.

After much thought and consultation with her father, she wrote an apologetic note to the school saying she'd changed her mind and wanted Caro to stay at home with her.

It was a frightening time for everybody. The population listened to every news broadcast they could, and studied what was said about the situation in the newspapers. Neville Chamberlain had pledged Britain to guarantee Poland's independence, and on 1 September 1939 the military might of Nazi Germany crossed the Polish border.

On Sunday morning, Nancy and her father heard with heavy hearts that Britain was at war.

BOOK TWO

CHAPTER EIGHTEEN

August 1940

FOR MONTHS LIFE had remained more or less normal in Birkenhead, though the sky filled with barrage balloons. Nancy told herself she'd made the right decision to keep Caro with her. The women and children who had been evacuated were drifting back. Billy and his family stayed away for only six weeks. It was dubbed the phoney war, and the schools, cinemas and theatres that had shut down reopened within weeks. There was a sense of anticlimax. As Miles reminded his pub customers, the war was being waged elsewhere.

Nancy felt her father's illness was following the same pattern. It was months since he'd spent a few days in hospital having tests, before being sent to the Radium Institute in Liverpool for treatment. Over a period of weeks Miles had made periodic visits to the Institute, but he went on running the pub, rarely complaining, rarely speaking about his illness.

Nancy could see that at times he still struggled to get his breath and knew he wasn't the sort to complain. She didn't think he was getting any better, and when the brewery wrote to him announcing a periodic inspection visit, she suggested he tell them about his illness.

'No,' he said. 'Not yet. I'll do it if things get worse.'

'Dad, I know you enjoy being the licensee of this pub, but you're sixty-three. You could retire early on the grounds of ill health.'

'No, Nancy. Where would I go? I have no other home.'

'We could find somewhere to rent nearby. You could come back as a customer.'

'No. Not when you've practically finished fitting up the flat on the second floor.' It was almost ready, but she hadn't moved into it yet because she didn't want her father to have to fend for himself downstairs. 'You'll lose your home too if I give up the licence to run the pub.'

'I can find somewhere else too, Dad. I don't think you're well enough to work.'

'I can get others to do the work. Besides, I'd be bored out of my mind if I didn't have the pub. What would I do all day?'

So for Nancy everything went on in much the same way. She still had Sunday lunch with Henrietta every week and felt no better about her.

*

Ration books were issued and food rationing had come into force last January, starting with bacon, butter and sugar. Meat was added to the list in March.

Jago was delighted when he heard that liver, kidneys and hearts, as well as products made largely from offal such as sausages, faggots and haggis, were to remain on open sale. With a shortage of meat, it meant the market for sausages would burgeon. He'd have a ready sale for all he could make.

In May, the Nazis invaded the Low Countries and swept through northern France with breathtaking ease, cutting off the lines of supply to the British Expeditionary Force which was driven back and had to retreat hurriedly to Dunkirk. The humiliation was redeemed by getting most of the Force back across the Channel to safety. France collapsed, which brought the German might within twenty-odd miles of the Kent coast, making an invasion of England a very pressing fear.

For Nancy, there was the added fear for Gavin's safety, especially as it was understood that Germany had to achieve control of the skies before a ground invasion could be sure of success. Since she'd last seen him, they'd been corresponding, but not very regularly. She'd heard about the life of a Spitfire pilot; how alert they needed to be and how quickly they had to respond to enemy action. She knew Gavin felt he was too old to react with the necessary speed, and that perhaps he should have asked to fly bombers.

All summer, Nancy had listened to the news of the daring exploits of Spitfire pilots as they engaged the Luftwaffe over the orchards and fields of Kent in the Battle of Britain. Charlie would have been out-standingly good at it, if only he'd walked away from that crash, but she wasn't so sure about Gavin, and whenever she didn't hear from him for a while she worried about him.

After a day when frequent dogfights and heavy losses on both sides were reported, she wrote him a long letter telling him how she and Caro were faring. He didn't reply over the following days, and that worried her more. Every day she listened to the wireless and heard of the number of planes being shot down. It was said that on average a new Spitfire pilot lasted only three weeks. She didn't know whether Gavin had been shot down or whether he was just too busy to write to her. She feared the first.

Then she had a letter and a birthday card from Helen, who was still at Hawarden, telling her that Gavin had won the Distinguished Flying Cross. From what she said, Helen seemed to have no doubt that he was still alive and Nancy was very much relieved. She started to write to congratulate him, but before she'd posted her letter she received one from him.

Please forgive me for not answering your last letter. I did start to write but was interrupted by a call to get airborne. None of us do anything but sleep and eat in our spare time. I wish you a very happy birthday, and I'm sorry I haven't had time to go out to get you a card. I hope you have a splendid day.

I can't believe I've been awarded the DFC because I haven't done anything out of the ordinary. We're all trying to shoot down as many enemy planes as we can, but it's a nice change to have the top brass pleased with my efforts for once.

Do please write to me, Nancy. I look forward to your letters and find myself thinking about you often.

Nancy was thrilled for him and wrote back saying Toby had given her a duck to roast for their dinner, but otherwise her twenty-eighth birthday had passed in much the same way as any other day.

Merseyside's own battle began on 9 August 1940. Early on that morning a stick of bombs fell on the Birkenhead suburb of Prenton, damaging the home of Mr Bunney, the owner of Bunney's department store in Liverpool, and killing a servant girl.

Thereafter the Luftwaffe came over regularly on moonlit nights, when the shining waters of the River Mersey acted as a marker for German navigators. They dropped their bombs on the docks and industries that lined both banks of the river.

It changed everything for Nancy. While she and her father did their best to appear calm and comforting,

Caro was clearly terrified. There was plenty of space in the cellar under the pub, which was said to be the safest place in the building, though it housed crates of bottles containing spirits as well as barrels of beer. Having failed to find camp beds for sale anywhere, Nancy tried to make it comfortable with chairs and blankets.

The staff had to be offered shelter too if a raid occurred while the pub was open, but customers were encouraged to go to the nearby public shelters. The safest was said to be in the underground railway station at Hamilton Square, not very far away.

Nobody knew when or where the next bombs would fall. Most districts were getting a share of the battering. Those evacuees who had returned from the country made haste to go back. A fire-watching rota was drawn up for civilians and Miles put his name down to do it.

One Saturday night, they had a raid before midnight and a worse one in the early hours. Nancy could hear the bombs exploding round them, some near, some far away. The bursts of return fire from the ack-ack guns on Bidston Hill was almost as alarming. Nancy felt very much alone spending her nights in the cellar with her arms round Caro trying to comfort her as best she could. Morning found her stiff with tension.

Miles only lasted through three nights of fire-watching. On the fourth he couldn't get his breath and fell, and was brought home by a civil defence worker. After that he accepted that it was beyond him to work both day and night and Nancy was very pleased to have him with her in the cellar. When they went out and about in the days that followed, the damage they saw all round them was terrifying.

'There's no need for you and Caro to risk life and limb here,' her father said, after a particularly bad night. 'You ought to take her somewhere safer.'

'But that would mean leaving you on your own.'

'During the day there's usually plenty of people in the pub. Nancy, I'd feel happier if you went. You're the younger generation; you've more to lose than I have.'

It was Sunday the next day and Toby telephoned to ask if they were all right, and confirm that he'd come as usual to pick them up for lunch at Henrietta's house. Nancy didn't want to go. She didn't think she was up to coping with Henrietta after a string of wakeful nights, and Toby had to persuade her. When he arrived, Nancy still felt sleep-sodden. Caro, clearly very frightened, described the horror of it only too graphically.

'The Lord Nelson's no place for you now,' Toby told them, appalled. 'You need to get away to the country.'

Nancy groaned. 'I know.'

'I can hear the bombs bursting before I go to sleep but it's all in the distance. I know I'm reasonably safe because they aren't aiming for anything near me. All the targets are along the Mersey.'

Nancy had heard Henrietta say that Toby had a house

that was bigger and grander than her own, and that his bachelor existence meant he had rooms that were never used. She said, 'As you say, Caro and I are in need of safe lodgings. Could you spare us a couple of rooms in your place?'

The look on his face told her he wouldn't. After her conversation with Kevin, she could guess why and kicked herself for asking.

He smiled at her and said, 'You'd be better in a little place of your own. I'll ask round, see if there's a cottage nearby you could rent.'

'Thank you,' Nancy said. 'I'd be very grateful if you would.'

When they arrived, Henrietta was complaining loud and long about the bombing and how it frightened her.

'Uncle Toby's going to look for a safe cottage for Mummy and me,' Caro said.

'Good. It's urgent, Toby; don't drag your feet over it. I always knew that pub was the wrong place for Caro to live. And while you're at it, I want you to find a suitable house for me. Jago is too busy in that factory of his to do anything for us. I'd like a period house if possible, with a few acres of land.'

'It's a bit late in the day for something like that,' Jago told her. 'You wouldn't hear of it at the beginning of the war when I wanted to look.'

'Not easy to find a place like that now,' Toby agreed. 'Not easy to find any sort of accommodation just outside an urban area which is being bombed. People are snapping it up, because it's possible to have undisturbed nights and still work in town.'

When they moved to the dining table to eat, Nancy was impressed by the great round of roast beef which Jago was starting to carve.

'It's from my farm.' Toby smiled. 'So are the roast potatoes and all the vegetables. There's no need for us to go hungry.'

For pudding, there was a choice of rhubarb pie or poached peaches with cream and ice cream. 'From my farm too,' Toby said. 'Except for the ice cream. Aren't we all being told we must be self-sufficient in wartime?'

Nancy didn't hold much hope of Toby's finding them a cottage. Caro's fear of air raids was making her feel guilty, particularly as she'd chosen not to send her to a place of safety. She decided she must make an effort herself to find a cottage and bought copies of the North Wales newspapers to see if any were advertised. As none were, she wrote out advertisements asking for safe accommodation, but before she'd posted them Toby rang her to say he'd found something for her.

'It's in a row of six cottages not too far from Hattongrove. All the others are occupied, mostly by retired people I think. It's a two up two down, quite pretty and in a good state of repair, but the rooms are tiny. There's running water in the kitchen but no bathroom and the lavatory is at the end of the garden. It's the best I can find. Would that be acceptable?'

'Yes,' Nancy said immediately. 'Thank you! I'll be glad of anything, you know that. We've had three quiet nights since Sunday, but we hear the planes throbbing overhead and other districts are catching it. Is the cottage furnished?'

'There's a table and a few bits and pieces there but not much. You'll need more to make it habitable. I suppose you should see it before you decide. Shall I ask Jago to send a car for you?'

'I could take the train, Toby. You and Jago have been so kind, I don't like to trouble you further, especially with the shortage of petrol. Will I be able to find it?'

'Yes. The nearest station is Formby – get off there and head towards the village of Great Altcar. Before you get there you'll see a terrace of small cottages along the lane. It's number four Rosemead Cottages, and you can pick up the key next door at number three.'

'I'm thrilled. Thank you. I'll go tomorrow morning on the train.'

It was the school holidays and she'd have to take Caro with her. She wished she'd asked Toby if he thought it too far for her to walk. But Caro had a fairy cycle; she could take that on the train. Nancy remembered then that she'd had a bike in her teens and went down to the cellar to see if it was still in reasonable condition.

She asked Kevin's opinion. 'Yep, it looks OK,' he said.

'I'll oil it for you, pump up the tyres and adjust the brakes.'

It would have been a long walk from the train station, so she congratulated herself on taking their bikes. She had no trouble finding the terrace, which had been built of pink bricks in the last century. Toby was right, the cottages were pretty.

She knocked on the door of number three, introduced herself to a very bent old man who said his name was Tom Wickham, and received a big key. It turned smoothly in the lock of number four and they stepped straight into the tiny living room, which had a Victorian parlour grate. Everything looked very basic but it had a welcoming air.

'It's lovely, Mummy,' Caro said.

Nancy decided she'd take it even before she saw the rest of it. The room behind was a little larger, and the grate was of the Victorian kitchen variety and included an oven and trivets for cooking. The ceilings were beamed, and the walls whitewashed.

There was a brownstone sink with a single cold water tap in the kitchen and a back door opening on a long but narrow garden. It was somewhat overgrown, with pink hollyhocks growing round a small building at the bottom which housed the lavatory, a coal shed and what had once been a pig sty.

The stairs going up from the kitchen were steep and

led straight into the back bedroom. Through the open door ahead, Nancy could see another somewhat larger room.

'A bedroom each,' she told Caro, and went to look at the other room. The window overlooked the lane. 'I'll have this one with the cupboard. I'll be able to hang my clothes in it.'

Caro opened it. 'What's this inside?'

It was a chamber pot. 'We might need that,' Nancy said.

The place was very plain, but Nancy thought it a sweet little cottage. She knew they would be safe here, and couldn't wait to move in. She'd brought a notebook and pencil and began jotting down the essentials she'd have to bring. She needed curtains, though the poles were here to hang them on. The windows were smaller than those at the Lord Nelson, so the curtains she'd made for the flat there would do fine. She felt more cheerful already.

Caro unpacked their picnic on the scrubbed table in the kitchen. There were two hard chairs for them to sit on, but not much else. They tried the privy at the bottom of the garden, which Nancy thought would be fine until Caro saw the spiders behind the door. After Caro had picked a few flowers to take home, they went back to the next door cottage. Mr Wickham came to the door, moving very slowly. He seemed to be well into his eighties.

'We like the cottage very much,' Nancy told him. 'I've decided to take it. Can you tell me where we'll find the nearest school?' He thought there was none nearer than Formby.

They cycled back to the train station looking for it, but didn't see it. As the train was due and Caro was tired, Nancy decided finding the school could wait. Once back at the Lord Nelson she rang Toby to tell him she was delighted with the cottage and wanted to move in as soon as she could.

He was pleased. 'Start collecting together what you need to live there,' he told her. 'I'll have a word with Jago, so if you ring him when you're ready he'll send a van driver over to move your stuff.'

'Toby, you're very kind. I can't thank you enough.'

'You don't have to. I don't like waking in the night and thinking that bombs could be dropping on Caro. Or, of course, on you. I'll come and see you at the cottage when you're in.'

Nancy went to find her father. Caro was excited about the move and already telling him about the cottage.

'I'm not going to spend as much time fixing this place up as I did the upstairs flat,' Nancy said, laughing. 'I want to get Caro away from here as soon as I can.'

'I expect you'll want to take a lot of what's in the flat with you. The cottage does have electricity?'

'Heavens, I didn't look!' Nancy's feeling of well-being and success vanished. 'It never occurred to me, and now

I think of it, I don't remember seeing any light fittings on the ceilings.'

'If it's out in the country . . .'

'Oh, dear. I was thinking of taking that new electric cooker I bought for upstairs.'

'Never mind, love. There was a lot to think of on your first visit. I could run you up tomorrow afternoon for another look. I'd like to see where you're going to live.'

'Thanks, Dad. I'll take you up on that.'

Nancy liked the cottage just as much when she saw it for a second time. But within moments of opening the front door, she said, 'There is no electricity. How did I miss that?'

'You're not changing your mind about the place?'

'No. It's got charm, hasn't it?'

'Then you'll need oil lamps and coal.'

They had a good look round and then Nancy went next door to ask Mr Wickham where he bought his coal. He gave her the address of his coal merchant and her father drove her there. She had to register with him to receive a coal ration and he told her he wasn't due to deliver in her area for another fortnight, but he'd bring her some coal then.

As they were in Formby, they drove round until they found the school for Caro, but of course it was closed for the summer holidays. Nancy noted the address and her father advised her to ring the Lancashire Education Department and ask if she could reserve a place. She felt she was making progress.

'All I have to decide now,' she said, 'is when to ask Jago to send a van.'

When she returned home she started putting together all the things she'd need: bedlinen, towels and clothes. She gave Caro some boxes and started her packing her own belongings.

She was up in the flat she'd never moved into when Kevin put his head round the door. 'I hear you're evacuating yourself and Caro. Your dad's sent me up to help. What d'you want me to do?'

'Thanks, Kevin. Would you help me collapse these beds? We'll need them there, and I want to take those armchairs, that rug and the pictures. Then I'd like you to help me carry them down to the lobby behind the side door. It'll make it easier to load into the van when it comes.'

They filled the lobby and stacked articles halfway up the stairs. That night the enemy bombers throbbed overhead again, and the sirens blared. They heard the crunch of bombs in the distance and thought it must be Liverpool that was getting it, but Caro was frightened anyway and couldn't sleep. It made up Nancy's mind for her. She'd ring Jago in the morning and see if he could send a van and driver that day.

'Yes,' he told her when she spoke to him first thing.

'The air-raid siren went three times here, but it was the docks that got the bashing, not us. The sooner you get away the better. There's just one thing, Nancy. It's Saturday today and the drivers have a half day. If I send the van over straight away, can you get the job done so the driver can return the van here by one o'clock and still have his half day?'

'Of course, Jago. I've already got most of the stuff downstairs ready to load, so we should be able to make a reasonably quick getaway.'

When she put the phone down, she ran to the market to buy enough basic foodstuffs to keep them going for a day or two. When she got back, her father was wheezing but he'd got breakfast for Caro and cut a pile of sandwiches for them to take with them.

'I've found some candles and two old oil lamps in the cellar,' he said, 'but one is without a lamp glass. I thought I might go out and see if I could buy another glass to fit it.' He broke off in a fit of coughing and wheezing.

'No, Dad, you aren't well enough. Anyway, nobody's used oil lamps here for donkey's years. A new glass would be easier to find in a country district.'

'You'll have to have a tin of paraffin. I'll ask Alma to get that for you.'

'What would I do without you? Will you be able to manage here, Dad? I feel I'm being an awful trouble to everybody.'

'I'll be fine, love,' he said, smiling.

'I worry about leaving you here, with you not being well and the bombing and everything. You could retire and come and join us. I wish you would.'

'My life is here,' he told her. 'Kevin's down working in the cellar. Go and tell him to leave that and help you get the rest of your stuff down. In fact, take him with you. You'll need help getting the mattresses up those narrow stairs at the other end.'

Nancy and Kevin worked hard, and when the van arrived they helped the driver load it as quickly as they could. When they were ready to leave, she found her father had packed two carrier bags with coal from his own supply, plus some sticks to start a fire.

'You think of everything,' she told him. 'I'm very grateful.'

'I'll feel happier when I know you and Caro are safe,' he said, as he kissed her goodbye.

Kevin had to sit in the back of the van but he was hanging on to the back of Nancy's seat. He kept them amused on the way by telling stories he'd heard in the bar. On arrival they hurried to unload and soon the front room of the cottage was full of furniture and packages. The van driver wheeled their bikes through to the back garden and then left.

'I'm hungry.' Caro opened the sandwiches on the table. 'There's cake too,' she said, 'but nothing to drink except water.'

'There is.' Kevin grinned. 'I've brought along a little

something for the feast as well.' He brought out two bottles of orangeade and a bottle of beer. 'Your dad said I could.'

Kevin helped Nancy carry the furniture to where she wanted it, make up their beds and hang the curtains. He filled the lamps with oil, trimmed their wicks and polished the single glass in readiness. He was laying a fire when Jago pulled his car up at the front door.

'It's Grandpa,' Caro rushed to open the door and danced round him with excitement. 'Have you come to see our new house? Isn't it lovely?'

'Yes. You look almost settled.'

'I just need to unearth the pots and pans,' Nancy said.

'I've brought you some sausages. I was afraid you might have forgotten to bring something for your supper.'

She smiled. 'I went out and bought some fish to bring with us. We'll have your sausages for breakfast, thanks very much.'

'And I'll come to fetch you for lunch tomorrow, or Toby will.'

'You've all been very kind. Very thoughtful on our behalf. I'm grateful, Jago.'

'Come on, Grandpa. I want to show you my bedroom.' Caro led him round, making sure he missed nothing. Not even the chamber pot.

'Not much bigger than a doll's house, Nancy,' he said when he came down.

'It's plenty big enough for us two,' she said. 'I love it already.'

She saw Jago looking at Kevin. 'Can I offer you a lift somewhere? It's quite a walk to the railway station and I expect you're tired.'

'That's very kind of you. I'm shattered,' Kev said. 'Nancy works me harder than her dad does.'

CHAPTER NINETEEN

K EVIN COULD HAVE danced out to the immacu-
lately polished grey Jaguar standing outside the
cottage. When Jago got in and signalled to him to do
likewise he slid into the passenger seat, his heart beating
wildly. Since the night Jago had come to the pub to see
Nancy, he'd felt an overwhelming tug of attraction
towards him.

'Thanks for offering me a lift. I was trying to pluck up
courage to cadge one from you.'

Jago laughed. 'I'm going to my factory. It's not far
from James Street station. If you're going back to
Birkenhead that would be convenient, wouldn't it?'

'It would be perfect.' Kevin was almost sure Jago was
interested in him. 'I do envy you this car. An SS Jaguar
sporting saloon, isn't it?'

'Yes, 1938 model, but the SS is officially dropped now.
The German military machine has given it bad
connotations.'

Kevin smiled. 'It's gorgeous.'

'Do you know a lot about cars?'

'I looked up the details of this one when I first saw you driving it.'

Kevin knew Jago was amused. He'd told him he was shattered but he'd never felt so alive. His fingertips were tingling as the blood raced round his body.

'I'd love to be able to drive it.'

'These days you need a licence to do that.'

Kevin smiled with satisfaction. 'I've got that. I saved up for ages for lessons.'

Jago looked at him for a moment. 'That shows self-discipline.'

'If you want something badly enough, it's easy.'

'I suppose you'd like to get yourself a car now,' Jago said.

'I've been saving and dreaming of that for years, but now petrol rationing has come in I'm too late, aren't I?'

'It makes it a lot harder,' Jago admitted. 'Got any other ambitions?'

'Loads of them, I'm afraid. I'd love to have a job as a driver. I don't suppose you need another in your business?'

'These days the government decides how many drivers I need. I already have all I'm allowed.'

'How many is that?'

'Two, plus five with sales skills. They have reserved occupations because they're working in food distribution.'

He turned and his gentle eyes smiled into Kevin's for an instant, promising more than a lift home. 'But yes, given time, I could probably fit you in.'

Kevin felt his heart race. He'd felt Jago's interest in him the night he'd come to the Lord Nelson. Now he felt their joint excitement fill the car. He could almost touch it.

'Tell me about yourself.' Jago looked the perfect gentleman with his soft hands and thick white hair. Kevin wondered how old he was. Probably very old; after all, he was Nancy's father-in-law. Incredibly, they were hitting it off – more than hitting it off. 'I know Nancy sees you as a friend and you work for her father.'

'I do. He gave me a job when nobody else would. He took pity on me.' Kevin sensed it would be better to come clean about the lapse he'd had in his teens, rather than let Jago find out later. He told him everything, sparing him none of the details. 'So you mustn't assume I'm as respectable as Nancy and Miles,' he finished.

'We can't all achieve their standard,' Jago said easily. 'Would you like to see the set-up at my factory?'

'I'd love to.'

They were approaching the outskirts of Liverpool. 'I'm hungry. Are you?' Jago asked.

'Starving.'

'There's a small restaurant I know that stays open late. We'll have something to eat first.'

Kevin waited until they were seated at a table. 'About

that driving job we talked about. I'd really achieve one of my ambitions if you'd give me that.'

'But I can't offer it as a reserved occupation. You'd be conscripted.'

'No I wouldn't.' Kevin grinned at him. 'With a prison record the army doesn't even want me as cannon fodder. They reckon men like me are more trouble than they're worth. That's why I've been able to keep working at the Lord Nelson.'

A broad smile lit up Jago's face. 'If that's the case I'd be happy to offer you a driving job, more than happy. I think we'd get along very well.'

Kevin could see big changes opening up in his life, and he was thrilled. He'd had a wonderful time last night, though he hadn't seen the sausage factory. Instead, Jago had taken him to Toby's farm for the night and dropped him back at James Street station on his way to work this morning.

But now he'd have to tell Miles he wanted to leave, and he felt terrible about that. He felt he was letting him down after he'd done so much to help him, but he couldn't let a chance like this go. Jago had agreed he must give notice and work on for as long as Miles wanted him.

He was half an hour late when he reached the Lord Nelson, but Miles was still upstairs. Alma was alone, working in the bar, and she told him he looked as though he hadn't been to bed.

Kevin indeed felt half asleep as he started on the routine cellar work. He knew Miles would be down before long and tried to think of a way to break the news to him.

When he heard the heavy footfall on the stairs and the cheery voice saying, 'Alma reckons you've had a big night out,' Kevin's mind went blank. He mumbled some reply.

'What's that?'

Kevin took a deep breath. 'I want to leave, to better myself. I want to thank you, boss. You've always been very decent to me. Took me on when nobody else would. I'm very grateful, but now I've got the chance to move on.'

'How d'you mean?' He could see Miles didn't understand.

'I've always wanted a job as a driver, and now I've been offered one. I'll work out as much notice as you want.'

'Oh, dear. I know that's always been your goal, but you've become a fixture here. How long is it?'

'Nearly seven years.'

'I'll be sorry to see you go. You're always cheerful and you can turn your hand to anything.'

'Can I have a reference?'

'Yes, you're entitled to that. Well, I wouldn't want to stand in your way. Who's taking you on? Is it the brewery? Will you be delivering the beer?'

Kevin found the next step hard, but he had to tell him. 'No, it's Mr Seymour, Nancy's father-in-law. He employs several van drivers, as you know, but he also has company cars. I'll be doing a bit of both.'

'Good gracious!' Miles's mouth had dropped open. 'I suppose I can blame Nancy for this?'

'No, don't blame her. I didn't ask her for help. He came to the cottage to see her yesterday, and I bummed a lift from him. I asked him straight out if he needed another driver.' Kevin rushed on before Miles asked; he wanted to phrase it his way. 'He said yes, because half his staff had deserted him for war work.'

'I suppose they must have. Staff are hard to get these days.'

'He's going to give me a lodging with his farm boys so I'll be near to hand.'

'So you'll get away from the air raids. You'll be evacuated too.'

'But he's worried about taking me away from you. He's afraid you'll be upset.'

Kevin could see Miles was pensive. 'I thought you'd stay for good,' he said. 'You're almost one of the family. Still, no doubt you'll still see something of Nancy?'

'I hope so. Sorry to do this to you, boss, but I couldn't resist. It's the job I was hoping for. How much notice d'you want me to give?'

'I don't know. Give me time to think about it. There's less and less work here now that I can't get all the beer I want. It's hardly enough to make it worth while keeping open all these hours.'

'There's a man lives next door to us, retired last year from Threlfalls. He'll know all about cellar work and I think he'd like a part-time job. Shall I ask him to come and talk to you?'

'All I need is someone to cover the cellar work. Alma and Polly and I can manage the rest. Yes, ask him. I wish you well, Kevin. I hope you find your new job is what you want.'

'Thanks, boss. You're a saint.'

Nancy was loving the peaceful nights at Rosemead Cottages and found her neighbours friendly and helpful with local knowledge. On their first morning, the two elderly spinsters next door at number five knocked to introduce themselves.

'I'm Dora Lucas, a retired nurse, and this is my younger sister Emma, who is a retired midwife.'

Caro clutched her mother's hand but edged forward on the doorstep to see them. They were both plump, with kindly eyes and lots of white hair.

'Are you free this afternoon?' the sisters asked. 'Come and have a cup of tea with us at four o'clock. Some of your other neighbours will be there. They're all eager to meet you.'

'Thank you,' Nancy said. 'I'll look forward to that.'

Caro spoke up. 'Are there any children living here? I'd like somebody to play with.'

'No, I'm sorry. Mr Wickham next door to you has a

married daughter called Rita who comes regularly to shop and clean for him. And Mr and Mrs Walsh at number six have three children, but they're all older than your mother. I'm afraid we're all getting on in life.'

At four o'clock, Nancy took Caro next door and the neighbours made a great fuss of her. Mr Walsh turned out to be a retired railway worker, and Miss Dickens from number one was a retired dressmaker. She seemed younger than the others, had brown hair and bustled with energy.

They explained that Mr Davies at number two had been a farmer and kept himself to himself, but Mr Wickham would normally have joined them, but today his daughter had taken him out.

The home-made cakes were first class and Nancy pointed out that they must have been baked in a similar Victorian oven to their own. Dora Lucas gave her useful advice on how it worked and she was determined to try it. When she was leaving, her neighbours told her to knock if they could be of any help, but they didn't press their company on her.

Very soon everybody connected with the pub knew Kevin was leaving.

'You've been called up?' the customers kept asking.

Before Kevin had time to answer, Miles would growl, 'Army doesn't want him. He's found himself a better job.'

He'd told Kevin that he intended to take on the man

he'd recommended part time, but he wanted to take a couple of weeks' holiday first. If Kevin would work out three weeks' notice he wouldn't be left short-handed. Kevin felt better about that, but he was still uneasy about Nancy. What was she going to say when she heard he was walking out on her father?

Now that the pubs were opening on Sundays, Kevin usually took his day off on a Wednesday. Jago had invited him over to see his factory and have lunch on that day, and as he was equally keen that Nancy shouldn't be upset, he suggested Kevin take one of the cars and go to see her afterwards.

He parked it in front of her cottage window, and knew she'd heard the news when she came to the door looking as though she was ready to do battle.

'I rang Dad this morning,' she said curtly, 'and he told me you'd given in your notice. I find it hard to believe you're going to work for Jago.'

Kevin was apologetic. 'I feel a real heel for leaving your dad, honest. But this is a job in a million as far as I'm concerned.'

'Is that all it is, a job?' Her bright blue eyes were staring at him.

'Perhaps a little more,' he had to admit. She wasn't as welcoming as usual, not so friendly either. He flung himself into one of her armchairs. 'Look, Nancy, I don't want you to be upset over this.'

'I'm not upset, I'm worried about it.' She sat down on

the other side of the fire. 'I don't want Jago to be hurt and I'm afraid that's what you're going to do.'

'It's the last thing I'd do!'

'You've hurt my dad. I thought he'd earned your loyalty, that you'd stay with him for ever.'

'I thought so too, but I've made my peace with him. He knows I've always wanted a driving job. I'll always be grateful for what he did for me.'

'Kevin, you aren't telling porkies to Jago, are you?'

'Course not. What d'you mean?'

'You said he was, you know, queer. That he likes men. Is that what he wants from you?'

He hadn't expected her to tackle him head on like this. 'What if it is?'

'Kevin! You haven't told Jago you're homosexual too?'

'Of course.'

She was indignant, and it came out strongly. 'But you aren't!'

That rather floored him. 'How d'you know I'm not?' He knew he sounded defensive.

'If you can't remember holding forth about how you fancied Gladys Hopkins, I can. You thought you were in love with her.'

'People can be both, you know. Queer and straight.'

'Are you telling me that you are?'

'No, I'm not.'

'I think you're making this up!'

'No, I'm not.'

'I've never heard of such a thing.'

'That doesn't surprise me. You didn't even know what being queer meant until I told you.'

Nancy was looking incredulous. He mustn't be rough with her. 'Look,' he said. 'I wanted you to believe I was normal. Didn't you wonder why I never made a pass at you?'

'We were just friends.'

'But why were we just friends?' His dark eyes were staring into hers. 'You were looking for love, Nancy. You wouldn't have fallen for Charlie if you hadn't been.'

'You weren't showing that sort of interest in me.'

'Exactly, but why not? You're better-looking and a lot more fun than Gladys Hopkins ever was.'

He could see her chewing on her lip at that. 'The sad thing is, Nancy, men interest me more.'

She gave a gusty sigh. 'I was afraid you wanted to get close to Jago because he's got money. I told you how generous he'd been to me and Caro, and I was afraid you were hoping he'd be generous to you too. I know you pretty well, Kev. Wasn't that it?'

He hesitated. 'To be honest, perhaps a bit. You and I spent a lot of time talking about money when we were young. I thought it the most important thing in the world then.'

'Not any longer?'

'I know now there are more important things. I liked Gladys Hopkins, yes, and every other boy I knew fancied her. I wanted to fall in love with her, because that would have made me normal.' He knew it sounded like a cry of pain. 'I wanted to be normal more than anything else. Jago says that being queer was what sent me off the rails when I was a kid, breaking and entering and stealing. He knows all about things like that. Psychology, he calls it.'

Nancy was frowning. He knew she was trying to understand. 'I wish you'd explain things to me.'

'I'll try,' he said. 'We don't choose to be like this, but we can't help how we feel. Which is that people of our own sex attract us and we fall in love with them.'

Nancy didn't look convinced, so he went on, 'You can remember how you felt about Charlie? Jago and I feel exactly the same about each other. He's the most important person in the world to me.'

'But it's all so sudden. And he's so much older than you.'

'You and Charlie didn't waste any time.' Kevin was smiling. 'It was fast, wasn't it? And sometimes there's an age difference between men and women who fall for each other. There's no rule about that.'

'I thought this being queer thing was rare, but now there's you, Jago and Toby. And nobody wants to talk about it.'

'Well, you have to remember it's against the law. We have to watch our tongues.'

'Yes. Sorry. I do understand that it makes things

difficult for you.' She suddenly looked at the clock. 'I've got to go. I've got to collect Caro from school! I'm going to be late.'

'I'll run you down there in the car.'

'No, I need my bike to ride back with her.'

'Where is it? It'll go in the boot. Come on, let's get going.'

Despite feeling she had done the right thing for Caro, Nancy missed her father and the hustle and bustle of the Lord Nelson pub. The war seemed miles away from these sunlit green fields, and she had no idea how it was progressing. She'd thought this was what she'd wanted, but she felt cut off and at times a little lonely.

On some days, she and Caro cycled into Formby to shop and she'd ring her father from a public phone box.

'Why don't you buy yourself a wireless?' he suggested. 'I find it good company when the pub's closed.'

'I thought of that,' she told him. 'We took the train to Southport yesterday to get one, but the shops were empty. There's almost nothing in them, not a wireless to be had anywhere. I don't suppose you could find me one in Birkenhead?'

A few days later, he told her there were no new wirelesses for sale anywhere, but Kevin had found her a second-hand Marconi that worked, though it would cost twice as much as it had when new. He'd also found her a primus stove so she could make tea when she had no fire.

'I'll see if he'll drive me up tomorrow afternoon. He might need to show you how the primus works.'

Her father was ill and no longer a confident driver. If he didn't come out to see her for several days, she and Caro would take the train to see him. Once they were almost caught in an air raid, and after that he was nervous about them coming over, even though Toby was bringing her so much food that she was usually able to take him a share. He was particularly fond of Toby's big brown double yolk eggs.

Nancy felt better once she had the wireless to listen to. A few days later, she put it on for the news while they had breakfast and heard Alvar Lidell, the news-reader, announce, 'Enemy aircraft made several raids on Merseyside last night. In Birkenhead, the Argyle Theatre, which for seventy years has been one of the country's leading music halls, was badly damaged. Four enemy planes were shot down.'

Nancy felt a shaft of horror run through her, and she saw Caro's spoon stop halfway to her mouth. The Argyle Theatre was in the same street as the Lord Nelson and only a few hundred yards away. The level voice went on telling them that many famous stars had started their careers at the Argyle. George Formby and Charlie Chaplin had each been paid thirty shillings a week to perform there. Harry Lauder had sung his Scottish songs there. Marie Lloyd, Wee Georgie Wood and many others had made their names on its stage.

'Does that mean Grandpops's pub has been bombed too?' She could hear the fear in Caro's voice. It echoed her own. Nancy forced herself to stay calm.

'No, not necessarily. Let's cycle into Formby and ring Grandpops. That's the only way to find out.'

But when she put her pennies in the slot, the operator told her she couldn't connect her. 'Owing to enemy action that line is down. Try again later,' she advised.

Nancy felt weighed down with a terrible dread. She was desperately worried about her father. Her other option was to take the train into Birkenhead to see him. He didn't like her bringing Caro into town, he thought it was too dangerous, but perhaps he wouldn't mind this once. Plastered all over the station, however, were notices saying that the service to Liverpool was temporarily suspended due to bomb damage to the track. They'd have to go all the way home to the cottage and make the journey again this afternoon in the hope that the telephone lines had been repaired.

After lunch, one of Toby's farm workers came with another delivery of milk. 'There's a note from the boss inside,' he said.

She expected it to be about the arrangements for Sunday lunch, but it read, *I've had a phone call from the Lord Nelson to tell you not to worry. The pub is still standing and nobody has been hurt – just a few windows blown out.*

She sank down feeling almost swamped with relief that all was well. The note had been hastily scribbled in pencil. How clever of Dad to know she'd be worried and to think of ringing Toby. But how had he been able to do that if the lines were all down? Never mind – somehow he'd managed to get a message through to her.

Nancy tried to ring again that afternoon but it was the following morning before the lines were repaired and she was able to speak to her father.

'Yes, we're all fine,' he told her. 'Just a bit shaken to find we'd had such a close shave.'

'I heard about the Argyle on the news and was worried stiff. Thanks for sending that message through Toby. It set my mind at rest.'

'What message?'

'Didn't you ring him?'

'No, I couldn't. The phones were out until this morning. We didn't have electricity until nine last night and the gas is still off.'

'Goodness!'

'The bombs fractured a gas pipe and started a big fire. I doubt the Argyle will ever open again. I'm glad you and Caro weren't here. It was very scary; I really thought we were going to cop it.'

After Nancy put the phone down she wondered who had got Toby to send her that message. She'd ask him next time she saw him. Whoever it was, she was grateful.

CHAPTER TWENTY

WAR WAS TIGHTENING its grip on everybody. It seemed that the Battle of Britain had been won but there had been no celebrations. Gavin wrote that his squadron was now trying to intercept the enemy bombers before they could reach their targets.

For most, the rations were meagre and what wasn't rationed was in short supply. Nancy had settled into the cottage and was enjoying it but found the housework took twice as long without modern facilities. She had to light her fire to boil a kettle for her morning tea. However, as the nights were blissfully quiet and their sleep unbroken, she thought it was worth it.

Over at Gateacre, because petrol was in short supply and drivers were conscripted or required to do war work, Jago had put Henrietta's car up on blocks for the duration.

'You'll have to ask me to send transport from the factory when you want to go out,' he'd told her.

Henrietta soon arranged that he send her a car every Friday morning to get her to her hairdresser by ten o'clock so that she could have her hair washed and set. She generally had a bite of lunch in town and then went shopping.

One Friday afternoon, Nancy heard a knock on her door and was alarmed to find Henrietta on the step.

'I've come to see what sort of house Toby's found for you,' she announced. She'd come uninvited and without prior arrangement. Nancy was not pleased to see her and felt quite fluttery. She felt Jago had brokered a truce between them so that on the surface they were polite to each other, but behind the social chitchat she could always sense Henrietta's cold dislike.

For her own part, Nancy couldn't forget how she'd whisked Caro away from school without telling her. She felt nervous in Henrietta's company and didn't trust her not to cause more trouble. She'd impressed on Caro that she must never allow herself to be taken anywhere without first letting her know.

Henrietta marched straight in and settled herself in the most comfortable chair in the front parlour, away from the heat of the kitchen. Nancy had filled the grate with a jug of flowers they'd picked during a walk down the lane. Caro was looking very pretty in one of the new dresses her grandmother had bought for her.

'I call this my birdie frock, Grandma.' It was a cotton print of brightly coloured birds. 'It's my favourite.' She twirled to flare out the full skirt. Then she sat on a cushion at her grandmother's feet to tell her what she'd been doing.

Nancy had to admire the clothes Henrietta had provided for Caro. They were expensive and well designed, not the austerity ones which were all she herself could find in the shops. She also wondered how she'd managed to scrape together the clothing coupons to do it.

'It's almost teatime, isn't it, Nancy? I had very little for my lunch.'

Clearly Henrietta was expecting afternoon tea and Nancy felt that after all the Sunday lunches she'd provided for her, she must offer it willingly. 'I was thinking about tea myself,' she said.

Luckily, she'd unpacked all the fancy china, tea knives and lace-edged tea napkins that she'd used at Hawarden and was able to set the little table in the front room in the way Henrietta would expect.

This morning, Caro had found some ripening raspberries half hidden in the overgrown garden and Nancy had tried baking in her oven for the first time. Not with total success – her sponge cake had refused to rise – but she was pleased with her raspberry tart.

She was glad the whole house happened to be spick and span, and she was able to rake the hot coals out from under the oven so that her kettle boiled for tea in minutes. She served home-made scones and the raspberry tart.

Henrietta's sharp eyes were darting round. 'Toby has found you a delightful little cottage,' she said. 'It wouldn't do for me, of course, but for you it has everything you could possibly want, hasn't it, Caroline?'

'I want to have children living nearby,' she said. 'I've nobody to play with here.'

'They're retired people,' Nancy explained. 'But everybody is very pleasant and they've gone out of their way to make us feel welcome.'

'I do wish Toby would find somewhere for me to live. I can't stand these air raids. The siren went twice last night, disturbing us, but no bombs were dropped.'

'But that was good, wasn't it, Grandma?'

'The sirens ruin my sleep, child. I'll be ill if I don't get my rest.'

'Cream with your tart, Mother-in-law?'

'Thank you. A little more than that, please. The shortages don't seem to be bothering you, Nancy.'

'No, Toby regularly sends one of his farm boys down with a box of food for us. The cream came from him.'

'Well, he doesn't want Caroline to go short. A child must have a nourishing diet.'

'Mummy taught me how to make pastry, Grandma. I made two little jam tarts myself. Would you like one?' She rushed to the kitchen and presented them on a plate. Caro handled pastry like Plasticine. The tarts looked a little grey.

'No thank you, dear. I won't, because if I do you and

Mummy won't be able to have one each at supper time. I'll leave those for you and have another slice of Mummy's raspberry tart now.'

Afterwards, Caro wanted to take Grandma upstairs to see her bedroom. Henrietta's well-rounded figure almost filled the narrow staircase and she found it a struggle to get up the steep rise.

When she was ready to leave, she sent Caro out to find her car and tell the driver to bring it to the door.

'His name's Alf, Grandma. He fetched us back from Folkestone, don't you remember?'

'The working class can be very cheeky these days, Nancy. They don't know their place. D'you know what he said to me? "I can't wait here, madam, I'll not only block the light to the cottage but I'll block the lane as well. I'll park at the end there. Come and get me when you want me."'

Henrietta's eyes raked the front of the cottage. 'A nice enough little cottage, much better for Caroline than the pub. You don't have much privacy, but I don't suppose that bothers you.'

'No,' Nancy agreed. She hoped that now Henrietta had satisfied her curiosity, she wouldn't visit them again.

September came and the schools reopened. Nancy had had a letter from the education department telling her there was a place available at the school in Formby and to take her daughter to see the headmistress on the first day of term. Caro had been looking forward to starting school, because she wanted other children to play with.

Formby was some distance away. Even on their bikes the journey took more than half an hour. Nancy had mastered the primus stove and could make a hot drink for Caro before taking her to school, but to provide her favourite breakfast of scrambled eggs on toast was difficult.

Rita, Mr Wickham's daughter, had knocked on Nancy's door to say hello during her first week here. She was a jolly red-haired girl, only a year or so older than Nancy herself, and Nancy had taken to her. Rita told her that porridge was what she'd had as a child before going to school. It could be made the night before and the saucepan kept in a haybox overnight. Rita pointed out a large cardboard carton under the stairs that would be suitable, and offered to give Nancy enough hay to fill it if she'd walk with her to the farm where she lived.

Nancy found it worked. Porridge and milk became their standard breakfast. She brought the milk almost to boiling point and that too was still warm in the morning.

The war was disrupting education for many children. Some schools had been gutted by bombs and teachers were going round their pupils' homes leaving work for them to do. To start with, Nancy thought Caro fortunate to be going to school, even though getting her there and back took a large slice out of her own day. But Caro said she found the lessons boring because she'd done much the same thing in Wilbraham Street. 'Playtime is good, though, and we have much more of that.'

It was on Nancy's conscience that she was doing nothing to help the war effort. She'd heard on the wireless that conscription was going on apace and that civilians were being directed into war work. Married women with children under school age were exempt, but those with older children were urged to fill any vacant posts they could.

She enquired at Caro's school, thinking she might help as an untrained teacher or perhaps a dinner lady, but was told they didn't need anybody. There was little apart from farm work in such a rural district and she knew nothing of that. She knew there were jobs in Liverpool and Southport and it would be possible for her to get to either place by train after she'd taken Caro to school. She very much regretted that she hadn't kept Charlie's MG and learned to drive. It would have made life much easier for her now. Gavin mentioned from time to time that the car was still giving good service.

The Luftwaffe was making more frequent and heavier raids. All through September it was the Liverpool side of the river that caught most of them. The war was waging furiously, and it made Nancy feel guilty that she was still enjoying a life of comparative leisure.

As he usually did, Jago had spent Saturday night at Toby's house. It had become routine for Kevin to spend Saturday nights with him. Mostly, on other nights, he used the room Toby had allotted him in one of the farm cottages. Colin was always invited too and Toby's housekeeper organised a good dinner for four, put it in the oven to cook and left them to dish it up themselves when it was ready. They'd had a very good evening.

Jago woke feeling a bit hungover; he'd drunk rather more than was good for him. Well, they all had, really, and normally it wouldn't matter as Sunday was their rest day. But this morning he needed to do a few hours' work and Toby had promised to help.

He and Kevin were late going down for breakfast and a delicious scent of frying met them in the kitchen. Colin was making bacon sandwiches, while Toby was fiddling with his wireless trying to pick up the latest news. Jago poured himself a cup of coffee and slumped down at the kitchen table to drink it.

'We've missed the news itself,' Toby said, and tuned in to a talk about the illicit trade that was beginning to flourish in large towns and cities. A measured formal voice said, *Mass shortages are creating a black market for clothes, petrol and particularly food. A thoroughly unpatriotic practice in wartime.*

Jago's attention was captured straight away, and soon they were all listening intently.

Black market goods are frequently sourced by pilfering from bombed shops and warehouses, although there are notices everywhere warning the public that pilfering carries the death sentence.

'I don't think they could get away with sentencing pilferers to death,' Kevin said. 'That's way over the top.'

'We don't pilfer,' Colin put in.

Evading rationing regulations is also a criminal offence and punishable by fines or imprisonment.

Toby pulled a face. 'This programme's making me feel guilty.'

'I'd never keep up with Henrietta's demands if we weren't doing what we're doing,' Jago said. 'She expects the best and I promised she could have it. But yes, I have my qualms too.'

A black market in meat was one of the first to be established. In order to control rationing and prices, the government has set up specialised marketing schemes for farm animals which are ready to be butchered, and all farmers are compelled by law to sell only to a government agency. But stock for rearing, for fattening or breeding can go to auction or to a stores market and be sold to the highest bidder. There is nothing to stop black market traders buying at this stage.

Colin slid into a chair and passed a large plate of fragrant sandwiches down the table.

'They'll surely think of some way of stopping that,' Kevin said.

Toby laughed. 'They employ officials who know nothing about the meat trade. They can't tell the difference between an animal that's ready for the table and one that needs two months' fattening.'

'It's easy to defeat them,' Jago said. 'Traditionally a

farmer keeps his prime specimens for breeding, and it's up to him to decide on the number he wants.'

Colin explained to Kevin. 'An extra ten per cent can easily be designated for breeding on the forms that have to be filled in, and later they can be sold privately.'

'And if, later, there's found to be less stock than expected,' Jago added, 'a farmer has the perfect excuse – the animals died.'

'An official went to my uncle's farm, saying his sheep breeding flock was smaller than expected,' Colin put in. 'He wanted to know why he'd lost so many when he hadn't reported any disease. Uncle Bob told him it was caused by the officials traipsing round his fields. One left the gate open and half the flock went out on to the road. One of his ewes was hit by a car and never recovered, and five more strayed and were never found.'

They all laughed. 'I can't use excuses like that,' Jago said. 'What I handle is already dead.'

'Butcher's meat, you mean?' Kevin asked.

'Yes, and bacon.'

Jago had taken him round the sausage factory and explained how it functioned. He knew Kevin had worked for a butcher in his youth and that he knew a lot about meat and how to sell it. Kevin's dark eyes smiled into his. 'Do you sell fresh meat through your sausage sales force?'

Jago was shocked. 'Is it that obvious?'

'It's just that it seems a possibility to people like me who've worked in the trade.'

'It is,' Toby said. 'You've hit the nail on the head.'

'Oh, dear!' Jago said. He found it unsettling to think Kevin had homed in on his scheme so quickly. 'It can't be as safe as I thought it was. What gave you the idea?'

'You did, Jago. You said your sales team sold your sausages to cafés and retailers like butchers, market stalls and corner shops. If they make regular deliveries they'll get to know them, and those are exactly the places where they could increase their profits by selling black market meat and bacon. I have a few contacts on the other side of the water. Relations, and people I know well. How about letting me handle a bit for you?'

'It's mostly pork,' Jago said.

'That's fine. Toby's pork?'

'Not necessarily. My factory buys in certain parts of the pig that nobody else wants. From pig farmers generally, in this part of the country.'

'It sounds like big business.'

'It is,' Jago said. 'Look, you won't go anywhere near the Lord Nelson with black market goods, will you? Not Miles Milton or his customers. You could end up in trouble there.'

'I know that. I admire his ideals. For years he's done his best to keep me out of what he calls "mischief". I wouldn't take anything black market near his patch.'

'Very wise,' Jago said. He felt he could rely on Kevin. 'We'll have another cup of coffee, Toby, and then you and I need to get our heads together and work on the accounts.'

'Don't you have an accounts department at the factory to do that for you?' Kevin asked.

'I do, but they look after the legitimate side of my business. I personally have to keep track of all the stuff that's being bought and sold off the cuff, so to speak.'

'I'm ready to help,' Toby said, dumping his used crockery in the sink on top of the detritus from last night's dinner. 'Let's go to my office. Get your figures and we'll work there.'

Jago paused. 'Oh, dear, I've forgotten to bring them. I was looking through them yesterday, and I've left them at home in my study.'

'Then we'd better go to your place.'

CHAPTER TWENTY-ONE

T HAT DAY, NANCY and Caro had to wait for some time for Toby to collect them. In the end, it was Jago's Jaguar that drew up outside.

'Sorry, Nancy. Toby came over to my place to help me work out some figures. We didn't keep an eye on the time.'

'Have you got a lot of work to do, Grandpa?' Caro asked, climbing on to the back seat.

'Yes. Half my staff have volunteered for the forces and all this rationing makes extra work for us.'

'Mummy's looking for a job,' Caro said. 'She wants to help the war effort.'

'Yes,' Nancy agreed. 'Could I come and work for you?'

She could see by the look on his face that he wasn't keen on the idea.

'It's quite a journey from the cottage. You'd have to come in by train and then bus.'

'Yes, and I couldn't work full time because of Caro. I'd have to see her into school and be back before quarter to four to collect her.'

'I know the way home. I could do it by myself now. I know I could.'

'We all know you could,' Nancy said. 'But I don't want you to, because it will be getting dark at four o'clock soon.'

She could see Jago frowning. 'I don't know how practical it would be. Public transport doesn't always run on time these days. As soon as the siren sounds, everything stops and people run for cover and an air raid can leave holes in the road and tear up rail tracks.'

'But we don't have many daylight raids.'

'It's this awful war,' Caro said, in the doom-laden tones she heard many adults use. 'It makes huge difficulties and there's a shortage of everything.'

Jago laughed. 'Isn't Uncle Toby sending you enough to eat?'

'Yes, but Mummy can't buy drawing paper for me any more.'

'Oh, dear. I might be able to find you some paper that's blank on one side. There'll be typing on the other, will that matter?'

'That'll be a great help,' Nancy said. 'Caro's been drawing on both sides of the paper for some time. In fact Mr Wickham next door gave her some wallpaper to draw on.'

'I've used all that. Grandpa, will yours be nice big sheets like Grandma used to get me?'

'I might possibly find you some big sheets if you don't

mind it having lines and columns printed on the other side.'

'You wouldn't mind, would you, Caro? It would be better than nothing, wouldn't it?'

'You're given paper at school, aren't you?' Jago asked.

'Yes, lined paper for doing our nature notes and paper with squares on for doing our sums, but it mustn't be used for anything else. I got into trouble for drawing a picture on the back of my nature notes.'

'How old are you now, Caro?'

'You know I'm eight,' she giggled. 'You gave me a book of puzzles for my birthday. I like doing them. I've brought it with me so I can do some today, but I've nearly done them all.'

'Good. Well, now you're growing up it might be better if you concentrated on your sums and your writing while you're at school and drew your pictures at home. You're very good at drawing and painting, but we want you to be good at other things too.'

'I'm good at sums too. I can add up and take away and multiply. I learned all that at my last school. It's easy. I'm good at reading as well, but they don't have nice books at this school. Mummy lets me choose books from the library to read at home.'

'I'm not altogether pleased with this school,' Nancy said. 'They don't seem to be pushing her at all.'

'Are you happy there, Caro?'

'It's all right.'

'Nancy, if you find you've made a wrong decision, you can always change your mind. It was the right thing to move Caro away from the air raids as soon as you could. But now you've got time to think again. It seems to me that either you stay where you are for the duration, devoting your time to looking after Caro instead of working, or we could find her a boarding school with high academic standards where she could also get a grounding in art. Then you could help the war effort by working full time.'

'I've worked that out for myself,' Nancy sighed, 'but it took me a long time. Which would you advise?'

'Nancy! Not so long ago, when Henrietta was pressing for boarding school, you were fighting against it.'

'I suppose it was Henrietta I was fighting. Sorry.'

'Yes, well, I understand that.' He glanced at her and gave a wry smile.

'I think I have made a mistake.' Nancy sighed again. 'Caro's bored at this school and winter's coming. It's a long way for her to cycle in bad weather.'

'If only you could learn to drive and get a car, that would solve a lot of your problems.'

'But I can't, can I? Civilians aren't entitled to a petrol ration unless they have important war work or a business to run.'

Nancy saw him glance at her again, as though he was going to say something but changed his mind. Instead, he said, 'Chopping and changing schools is never a good idea, but in wartime safety must come before education. Caro can catch up later. But this, Nancy, is a decision only you can make.'

'I know nothing about boarding schools.'

'If that's the way you want to go, we can find one to suit. You could go to see one or two before you decide. Would you like to go to boarding school, Caro?'

'I don't know.'

'Uncle Toby and I went to boarding school and so did your father. Once you're there, if you like it, you wouldn't have to move schools again. You'd make friends and be able to stay with them whatever your mummy did.'

'I lost my friend Billy when we came here.'

'We enjoyed boarding school . . .' he dropped his voice, 'on the whole.' The car turned into the drive of Carrington Place and pulled up by the front steps. 'You and your mummy need to talk it over.'

'We will,' Nancy said, thinking again what a lovely house it was; the sun was glinting on the large windows, and the front garden of lawn and flowers looked almost manicured.

They followed Jago to the drawing room, where Henrietta was already sipping a glass of sherry. He poured a glassful for Nancy, who gave her mother-in-law the dutiful peck on the cheek expected of her and sat down on the sofa. Caro kissed her grandmother and pushed her small body on to the seat of the armchair beside her.

'You'll have to excuse us for ten minutes,' Jago apologised. 'Toby and I are doing a little job we need to finish.'

'For heaven's sake,' Henrietta exploded. 'You're not going back to your study now? This is Sunday.'

'Blame the war,' Jago said, smiling at Nancy. 'It gives me a lot of work.'

'You don't have to do it!'

'If you want us to earn a reasonable profit, we do. We won't be very long.'

'What good is money these days?' Henrietta complained. 'There's nothing I can buy with it.'

After a few moments, sensing her grandmother's bad mood, Caro struggled to her feet and ran after Jago.

Jago crossed the hall to his study. 'I'm back,' he said. 'How far have you got?'

Toby vacated the chair in front of the desk, taking his tankard of beer with him, and settled himself on to a more comfortable tub chair.

'I've checked everything over,' he said. 'You knew the official figures were fine, and I can't see anything wrong with the black market ones. What a complication it makes, having to run two different sets of accounts.'

'But very necessary. One for the tax inspectors and the ministry advisers, and the other to keep track of how much fresh meat is being delivered to my factory.'

'And who in your sales team is selling it on, and for how much.'

Jago sat down beside his twin and reached for another bottle of beer. 'Paying cash to each farmer for the prime cuts as they deliver does cut out some paperwork, even though I have to bill the same farmers for the offal used in sausage-making which they deliver at the same time.'

The door clicked open and Caro came in. 'Hello, Uncle Toby.'

Jago smiled at her. 'Caro's thinking that she might like to go to boarding school after all, aren't you, love?'

'Yes, Grandpa. You said you had some paper I could draw on.'

'I meant at the factory.'

'But you've got a lot of paper here.'

Jago got to his feet, closed the account books he'd brought home from the factory and turned over the two pages of calculations they'd been working on, pushing them to the back of his large partners' desk and pulling some others to the front.

'All right. There are a few sheets here we've finished with. You can draw on the back of them.'

'Thank you, Grandpa.' Caro sat on the desk chair. 'I haven't brought my colouring pencils. Do you have any I can borrow?'

'No.'

'You had a red one last time I was here.'

Jago opened a drawer. 'I think you must have taken it away with you. I haven't seen it since. I've only ordinary lead pencils. I hope they'll do.'

'What are you going to draw, Caro?'

'Your pigs, Uncle Toby. I'd like to come to your farm to see them some time. Can I?'

'My farm can be very muddy and dirty, and frankly it isn't a healthy place for little girls to play. You've seen pigs before, you can draw them from memory.'

'I can, but I don't know if they're quite the right shape.'

Jago pulled a face at his twin. 'I think this means we've done all we can here for today, Toby.'

'What more is there? You've got the book-keeping under control.'

They finished their drinks in peace while Caro drew busily. Fifteen minutes later, Jago decided it was time to join the ladies in the drawing room. They found Nancy quiet and withdrawn and Henrietta more churned up than ever.

'Jago, I do wish you wouldn't hide yourselves away. I hardly see anything of you these days. You come in and eat an occasional meal and then you're off out again.'

'Well, I am busy, dear. There is a war on.'

'And don't I know it. All last night you left me alone in this glass house. We had two air raids and if a bomb had fallen anywhere close I could have been cut to ribbons. I might have been in need of your help.'

'You weren't alone,' Jago protested mildly. 'You had two other women with you.'

'Servants,' Henrietta snorted.

'You have the Anderson air-raid shelter in the garden to keep you safe.'

'It's horribly cold and damp, and I find it impossible to get to sleep in there. And there are spiders in it. I do wish you'd find me a safe house like the one Toby found for Nancy and Caroline. I do envy them that.'

'It's harder now to find anything within reasonable distance.'

'I don't care how far away it is. I couldn't see much less of you if I went to Timbuktu.'

Nancy was feeling uncomfortable and was glad when Caro snuggled up alongside her on the sofa. 'Are you going to show me your drawings?' she asked.

'They're of Uncle Toby's farm animals.' Caro held them up one by one for them all to admire. 'Here I've done three pigs in front of their sty. Do their sties look like this?'

'Exactly,' Toby assured her swiftly, though they bore little resemblance.

She held up one of two cockerels showing all their feathers, and one of Dash the border collie with his fur beautifully detailed.

'I like this one best,' Toby said. 'It's my dog Dash. Quite a good likeness, too.'

'That's because I've seen him,' Caro said pointedly.

'I think they're all very good,' Toby added hastily. 'I'm really impressed. The pencil shading you've done makes the animals stand out. You draw with great skill, Caro.'

The girl was smiling at his praise. 'You can have the one of Dash to put up on your wall.'

'Thank you,' he said gravely.

'Grandma, you can have the pigs.'

Henrietta frowned. 'I've nowhere suitable to pin it up, dear. Though it is a good picture.'

'Then I'll give them to Mummy. She likes to put them up in the kitchen, so she can look at them all day while I'm at school.'

When lunch was over, it was decided that Toby would take Nancy and Caro home. Jago went out to the steps with them to see them off. Once the car was out of sight he returned to Henrietta, who was somewhat mollified following an excellent lunch. She was looking through some estate agents' brochures.

'I saw these houses advertised in the papers and telephoned for more details. There are two I'd like to see. You did say you'd take me to look at houses this afternoon.'

Jago knew what Henrietta sought from him was companionship and attention, not things he found easy to give. Now, without a car and driver standing by, she found it harder to get out and about on her own. He'd decided a while ago that the best way to keep her happy was to put aside time to devote to her, and Sunday afternoons were convenient for them both.

Today, he was in a buoyant mood and ready to humour his wife; the calculations he'd made this morning showed he was doing more business than he'd ever envisaged. He and Toby would be set up for life once the war was over.

'Where are these houses?' he asked.

She passed over the two brochures. 'They sound very comfortable. One has six bedrooms and the other four. The agent says they're both in very safe districts.'

Jago read the details, and his good humour was swamped by a wave of irritation. 'We can't possibly see this one – it's six miles from Bakewell. That's the other side of the country, much too far for you to think of living there. Anyway, we'd need a full day to get there and back.'

'Oh, dear. I didn't think of that.' Privately, he and Toby had agreed that Henrietta's disastrous attempt to take Caro to France had rocked her confidence and made her more difficult. 'What about the other, then?'

'Where's that? Whitworth? I don't know where that is.'

'Here's your road atlas. I got it out.'

'That's a long way too, practically up in the Pennines.'

'It's the one with six bedrooms; a gentleman's residence, it says.'

'Six bedrooms? With empty rooms you might get evacuees billeted on you.'

Henrietta was indignant. 'I shall refuse point-blank.'

'These days you wouldn't get any choice, but we can go to look at it if you want a run out. I doubt if you'll like it.' He'd driven Henrietta to see several houses she thought sounded hopeful, but after one quick glance inside she'd dismissed them as not being up to the standard she wanted.

Jago found he was right: the house was too far off the beaten track for Henrietta, but it was quite a pleasant trip out. They stopped at a tea shop on the way home and had a high tea, which was all they needed after their substantial lunch.

With one thing and another it was nine o'clock the next morning when Jago went to his study to collect his official account books to take them back to his factory.

He picked them up and then looked for his black market accounts. For security reasons, he always worked out his figures on loose sheets of paper and burned them when the need for them had passed. He was ultra careful about such things. His father's business had once come under scrutiny from tax officials and he'd found it impossible to wriggle away from his accounts. Jago didn't keep a book full of incriminating figures in case his affairs ever came under the official spotlight.

It didn't take him long to realise that the papers he was looking for had gone. Full of trepidation, he sat down at his desk and tried to think through what he'd done with them. Caro had come into his study and asked for paper to draw on. He'd closed his accounts books and turned over the sheets he was now looking for. He'd moved them over to the far end of his desk, but they weren't there now.

He looked in the desk drawer where he usually kept them, but they weren't there either. He flicked through the pages of his factory account books, but still no luck.

Slowly, and with mounting dread, he went through every sheet of paper on his desk. He was not a tidy person, and there was a lot of it. He made one pile he needed to file away, and another pile of assorted figures they'd entered on the missing sheets and would need again if he failed to find them.

The rest he destroyed one by one: little reminders he'd scribbled to himself; figures he jotted down during telephone calls and no longer needed. Preliminary workings, some with so many figures crossed out and altered they were hardly readable. Even a half-finished drawing of a horse abandoned by Caro. His black market records did not come to light.

He leaned back in the chair and told himself to stay calm. Had Caro drawn those damned pigs on the back of his important figures?

He rang Toby. The housekeeper answered and it took her a long time to get Toby to the phone. All the while Jago grew more anxious. He was hardly coherent by the time he spoke to Toby and it took him some time to make his twin understand what he was worried about.

'I think Caro must have drawn on the back of our figures. I don't suppose you turned over that drawing of a dog she gave you?'

'Well – I think there were figures on the back, now you mention it.'

'Yes, but were they our final figures?'

'I don't know. I didn't really look at them.'

'Well, can you?'

'I'm not sure what I did with it.'

'This is important, Toby. At the very least, if they're lost I'll have to do them again. Before I can collect any money, I have to know who owes it to us and how much.'

'I'll have a look for that drawing. It might be in my car. I'll ring you back.'

'As soon as you can.'

Jago sat down to wait, drumming his fingers on the arms of his chair. It took Toby a long time to let him know that the figures behind the dog drawing were just rough calculations.

'Damn,' he said. 'I wish I knew where our final figures had got to.'

'Jago, don't panic. Nobody would recognise what they refer to. We only used the initials of the lads who sold the black market meat and the buyers who hadn't paid cash for it. There were no full names that strangers could identify.'

'I'm not so sure. We wrote down words like pork loin and leg and sirloin steak with their weights and the amount of cash owed to us. If they fell into the wrong hands . . .'

'It might be possible for someone to deduce what the calculations mean, but it's hardly likely, is it?'

Jago ran his fingers through his thick white hair, a habit he had when he was worried. 'I'll have to work the figures out again. As if I haven't enough to do.'

'If you're sure they've really gone from your study.'

'I'm certain, Toby. They aren't here.'

'What about your maids? Could they have taken them? Would they know what they were?'

'I don't think so. What use would they be to them? Anyway, they both have a half day on Sundays. They can't clear up fast enough after lunch to get out.'

'They can get in again. They live in your staff annexe.'

'Gertie never moves anything when she dusts.'

'Then Caro must have thought it was paper to draw on and taken them home. Do you want to call on Nancy? She'll give them back to you if they're there.'

'She knows nothing of this side of our business. Better if we keep it that way. You take her milk regularly, don't you? She wouldn't see it as out of the ordinary if you went.'

'I don't go that often. Usually somebody else takes the milk.'

'But you go more often than I do. You could have a

look round her kitchen walls. Caro said she pins her drawings up there.'

'All right.'

'Try to be discreet.'

Jago heard his twin sigh. 'What if I have to ask outright? Shall I? Or do I come away empty-handed and no wiser?'

'I'll have to leave that to you. Play it by ear.'

CHAPTER TWENTY-TWO

Toby was reluctant to go down to Nancy's cottage. He couldn't really spare the time; running a big farm like his took a lot of organisation. His main crop potatoes were not all lifted and he ought to start somebody ploughing to get the ground ready to sow winter wheat.

But he'd have to go; he could tell Jago was worried stiff. Why on earth had he allowed Caro to sit at his desk? He could quite easily have given her a few bits of paper and sent her back to her mother.

Toby started putting together some fruit and vegetables for Nancy. If he had a large box of stuff for her, it would seem normal to carry it into her kitchen himself instead of handing it to her at the door. That would give him an opportunity to look round for Caro's drawings.

He put the box in his car. He was ready to go, but it was too soon. He needed to give Nancy time to cycle back from Formby after seeing the child into school, and possibly she'd do a bit of shopping before coming home. He went out to find Colin to give him a few instructions to hand on to the others.

He'd barely waited long enough. Nancy was just getting off her bike in front of the cottage when it came into view.

'Hello, Toby,' she sang out. Her hair had blown into a tangle and her cheeks were pink. 'I'll be with you in a minute.'

She was lifting her bike through to the back garden, leaving the doors open for him. He was in with the box by the time she was closing the back door.

'You're very generous. I can't thank you enough for all the food you bring us. Those pears look gorgeous.'

'You'll have to keep them for a week or two; they aren't ready to eat yet. There's potatoes and other stuff you might find useful underneath.' Toby was casting round for a natural way to turn the conversation to Caro's drawings.

'Are you busy on the farm, Toby?'

'Yes. There's always plenty to do.'

'I've been thinking of getting a job. I'd like to feel I'm doing something towards the war effort. Could I come and work for you? I could cycle up.'

Toby knew immediately he should not have told her the farm was busy. He couldn't afford to have Nancy there every day. He didn't want her to see the set-up and know how much time Jago spent there. In particular, he didn't want her to know about Kevin and Colin.

'Women are being urged to take work outside the home,' she said, smiling at him. 'Besides, I'd like to.'

That was worse. He was casting round desperately for some way to put her off without arousing her suspicions.

'It's not the sort of work you could do, Nancy,' he managed at last. 'We're lifting carrots and cutting cabbages; that's back-breaking and heavy on the hands. When the weather's bad you'd get cold and wet. You'd hate it.'

'I can do simple book-keeping. Don't you have a lot of paperwork to do? I heard a farmer on the wireless this morning complaining about the extra form filling the war was giving him.'

Toby knew he'd complained of the same thing. He must watch that in future.

'I could help with your paperwork. I used to do Dad's accounts at the pub.'

He couldn't look at her eager honest face. 'I do as little of that as I possibly can,' he said, and tried to laugh it off. He knew he failed. 'It's kind of you to offer, Nancy, but I'm sure you have enough to do here, looking after Caro.' That sounded limp. She looked quite downcast. He wished he hadn't had to put her off.

He turned hastily to the sheets of paper pinned on the wall. 'What a lot of drawings Caro does.'

Hadn't they all said that to her a thousand times already? He must do better. 'Caro's drawing is improving, isn't it? I thought those pigs she did yesterday were very good indeed.' That was better. He'd got round to the right subject.

'Yes,' she agreed, striking a match and setting light to the fire she'd laid in the grate.

Toby could see no sign of pigs or cockerels in the drawings. He went back to the beginning and went through them again more slowly.

'I might do some baking today,' Nancy said. 'Those apples you've brought make me think of apple pie. Caro loves that.'

Toby told himself he must not be deflected from his purpose. 'It would be nice to compare Caro's early drawings with her most recent ones, wouldn't it? Then we could see how much she was improving. But I don't see those she did yesterday. D'you know what she did with them?'

'Erm . . .' Nancy sat back on her haunches. 'Sometimes she puts them up in her bedroom.' After a pause, she added, 'Do you want to go up and look?'

Toby knew he was pushing too hard but he said yes, and followed her. The stairs were steep and led straight into Caro's bedroom. The window was open and the curtains were fluttering slightly in the breeze. The bed had been made, but there were books, toys and drawing paper everywhere.

Toby began checking the drawings pinned on the wall. 'Here's one of pigs.' A note of excitement had crept into his voice. He saw Nancy look up in surprise. Black mark; he must be more careful. She came closer to look.

'That's quite an old one. Caro did that months ago.'

For heaven's sake, what was he thinking about? The paper he was looking for was what Jago used in his office. Without going any closer Toby could see all this was standard drawing paper, a different quality altogether.

'This drawing of monkeys is more recent and it's very much better,' Nancy said. 'I think it's really good, don't you? All this feathery shading.'

'Yes,' he said, feeling a shaft of disappointment that yesterday's drawings weren't here. But he must not let her see that.

Nancy began collecting all the drawings together. 'She's done a few landscapes. Here's one of the view from this window. They're the best she's done.'

He had to show more interest in them now, or she'd think he was mad. He sat on the bed and took the sheets of paper from her. If Jago's figures weren't here, where had they gone? It was worrying. He hoped they hadn't fallen into the wrong hands.

Nancy said, 'Caro and I had a long talk last night. I think she's ready to say she'd like to try boarding school. I don't think I have much choice, because this school isn't doing her much good. Jago said he'd help me get some information on boarding schools so I could choose the right one for her.'

'Henrietta has all that information at her fingertips. I

think she sent for a book listing girls' boarding schools last year. She was very keen Caro should go then.'

Nancy said quickly, 'It was Jago I talked to about that. I'll ring him and tell him we'd like his help.'

After collecting Caro from school that afternoon, Nancy made up the fire and was lowering the kettle on to it when she heard a tapping on the front window. She looked up to see Henrietta beaming at her and lifting an attaché case to show her. Nancy stifled a groan. She guessed Henrietta meant to help them choose a school.

It was Caro who let her in. She swept the child into her arms for hugs and kisses. She was in a very different mood today.

'Nancy, I'm so glad you've changed your mind about boarding school. Much the best thing, as I've said all along.'

She opened her case on the table and tipped its contents out. Bringing up a chair, she pulled Caro down beside her. 'Now, my love, I'm going to tell you all about boarding schools.'

Like the twins, Nancy had thought Henrietta's disastrous attempt to take Caro to France had reduced her self-confidence, but it was as though she was feeling a resurgence of power because they'd changed their minds about the local school. However, Nancy was determined not to let her get the better of her again.

'It's very important that you and Mummy choose the

right school, my pet. I'll help you, because it was my idea that you should be a boarder. A boarding school is a different world, a much more interesting world, with plenty of nice girls around to make friends with. And there'd be games for you to play, tennis and lacrosse. You'd like that, wouldn't you?'

'Yes,' Caro said. 'Mummy started to teach me tennis at Hawarden and I'd like to have lots of girls to play with.'

'You shall, my pet. Nancy, look through the schools in this book. All the information is set out for you; how many pupils in the school, the subjects they teach and the examinations the girls are entered for.'

'Won't there be any boys there?'

'No, not the school you'll go to, darling. Boys have their own schools.' Henrietta was shuffling through the pages. 'Nancy, this is St Monica's, this is the one I'd choose. I've considered them all carefully and I think it would best meet Caroline's needs.'

Nancy went to sit at the table with them. 'I've got very firm ideas about what I want this school to provide.' She started to list what she thought of as essentials. 'It mustn't be too far away. It must be in a safe area, have high academic standards and teach art. I want Caro to have experience . . .'

'St Monica's has all that,' Henrietta said smoothly. 'It's in open country a few miles north of Chester, so well away from industrial cities. Look, Caroline, this is a picture of the school. The main building is a lovely stately mansion in twenty-six acres of gardens and playing fields. They've built extra classrooms in the grounds. You'd like to go there, wouldn't you?'

The picture was flashed in front of Nancy. Henrietta smiled at her. 'I could ask Jago to arrange a car for tomorrow morning and we could go and look it over. Would you like that?'

That put Nancy on pins. 'Do we need to be in such a hurry?'

'Yes, I think we do. The new term will start in January, which doesn't give us all that much time to get ready. You don't want her to spend the hardest winter months cycling to the place she's at now? Really and truly, it would have been easier for her to start in September, at the beginning of the school year.'

Nancy was brimming with resentment. She didn't trust her mother-in-law's choice. 'What are the fees for St Monica's?' She'd be bound to want the most expensive one.

'You don't need to worry about the fees, Nancy. I've already told you that the trust fund will cover them. As well as all Caro's other expenses, such as uniform, books and games equipment.'

Nancy took a deep breath. 'Caro and I would like to look through all this information you've so kindly brought,' she said. 'Quietly and on our own, so that we can make our own choice.'

She'd had no option but the Formby school for Caro

when they first moved here, but she was nervous of making the wrong choice now. At the same time, she knew that if she gave her mother-in-law half a chance Henrietta would bulldoze them into accepting what she wanted.

It certainly sounded as though she'd taken offence now. 'In that case, I'll leave everything with you. But you'll find I'm right.'

That night, Nancy made an exhaustive study of the literature Henrietta had brought, and reluctantly admitted that St Monica's did seem to be the school most likely to suit Caro. The next day she spoke to Jago on the phone and found he understood her problem with Henrietta.

'Look,' he said, 'pick out two or three of the schools you think most suitable. Ring them up to see if they'll take another pupil after Christmas, and then make arrangements to see them as soon as possible.'

'I'd like to go on a Saturday so I can take Caro with me. I want her to see them and have some choice as to where she goes.'

'Let me know what time you want it and I'll send you a car and a driver,' he said.

Nancy found it an exciting expedition. They visited St Monica's first and toured the classrooms, dormitories, library and sports facilities. Then Caro was left in the splendid art room with the art mistress and a few of the pupils, who showed her some of their recent work. The headmistress took Nancy to her study to tell her more about the school. It was clearly a friendly place.

Afterwards, they went to see Hillsdene. Nancy tried hard to prefer it because it was not Henrietta's choice, but she had to agree with Caro that St Monica's seemed to have exactly what they wanted. She asked the driver to return there and was able to arrange with the headmistress that Caro enter the school at the start of the spring term, which began on 9 January. Nancy said she'd bring her on the afternoon before.

Caro was excited but the satisfaction Nancy felt at getting everything sorted soon faded on the journey home. She knew her life would seem empty without her daughter.

At Sunday lunch the next day, Jago was amazed to hear that Nancy had already finalised arrangements for Caro to start at St Monica's. 'You certainly don't let the grass grow under your feet,' he told her.

'It's a nice school.' Caro smiled round them all.

As it was the one Henrietta had chosen, she didn't seem too put out that they'd gone to see it without her.

'I knew it would suit Caroline,' she said. 'You should have gone there last year instead of wasting time in those council schools. You'll be very happy there, my pet.'

Jago got to his feet to refill their sherry glasses. He was afraid Henrietta was pushing Nancy aside again.

'I'm going to have such a lot of new clothes, Grandma, and I'll need a lacrosse stick.'

'Did you get the school list, Nancy?'

'Yes, and it seems impossibly long. I don't know if I'll be able to find everything.'

'Which shop stocks the uniform? I'll come with you. I'm good at finding what I want in the shops.'

Jago held his breath, hoping Nancy would agree. The last thing he needed was more friction between the women of the family.

Nancy did, and even consented to keep Caro off school on Monday, so they could do it straight away and on a slack morning in the shops. Relieved, he allowed Henrietta to cajole him and Toby into giving up their clothing coupons to help fit Caro out. He was glad Nancy had been able to forgive Henrietta for snatching Caro and taking her away.

Gertie had put the soup tureen on the table and they were going in to lunch when Henrietta said, 'Nancy will be able to work for you, Jago, once Caroline's away at school. You're always complaining you're short of staff.'

Jago didn't want Nancy around his factory. The sausage business was all above board, but he'd set up an efficient team from amongst his staff to sell fresh meat into the black market, and his instinct was to keep her well away from the place.

'We'll have to see,' was the best he could manage on the spur of the moment.

'I do want to help the war effort,' Nancy said. She looked eager and innocent. 'I can do basic book-keeping and I used to do shorthand typing, but I must be a bit rusty at that by now. I don't suppose I could borrow a typewriter from your office so I could work up my speeds?'

'Yes, of course.' Jago felt he could agree to that. 'I'll send one with the driver when he comes to take you and Caro shopping tomorrow.'

'Thank you. You're very good to me.' Nancy looked him in the eye as she went on. 'There are plenty of jobs in Liverpool that I could do.' Jago could see she'd taken on board that he was not keen to have her services. 'But I can't work during the school holidays as I need to be with Caro when she's at home. It might not be so easy to find an employer who'd be willing to let me take time off like that.' She was smiling at him, willing him to offer her work, and he didn't know how to refuse.

Henrietta dropped him in it. 'Jago could do that, of course, but you needn't worry about the holidays. I could look after Caroline whenever she's home from school, couldn't I, pet?' She rumpled the child's blonde curls. 'You wouldn't need to give Nancy time off work, Jago.'

He cast around for another reason not to take Nancy on. He knew he was scraping the bottom of the barrel here. 'You're part of the Seymour family,' he told her, 'and you'd not have a senior position in my office. My other employees might have trouble accepting you. It wouldn't be fair to you.'

'I don't think that would matter.' Nancy was still smiling at him. 'I get on with most people.'

'For heaven's sake,' Henrietta burst out. 'You don't have to tell your workers everything. She can use her maiden name, can't she? Probably be better if she did.'

Jago shuddered. Keeping the womenfolk happy and everybody on good terms was not easy.

For Nancy, the war seemed to be getting closer. It was not just Merseyside that was suffering more air raids; other ports and industrial areas were too. In November, Coventry took a hammering. She was anxious to get Caro into school so she'd be able to start work.

Gavin wrote to say he'd been to Buckingham Palace to receive his medal and everybody had made a big fuss of him.

I wish you could have come with me, you would have enjoyed the party. The whole squadron is shattered, we're all overdue for leave, and there's a rumour going round that we'll all get it soon. If so, I'd like to come up and see you. Could you find me somewhere to stay near you?

Nancy was thrilled. She was thinking about him a lot. She cared about him, but what she felt for Gavin was different from what she'd felt for Charlie, so she was not sure that she loved him. She wrote back to say she'd find him lodgings and was looking forward to seeing him. She wondered if she dare offer him Caro's bed if she'd gone by then. She was afraid Henrietta and Jago would not approve of their relationship; he was signing his letters *With love from Gavin* and making it clear that once the war was over he hoped they'd not be parted again.

The second Christmas of the war came round. Most people had been hoarding food for months so they could have something special over the holiday. Nancy felt quite guilty that she had so much. Toby brought Caro a Christmas tree and Nancy helped her find decorations for both that and the living room. It was mostly holly and mistletoe from the lanes and a few late flowers from the garden. She'd invited her father to have his Christmas dinner with them, but at the beginning of that week he wasn't feeling well and was afraid he'd not be able to drive.

Nancy rang him every day to find out how he was. On Christmas Eve he asked if he might invite John Tennant to come with him. As he'd been a bus driver before he'd retired, he'd be able to drive his car.

Nancy knew John well. He was a widower living alone and a regular customer at the Lord Nelson. He and Dad spent many hours discussing the war and putting the world to rights. She was happy to invite him to come too, and glad that Dad would have somebody to see him safely home.

When they arrived, she had a log fire roaring up the chimney and the cottage looking cosy and festive. The capon Toby had given her was roasting in the oven, filling the whole place with delicous scents. But her father looked very frail. It saddened her to see his health deteriorating like this.

He said he very much enjoyed the traditional Christmas dinner with all the trimmings that Nancy had cooked. He brought a bottle of wine and some hazelnuts he'd gathered in the lane that autumn, which were now ready to eat. John Tennant brought a gift of chocolate biscuits. He was in a jolly mood and made it a happy occasion.

The visitors left early because her father feared another air raid. Soon after they'd gone, Toby came to take them to Carrington Place to have a special Christmas night supper. Henrietta had managed to find extravagant presents for them all, especially for Caro.

CHAPTER TWENTY-THREE

WHEN THEY WENT to Lexington Avenue for their last Sunday lunch before Caro went away to school, Nancy found Jago still working in his study.

She slid into a chair near his desk and said, 'I really want a job. I have to have something to do. I want to help the war effort and I feel everybody else is working their guts out while I'm sitting back doing nothing.' She knew there was some reason he didn't want her in his factory, though he wouldn't tell her what it was. 'Are you afraid your workforce will see me as a management spy or something?'

He straightened up. She could see that she had surprised him.

'I could use my maiden name if you prefer it to be a straight business arrangement, and I'd be very happy to work for nothing.'

Jago seemed somewhat at a loss. 'You put me to shame, Nancy.'

'After all,' she went on, 'you've already arranged that I

have a very generous income. It wouldn't be fair to expect you to pay me a salary on top.'

'Of course it would. If you work, you must be rewarded for what you do.' After another moment's hesitation, he smiled. 'All right, if you want a job that badly I'll give you one. The accounts department is short-staffed. You'll find plenty to do, and I'll do my best to give you time off in Caro's holidays.'

Nancy sighed with satisfaction. She'd got what she wanted. 'Thank you.'

'I'll put you on the payroll as Miss Milton. Same terms and conditions as the rest of the workers.' His smile broadened. 'I'll expect you to report any subversive activity amongst the staff to me.'

Nancy was very pleased. 'I know you're just teasing me. The cottage will seem very quiet once Caro's at school. I'd be lonely there on my own with nothing to fill my day.'

Taking Caro to St Monica's and returning without her tore Nancy in two. She told herself it was for Caro's benefit and under the circumstances the best thing for them both. She missed her terribly during the first day or two and was very glad to start work in Jago's office, even though she found the journey tedious. She had to cycle to Formby to catch the train into Liverpool. According to the timetable the trains ran at half-hourly intervals, but December had been a month of heavy air raids. Several trains had been gutted in their sidings and the track was damaged in many places. Trains ran when and where they could. Nancy's journey was fragmented and the route could change from day to day. It took a long time.

She'd always been curious about Jago's sausage factory. On the day she started, he took her round it, and she was very impressed. She'd known it was recently built but was still surprised by all the stainless steel and white tiles. It was a busy and noisy place, with the latest machines pumping sausage filling into skins then twisting them into identical lengths. The sausages were automatically moved on to be weighed and wrapped in greaseproof paper and finally labelled. It all looked very efficient and hygienic.

The office was modern too and equipped with the latest typewriters and comptometers. It was light and airy, with a good view of the Mersey. Nancy's heart turned over as she surveyed the extensive damage that had been done to the docks.

He allotted her a desk in the accounts department and introduced her as Miss Milton. The girl occupying the desk next to hers was young and pretty.

Jago said, 'Help is here at last, Miss Jones. You can hand over the account books to Miss Milton now and explain our system to her. Jill Jones is one of our most versatile workers, Miss Milton. She stands in for everybody. She's virtually been doing two jobs for the last few months.'

Miss Jones giggled, and when Jago had gone she said,

'He's a great boss, easy to work for. Very understanding.'

Within hours, Jill Jones had noticed Nancy's wedding ring and asked if Jago had got it wrong and she was really Mrs Milton.

'No,' Nancy said. 'Milton is my maiden name, and I've decided to use it again. I'm a widow now.'

Jill wasn't satisfied until she'd heard all about Charlie's death. Like everybody else, she assumed it had happened in the Battle of Britain and that Charlie had been a hero. 'I don't even have that comfort,' Nancy had had to say.

She found the people in the office friendly and gradually got to know them and to understand the accounting system. Jago was popular with them all; they liked his gentle manner and encouraging smile.

The sales team drifted in and out of the office leaving figures in her in tray for her to enter in the books. Miss Jones introduced her to them. Zac McEllery was a good-looking man of about thirty who stayed talking to Jill Jones for a long time, but he chatted up all the girls, and even tried to flirt with Nancy. She decided she didn't care for him. At the same time, Nancy learned a good deal about sausages.

'They aren't what they were,' Zac McEllery said. 'But I don't say that to the customers. If they're not on ration the customers can't expect to find much meat in them, can they? The tenderloin or fillet was traditionally used to make them, but not any more.'

'They don't even look the same,' Jill said. 'The wrapping used to be bound with a red and gold band, printed with a picture of them browning in the pan. Now it's a plain white strip with *Seymour's Sausages* printed in black.'

Nancy had to ask Jago what the wartime sausage was made from.

'It's a deep secret.' She could see he was teasing her. 'One you mustn't share with my customers. We still use the casings from the pig, nothing has changed there, but we now put a lot more grain and internal fat from the carcass into the filling.'

'You make it sound as though they'll taste awful, but they don't. I quite like them.'

'Because we also use trimmings of meat and the offal: heart, spleen, lungs and liver.'

'What sort of grain?' Nancy asked, trying hard not to pull a face.

'It depends what's available; bread sometimes but I've used barley meal, wheatmeal, ground oats, flaked maize and brewer's grains left over from making beer. Anything I can get like that.'

'But doesn't that mean they won't always taste the same?'

'Yes, that's a problem. Sometimes they taste better than others, but while everything is in short supply I have to use what I can get. The government allows me to have supplies of whale meal . . .'

'What's that?'

'It's prepared from the residue of the whale after the blubber has been removed. It still has a high oil content, and I don't use it unless there's nothing else. It can give my sausages a fishy taint.'

The Luftwaffe was kind to them throughout the month of January, coming over much less often. In February, they didn't come at all. The population caught up with their sleep and many were heard to say that they thought the worst of the raids were over.

Now Caro was away at school, Nancy felt she spent a lot of time writing letters, not only to Gavin but to her daughter too. Today she'd had another long letter from Gavin, telling her how much he loved her and wanted to be with her. Nancy kept reading it through. It had made her day.

Without Caro, she found her cottage too quiet, and as the sausage factory was just across the river from the Lord Nelson and the train lines ran underground and so had not been damaged, when she finished work for the day she took to going over to see her father. Miles said he'd recovered from the bad bout he'd had at Christmas, but Nancy felt he hadn't regained his strength.

She could spend time in the bar with him now and even help a little if they were busy. Chatting with Alma and the other barmaids was like seeing old friends again. She enjoyed it, but her father always insisted on her taking the train back to Formby in case the enemy planes came over in the night. It seemed a long ride home on her bike in the blackout.

Everybody welcomed the lighter evenings and milder weather in March, but it brought renewed attention from the Luftwaffe. One night Liverpool would get it and the next it would be Birkenhead's turn, or Wallasey or Bootle.

'Go straight home,' Nancy was told by her father. 'You're safer there.' These days the planes were coming over in daylight too. In the mornings, it shocked Nancy to look out of the windows of her office and see fires still burning. There were growing areas of total destruction. The death toll was rising and the hospitals were full of people who had been injured in the raids.

She usually tried to ring her father as soon as he reached the office to find out what sort of a night he'd had, but many times the phone lines were down and she had to tell herself that it didn't mean that anything had happened to the Lord Nelson.

Her colleagues didn't always come to work, making those who did wonder if they'd been bombed out. She knew Jago was exhausted, deprived of sleep by the noise and the fear.

Easter came and Caro had three weeks' holiday. Nancy loved having her back at home with her. 'Don't bring her into town,' the family told her. 'It isn't safe.'

Nancy put on a Sunday lunch for her in-laws at the

cottage, for which Toby supplied a large joint of pork. It took her over five hours to roast it in the Victorian oven, but it turned out well with crisp crackling. Five of them in such a tiny house was a bit of a squash, but Henrietta envied her.

'I do wish I could have found a safe bolt-hole,' she said, 'but they've all been snapped up now.'

Nancy was discovering at first hand how busy the sausage factory was and how short-handed they were. In order to keep the work under control during the school holidays, on several days each week Jago sent a car to take Henrietta to the cottage and then run Nancy into work. It would go back to take Henrietta and Caro on little jaunts until it was time for Nancy to be fetched home. Nancy considered it a great luxury to be driven in and out of work.

Once Caro had returned to school, Nancy started cycling direct to the factory. It was a long way but at least she didn't need to rely on public transport. She saw appalling damage, and on the way home there were long trails of people leaving the city for the night.

In May the blitz intensified. Nancy could hear the distant crump crump and see the flashes of fire in the skies over Merseyside. Often there was a huge pall of smoke when daylight came.

Toby was enjoying his regular visits to the busy livestock market at Beeston, where he was selling off most of his milking herd. He and Colin had brought six cows to sell today, Herefords of three and four years of age. They'd walked round the market comparing the quality of their cows with the others offered for sale.

Toby was pleased. 'There's nothing better than ours.'

'Nothing as good.' Colin was as pleased as he was.

The auctioneer praised the stock from Hattongrove. Toby was gratified and raised his cap in response.

His cows were being driven into the ring one at a time to be sold and were making good prices. Toby believed that now fresh milk was rationed and had by law to be sold at a controlled price, he could make more profit by using the land for other enterprises.

A man sidled up beside him. 'Good morning, Mr Seymour. I see you're selling?'

'Good morning.' Toby was concentrating on the bidding. 'This next cow has recorded outstanding milk yields.'

That fact was immediately echoed by the auctioneer. The bidding was going up and up. It made an excellent price.

'I'm delighted with that.' Toby turned with pleasure from Colin to the man beside him. 'A good price for a good cow.'

This big man looked vaguely familiar but Toby couldn't place him. He was tall as well as fat, but he wasn't wearing the clothes of a farmer. A dealer perhaps?

'Do I know you?' he asked.

'Robert Bellamy.' The man was smiling at him.

Toby gasped. He felt his heart jerk into overdrive and start thumping like an engine. He certainly recognised the name.

So had Colin, and he wanted nothing to do with the man. 'Just seen a friend over there,' he said to Toby. 'I'll be back in a minute.'

Bellamy stood back to let him go, saying, 'I understand I must thank your brother for taking me to hospital when I had that accident on your farm.'

Toby shivered. Was he imagining an emphasis on the words 'that accident', as though the fellow was questioning it? Astute brown eyes were watching him closely, making him more nervous.

'Sorry I was a trouble to you.'

'It was no bother,' Toby murmured. 'But there wasn't much else we could do, under the circumstances.' Was he was being too defensive? After all, this fellow had been trespassing. He went on the attack, saying, 'How did you come to be near my milking parlour?'

'I was heading for your house, but I was early for our appointment, so I thought I'd do two things. I hear you employ a young man by the name of Leslie Gibson. I thought I'd look him up.'

Toby could feel himself quaking. Hell! Bellamy had prepared for this meeting and he was definitely on the offensive.

He told himself to keep calm, betray nothing. 'Leslie

Gibson?' He'd known that lad was trouble from the moment Jago took up with him, and they hadn't got on very well. 'He used to work for me, but no longer. Left some time ago to join the forces. Did you know him?'

'My son did; he wanted to get in touch. I don't suppose you know where he is now?'

Toby shook his head. 'No, 'fraid not.'

'Was it the army he joined? You wouldn't know which regiment?'

The damn fellow was still smiling and pushing hard. Did he know it was Leslie who'd knocked him out?

'No,' Toby said carefully, 'it might have been the Navy, now I think about it. You said there were two reasons?' He thought he'd caught the man off guard. 'Why you went to my milking parlour?'

'Oh! To have a quick look round first to get an understanding of your business. Then I could be of more use to you.'

Toby's eyebrows lifted. Bellamy looked like a civil servant used to pushing paper round a desk. He'd be no use to him at all and probably not to any farmer.

'That's right, I remember now. You work for the Ministry of Agriculture, don't you?'

Bellamy's enquiring eyes were studying him again. 'That day I came to your farm, was it you who found me?'

That pulled Toby up short. He was being questioned minutely. He would have liked to tell the man to get lost but he knew it would be better to quieten his suspicions if he could. What exactly had Jago told them at the hospital? He couldn't remember, but he must make it sound logical.

'I was waiting for you up at the house. My brother found you and sent one of my cowmen to fetch me.'

'I don't understand exactly how I came to fall and strike my head.'

Toby felt scared, but knew he mustn't show it. This was the ninth degree. 'Neither do we really,' he said. 'But it was raining and turning the farmyard to mud, making it slippy. You were wearing shoes more suited to town pavements.'

He looked pointedly at Bellamy's feet now. Farmers wore strong boots or wellingtons here in the market, but this man was still wearing city shoes. 'I trust you've fully recovered?'

'Yes, thank you. Sorry I didn't get to discuss your farming policy with you. I'd like to pay you another visit to do that. Shall I get the office to ring up and make another appointment?'

Having him poking around again was the last thing Toby wanted. 'I've already decided on the best route forward for me.'

'Oh. I see you're selling quite a few of your milking cows. You're reducing your herd?'

'I am,' he said firmly. He didn't like these damn bureaucrats poking their noses into other people's business.

'Could I ask your reasons?'

Toby swallowed hard. He had to flannel this fellow. 'It's probably what you'd have recommended, had you come to talk it over with me. Here in Cheshire it's cattle country, but on the Lancashire coast where I farm the land is better suited to market gardening.'

'Well, that's true.'

'I'm glad you agree with me.' Toby hoped that would appease the man's ego. 'I've decided I'll get more from my land if I concentrate on that and my pigs.'

'Pigs? I didn't know you kept pigs.'

'You should. I declare them on all those forms I have to fill in.'

'Sorry. I'd have had all this at my fingertips if I'd known I was going to talk to you. You'll be needing animal feed to fatten them, then. Have you applied for a permit?'

'No. I grow my own fodder, but I've applied for extra fertiliser. The pigs eat the small potatoes the greengrocers don't care for, and there's a lot of waste leaves cut off cabbages and the like. I like to run my business economically.'

At last, Toby watched Bellamy walk away. It seemed Colin had too, for he came back straight away. 'What did he want?'

'He was asking about Leslie. We were right to get him out of the way as soon as possible. It makes me wonder if he realises he got a bash on the head with a spade.'

'He can't,' Colin said. 'He was out cold.'

'How does he know Leslie's name? Has he been spying on us?'

'If he has,' Colin grinned at him, 'he got his just deserts.'

'Possibly,' Toby said. 'Let's go. That's taken all the pleasure out of our day out for me. You can drop me at Jago's factory. He'll provide me with transport home.'

It always eased his worries if he shared them with his twin. He found Jago working in his office, looking concerned. 'Toby! For the last few hours, I've had a terrible feeling that all was not well with you.'

'It wasn't.' They seemed to share a sixth sense and know if the other was in difficulties. 'It still isn't.' Toby slid on to a chair. 'Remember that fellow Robert Bellamy you took to hospital? He buttonholed me in the market today.'

'Is he all right?'

'As right as rain. But he was trying to find out more about what happened to him that day.'

'Glory be.'

He could see that worried Jago too. 'And then he asked about your friend Leslie Gibson by name. How could he know about him?'

'D'you think he knows Leslie bashed him?'

'Colin says no, he was unconscious.'

'Then he must have been spying on you. That day I prayed hard that Leslie hadn't killed him, but now I wish

I hadn't bothered. It might have been the better option.'

'No,' Jago said. 'It wouldn't. Anything's better than manslaughter in your farmyard.'

'This is scary, isn't it? I'm afraid he's trying to dig up more trouble for us. What can he possibly remember?'

CHAPTER TWENTY-FOUR

Henrietta felt at the end of her tether. The war was wearing her out. She no longer had the energy to look after Caroline. She'd had to do it during the recent school holidays to help Jago, but he was nine years younger than she was and didn't appreciate that their granddaughter demanded almost constant attention. In two years Henrietta would be seventy. She needed a quieter life at her age.

Recently, Jago had not been at all helpful. Toby had found Nancy a country cottage but her husband had done nothing for her. He went his own way and thought more of his twin brother and his factory than he did of her.

She'd agreed as a favour some years ago that he might spend one or two nights a week with Toby, but now he was stretching it to five or more. He made the excuse that he was fire watching, but he could surely have paid some-body else to do that for him. Henrietta did not like being left alone at night, not when bombs were dropping all round her.

'You'll be as safe as we can make you in the Anderson shelter,' was all Jago had to say about it. She hated the shelter. He'd arranged to have four bunks inside but Henrietta had found hers so hard it had hurt her back. She'd managed to find herself a camp bed that would take a decent mattress and move that in, but it was wider and left little space for anything else.

When the servants brought out her hot water bottles, if Jago was with her he'd insist they come inside and lie down. They slept in their siren suits, but Henrietta found it easier to get to sleep if she undressed and wore her nightdress, and then of course she couldn't have the servants too close. Anyway, Mrs Trott's feet smelled and Gertie snored. She always sent them back to the house.

Late in the evening of 1 May, the air-raid siren wailed while she was still downstairs listening to the wireless and she had to run to the shelter in her day clothes. Jago was at Hattongrove and she found it frightening and impossible to settle down to sleep. It was one in the morning when the all clear sounded, and she went indoors to make herself more comfortable for the rest of the night, which she hoped she'd be able to spend in her bedroom.

She knew that Mrs Trott and Gertie had made up beds for themselves under the stairs and very comfortable they looked. She woke them up by coming indoors and Gertie got up to make them all some tea.

'I'll have a tray up in my room,' she told her. 'And perhaps a biscuit with it.'

Henrietta had got into bed and was sipping her tea when the siren sounded again and she had to rush back to the Anderson shelter. The night sky was lit up by roving searchlights.

Mrs Trott brought her a flask of tea, 'in case you didn't get round to drinking the pot Gertie took up to you.'

'Thank you, that's thoughtful of you,' she told her though she couldn't drink Thermos tea, it gave her indigestion.

Henrietta found sleep impossible. She could hear the planes throbbing overhead and there was no more terrifying sound on earth. She quaked, pulling her bedclothes over her head.

This time, the bombs seemed to be falling very close and the night was full of heavy gunfire, clanging fire engines and screeching ambulances. The noise gave her a thumping headache.

Then, without warning, there was an almighty crash that shook the foundations of the shelter. Henrietta felt as though she was tossed three inches into the air. The deafening noise of shattering glass and tumbling masonry hurt her eardrums.

She lay back against her pillows paralysed with terror and wondering if her house had been damaged. Within minutes, the shelter door was thrown back and a gibbering Gertie was screaming at her.

'It's Mrs Trott. The stairs have collapsed on her. She's pinned down by rubble.' The woman was almost hysterical. 'She's crying out in pain. She's really hurt. I need help to lift the weight off her; I can't do it. Not by myself.'

A wave of horror washed over Henrietta. She shone her torch on Gertie, who was covered with grey dust; blood and tears were running down her face. The sight made Henrietta huddle further down her bed.

The apparition at the door croaked, 'We've got to help her. Will you come?'

Henrietta pulled her blankets closer. 'What can we do? We haven't the strength. Better if you telephone the civil defence and ask for an ambulance.'

'You know I can't,' Gertie wept. 'The phone's been off since teatime.'

'The neighbours? Run next door to Westonryn. They'll help you.'

At seventy-seven Gertie Bell was past being able to run anywhere, but Mrs Trott's plight made her jog down the gravel drive with all the speed she could. She found it hard going in her slippers. She was shocked that Mrs Seymour had refused to help, though Mrs Trott had said she was a lazy bitch who wouldn't stir a finger if she could help it.

The night was alive with noise and flashing lights. As she reached the road and turned left for the next driveway, she ran into three civil defence workers who were coming to investigate the recent bomb damage. Gertie was so breathless she found it a struggle to get the words out to tell them about Mrs Trott.

One ran off to the nearest air-raid warden's post to telephone for an ambulance. The other two supported Gertie between them as they walked her back up the drive. They paused for a moment to view the front of the house. 'At least it hasn't gone on fire,' one of them said, but Gertie burst into tears as she took in the destruction wrought upon the once handsome building.

'Don't worry, we'll see to your friend,' they assured her. 'Whereabouts in the house will we find her?'

'In the entrance hall. We were under the stairs,' she gasped, 'but they fell in on us.'

'You should have been in a shelter. Don't you have one here?'

'Yes,' she croaked, 'in the rose garden at the back, but Mrs Seymour likes to have it to herself.'

'Right, I'll have a recce inside. Tom, you take this lady to the shelter to wait for the ambulance.'

'It's for me?'

'Of course. You're still bleeding from that cut on your forehead. There's a raid on and you can't walk round in your nightdress. You'll catch cold.'

Gertie found herself escorted to the Anderson shelter, where an indignant Henrietta sat bolt upright when the door suddenly opened.

'Hello, missus,' Gertie's escort said. He threw back the

covers on Jago's bunk and pushed Gertie down on it.

'I'm sorry,' Gertie muttered, knowing Henrietta wouldn't like this. Another blanket was whipped off a third bunk and thrown over her.

'Stay there. We'll let you know when the ambulance gets here.' He went out, pulling the door shut behind him.

'That man was disrespectful, coming in here without so much as a knock.'

Gertie's teeth were chattering. She would have liked to say, 'Don't you know there's a war on?' but she didn't dare, not to Mrs Seymour, not even after working for her for thirty years.

It was a lovely spring-like morning but Nancy could see a huge smoke cloud crowding the sky over Liverpool, which meant fires started by the bombs were still burning. She'd eaten her breakfast and was cutting a sandwich to take to work with her when she saw Toby's car pull up outside her door. She went to meet him.

'Hello, Toby. You're out bright and early this morning.' He paced blindly inside, carrying a large box which he slid on to her table.

'Thank you, you're very kind, but I've got plenty of milk. You're over-generous now Caro isn't here.'

She noticed then that he looked stricken. 'Carrington Place got a direct hit last night,' he said.

'What!'

'The cook was killed. Gertie was inside with her but she escaped with a cut on the head.'

Nancy was horrified. 'Oh, my goodness! Is Henrietta all right?'

'Yes, but the house is gutted; just a shell left. Impossible to live there now, which means we're very short of living space. I had an empty cottage because three of my farm boys gave notice and went into the forces and Jago has tried to persuade me to let Henrietta have it, but I have two land girls arriving today to work on my market garden and I have to provide accommodation for them. I've applied for four girls, actually, and am expecting the other two shortly. I've had to move Kevin and Colin into my own house.' His eyes were searching her face. 'Jago and I have a favour to ask, Nancy.'

She turned cold but had to say, 'Anything.' They'd been so good to her when she needed help, but she could guess what was coming. 'It's Henrietta?'

'Yes. Can you take her in for a few days until we can find her somewhere else?'

Her stomach muscles contracted. Henrietta was the last person she wanted with her. She couldn't stand her as a permanent guest.

'I'm afraid there's Gertie as well. Ordinarily, she'd be a help, but I'm not so sure now.'

Nancy's mind was racing. How could she possibly fit them in? 'Is Gertie badly hurt?'

'She's confused, I think. She was taken to hospital but sent home with stitches in her head. The hospitals are full to bursting. Liverpool had a terrible night. It was bedlam. Did you hear it?'

'No, I slept through.'

'Lucky you. It kept me awake.' He paused. 'Thank you for taking them in.' He stood looking down at her, and then said awkwardly, 'I suppose you know why I can't have them at Hattongrove?'

Kevin had made that clear to her. 'The same reason you didn't want me or Caro there?'

He nodded.

'What about Jago?'

'He'll stay with me, you've no room here. Even two guests will be a tight fit. Henrietta won't want to share a room.'

Nancy looked round her front room. 'I could push these two armchairs together and sleep here at a pinch.' Then she thought of something better. 'No. Without Caro, I could go home to Dad.'

Toby looked indecisive. 'That's a hell of a lot to ask of you, Nancy.'

'You've always done a lot for me.'

'Oh, there's another thing. Jago wants to know if instead of going to the factory, you could help him salvage whatever's possible from the house? He's taken Henrietta and Gertie to his office at the factory, and if it's all right with you he'll put them in a car and send them over. He says will you then ask their driver to take you to Carrington Place?'

'All right.'

'You're the tops, Nancy. I'll go home and ring Jago, let him know you'll give them a roof over their heads. I hope it won't be for long.'

Nancy felt shocked at the turn of events and the upheaval it was going to mean for her. Even her plans for today had been drastically changed. There were things she'd need to prepare, but what? She couldn't think straight. Yes, the beds. She must change the sheets on hers and tidy her room so Henrietta could use it. Fortunately, she'd cleaned Caro's room thoroughly as soon as she'd gone back to school, but it was full of her toys and clothes. She'd need to take away some of their belongings. There was little enough room for anything here.

Kevin was pulling the car up at her front door before she was ready, but she ran down to welcome her two guests. Henrietta marched past her into her living room and collapsed on the most comfortable armchair. She'd wrapped herself in a car rug.

'You'll need to light the fire, Nancy,' she said. 'There's a chill on this room.'

Kevin had to assist Gertie out of the car. Nancy could see her swaying on her feet and went to help him.

'Steady, missus,' he said. He was having to hold her upright. 'Jago asked me to do what I could to help,' he told Nancy, giving her a cheeky grin.

'How d' you feel, Gertie?' Nancy asked. The maid had a large dressing strapped on her forehead, but the rest of her face looked paper white. 'Would you like to lie down? I think that's best. Let's get her up to Caro's bed, Kev. Now, while I've got you here to help.'

The narrow stairs made their task difficult and Gertie was breathless when they got her up. Nancy threw back the bedcovers.

'The bathroom,' Gertie choked. 'I'm all dirty. Covered in that awful dust. It'll make the bed dirty.'

'There's no bathroom here, I'm afraid,' Nancy said. 'Oh, Lord, should we have taken you down the garden first?'

'Too late,' Kevin murmured. 'Not back down and then up again.'

'Sit on the chair here,' Nancy said. 'I'll bring you a bowl of water so you can wash.'

'Tell me what you want me to do,' Kevin said as they clattered down the stairs.

'You could put a match to the kitchen fire, it's already laid, and bring in another bucket of coal from the coal hole.'

There was hot water in the kettle intended for washing up after Nancy's breakfast. She poured it into a bowl and took it upstairs to Gertie, found her a comb and a clean nightdress and helped her to use the chamber pot.

'Are you hungry?'

'You're very kind. No, I couldn't eat anything,' Gertie gasped.

'A cup of tea?'

'We had some at the factory, thanks. I just want to lie down now. I ache all over.'

'A sleep might help. I'll leave you so you can.' Nancy drew the curtains and went downstairs. The fire in the kitchen was blazing up and a full kettle swinging on the chain.

Henrietta was pulling her rug closer. 'I can't feel that fire from here. I need another lit in this grate.'

Nancy had kept a vase of flowers in the little parlour grate all summer. 'Sorry,' she said, 'but the coal ration won't run to two fires.'

Henrietta was irritable. 'Why didn't you light this one then?'

Nancy told herself to turn the other cheek and be patient. 'We can't cook on that one, Mother-in-law.'

'Well, you're doing nothing to make me comfortable. I've been bombed out. I'm cold and I can't get dressed because I've no clothes.'

'Let me think. What have I got that would fit you?' Henrietta was a heavily built woman, while Nancy's clothes were size twelve. 'Not a lot. Possibly a cardigan; would that help?'

'Anything would help.'

'We could move your chair into the kitchen,' Kevin suggested. 'Get up and I'll push it through.' He did it, but it meant furniture in the kitchen had to be rearranged. 'You're near enough to this fire now to feel the warmth.

Anyway, it's a sunny day. It's going to be one of those days when it's warmer outside than in.'

Nancy crept back upstairs. She had to pass through Gertie's room, but luckily she wasn't yet asleep. She found her largest cardigan and some thick socks for Henrietta and helped her put them on.

'Where's your bathroom?' she demanded.

Nancy pointed to the little shed at the bottom of the garden. Henrietta shuddered. 'I can't go down there.'

Nancy smiled. She was pleased to be able to say, 'I'm afraid there's nowhere else. No mod cons here.'

Henrietta's face went puce. 'I can't stay here. This place isn't at all suitable.' She pulled her car rug more tightly round her, pushed past Kevin and waddled down the path.

He giggled. 'I don't think you'll have to worry about her overstaying her welcome.'

Nancy smiled ruefully. As far as she was concerned, Henrietta wasn't welcome at all.

When Henrietta returned, she said, 'I wanted to go to Toby's farm. It's well away from any air raids and I'd have Gertie to see to my needs, but he thought we'd be better here. Nancy, this won't do. I don't think I'm going to be comfortable.'

Nancy made herself say, 'Yes, you will. We'll soon have things as you want them. Are you hungry?'

'I feel empty. I've had nothing since dinner last night.'

'I have Force Breakfast Flakes or bread and marmalade.'

Henrietta pulled a face. 'No, thank you.'

'Toby brought a fresh loaf this morning, and you'll soon be able to make toast on this fire.'

Henrietta was shaking her head. 'What d'you have for lunch? Perhaps I'll wait till then.'

Kevin had made a pot of tea and was pouring it for them all. He took a cup up to Gertie.

Henrietta sipped hers reluctantly. 'I prefer Earl Grey. I don't suppose you have any?'

'Afraid not.' Nancy picked up the sandwich she'd cut for her own lunch and put it in her bag.

Kevin said, 'Mr Seymour gave me a pound of sausages to bring. I'll fetch them from the car.'

'I don't care for his sausages.' Henrietta's lip was curling in disgust.

'Well,' Nancy was making a big effort to remain polite. 'If you prefer, there's eggs and a bit of bacon, or salad with hard boiled eggs. Do help yourself, Mother-in-law.'

'You're not going? I don't know whether I can manage here by myself.'

'I'm meeting Jago at Carrington Place. I'll try and find your clothes and personal possessions and bring them for you. Is there anything you particularly want me to look for?'

'My fur coat. Oh, I need clothes to wear, everything.'

Nancy unwrapped the sausages, placed them in a baking tin and shut them in the oven. 'Everything takes a long time to cook in here,' she said, using the poker to push hot coals under the oven. 'Look at them after an hour, but it might be twice that depending on the fire. Just take them out when they're cooked.'

'How will I know when that is?'

'They go nice and brown, and look appetising,' Kevin told her. He'd brought in another bucket of coal and was backing up the fire. 'And they smell delicious. Turn them over, get them brown all round and they'll taste fine.'

'Right,' Nancy said. 'I think we're ready to leave. Would you like to listen to the wireless, Mother-in-law?' She edged Henrietta's chair closer to it and showed her how to put it on. 'Goodbye.'

'When will you be back?'

'As soon as I can.'

'Phew,' Kevin said as he and Nancy got into the car. 'Lady Henrietta! How does the woman get away with it?'

'Jago's too kind and generous to her.'

'So are you.'

Nancy pondered on Henrietta. 'Bombed out and with nothing but her nightclothes, she's even more demanding.'

'She's going to be a real handful as a house guest.'

CHAPTER TWENTY-FIVE

A S THE CAR TURNED into the drive of Carrington Place the utter destruction took Nancy's breath away. The beautiful facade was gone, as was one wall of the house. Roof timbers were hanging loose, looking like broken bones, and torn curtains, clothes and household bric-a-brac were scattered over the front garden.

'Oh my God,' Kevin said as he pulled up amongst the group of vehicles already there. 'What a mess. There's Jago. I'd better see what he wants me to do now.'

Nancy followed him. Glass crunched under their feet as their weight drove it through the layer of grey dust that had settled everywhere. Several men were pulling out pieces of furniture that could be salvaged.

'D' you want me to go somewhere else, boss?' Kevin wanted to know. He didn't address him as Jago if there were other staff close enough to hear. 'Or shall I give a hand here?'

Like the others, Jago was covered with the horrible

dust. It was sticking to his face, and smelled disgusting.

'Give Nancy a hand to collect what you can of Mrs Seymour's belongings. Gertie's things too. We found a few bits and pieces and piled them up over there, where it's reasonably clean. You could start loading them in the car now.' Jago turned to Nancy. 'If we don't strip out everything that's usable now, I'm afraid it'll get looted. Everything's in such short supply.'

'Where will you store it?' Nancy asked.

'Toby's got a barn that'll be empty until harvest time. I can put stuff there for the time being. Thanks for taking Henrietta in. Sorry to burden you with her,' he said. 'I've left Miss Farthing, my secretary, ringing round trying to find rooms somewhere else for her and Gertie, but not a lot of hope I'm afraid.'

'Don't worry about it, Jago,' she told him. 'Henrietta and Gertie can have the cottage. I've decided to go back to the Lord Nelson and live with Dad.'

'No, Nancy. That would put you in the thick of the bombing again.'

'There's only one and a half bedrooms in the cottage. I've put Gertie in Caro's bed and that's on the landing at the top of the stairs.'

Jago was aghast. 'We didn't mean to push you out.'

'I'd rather go and leave it to Henrietta. The Lord Nelson has advantages for me; it'll be easier to get to work from there. Not that I've been able to tell Dad yet, but he won't object.'

'This makes me feel terrible. He'll think we're pushing you out to make room for Henrietta.'

'Well, I don't think that. It's my choice.'

'But you've fixed the cottage up nicely with your own furniture and things.'

'Yes, but all that came from the flat I was doing up on the second floor. I'll still have my old bedroom in Dad's flat.'

'I'm very grateful. Nancy, I want you to sort through these things we're getting out. They all look pretty dreadful but most of this dirt will clean off. Take anything you want to refurnish that flat.'

'But a lot of your furniture is antique. Mine was common or garden stuff.'

'A lot of mine is too. I insist. Take anything you think you can use.'

'Thank you. I told Henrietta I'd try to find her clothes and personal possessions. She's got nothing to wear.'

'Her bedroom was on this side of the house, so she might be lucky. Gertie slept over the kitchen there, and so did Mrs Trott. I feel terrible about her being killed. Gertie was lying within a few feet of her. Is she feeling better?'

'No, I don't think so. She's not over the shock yet.'

'Kevin, be careful,' he called. 'The house isn't safe now. All that rubble can collapse on you. Nancy, pack their belongings into the car and then he can run you back with it.'

'There isn't much room in the cottage. I'll need to move out all our things before they'll be able to get theirs in.'

'Kevin will help you. Get him to take you and your things over to Birkenhead. I'm expecting a furniture van here any minute to load my things in. It's chaotic, isn't it?' Jago wiped a weary hand across his forehead. 'I'm spent. I've been up all night fire watching and it was a busy night.'

'I don't suppose you've had any breakfast either?'

'Well, tea and ginger biscuits in the office.'

Nancy got out her sandwich. 'Here, have this. It's egg and lettuce. You'll have more energy if you eat.' She twisted the paper wrapper round it and handed it to him. 'Your hands are too dirty to touch it.'

He bit into it with relish. 'I feel filthy.' He sighed. 'Thanks, but I shouldn't be eating your lunch.'

'Yes you should. I can make myself something else when I get back to the cottage.'

'You're one in a million, Nancy. Your head still works in a crisis.'

She smiled. 'It doesn't always.'

Nancy was equally tired, dirty and hungry by the time she and Kevin were returning to the cottage.

'Is the job all you hoped it would be?' she asked him.

'More.' He wriggled his nose. 'More a new life than a new job.'

'I'm glad. Is Jago happy with you?'

Kevin gave her a smile. 'I think he was until he got bombed out.'

The car was packed tight with things Henrietta and Gertie would need. Outside on the doorstep, Nancy and Kevin took off their dust-caked shoes.

'I'll have to wash before I do anything else,' she said. 'This dust is sticking to me.'

'Same here,' Kevin said. 'It's in my hair and up my nose.'

There was a delicious smell of sausages and Henrietta was just waking up. 'Did you get all my clothes?' she demanded.

'Most of them, I think. Kevin found your coffee and your special tea in the remains of the kitchen.'

'Thank goodness. What about my sherry? Did you find any of that?'

'Jago pushed some bottles into the car for you just as we were leaving.' Nancy splashed plenty of cold water over her face, and began to feel better.

Kevin backed up the fire before joining her at the kitchen sink to do the same.

'I'm starving,' he said. 'We've got to eat. I'll make some tea and some hot sausage sandwiches before we do anything else. Didn't you take the sausages out of the oven, Mrs Seymour?' He made haste to do so. 'A bit overcooked, I'd say, and they'd have benefited from being turned over, but my, don't they smell gorgeous?'

Nancy found him the fresh loaf, butter and mustard. 'How's Gertie?' she asked.

'How would I know?' Henrietta was irritable. 'I haven't heard a peep out of her.'

She wouldn't lift a finger to help anyone else. Nancy felt repulsed by her selfishness.

'I'd better go and see,' she said and shot up the stairs. Gertie was just opening bleary eyes. 'Good,' Nancy said. 'You've had a little sleep. Would you like something to eat now?'

'Yes, please.' She sat up in bed. 'I feel better. I ought to get up. I can't have you waiting on me like this.'

'Stay where you are for today, Gertie. You need a rest after what you've been through.'

'But what about Mrs Seymour? She's nobody else to wait on her.'

'She'll have to manage with me,' Nancy said. 'And I'm not doing it to your standard. You'll find it hard going if you try to wait on her hand and foot here. Without Mrs Trott and modern equipment, you'll find everything takes twice the time. Henrietta's perfectly capable of doing more for herself and from now on you should let her.'

Henrietta had scarlet patches in her cheeks and her lips were set in a tight straight line. She was in a bad mood. Nancy knew she'd sensed she and Kevin were on friendly terms and didn't like it.

She'd taken against Kevin. She thought it wrong that he'd shared their lunch, though he'd made it. He was a driver and should eat elsewhere. Neither did Henrietta like the idea of Gertie lying in bed and being waited on. She was throwing her weight about, rather like a spoilt child, Nancy thought, trying to attract attention to herself.

'This is a difficult day for us all,' Nancy tried to explain. 'I'm going upstairs to remove my clothes from the bedroom you're going to use, and Caro's from Gertie's room. Kevin will bring all your things in and stack them in the front room, so my stuff can go straight out to the car. Then we'll carry your things up the stairs. If you want to speed things up, you could wash up the lunch dishes.'

'I wouldn't know how,' Henrietta said disdainfully. 'I've never washed up in my life.'

'Now's your chance to try it,' Kevin said, winking at Nancy as he went out to the car.

Nancy went up to her bedroom, opened her two suitcases and stuffed in as many of her belongings as she could. Then she draped the clothes hanging in the cupboard over her arm and ran down to the car with them. Shoes, books and make-up she swept into carrier bags and took downstairs.

Gertie's gaze followed her as she went back and forth through her room. 'I shouldn't be sitting here like a lady watching you do all this on your own.'

'If you rest,' Nancy said, 'you'll feel better tomorrow and be able to potter round again.' She started packing Caro's belongings, but found things she'd have no further use for.

'All this paper can be used to light fires,' she said, sorting things into piles. 'Caro won't want these drawings, or all these painting books she's filled up.' There were soft toys and clothes she'd grown out of but some other child might like to have.

Nancy paused to look at a puzzle book. This was the one Toby had given Caro for her last birthday. She'd worked through it very quickly. Nancy flicked through the pages to see if there were any puzzles left for her to do, and two sheets of paper flew out. She was sweeping them on to the pile of waste paper when something made her look at them twice.

These were the pencil drawings Toby had been so keen to see that Monday morning. She remembered how awkward his manner had been. Caro must have put her drawings inside the pages of the book to bring them home. What better place was there to keep them clean and flat? Nancy sighed. Why hadn't she thought of that when Toby was looking for them?

There was nothing special about them. Caro had produced loads of drawings like these; one was of cockerels feeding and the other of pigs in front of their sty. She could do better ones if she took more time over them. Nancy turned them over. On the other side were neat rows of figures written by an adult hand. Instinct told her these were what Toby had been looking for.

They were laid out in a similar style to the accounts she worked on in the office, but she knew enough about them to see that these were different. She had neither the time nor the energy to study them now, so she unzipped a bag and slipped them inside. She wanted to take her things and get away from Henrietta. Although she and Kevin had been doing their best, she'd been sending malicious looks in their direction all day.

Kevin was running up and down the stairs now, taking Nancy's things down and carrying Henrietta's belongings up. He dumped a lot of Gertie's belongings on her bed and she cooed with delight to see them. 'They're still clean. I've got plenty to wear after all.' She put on a dressing gown and started trying to fit her clothes into Caro's small cupboard and chest of drawers.

'That's the lot,' Kevin said, coming up with a pile of shoes and dropping them on the floor. 'You'll have to sort them out later. I don't know which are yours and which belong to Mrs Seymour.'

'Thank you. You've been ever so good.'

'Nancy, the car's packed tight. There's no room left for your bikes, but I've got just about everything else in.'

They went downstairs, Gertie trailing after them.

'We're about ready to leave,' Kevin said.

Henrietta was staring stonily at him. 'The fire needs making up,' she said frostily.

'Sure,' he said, obligingly poking it into a blaze and tossing on coal. 'Nancy, I'm getting peckish again. Mr Seymour gave me these cake tins; he said there was cake in them. Shall we have a slice and a cup of tea before we go?'

'Why not?' Nancy filled the kettle and hung it over the fire to boil.

'Wow! There's a cherry cake and a chocolate cake.' Kevin was cutting slices. 'Bet you could manage a slice of cake, Mrs Seymour. Which do you fancy?'

'I'll have mine later,' she said haughtily.

'Gertie? What about you?'

The tears were rolling down her face. 'Mrs Trott made those cakes yesterday,' she choked. 'We've worked together for over thirty years. I can't believe . . .'

Nancy put an arm round her shoulders, led her to a chair and made her sit down.

'She made very good cakes. Come on, she'd want you to eat them, wouldn't she? You'll feel better if you do.'

'It's been a helluva day,' Kevin said, pulling a stool closer to Henrietta before putting a cup of tea on it.

'No thank you.' She gave a theatrical shudder. 'I can't possibly drink that.' Glaring round the room, she said, 'Look at your table, Nancy. There's no room to eat at it. All this stuff needs to be put away before you go. How can Gertie work when it's spread out like that?'

'We're all clapped out,' Kevin said, taking Nancy's best teapot from the dresser. 'We've overdone it and it's high time we stopped for today. But as I managed to salvage your tin of Earl Grey, I'll make you a cup of that before I go.'

Nancy was having to move boxes in order to open the front door so they could get out. 'Things will look better in the morning,' she said.

'Hey, Nance, look, that's half a case of sherry you're shoving.' He took a bottle out and stood it on Henrietta's tea tray. 'Do you both good to have a glass of this. Where d'you keep your glasses?'

Nancy took two from the dresser and added them to the tray. She went to rest her head wearily against the door frame.

'I know my cottage is a chaotic mess today,' she said. 'But what's on the table is food and all this other stuff is yours, Mother-in-law. Kevin and I salvaged it and brought it here for you.'

'But what about my dinner?' Henrietta's voice was plaintive. 'Have you told Gertie what she must cook?'

'Gertie's still feeling a bit groggy. I don't know if she'll be able to do much for you tonight. The food is all here on the table so you can choose what you want to eat. You'll have to help yourself.'

Kevin said cheekily, 'Why don't you have a go at cooking, Mrs Seymour?'

Indignation made her straighten up in her chair.

Hurriedly, Nancy said, 'Good night. I think you'll be all right now.'

'What is the world coming to?' Henrietta glared at Kevin. 'I've never known such impudence. You think because you're asked to help out in a crisis, you can presume to be our equal. You even sat down and ate with us. You're a paid servant, a . . .'

'A fully licensed driver,' he said. 'And a good one.'

'A rude, half-civilised lout.'

Kevin was pulling the door shut behind them. 'And your husband's lover,' he said.

Henrietta's mouth fell open with shock, her face swelling with boiling rage.

'That's right, missus, you heard correctly. I'm your husband's lover. Good night.'

He ushered Nancy to the car. She was horrified too. 'Kevin! You shouldn't have said that! She'll blow her top!'

'She asked for it. What an ungrateful old witch she is.'

Nancy flopped on to the passenger seat, lay back and closed her eyes. 'Henrietta will never get over that. She'll not have you near her in future.'

'Suits me.' Kevin started the car and pulled out into the lane.

'But what will Jago say? You've told her . . .'

'She knows he has lovers.'

'Yes, but now she knows it's you, and she knows I know too, and what about Gertie? Henrietta will be mortified.'

'She drove me to it. Even a worm will turn. It needed doing, anyway. She thinks she's so superior to everyone else.'

'Oh, my godfathers! She'll go berserk.'

'Calm down, Nancy. Why don't you snatch a few minutes' sleep while you can? You must be exhausted.'

'I am.' She realised he was calm, and it surprised her. They'd both worked very hard today and it had been emotionally draining. He'd tried to humour Henrietta as they all did, but she'd gone out of her way to be nasty to him. She couldn't blame Kevin; he must feel totally shattered too.

She heard him chuckle. 'If looks could kill. Did you see the way she looked at me? Full of malevolence.'

'She hates us both.'

'All day, we did our very best for her. Enough to make any normal person love us.'

Nancy sighed. The engine hummed soothingly but she'd long passed the point where she could sleep. Kevin was slouched silently over the steering wheel, straining his eyes into the murk of a rainy dusk. There were no lights anywhere.

Nancy's feet were wedged up against something, and realising it was her zipped bag, she slid her hand inside to take another look at those figures. To Toby and Jago they were important calculations, or they had been when they were lost.

She took out the torch they all carried in their pockets these days, and shone the pencil of light on the figures for a few moments.

She was used to seeing the initials ZMcE. Jago had

told her Zac McEllery was one of his best salesmen, and he stopped at her desk several times a week to throw pages of figures into her in-tray. He tried to chat her up, too. Twice he'd asked her out for a drink but she didn't care for him and hadn't gone.

She shone her torch again and recognised the initials of other men working on the sales team. AB was Anthony Best, and JF was John Fadden. It was easy when she knew the men, but they were employed to sell the products from the factory, and here clearly set out were cuts of fresh meat: pork leg, pork loin, sirloin and even different types of steak, with weights and cash values beside them.

The factory didn't handle any rationed meat. The best thing they made, and then only occasionally when they had an excess of offal, were faggots. Nancy enjoyed those: they had onions and sage added to give them flavour. So what was the connection between fillet steak and Zac McEllery?

She gave a little gasp as it came to her with the force of a bomb blast. These figures must refer to black market sales. They could be nothing else. Jago must be in it up to his neck because they were being run through his sales team alongside the sausages.

Gentle, generous Jago was a black marketeer. And Toby too, of course.

Guiltily, she glanced at Kevin. 'What are those figures?' he asked.

'I'm not sure. Just trying to make them out,' she said, hastily folding up the sheets and stuffing them back inside her bag.

He was concentrating on the road again, but Nancy felt cold with shock. She found it hard to believe that Jago and Toby could be involved in anything illegal. But hadn't Charlie said something about his grandfather being sent to jail for fraud? So his family had not been so honestly upright as hers.

She'd found them friendly and generous to a fault. The allowance they'd said she needed was being paid into her account without fail They'd given her a regular supply of milk and eggs, which were rationed, as well as the occasional piece of meat. She'd gladly eaten them without much thought. Toby was producing the food, wasn't he?

They both treated her with affection and she was fond of them. It bothered her to think of them doing something like this. She could talk to Jago about it, get it all out in the open, ask him . . .

No, she couldn't. Dealing on the black market was cheating their fellow countrymen and a criminal offence. She thought of discussing it with her father but he had very strong views about honesty and would be terribly shocked if he knew. He might want her to report it, say it was her duty, and she couldn't do that.

Nancy felt torn in two, in something of a moral dilemma. She decided she'd forget about it. After all, it was nothing to do with her. It was just something she'd stumbled on. She didn't want to think of Toby and Jago handling black market goods. She didn't want to know any more about it. Perhaps she'd got it all wrong and the figures were totally innocent. Yes, she must forget about it. Put it out of her mind.

CHAPTER TWENTY-SIX

HENRIETTA WAS ALMOST exploding with fury as the front door closed behind Kevin and Nancy. How dare he say such a thing to her? Another queer! She might have known. But she found it hard to believe that Jago would want an uncouth youth like Kevin near him. The cheek he was giving her! He had no respect for his elders and betters. Jago's lover indeed!

Here she was, bombed out, homeless and without any real help. She had a migraine and her nerves were raw. It would be enough to finish off most women, but she was made of stronger stuff. She needed rest and pampering to get back on her feet, and then she'd deal with them all.

'Gertie,' she said, 'pass me another slice of that chocolate cake. Thank you, but what a miserly portion. Perhaps a little more.'

Gertie was trying her patience; she'd had just about all she could stand from her too. But Gertie was easy to control. She could fluster her so easily it was no longer much fun. She'd get round to Nancy, and she'd separate

Jago from Kevin. She was not going to put up with him saying such shaming things. She'd make them both sorry they'd not treated her with more kindness and respect.

But Nancy first. If she could get rid of her, she'd be able to bring Caroline up herself. She could turn her into a little lady. She'd have somebody to love her and look after her in her old age.

Miles welcomed Nancy home as she'd known he would, though he said it would have been safer for her to stay with Henrietta at the cottage.

'Dad, I couldn't possibly,' she said. 'She'd drive me round the bend.'

As soon as the pub opened and she was alone in her father's living room, she got out those sheets of figures from her bag and studied them. Then she threw them on the fire and watched the flames scorch through and shrivel them up.

The siren blared at ten o'clock and Nancy spent most of the night in the cellar. She'd forgotten how terrifying an air raid could be, though her father said in the morning, 'Nothing fell too close, thank goodness.'

When she got to the office, Nancy noticed several desks were still unoccupied after nine o'clock. She was afraid her colleagues had been injured in the raids during the night, and was on tenterhooks until they turned up. All of them looked weary and complained they'd been unable to sleep.

Zac McEllery came in, looking more awake than anyone else, and dropped his figures in Nancy's in-tray.

'Is the boss in yet?' he asked.

'I haven't seen him, but his car's outside.' She watched him bound over to Jago's office door and knock, stroke his handsome hair in place, then disappear inside.

Nancy yawned, feeling sleep-sodden too, and reached for his figures. What she'd learned made her look at them in a new light, but they referred to standard factory products. She opened up her ledgers and started work.

Some twenty minutes later, Jago came out of his office with Zac, but while the latter winked first at Jill Jones and then at Nancy before striding out, Jago came to her desk. He was grey-faced.

'I'd like a word,' he said. 'Come to my office.'

She followed him back, saying, 'Are you all right?'

'I'm shattered.' He closed the door. 'I went to the cottage last night to see how Henrietta was getting on. She'd worked herself up into a fine old state.'

Nancy thought of what Kevin had said last night. 'She's bound to be upset.'

'It wasn't about being bombed out. She seemed to have accepted that. No, Gertie had put a small joint of pork and some potatoes in the oven to roast but it was eight o'clock and they still looked half raw. Henrietta said she was starving hungry and had had virtually nothing to eat all day.'

'Kevin made us all hot sausage sandwiches for lunch.'

Had she not complained about him? 'And she had cake at teatime.'

'She insisted I take her out for a meal, but there wasn't a restaurant open nearer than Southport. It was very late by the time I got to sleep, and of course I'd hardly been to bed the night before. There's nothing worse than digging about in the rubble of one's own home, trying to salvage one's possessions. Did you have a bad night in Birkenhead?'

'My dad seemed to think it wasn't too bad. Was Gertie all right?'

'I had to ask her to come out to dinner with us, didn't I? Henrietta didn't like that, but thank goodness Gertie didn't want to. She said she didn't feel well enough, and she'd boil herself an egg and warm some milk and go to bed. There were no lights on when I took Henrietta back.'

'I don't think she's going to be happy there with only Gertie to do all the work.'

Jago sighed. 'Gertie's nearly eighty, and after having the house collapse round her and kill her friend I was surprised to find her still on her feet.'

'She was very groggy earlier in the day.'

'Nancy, would you mind going down this morning? I'm afraid they both need sorting out. Perhaps you could teach them how to cook a few simple meals?'

Nancy's heart sank. 'Teach Henrietta to cook? That's not going to be easy.'

'I know.' Jago smiled and patted her shoulder. 'Please?'

'All right, I'll try.'

'I'd be grateful if you would. Please do your best. I've got to get Henrietta settled or there'll be no peace for anybody.'

Nancy went to the car park, wondering if she dare ask Kevin to take her, but he said, 'I'm standing by to drive Mr Seymour home. He says he won't be staying long this morning. He's asked Alf to take you.'

Nancy found Alf pleasant and obliging. 'How is Mrs Seymour?' he asked, opening the car door for her. 'A bit of a battleaxe, that one. I bet it's knocked the stuffing out of her to be bombed out of her home. Can't help feeling sorry for her; she'll never find another house as good as that.'

'She's in my house now. I've gone back to live with my dad. Would you mind helping me get her organised? Kevin was awfully good, cooking sausages and carrying in coals.'

'Course I will, you just tell me what wants doing. We've all got to help each other at times like this, haven't we? How's your little girl?'

When they arrived, Nancy found Henrietta occupying the same armchair near the kitchen fire, while Gertie was struggling in from the back garden with a bucket of coal.

Alf snatched it from her. 'Let me do that,' he said.

'Thank goodness somebody's come to clear up this mess,' Henrietta said sharply, looking at Nancy. 'Do get this stuff put away. It's impossible to feel comfortable here when it's like this.'

'I will.' Nancy looked round. Her cottage was a shambles. 'And I'll show you how to cook a meal for tonight.'

'No, you tidy up and show Gertie how to cook. I think I'll take the car and go into Southport for a bit of shopping.'

Nancy was shocked. Alf was tossing coal on the fire but turned round to grimace at her. She took a deep breath. 'I want to show you how this oven works. Jago has found your ration books but you'll need to register with a butcher and a grocer. Formby is the most convenient place. I'm still registered with shops there and they'll have rations that you can collect.'

'I'll leave that to you, Nancy. I was reading a very good novel, but it doesn't seem to be here and I must have something to read. Come along, driver.'

Alf turned to Nancy. 'What time do you want me back?'

Henrietta answered for him. 'We'll be back when I'm ready to come,' she said firmly.

'Three o'clock,' Nancy said with equal firmness. 'Jago needs me to get back to the factory. I have work to do there too.'

As soon as Henrietta slammed the door behind them, Gertie burst into tears.

'I can't stay here,' she wailed. 'No electricity, no

bathroom and no hot water. Mrs Seymour doesn't like it either. She hates the lavvy down the garden.'

'The place has a certain charm, Gertie. It's safe here, and quiet at night.'

'It's too quiet in the day. She hates it because there's nobody here but me. She has nobody to talk to and she can't get away now she has no car.'

Nancy had seen it stored on blocks in the garage. It had been so badly damaged in the raid it would never be driven again.

'If I had somewhere else to go I'd be off like a shot, I can tell you.' Gertie was mopping at her eyes. 'But I've no relatives I can ask to take me in.'

'You might grow to like it here in time.'

'No, not with her. I've never lived in the country. I can't please her. I can't cope.'

'I can show you,' Nancy said gently. 'It's all very old-fashioned. Just like it would have been when you were a girl growing up at home.'

'I've never had a home. I was brought up in an orphanage.'

'Oh, dear! I'm sorry.'

'I've always done domestic and lived in. I've been with the Seymours for thirty years. I can do parlourmaid and personal maid but now Missus wants me to cook and I can't. I've never done that.'

'I know, but let's hope it won't be for long. You've looked after my mother-in-law too well, Gertie, that's the trouble. She can't do anything for herself.'

'She makes me feel such a helpless fool.'

'She probably feels just as helpless.'

'Not her. She doesn't want to do anything. She never stops ordering me about, do this Gertie, do that, we'll have dinner at seven Gertie, roast pork with stuffing and apple sauce, and make a nice pudding for afters.' Gertie's voice was rising up the register towards hysterics. 'But I can't! I've ruined a good joint of meat!'

'No, you haven't,' Nancy said soothingly. 'You took it out of the oven and it's still here. I sometimes half cook a joint the night before.'

'Do you?'

'Yes. I'll show you how to finish it off. You and I will have a good lunch and there'll be enough cold pork left for you and my mother-in-law to have for dinner tonight.'

'She won't like it cold.'

Nancy filled the kettle and swung it on to its chain. Gertie was going to need a cup of tea to calm her down.

'She will, with salad. Everything takes hours longer to cook than with electricity or gas. How long did you cook this pork for?'

Gertie mopped at her eyes. 'About four hours, I think.'

'That's what I'd have given it.' Nancy pushed the dish back in the oven. 'Now, you have to build the fire up, which Alf did for us, and push the hot coals under the oven with the poker, like this.'

'She said I was to be sure to get the crackling crisp.'

'It can be done if you get the oven hot enough. I'm not sure if these potatoes will be all right, but they might be. It's a very forgiving stove. Let me show you an easy way with potatoes. Just scrub a couple of big ones clean, prick them over and put them on the oven shelves. You can leave them for hours. When you take them out they'll have hard crisp skins, and you just cut them open and let a lump of butter melt into each one.'

'That's all?'

'That's all. And if they're still hard and you want to hurry them up, you can use the tongs and put them straight on to red hot coals.'

'I could do those tonight, couldn't I?'

'Yes. Knowing how to manage the oven is the main thing. Vegetables can cook in a saucepan on this trivet. And there's fresh fruit and cheese and biscuits for afters. Let me show you where I store all my food.'

'She can be hard to please.' Gertie's lip quivered. 'She used to upset Mrs Trott by turning her nose up when she took the food to the table.'

'Tell her she'll have to eat what you've made or go without. She knows there's a war on.'

'I can't answer Mrs Seymour back like you and Kevin do. She scares me.'

Nancy laughed. 'She scares me too. Don't let her get to you.'

*

Alf returned Henrietta to the cottage and helped her carry in her parcels well before three o'clock.

'Tell Jago I'm quite put out that I had to return the car before I was ready,' she complained. 'I'd have liked to go to a cinema matinee. Tell him to send a car for me again tomorrow.'

When she returned to the factory, Nancy went to Jago's office to bring him up to date. He was sagging over his desk with his head in his hands. He looked ill.

'Are you all right? I thought you were going back home this morning.'

'Is Henrietta all right?'

'She never stops complaining. Nothing is ever right for her,' she told him. 'It's Gertie I'm worried about. She feels she can't cope with her.'

'Can any of us?'

'You can.'

He looked at her with exhausted eyes. 'Once I could. I try to keep the peace, but she's bound to be upset at losing her home. She's used to being waited on hand and foot by me and a battery of servants.'

Nancy wanted to tell him that he'd spoiled her for ordinary life, but he looked miserable enough without that, so she contented herself with describing how Henrietta had hijacked Alf and the car.

He sighed. 'You'd better ask Alf to go again tomorrow and stay as long as she wants him.'

'I will, and I'll ask him to carry in more coals for them.'

'Do they have enough food?'

'Yes. I've arranged a menu for tonight that Gertie can cope with.'

'Good. So I won't need to take her out for dinner?'

'No, and she had lunch out anyway. They'll probably be all right tomorrow because I've shown Gertie how to manage the oven. Henrietta refused to stay for the lesson.'

'You've been very patient with them, Nancy. If we found another house for them, it probably wouldn't please Henrietta any better. I don't feel there's much more help we can give. They'll simply have to get on with it.' Jago broke off in a fit of coughing. 'Perhaps they just need time to settle down in their new quarters.'

'Jago, you sound in need of help yourself. You aren't well.'

'I think I'm getting a cold or flu or something.' He blew his nose. 'I don't feel too good.'

'Go home now and go to bed.'

'I think I might as well. I'm not achieving anything here. I'll ask Toby to pop down tomorrow to see if they're all right.'

Nancy felt uneasy as she went out to find Alf. Henrietta seemed to be behaving like a volcano getting ready to explode. She was turning Gertie into a bag of nerves and even Jago no longer seemed able to cope.

CHAPTER TWENTY-SEVEN

BOB BELLAMY HAD spent the morning working at his desk in the office he shared with other ministry advisers. He'd been giving thought to what Toby Seymour had said about his farm, and decided he was right to concentrate on pigs and market gardening. The black loam of coastal Lancashire and the proximity of Hattongrove to a large urban population lent itself to them.

Bellamy enjoyed putting his ideas to farmers and jollying them along until they accepted them. That was his job, and it gave him a sense of power to have the law on his side and be able to insist they ran their farms according to his instructions. Then, when they were ready to admit his ideas had increased their production, he received their accolades.

He didn't care for Toby Seymour. The man was too self-confident. He'd also been quite aggressive and tried to put him in the wrong for being found in his farmyard.

Bob Bellamy had in front of him the forms all

farmers, Toby Seymour included, were required to fill in. Seymour had invested in pigs in a big way and apparently meant to increase his number of breeding sows. Bob couldn't help feeling a pang of envy, and wished he'd had the wherewithal to go into farming on this scale.

To use the floor space to the best advantage in this small office, his desk was pushed straight up against that of his immediate boss.

'Dave,' he said, 'have you ever had any dealings with Toby Seymour of Hattongrove?'

'Yes. Smashing set-up, over seven hundred acres. He's a hobby farmer, got a manager there running the place.'

'He seems to know what he's doing.'

'Well, he knows what to tell others to do.'

'He seems to have a special marketing contract with Henry Ipcress and company. Seymour says on this form that his carcass meat goes to them, but his offal goes to J. C. Seymour and company, sausage makers. Isn't he related to them?'

'Yes, I believe that's his brother. If you want the low-down on them, speak to Orlando Donkin in food.'

'Thanks, I will.' There was something about Toby Seymour that roused Bob's suspicions.

As Orlando Donkin had an office at the other side of the same building, Bob sought him out straight away. He knocked and put his head round the door.

'Bob Bellamy, from agriculture,' he said, putting out his hand. 'Can you spare me a few moments?' Donkin had a cup of tea in front of him and was tucking into a sandwich. He was a small gaunt man with a large roman nose.

'Yes, if you don't mind me eating my lunch at the same time. I'm going out this afternoon and I want a quick getaway.'

'Not at all. That sandwich smells good.'

Donkin waved it at him. 'Not all that good. Bloater paste. What can I do for you?'

'I'm looking for information. I have concerns about a pig farmer called Toby Seymour. He states that his stock is slaughtered by Henry Ipcress and company, who handle the sale of the carcasses.'

'Yes, I know the firm. Some goes to be cured for bacon and the fresh pork is bought up by the ministry.'

'Have you any suspicions that they aren't following the letter of the law?'

'Suspicions?' Donkin's sandwich paused on the way to his mouth. 'Nothing specific, but it's common knowledge that the meat flooding the black market comes from farmers and smallholders. Catching them and proving it isn't easy.'

'Seymour has a brother who runs a sausage factory, J. C. Seymour. Do you have any dealings with him?'

'No.' For a moment Donkin chewed silently. 'I take it you have suspicions about this farmer?'

Bob hesitated. He wasn't proud of knocking himself out in Toby Seymour's farmyard. The story had swept through the ministry offices as hot gossip, making him a three-day wonder. He didn't want a repeat performance of that, but he was going to say it anyway.

'It's not part of our remit to find homosexuals, but I bet Toby Seymour is one. About providing black market meat, yes, vague suspicions, nothing concrete.'

'What sort of vague suspicions?'

Bob Bellamy paused. 'It's this job, isn't it? When we see the sort of set-up where it could be possible, don't we all sniff round wondering if it might be happening this way or that? Is there anything else you can tell me about these two businesses?'

Orlando Donkin said, 'Henry Ipcress provides Seymour's Sausages with meat trimmings and offal from all the animals they slaughter, not just those from his brother's place.'

'Right, but they can do what they like with offal and trimmings, they're unrationed. It's the fresh meat I'm interested in.'

'It's the fresh meat we're all interested in, Mr Bellamy. You could be right. They're all into backhanders.'

'I was thinking of something more substantial than backhanders.'

Donkin felt for his teacup. 'Sorry, can't help you there.'

'I find that comparing our findings often brings a breakthrough in a job like this. Two brains better than

one, sort of thing. Would you take another look at them
and let me know what you think?'

When Bellamy had gone, Orlando Donkin sat back in his
chair to think. He liked to keep his suspicions to himself
until he had proof. When he'd first been directed into
this job he'd been too open in what he'd said to his
colleagues, and they had used his information to
prosecute clients. Promotion was based on how efficient
one was in controlling the black market, and to initiate
successful prosecutions helped.

Now he had suspicions that he'd not mentioned.
Henry Ipcress handled a lot of fresh meat and for a
company like that it would be easy to leak a proportion
into the black market where it would command a much
higher price. Donkin had paid several visits to Henry
Ipcress's premises as he was required to do, and found
him tense and cagey.

In Donkin's job, that made him suspect guilt, but the
Ipcress accounts were impeccably kept and there was no
evidence that anything illegal was taking place. But
evidence could easily be kept out of the company
accounts, and Donkin thought the chances were that the
company was dealing in the black market.

It was Bellamy's mention of the Seymour sausage
factory that had set his mind running along a different
tack. He hadn't asked whether Ipcress delivered or
Seymour's collected the casings, meat trimmings and

offal, and perhaps he should have done.

Now he thought about it, he seemed to remember seeing in the Ipcress accounts the charge for making deliveries to J. C. Seymour's factory. But he'd also seen a van with the Seymour name on it in Ipcress's loading bay, though it had looked too small to transport all the casings and bits the sausage factory would need.

Donkin drained his teacup and decided he'd delay the plans he'd made for the afternoon and pay another visit to Henry Ipcress and company.

He went to the yard first and was very pleased to find there another van with the message *Buy Seymour's Sizzling Sausages* emblazoned on its sides. He was out of his car and across to the van in an instant.

The van was completely loaded and he knew he'd taken them by surprise. The Ipcress workers looked as though he'd routed them, and after getting the van driver to sign for what they'd loaded in his van they disappeared poste haste back into the building.

Orlando Donkin introduced himself to the driver and asked to see his credentials.

'Your name is Zachary McEllery and you work for Seymour's Sausages?'

'That's me.'

He looked a wide boy if ever there was one, Donkin thought. He was flashily dressed, and, in these times of clothing coupons, without an apron or overall to protect his fine clothes. He must be about thirty, and he was grinning at him, apparently not one whit put out to be questioned by an official of the ministry of food.

'You're employed as a van driver?'

'I'm a salesman,' he said. 'This van is allotted to me. I deliver sausages to shops and markets and take their orders for the following week.'

Donkin could see a straw hat with an orange band round it on the seat in the van. This fellow looked the sort to be doing a job like that. 'So what are you doing here?' he asked. 'They don't sell your sausages here, do they?'

McEllery laughed easily, as though Donkin had made a joke. 'No, I've been sent to collect more of the stuff to make the sausages. Supplies at the factory are running low, and the boss gets cross if the shift can't keep working.' He grinned at him again. 'I suppose you want to inspect my load?'

Orlando thought him either innocent or very self-possessed. 'Yes please.'

The van was packed up to the roof with large tightly lidded metal containers, each with a decal on the side bearing the sausage factory name.

'Give us a hand to lift them down, will you?' McEllery asked. Donkin felt he had to oblige though his back was playing up. The first container was heavy and difficult to open, and when the contents were revealed they were indeed pigs' hearts. They didn't look inviting.

McEllery wanted the lid of the first fastened down

securely before he'd open another, and he was taking his time over it.

'It's food, and we all know how scarce that is,' he said. 'My first duty is to make sure it's kept clean and wholesome.'

After inspecting the contents of four more containers, two filled with liver, one with kidneys and the other with fat and meat trimmings, Donkin began to feel a little queasy. At this rate it would take the rest of the afternoon to open all the containers in the van.

He decided there must be an easier way than this, and signalled to McEllery that he'd had enough. The containers went back in the van at twice the speed they'd come out.

'What are your sausages like?' he asked.

'Not bad if you're hungry.' Another friendly grin. 'There's a war on, you know. But I recommend our faggots. They're really tasty, full of herbs and onions. Have you tried them?'

'No, but now you've said they're good, I will.' But first he'd have to put all that raw offal out of his mind.

He needed a different approach to crack this. He followed Seymour's sausage van at a distance. It drove straight to the factory and went round the back where it could be unloaded. Donkin decided to return the next day and speak to the manager if he could. He could interview anybody in his search for black market traders. The problem was that he'd found no grounds to be suspicious of Seymour's sausages, and all the food produced here was unrestricted and unrationed.

Jago had spent two days in bed nursing a runny nose and a sore throat with nothing to do but listen to the wireless. It had given him too much time to worry and fret about what could be happening at the factory. Though he'd heard that Merseyside had continued to suffer heavy bombing, he'd been able to have his sleep out, so had decided this morning that Kevin could drive him to work.

He passed through the office to a chorus of good mornings. Jill Jones's red head was down and she was typing hard, but a moment later she came to his room. 'Are you feeling better, Mr Seymour?'

'Yes, thank you,' he said, though by now he wasn't so sure.

'Miss Farthing hasn't come in,' she said, and went on to tell him his secretary had been bombed out the night before last.

'Oh, no!' Jago felt sick. 'Is she all right?'

'Yes, and so are her family. They've been taken in by relatives in Blackpool. She's shaken up and upset and worried that if she can't find lodgings in Liverpool she won't be able to come back to work.'

'That's the last thing we need. Did you get her address in Blackpool? I'd better write to her.'

'Yes. I've opened all the incoming post and sorted out

what other people can do for you,' Miss Jones went on. 'And I've taken some of the routine stuff to type replies myself.'

'Thank you for taking over Miss Farthing's work. It looks as though you and Nancy will have to carry on doing it.'

'Now you're in, shall I bring the routine letters back to you?'

Jago could see the work had piled up on his desk. 'No, you do what you can. I don't know how long I'll stay.' He had a thumping headache and was feeling a little dizzy. 'I'll read them through and sign any replies you have ready before I go.'

Since he'd seen Nancy at her desk and knew she'd been brushing up on her shorthand typing, he said, 'Ask Nancy to come in and give me a hand.'

Nancy looked alert and fresh-faced. 'I didn't think you'd be back so soon,' she said, putting her shorthand pad on his desk. 'You don't look yourself even now.'

'It gets out of hand here if I stay away too long. And I've got a letter for you. Toby collected it from the cottage yesterday.' He pushed it across the desk to her.

Nancy picked it up. 'It's from Gavin Freeman, Charlie's old friend.' Jago noticed that her cheeks were growing deeper pink as she studied it. 'I wrote to him about my change of address but he must have posted this before he got mine. Oh, this is number fifty-seven. I picked up fifty-eight the last time I went to the cottage.'

'The post isn't as reliable as it used to be.'

'No, but considering the bombing, it isn't too bad. Number twenty-one has definitely gone missing. Often days go past and I get nothing, then I get three at once. That's why Gavin started numbering them, so I can read them in the right order.'

'Have you got yourself another admirer, Nancy?'

'Another boyfriend, you mean?' She smiled at him. 'Would you mind?'

'No, why should I?'

'Wouldn't it make you think I've forgotten Charlie? I'm sure Henrietta would hate me to have someone else.'

Jago pondered that for a moment. 'It would be much the best thing for you. You're young enough to start again.'

'Jago, you're the best father-in-law anyone could have. You tell me I'm one in a million, but so are you.'

He took out his handkerchief and blew his nose hard. 'I'd see it as another chance of happiness for you. We all need somebody to love us and put us first. You don't want to spend the rest of your life alone, do you?'

'No, I don't.' He could see her doodling on her pad. 'But I'm scared of counting my chickens before they're hatched. I haven't seen Gavin for ages and almost every time he writes he tells me another friend of his has bought it. He says he's almost scared to pal up with anybody because they'll be the next to be shot down.'

'He's very brave to keep going all this time.'

'They all are. Gavin says he has a charmed life and he'll come through everything unscathed, but I think he's saying that to buck me up.'

'Does it?' Jago's soulful eyes were full of sympathy.

'In the middle of the night, no. I'm on tenterhooks all the time, dreading to hear that he's been shot down.'

'You're brave too, Nancy.'

'No, I'm a shaking coward inside. I can't even let myself think of the future. I just wish this war would be over so we can get on with our lives.'

'We all wish for that, my dear, but you must hope for the best too. I hope life will give you everything you want and that you'll be happy.' He thought she was looking a little tearful. 'Forgive me,' he said. 'I'm getting over-emotional. Everything seems to be getting on top of us, doesn't it?'

He pulled the pile of letters and files closer and started to dictate, but he couldn't think straight. If he paused, searching his fogged brain for the word he needed, Nancy would suggest one that sufficed. He kept doggedly on, as he really needed to get some work done. If he could clear this little pile he'd go back to bed at Hattongrove and Nancy could type them and send them with Kevin for him to sign.

There was a tap on his door and Miss Jones's head came round. 'There's an official from the ministry of food here asking to see you,' she said.

Jago was alarmed. His mind leapt to the figures he and Toby had drawn up and subsequently lost. Had they somehow fallen into the hands of the ministry? In a court of law, would they be considered sufficient proof of black market trading? Only last night, Toby had chortled over the amount the trade was bringing them.

'What does he want?'

'He says he's just making routine enquiries.' Miss Jones pushed a visiting card across his desk. *Mr Orlando Donkin*, he read.

Jago considered saying he was too ill or too busy to see him, but that would only put it off. Better if he faced him now and looked as though he had nothing to hide. Also, he'd then know what he had to deal with. If nothing else, the shock had woken him up. 'Better send him in,' he said.

'Shall I leave you?' Nancy stood up.

'No, I want to get these letters done. I'll get rid of him as soon as I can.'

When Orlando Donkin came in, Jago pulled himself to his feet to shake his hand. He was a weedy-looking fellow, but his sharp dark eyes were sweeping round his office, missing nothing. They came to rest on his face. 'Sorry to disturb you, Mr Seymour.'

'I'm rather pushed for time. I've been off sick and have a lot to catch up with. You don't mind if Miss Milton stays?'

'Not if you don't.' He smiled at Nancy, who got up and brought another chair nearer the desk for him. 'I won't take up too much of your time.'

Jago made himself say, 'This is something of a surprise. We don't deal with rationed food at all.'

'I know. I'd just like to ask you a few routine questions.'

Jago felt stiff with tension. It sounded as though he was being investigated. He and Toby couldn't stand anything like that. To be charged with black market trading would be a disaster. Even worse if they found grounds to charge them with homosexual practices. 'About what?'

'On several occasions I've seen your vans in the yard of Henry Ipcress's premises. I believe you have a business connection with that company?'

The mention of Henry Ipcress sent a cold shiver down his spine. 'I do. They provide us with ingredients for our filler. To fill our sausages.'

'Can you tell me whether they deliver to you or you collect?'

'They deliver.' Jago wanted to bite his tongue out the moment he said those words. *Had his vans been seen in Henry's yard?*

With what seemed a spark of triumph, Donkin was opening a notebook. 'Yes? Then why—'

'Actually, it's both,' Jago added hurriedly. 'They deliver in bulk at set intervals, but my factory can run out of offal and rather than let the plant lie idle we sometimes collect.'

'Oh, I see.' Donkin was biting the end of his pencil. 'Then let me tell you that this afternoon in the course of my duties I searched the van of an employee of yours, a Mr Zachary McEllery.'

'Yes?' Jago felt as though a hole was opening up at his feet. Had Zac been caught? His thought processes were spiralling out of control.

'In what capacity do you employ him?'

'He's a salesman, one of our best salesmen.'

'And his duties?'

'To sell our products.' Jago had a fit of coughing, which gave him time to think. 'Before the war he went round trying to raise orders, and he had to sell hard. But now . . . well, orders come flooding in. He delivers sausages to the shops and markets and takes their orders for the following week.'

'And collects ingredients from Henry Ipcress?'

'Sometimes. Like everybody else in wartime, he has to turn his hand to whatever needs doing.' Jago had another thought. 'It's more economical in time and fuel if after he's made his deliveries he can make a collection from Ipcress's on his way back.'

Jago froze, panic-stricken. There was a golden rule to follow when being interviewed like this, and he'd just broken it. Answer the question and volunteer nothing else.

He shivered again. What if McEllery had been seen to load up at Ipcress's and drive off somewhere else?

'On what day do they deliver offal here?'

He was sweating now. Keep it vague, he cautioned himself. Don't pin it down.

'It varies for several reasons.'

'Such as?'

'The number of animals going through their abattoir, and therefore the amount of stuff they have for us,' he said. 'And the amount of fuel they have. The product has to come fairly promptly, as you can imagine.'

'Yes. I wonder, as I'm here, if I could take a quick look at McEllery's sales figures?'

Jago was taken aback. This was scary, though he didn't think this nosy fellow would find anything wrong there.

'Nancy,' he said faintly. 'Show them to him, would you? And perhaps you'd ask Miss Jones to rustle up a cup of tea for me while I wait for you to come back?' Donkin was going to leave him alone at last.

'Thank you for making time for me,' he said as he followed Nancy out. 'I won't keep her long. I can see you're busy.'

Jago was gripped by a series of uncontrollable sneezes. 'I do hope I haven't passed on a dose of flu to you,' he said.

Once he was alone he slumped back on his chair, feeling both anxious and angry. This must mean McEllery was being investigated. How many times had he told him to be careful not to flash his money about; that he must not be seen to live above his normal income. Jago mopped at his face with his handkerchief. Or was he barking up the wrong tree and it was those figures he'd lost that had brought on this grilling?

A girl from the canteen brought him a cup of tea with a ginger biscuit in the saucer. His mouth was dry and his throat sore, so he drank it down quickly. The girl had left his office door ajar, and through the crack he could see Nancy at her desk with that fellow sitting beside her, the account books open in front of them. His finger was pointing something out; he was questioning her. Nancy half smiled at him as she answered.

Jago had never admitted anything to Nancy, told her nothing about what he and Toby were doing, but she was familiar with what was going on here as well as in his home life. She'd probably picked up enough to drop them in it. He should have warned her to be careful. He felt defeated, ready to snap. Nancy had an expressive face; he couldn't watch her any longer. He got up and closed his door, and then, feeling a tear of desperation roll down his face, he wished he hadn't.

This was the first time any official had shown any interest in his business, though Toby was always sounding off about present-day bureaucracy that allowed ministry advisers to poke their noses into how he ran his farm.

Jago could feel himself shaking. As if he didn't have enough to worry about without this. He'd been on edge from the day Leslie had cracked that fellow Bellamy on the head. But so many things had gone wrong since then; his house had been gutted, and poor Mrs Trott who'd cooked for him for years had been killed. Henrietta was becoming an impossible problem without a home and servants to look after her. Now there was the added worry that their black market activities were about to be laid bare.

Jago knew that if this fellow unearthed one solid fact to confirm his suspicions, a whole army of investigators would descend on them to search for more, and total disaster could follow.

He was scared. He shouldn't have agreed to see the man. He hadn't been up to it; he hardly knew what he'd said. His mind wasn't working as it should. He closed his eyes. He'd have five minutes and try to pull himself together.

CHAPTER TWENTY-EIGHT

NANCY WALKED OVER to her desk knowing that Jago was terrified of what this man might find out. She'd felt his fear, cold and solid. Surely Donkin had too? She wiped the perspiration from her forehead, sat down at her desk and took out the account books.

She took a tight hold of her nerves. 'Pull up a chair,' she said as calmly as she could. 'Poor Jago has the flu. It's going round the office. He shouldn't have come to work today, but we're so busy. Half the staff are off sick and the rest have been bombed out of house and home.'

Donkin's weedy frame lowered itself beside her. 'It was good of him to see me without an appointment,' he said politely.

'That's Jago all over, always thinking of others, never himself. Now what exactly was it you wanted to see?'

She knew Donkin was probing for information but she knew nothing for sure about what Jago and Toby were doing, only what she could guess. She knew she mustn't voice those guesses to this man. 'I'm afraid I don't know all that much about these figures,' she said disarmingly. 'I haven't worked here very long.'

'How long would that be?'

'This is my third week, and with the bombing and all that it's been a bit chaotic. Miss Jones did them before me; she might be able to tell you more.' She pointed Miss Jones out to him. She was typing away at twice the speed Nancy could manage.

He asked a few more simple questions and then got to his feet. 'Thank you Miss Milton,' he said. 'And tell Mr Seymour I appreciate the co-operation he's shown.'

Jago was glad to see Nancy come back to his office, slide into the chair and pull her shorthand pad and pencil closer. 'He's gone,' she said.

'What did you tell him?' Jago knew it was his nerves that made him jump at her like this. He took a deep breath and said more quietly, 'What did he want to know?'

'How the figures are made up, that sort of thing. The same sorts of questions he was asking you.' Her blue eyes met his, full of concern. 'Jago, you look grey. You're not well enough to be in work.'

'I know.'

She smiled at him. 'Mr Donkin doesn't know what he's looking for. He's just feeling round hoping a clue will pop up. There aren't any in those account books. The figures are all true blue, but you know that, don't you?'

He stared at her in surprise. It sounded as though she knew there were other figures, and . . . He groaned. 'I'm worried.'

'I can see you are.'

'I wish I knew what had made him come here.'

She was doodling on her pad. 'There's something I think I should tell you. Those drawings of pigs and cockerels Caro did in your study, the ones Toby was so eager to find . . .'

Jago felt fire shoot through him. He couldn't take his gaze from her face now. 'I found them when I was moving out of the cottage. They had figures on the back. Caro took something you and Toby were working on, didn't she?'

'What did you do with them?' he demanded.

'I burned them in the fireplace at the Lord Nelson. Nobody saw them but me. They led me to believe you and Toby are trading in the black market.' He stared at her, feeling stunned. 'What else could they mean?' she asked.

He sighed. 'Why didn't you tell me?'

'It was all assumption on my part. I didn't want proof. I didn't want to know what you were doing.'

'Nancy!'

'I didn't want to share a secret like that. You've both been so good to me and Caro, so friendly and kind. I didn't want to believe you were capable of black marketeering.

It's wrong, Jago. You're helping some people to get more than their fair share of rationed food, and you're making money by doing it.'

'Yes,' he admitted, wondering if she knew their other secret. 'Kevin said you'd play everything straight up and honest, like your dad.'

She smiled wryly. 'Give me a child until he is seven, and all that.'

'You could say the same about me and Toby.'

'Yes, well, you've had a nasty fright, but I don't think Mr Donkin learned anything today. Why don't you stop selling on the black market now while you're still in the clear? I'd like you to do that.' Her cornflower blue eyes were looking straight into his soul. 'You look ill. Go home and talk it over with Toby. You've got lots of money, you don't need more, and you could do without the worry of this.'

'You're certainly right about that. It's more than a worry; I dread that we're going to be found out. But you know what Henrietta's like. There's always something else she has to have. It isn't just the money, it's everything else. Dealing on the black market allows us to barter food for the things she wants.'

'Henrietta is making unreasonable demands on you. Totally unreasonable. You shouldn't feel obliged to fulfil her every wish.'

He sighed. 'She always has. She makes demands on us all.'

'And we all rush to do her bidding, which encourages her to ask for more.'

Jago played with his fountain pen. What Nancy had said was something of a revelation. Henrietta *was* becoming impossible. She would never be satisfied, she'd always want more. It was like trying to fill a bucket with water when it had a hole in the bottom.

'Toby and I . . . the business . . . we know it's wrong and we do have our moments of remorse. We must think of calling it a day.'

'Do that, Jago, before you're caught.'

'If it isn't already too late.'

'The sooner the better, I'd say.'

He pulled himself to his feet. 'You're right, of course, Nancy.' The problem for him and Toby was that they'd still be criminals if they did stop. The only thing that would make them honest citizens was to change the law and decriminalise homosexuals. 'I'll take these letters home and dictate answers over the phone when I'm feeling better.'

At the door he paused. 'Thanks for everything, Nancy.'

Back in his office, Donkin blew his nose and hoped he wasn't in for a dose of flu. He made some notes about his visit to Seymour's sausage factory and thought about what he should tell Bellamy. There was nothing wrong there he could put his finger on.

Jago Seymour was a bag of nerves. Normally he'd

think of that as a possible sign of guilt and keep a close eye on him. But he was ill, and really quite willing to open everything for him to see. He'd had no sense of things being hidden from him, and the accounts appeared above board.

The only member of the sales force he'd seen was McEllery. To look at, there was nothing saintly about him, but what he'd said and done seemed straight up.

He had no intention of being helpful to Bob Bellamy. He didn't like him. He stood head and shoulders above him and made him feel a weakling. It was satisfying to think he could be completely honest with him knowing it would get him nowhere.

He sauntered along to Bellamy's office to tell him he'd drawn a blank.

'Was he aggressive towards you?'

'No, quite the opposite. But I always try to make a friend of people I interview. I find that can help.'

'Did you see any evidence of homosexuality?'

Donkin's mind had been on black market meat. He'd forgotten all about the other angle.

'That's the last thing I'd suspect of Jago Seymour.' He smiled. 'I'd put him down as one for the ladies. I spoke to a girl who said she'd only been working there for three weeks, but they seemed on close terms. She was full of admiration for him, kept saying Jago this and Jago that. A pretty girl too.'

'Really?'

'Yes. You know how you sometimes get the feeling that people are very comfortable together? As comfortable as a pair of old shoes, I'd say.'

'He's married, but estranged from his wife, I understand.'

'Ah. He could be finding solace with her.'

The Easter holidays had come and gone. For Nancy, having Caro home from school had brought a problem. Merseyside was still suffering frequent bombing raids and though she was growing used to sleeping in the cellar at the Lord Nelson, nobody in the family thought she should take Caro with her.

It was Toby who found the solution. Colin's mother ran a boarding house in Ainsdale and he booked them both in there for three weeks. Jago wasn't able to give Nancy the whole holiday off, but they were still able to spend a lot of time there. The weather held fine but was blustery and cool, but they could find shelter from the strong breeze in the sand dunes, and when the sun came out it was marvellous.

Caro made drawings of the different types of grasses she saw thriving in the sand, and the tiny marine creatures they found in the tide marks at low water. Nancy saw those days as holidays and a complete rest. On other days she went to work, and Caro stayed with her grandmother at the cottage.

When Caro went back to school Nancy returned to

the Lord Nelson. On the first night back she got home
from work to find her father asleep in his armchair. He
woke up as she came in, but he looked really ill. Jago was
sick, but her father's illness was harder to bear because
she could see he was slowly going downhill. He was losing
weight and strength and no longer had much appetite.

Nancy started making soups for him as he said he
found those easier to get down than anything else. She
would prepare one recipe for his lunch and a thicker,
meatier one for his evening meal. It was usually about
quarter to six when she got home, but all she had to do
was to warm up the soup and they could have it together.

Nowadays it was usually Alma who opened up the pub
at six o'clock, but Miles would go down as soon as he'd
eaten. Nancy tried to persuade him not to, but the jollity
in the bar seemed to cheer him up. Down there, he
always had somebody to talk to, and Alma told her he'd
sit down when he felt tired.

Nancy had washed up and was preparing soup for the
next day when one of the younger barmaids came
clattering upstairs to say Gavin Freeman was on the
phone and asking to speak to her. She dropped
everything and ran down to the bar. There had been a
time when she'd been shy of speaking on the phone in
front of staff and customers, but now she was so pleased
to hear his voice she no longer cared.

'Gavin, hello. How lovely to hear from you. How are
you?'

He too seemed to be bubbling over with high spirits. 'I've got two whole weeks' leave,' he said.

'I can't believe it! Fourteen whole days? That's wonderful. When does it start? You'll be coming up to see me, I hope?'

'Try and stop me,' he laughed. 'I can think of nothing else. I want to spend a day in London on the way up, to see my father's sister. She's my last living relative, but I'll drive up to see you on Sunday. I'll arrive some time in the afternoon.'

'I can't wait.' Nancy was immediately uplifted. She'd felt tired but was suddenly invigorated. She brought him up to date with her news and talked on for a long time, reluctant to put the phone down and cut herself off from him.

Eventually, she had to, but she was left fluttering with excitement at the thought of his coming. They'd been writing to each other regularly over the months, and his letters had provided support and comfort when she was struggling with her own difficulties. He wrote of a future when they could be together all the time, but her life had changed so much, and it was so long since she'd seen him, that she didn't feel sure about that.

She rushed upstairs to the flat on the second floor and started to make up the bed for him. When she'd seen the dust and the mess at Carrington Place, she'd been in two minds whether she wanted to accept Jago's offer of salvaged furnishings, but she'd been in need of mattresses for the beds having taken her own to the Rosemead cottage. Jago had had everything wiped clean and she'd been surprised at the luxury of the things he'd sent her. The flat was much improved and she had a huge stock of bed linen and towels.

Gavin's visit put everything else out of her mind. At work the next morning she felt a bit shy of asking Jago for more time off. 'I feel as though I've just had a break with Caro,' she told him, 'and I should settle down and work now.'

'You came to work on three days a week, Nancy, and did a lot for Henrietta as well. You deserve a real break,' he said. 'I'll ask Miss Jones to keep the accounts up to date. Are you planning to go away for a little holiday?'

'I haven't got round to making plans, but I'd love a real holiday. Dad isn't well, though. I'm glad now that I went back home to live with him. I feel he needs me.'

'You can leave him for a few days, can't you? There are times when you have to think of yourself.'

And Gavin, Nancy thought. 'I'll see how things go.'

She was counting the days to Sunday. Never had they seemed so long, though not only did she receive two more letters from Gavin, but he rang again and they were able to talk over their plans.

'I'd like to go where there'll be no air raids,' Gavin said. 'I fancy walking in the Lake District.'

That sounded marvellous to Nancy. Her father seemed a little better and said they should go.

Sunday was a lovely summery day. She spent it preparing a special dinner for the three of them and ironing her summer dresses, but she felt restless and on edge and as the afternoon wore on she kept drifting to the window. She was standing there staring down when she actually saw him draw up outside the side door. She felt her heart turn over and raced down to let him in.

To see him again, whole and well despite the dangers he'd lived through, made her feel over-emotional, and she had to blink hard. For once he was not in uniform. His hair was ruffled by the wind and his dark eyes smiled into hers. He almost leapt from the car and wrapped his arms round her in a bear hug, raining kisses on her face. She loved him. Of course she loved him. How could she ever have doubted that?

They'd never done this before but somehow it seemed the most natural thing in the world. Here, in broad daylight, outside the pub, where everybody knew her.

'How are you? Nancy, you look wonderful.'

'So do you.' She stared up into the face she'd known so well. He'd never been handsome in the way Charlie had. His features were not so even, but he looked kind and considerate and he was very brave. She added, 'Well, perhaps you look tired and a little older.'

'Being here with you will solve that.'

'Charlie's car hasn't changed a bit.'

'I try to look after it.'

'He didn't.' Tears were welling in her eyes despite her

efforts. 'Driving it was what he wanted to do.'

'I'm a very different person,' he said gently, pushing a handkerchief into her hand.

Nancy mopped at her face. 'What will you think of me, bursting into tears as soon as you arrive? I meant to give you a big welcome.'

'You have.'

'It's just that I'm reminded . . .'

'Of Charlie?'

'Yes. It's the car, too. Come on, I ought to get you inside.' She watched Gavin pull a couple of bags from the MG. 'I want you to know . . . I'm over Charlie now. I'm over the grieving and the looking back.'

He kissed her again, more gently, on her cheek. 'Thank you for telling me. I am too.'

Nancy felt she'd found love again. 'Come on inside and say hello to Dad.'

It wasn't until she was pouring out the tea she'd made that she said, 'Fourteen days' leave in one go. You're jolly lucky to get all that at once, aren't you?'

'It's embarkation leave,' he said, suddenly more subdued.

'You've got another posting?'

'It's not just me, there's six of us moving on. We've all been in the front line for a long time.'

'Ever since the beginning of the war,' Nancy agreed. 'You fought right through the Battle of Britain. Won it and carried on trying to shoot down the German bombers coming over. Where are they sending you?'

He shook his head. 'They won't tell us until the very last moment. Careless talk costs lives, as the posters keep warning us. Your guess is as good as mine. All we know is we've been issued with hot weather kit.'

'Oh, heavens. Tropical kit? It could be the Far East.'

'It could be anywhere. The other lads are hoping for Canada. They train aircrew over there now, so perhaps it's possible.'

'But is it all that hot in Canada?'

Gavin shrugged. 'Summer's almost here. I rather fancy India myself, but who knows? Anyway, I'm not going to worry about that yet. I've got a fortnight first in which to please myself.'

Nancy spent the early part of the evening in a daze. She was very conscious of Gavin's love: she could see it in the way his eyes followed her, in the way his hand kept reaching out to touch her. He was just as intoxicated by it, sweeping her into his arms at every opportunity.

Toby had given her a chicken to make a special dinner for Gavin. She had everything prepared and put it in the oven as soon as he arrived. While it roasted, she took Gavin down to the bar for a drink. Dad had asked her to; he said the staff talked about him, sometimes asked questions about him, and he thought they would like to see more of him.

'I'm disappointed,' Alma declared. 'You're not in uniform.'

'I'm on my holidays,' he told her.

Nancy kept nipping upstairs to deal with the dinner, and when it was ready she swept Dad upstairs to eat with them. He was cheerful and quite chatty but he didn't eat much. She knew he must guess how she and Gavin felt about each other. Surely he could feel it in the atmosphere, as she could?

Afterwards, Dad went down to the bar again and Gavin helped her wash up. It was a beautiful spring evening, and they went out in the last rays of the evening sun for a stroll. He was shocked at the amount of bomb damage he saw.

'It'll be a clear night,' Nancy said, worried. 'That means we'll probably have another visit from the Luftwaffe. Now the light evenings are here, the raids tend to start around ten thirty, as soon as it's dark.'

'Had we better get back?'

Nancy took him back to the bar for a nightcap, but the air-raid siren went before he'd finished it. The customers streamed out towards the deep shelters at Hamilton Square station.

'Get off home,' her father was telling the staff. 'Go on, get away before the bombs start falling.' Having radar meant they had a few minutes' warning. 'I'm going to close the pub. No, Alma, leave that. We can tidy up in the morning.'

'Get yourself ready for bed,' Nancy said to Gavin. 'That's what we do now, except we go down to the cellar instead of tucking ourselves up between the sheets.'

'So I won't get to sleep in that very nice bedroom you prepared for me?'

'Perhaps later, if we're lucky.'

Nancy rushed to fill a couple of Thermos flasks with tea to take down with them. Gavin said it all looked quite comfortable in the cellar, where they had old armchairs, footstools and plenty of pillows and blankets.

Miles continued to cough and wheeze. He said it was impossible for anyone to sleep with all the noise. They could hear the drone of German planes overhead and the ack-ack guns firing at them. Ambulances and police cars whined past and every so often explosions shook the ground.

'It isn't the noise that keeps me awake,' Nancy said. 'It's the worry that the next stick of bombs will bring this building crashing down on us.'

'No,' her father said, 'they're not falling that close. I think it's Liverpool's turn to get it tonight.'

'A terrible thing if we got a direct hit, Gavin, while you were here,' Nancy said. 'After you've survived all those dangerous dogfights in the air.'

'There won't be a direct hit tonight,' he said in his calm voice. 'I keep telling you, I lead a charmed life.'

They talked on and off until the all clear sounded at half past one. Then, sleepily, they dragged themselves upstairs to more comfortable beds.

'Good night, Nancy.' Gavin yawned. 'I think it would be a good idea to set out for the Lake District in the morning.'

CHAPTER TWENTY-NINE

NANCY SLEPT UNTIL half past nine the next morning. She got dressed quickly but was surprised to find the only sounds were those of the cleaner down in the pub.

She tapped on her father's door. 'Are you awake, Dad?' He didn't answer, so she peeped inside. He was still flat out. She crossed the floor and pulled back his curtains. Bright sunshine flooded into the room.

Miles was pulling himself up the bed to peer at his clock. 'Oh dear, is that the time? I've overslept, haven't I?'

'We all have, Dad. I'll make some tea.'

From the bottom of the stairs to the second floor Nancy called up, 'Are you awake, Gavin?'

A shadowy figure came out on to the dark upstairs landing. 'Just about. I've only just come to.'

'We've all overslept,' she said. 'I'm making some tea. Come down to the kitchen when you're ready.'

Nancy was still half asleep, but while the kettle boiled

she went round checking that the windows were unbroken. Her father called down to Alma, 'Is there any damage down there?'

'Not that I can see.'

He collapsed on a kitchen chair. 'It's nice not to have to rush down to do cellar work,' he said, pouring himself a cup of tea. 'Alma and Ted see to all that these days.'

They all felt somnambulant. Nancy was the first to get to her feet. 'We're on our holidays, Gavin, so we'll have a leisurely start. I'll make us a brunch first. Seymour's sausages and fried eggs?'

'Not for me, love,' her father said. 'I'm not hungry.'

'Dad, you must eat. Scrambled eggs on toast, then?' She set about cooking it.

They ate and afterwards sat about talking and drinking more tea until Miles asked: 'Gavin, d'you want to go down to the phone to try and book a hotel?'

Nancy saw him hesitate. 'No, because then we'd have to find the place. It's easier to look out for a nice one as we're going along, and then pop in to ask if they have any rooms.'

'Right,' Miles said. 'Then I'll leave you two to get yourselves packed up and out.'

'We'll pop into the bar to say goodbye,' Nancy told him.

'I think I can hear Alma opening up. Where has the time gone?'

Nancy listened as his footsteps clattered on the stairs and the bar door clicked shut behind him. When she looked up, Gavin was looking pensive on the other side of the table.

'I didn't want to ring up,' he said, 'because I'd have to ask in that public place for either one double or two single bedrooms, and I haven't asked you yet.'

Nancy was somewhat taken aback by so blunt an approach. 'Well . . .'

'I've been wanting to tell you that I love you since I got here. I've been in love with you for ages. But you know that, don't you?'

'Yes.' She started to get to her feet, meaning to go round to his side of the table.

'No.' He held up his hand. 'Let me have my say first. If you come close I'll kiss you and forget everything else. I want to marry you. No, that's not what I meant to say. Will you marry me?'

Nancy was almost overcome. She nodded. 'Yes, but . . .'

'I know, there's that big but. That's what I'd like us to do, but with only twelve more days to go, would it be sensible, or even possible?'

Nancy didn't know what to say, but he wasn't waiting for answers. He just wanted to get the words out.

'I want things to be completely understood between us. I've spent half the night wondering about this and that. The thing is, I'm being sent off to some war zone or other and you might never see me again. I don't want to make you a widow a second time.'

'Don't say that!'

'I'm trying to be realistic. I know I said I had more lives than a cat, but I must be coming to the end of them now. And I haven't much to offer you. I've felt like this about you for a long time. In fact, when I first set eyes on you, I envied Charlie for having such a beautiful wife. I know how you felt about him, and I didn't want to put you off by telling you all this too soon. Before you were ready, I mean. While you were still grieving for him.'

'I've told you that I'm over Charlie.'

He was silent for a moment. 'I think not quite, Nancy. You were a bit tearful yesterday.'

She sighed. 'Perhaps I'll never be completely over him. He's Caro's father, and I see his likeness in her face sometimes. But I'm ready to move on.'

'If you don't want to take things any further,' his dark eyes searched into hers, intense and serious, 'if on this holiday you want a room to yourself, that's how it'll be.'

Nancy was shaking her head. 'That's not what I want at all. Recently I've been thinking a lot about you.'

He smiled. 'You're never out of my mind.'

'Now it's me trying to tell you something. You told me in your letters that you loved me, but I wasn't sure. I hadn't seen you for a long time. But now I have and I am.'

It was Gavin who leapt out of his chair to take her in his arms.

'I love you,' she told him. 'I want to be alone with you, I want to get to know you properly.'

'You're sure? Quite sure?'

'Yes, quite sure. I'm not a young virgin, Gavin. I was a wife for seven years. I know how to avoid ending up in the predicament I did with Charlie.'

'I know all about that too,' he said. 'I was married to Colleen for nine years.' He held her close. 'I'll take good care of that side.'

'We've both had hard times,' Nancy said, remembering that Colleen had died of TB after a long illness. 'I think we're entitled to grab what happiness we can when we can. We don't get many chances.'

She wanted him to love her, wanted to be completely his. 'When you've gone I shall have something to remember. Then I'll just have to keep my fingers crossed and hope you come back safe and sound.'

Gavin had a wide smile on his face. 'What a sensible girl you are. I'm going to buy you an engagement ring, Nancy. So that when I've gone, you'll at least have a memento of me.'

'Is the Lake District the best place to buy jewellery?' Nancy smiled. 'I'm hardly likely to forget you, anyway.'

'No, I want to do it. I want to get away from Liverpool. Last night wasn't much fun, and much as I like him I find your dad's presence inhibiting. It stops me holding you or kissing you, and I can't even say what I want to. It would be embarrassing for all of us.'

'There's no privacy here,' Nancy said. 'And it's worse down in the pub.'

Gavin caught at her hand. 'Why don't we stay overnight in Southport? I don't feel like rushing and that's just a gentle drive away. We'll be there in plenty of time to look round the shops.'

'Good idea. It's sufficiently far away from big ports and docks to make it unlikely we'll be bombed, and it's the right time of the year for the seaside. It'll be lovely.'

When she was getting ready to leave, Nancy pulled off Charlie's sapphire ring and put it in the little pot on her dressing table. She hesitated over her wedding ring, but left it where it was.

Nancy was tingling with anticipation. She'd been thinking of this trip with Gavin as a thrilling adventure and a welcome escape from everyday routine. Her father came out to wave them off, but seeing the MG Midget parked at the kerb distracted his attention.

'Charlie's old car! It's a real beauty, isn't it? You've kept it in very good condition. Looks better now than when he had it.'

'Shall we put the hood down?' Gavin asked. 'It's a lovely sunny day, but it'll blow your hair about.'

Nancy remembered that only too well. 'Yes,' she said,

and gave him a hand. She hadn't forgotten how to fold the canvas top away.

Her father stood watching them. 'I think I'm too old to enjoy a car like that now,' he said.

'Nonsense, Dad, you'd love it.' Nancy kissed his slack cheek. 'Look after yourself.' His face was grey in the morning sun, and he looked ill and tired.

'Don't you worry about me.'

She slid on to the small bucket passenger seat knowing she would. Dad was looking very frail. She'd asked Mildred, the pub cleaner who'd been tidying up his flat ever since Nancy was a child, if she'd get his rations in for him and make him some soup. Like everybody else, Mildred wanted to do her best for Dad.

'Should I be taking you away?' Gavin asked in a low voice. 'Can he manage without you?'

'He says Alma and Mildred will look after him, and he'll be fine.' But it was on Nancy's conscience. 'I've been running around helping Charlie's relatives but I've done virtually nothing for Dad. Yet he's the one who's ill and needs it.'

Gavin drove through the tunnel to Liverpool. Nancy turned and let her gaze travel round the car. Everything was so painfully familiar, she could almost feel Charlie here between them. She told herself that Charlie would always be with her, and she must accept that.

'About the car,' Gavin said. 'I'm being sent overseas so I'll have to part with it. Can I leave it with you?'

'Well . . . Yes, I expect Toby will find somewhere on his farm where it could be kept.'

'Thank you. Why don't you learn to drive it? You'd be able to get about more easily, wouldn't you?'

'There's no petrol ration for civilians unless they need it for their work. It would have been very useful while I was living at the cottage but now, no, it's easier to get to work and back on the underground and it would have to be parked on the street outside the pub.' She sat back in the seat. 'But I'd love to be able to drive it.'

Once they were out on the road to Southport the wind caught at her hair and the sun gleamed on the bonnet. She began to feel better. They were cruising up Lord Street in Southport sooner than she'd expected.

'There're two or three hotels along here,' she said.

'Keep a lookout,' Gavin said. 'If you see one that looks good, I'll turn round and go back.'

In double quick time, Gavin had booked them into the Scarisbrick Hotel, parked his car in the hotel car park, wrapped her arm through his and was strolling with her past the expensive shops on Lord Street.

'I glimpsed a jeweller's shop along here as I drove,' he said. 'Yes, here we are.' He ushered her inside.

'Engagement rings, sir?' the assistant said. 'I'm afraid we don't have a large selection, they aren't being made at present. But we have a few second-hand ones.'

Two black velvet ring pads were slid on to the counter

in front of Nancy. 'This is a rather nice sapphire with a diamond on each side.'

'Not a sapphire,' Nancy choked. 'Charlie gave me a sapphire.'

'Right,' Gavin said. 'Do you have any diamonds? A solitaire perhaps? A large one.'

'We have a few solitaires.' Another ring pad slid in front of them.

'These are a bit small,' Gavin said.

'We have a rather nice three stone diamond ring. Yes, here we are. Traditional styling, made about 1936. Eighteen carat gold with brilliant-cut diamonds set in platinum with platinum shoulders.'

Gavin picked it up to look at it more closely. 'Yes, I like that.'

Nancy knew he was feeling for her left hand; his touch made her tingle. He slid the ring on to her third finger, where it gleamed and glistened, throwing rainbow shafts of light up at her. 'It's absolutely beautiful,' she breathed.

'We'll have it,' Gavin said, drawing out his cheque book.

'Let me just make sure that it fits,' the assistant said. 'Does it feel comfortable? Yes? I don't think it needs any adjustment. It could have been made for you.'

Nancy walked back to the hotel with Gavin, feeling as though she was walking on air. 'I love it, but it's very extravagant of you.'

Gavin laughed. 'I haven't exactly had much opportunity to spend any money since the war started. Besides, it's perfect, isn't it? Different from Charlie's but perfect for us.'

Nancy smiled and gave herself up to enjoying the present: being waited on in a comfortable hotel, but most of all to having Gavin here beside her. She felt young again, in love again, thrilled about it and up on cloud nine. She wasn't going to think about his being sent overseas or wonder if or when he might come back.

After dinner they walked along the promenade arm in arm. They could have gone to a cinema, a theatre or a concert party on the seafront, but they just wanted each other.

When they returned to the hotel, she was surprised by Gavin's passion. Surprised too by her own. 'It's been a long, long time,' she said. 'And I've missed it.'

'No air raids tonight, thank goodness,' Gavin whispered. But they got even less sleep than they had the night before. Their need for love was greater than their need of sleep.

The next morning, they listened to the news on the wireless in their room and were told there had been heavy raids on Merseyside during the night. Nancy shivered at the thought of her father alone in the pub cellar.

'It must be very worrying for you.'

'It is, but I couldn't persuade him to move. He can be quite obstinate.'

'Nancy, he wouldn't be happy anywhere else. The Lord Nelson's his life.'

Before they left the hotel, Nancy rang him to make sure he was all right.

'We had a couple of warnings but it wasn't too bad. I slept quite well,' he told her. 'Better than last night, when we never stopped talking.'

They drove on north, and despite her lack of sleep Nancy had never felt so alive. They had sandwiches and coffee in Carnforth, before starting on the final leg of their journey. They'd left the towns behind and the countryside was the lush green of early summer.

'Will you have enough petrol for a long trip like this?' she asked.

'We're allowed a small ration, and I've been saving my coupons for months.'

They spent their second night in a small country hotel on the edge of Lake Windermere and slept soundly. Their bedroom had no wireless but at breakfast time Nancy rang home to see how her father was.

'I'm fine,' he told her. 'No air raid last night. Don't you worry about me.'

'The bombs are dropping all round you, Dad. I can't help it,' she told him.

The lake and the town were lovely, but they wanted to

get right away from civilisation and see the hills and the wild fells.

'I think we'll head for a place called Glenridding on Ullswater,' Gavin said. 'If we can find somewhere nice to stay, we'll spend a few days there.'

Nancy thought the little country inn was idyllic. They walked the hills all day, taking a packed lunch, and though the weather wasn't as warm as it had been it stayed dry. They feasted their eyes on the wide empty beauty of the landscape.

They savoured each day and each night as it came. On the sixth day, after he'd eaten his sandwiches, Gavin lay on his back in the heather and said, 'There's utter peace here. Nothing but us and a few sheep.'

'And the birds. I think that was a curlew,' Nancy said.

'It's perfect, absolutely perfect. If only we could stay here for ever.'

In the late afternoon they'd return to the inn, feeling tired and windblown, and though they were trying to forget the war there was no getting away from it. The wireless in the bar was turned on for the news at six o'clock and other guests could be heard discussing it all the time. Recently there had been heavy raids all over the country, and in particular the major ports were being hit. They learned that Merseyside had endured repeated raids of growing severity over the last eight nights. It seemed that by battering the docks the

Luftwaffe was aiming to put the port out of action.

The next morning, when Nancy tried to ring the Lord Nelson, she found it impossible. She was told the lines were down due to enemy action.

Gavin was sympathetic. 'You're worried about your dad, I know. I would be in your shoes, but it doesn't necessarily mean anything is wrong.'

'I know. It isn't the first time this has happened, but all the same it bothers me. What can I do when I'm this far away and nobody knows how to reach me?'

Gavin thought for a moment. 'Ring your father-in-law, he might know. If nothing else you can give him this number so he can contact you.'

'I don't like to worry Jago, he's got such a lot to think of, but if I don't I shall be on pins all the time. It could take ages to get the line repaired.'

Nancy got through to the sausage factory and Jago's voice was reassuringly firm.

'We've had a couple of terrible nights,' he told her. 'Half Liverpool is ablaze, and it's proving difficult to put the fires out. I've heard nothing from your father. Perhaps I can raise the Lord Nelson from here. What is the number, Nancy? I'll see what I can find out and ring you back. It'll take me a few minutes.'

Nancy sat with Gavin in reception waiting for the call for nearly ten minutes before it came. She heard Jago say, 'No definite news yet, Nancy, I'm afraid. The Birkenhead telephone exchange has been knocked out. Miles could be as right as rain, but I've sent Kevin over to check on him. I don't know how long that's going to take, but I couldn't think of any other way. I'll be in touch when I have news.'

'Thank you, Jago. If I've gone out will you leave a message for me?' She chatted on for a few moments and heard all was well with the Seymours except that Henrietta was fed up with the cottage and complaining that Gertie was getting on her nerves.

When she put the phone down, Gavin said, 'We'll go out for a walk, but we won't go far.'

The hotel owner said he would take a message if there should be a phone call for them. When they returned to the hotel at lunchtime they were surprised to find a written message for Gavin at reception, asking him to ring a number they didn't recognise.

'You, not me,' Nancy said, and went upstairs to freshen up for lunch, hoping she wasn't going to hear that Gavin's leave was being curtailed. She was splashing water on her face when she realised that Jago was the only person who knew where they were. That could only mean . . . Full of dread, she sank down on the side of their bed. Gavin came up a few minutes later and she could tell from his face that the news was bad.

She stood up and felt her heart turn over. 'What's happened?'

He gathered her into his arms. 'Terrible news, Nancy. I'm so sorry. That was Kevin.'

She could feel herself shaking. She could guess what was coming. 'Didn't he want to speak to me?'

'No, he thought it would be better if I broke it to you.' His arms tightened round her. 'The Lord Nelson was hit last night. It's badly damaged.'

Nancy felt her stomach muscles contract painfully. 'Dad?' she whispered.

'He was killed. So was Alma.'

'No, no!' She clutched at Gavin, put her head down on his shoulder. She felt devastated, hardly able to take any more in.

'The siren went off early, just before ten o'clock. They emptied the pub and sent the two young barmaids to the shelter at Hamilton Square station. Your father and Alma didn't even have time to get down to the cellar. It seems they didn't get much warning that time.'

'Oh, God!' Nancy felt icy cold although she was being held close against Gavin's firm warm body. Hot tears started to her eyes and she knew she was wetting his pullover.

'Kevin said the building went on fire. The civil defence workers are still there sifting through the rubble. He doesn't think it'll be possible to salvage much, but he'll collect what he can. He said Jago would send a van over for it.' Nancy felt a handkerchief being pushed into her hand. 'He and Jago both say we should carry on with our holiday, but . . .'

'No!' Nancy felt anguished. She couldn't do that.

'Do you want me to take you home?'

'Yes, I want to see Dad. See the pub. I must go home.' She broke free from his arms. 'I'll just throw our things in the bags. We'll go straight away.'

'All right.'

Gavin drove all the way back to Birkenhead without stopping.

CHAPTER THIRTY

A S SOON AS THEY reached the outskirts of Liverpool they saw isolated pockets of bomb damage. The closer they got to the docks the more frequent these became, while in the centre of the city the destruction was appalling. The road they were on was blocked with bricks and rubble in several places and they had to make detours. Fires were still burning and they passed gutted buildings now no more than broken walls with bare roof timbers sticking up into the sky or tossed like matches about the streets. Broken slates and glass were everywhere. The Birkenhead tunnel was open to traffic.

'Thank goodness they didn't damage the entrances,' Gavin said. 'I expect it's safe under the river bed with the water providing a cushion on top.'

Nancy swallowed hard. She could imagine now what she was likely to see when they drew up outside the Lord Nelson.

'I hope it was wise bringing you here.' Gavin echoed

her thoughts. 'I'm beginning to think we should have stayed where we were.'

'No, I had to come.' She felt sick when she saw the gutted shell of the Lord Nelson. 'My God!'

Both she and Gavin remained sitting in the car, stunned at the destruction spread before them. Several figures were working with picks and shovels; everything and everybody was covered with the usual layer of thick grey dust.

On the other side of the building, the second floor was still attached to one wall but unsupported on the other, so that it dipped down to the level of the pub lounge. She could see what remained of the flat she'd made for herself and Caro: the new paintwork on the bedroom walls, the Victorian grate still set firmly into the one wall of the living room that remained.

'Nancy?' It was a grimy and exhausted Kevin who tapped on the car window. 'What an awful thing to have happened.'

'Poor Dad! Where is he?'

'They've taken him to St Werburgh's church for the time being.'

'I must go and see him.'

'No, Nancy, please don't. Remember him as he was when you last saw him. I've officially identified both him and Alma.'

'I can't believe . . .' Nancy couldn't stop the tears. She was agitated and could no longer sit still, so she got out of the car. A heavy stench of burning and dust and ancient plaster hung in the air. It choked her, making her feel for her handkerchief to cover her nose.

'Poor Dad. I'm glad he can't see the old pub like this.'

The public bar just wasn't there any more; a great hole had opened up into the cellar below. She could see the twisted remains of the armchairs they'd slept on, and remnants of the torn green eiderdown under which she'd huddled.

She thought of herself then. 'I've lost my dad, my home – everything.'

'I managed to salvage something of yours.' Kevin was feeling for her hand and she felt him press something into her palm.

'My ring!' Charlie's sapphire surrounded with diamonds sparkled up at her.

'There's more.' He fished from his pocket the pearl necklace and a gold brooch he'd given her too. 'And I thought you'd want this.' It was her father's gold pocket watch, a half-hunter. Nancy turned it over in her hand. The glass had been broken and the case was slightly dented. It had stopped at ten minutes past ten.

'Oh, God, Kevin!' She was brimming with tears. 'Dad always had this with him.'

'Yes. It was the pub timekeeper.'

Now Nancy knew the exact time the pub had closed for ever and Dad had . . .

'I don't want it,' she said, pushing it back at him. 'I want you to have it as a memento.'

It was Gavin's arm that slid round her waist and pulled her closer.

Kevin went on, 'I've found some of your clothes and a photograph album. I'm afraid most of the stuff is dirty and battered, but you can sort through it later and see if it's any good to you.'

'Thank you,' she choked.

'So you haven't lost everything. You're alive and un-hurt, so is Caro and so is Gavin and so am I. You've still got family and friends, Nancy. You aren't alone. Think of Alma's poor husband, waiting for her to come home from work.'

Nancy felt overwhelmed by shock and grief. 'If we hadn't gone away for that little holiday,' she said to Gavin, 'we'd have been here when it happened.' It was a sobering thought.

'Yes,' he said. 'We'd have been killed too.'

Nancy went cold. 'I owe my life to you.'

'No, you owe it to luck. So do I. I told you I had nine lives.'

'But poor Dad!' Seen through her tears, everything was swimming round her. 'I can't get over . . . that he's dead.'

'He was ill, Nancy,' Gavin said. 'He might have preferred to go this way.'

'He was losing strength,' Kevin added. 'He couldn't

have carried on as the licensee much longer. At least his end would have been quick.'

'Yes.' She shuddered.

'Left to nature, he might have suffered a lot longer.'

She knew her father had already been suffering. He'd never complained, but she'd seen him take pain-killers and there'd been times when he'd had to fight to get his breath. His condition had been deteriorating, there was no doubt about that. She ought to feel glad he'd been spared a lingering death.

'But Alma? I've known her for years. She was in good health. Dad thought highly of her.'

Kevin led her back to the MG. 'The best thing you can do, Gavin, is take her away before the Jerries come back to have another go at us.'

'He's right, Nancy. This is no place for you, not now. This has knocked me for six, and I'm sure you must feel even worse.'

'This might help.' Kevin was pushing half a bottle of brandy through the car window. 'Believe it or not, we've found a few bottles of spirits that haven't been opened, but they'll have to go back to the brewery. We've salvaged just about all we can. There's nothing much more anybody can do here.'

'The best thing for us to do is to go back out on the Southport road and try to find a hotel for the night,' Gavin said. 'Perhaps even the Scarisbrick again.'

'I don't mind,' Nancy said, meaning she didn't care.

As Gavin put the car in gear, Kevin said, 'Ring Jago tomorrow. He'll want to know how you are.'

They were given the same room in the Scarisbrick Hotel but their mood was very different. On Nancy's mind was how best to tell Caro.

'She's only nine and it's not that long since her father died. I told her that Grandpops was giving us a home and a new way of life. She saw a lot of him – they were fond of each other.'

Gavin felt for her hand. 'It'll be very hard for her.'

'It's not something I can tell her on the telephone.'

'No, but I could take you to the school tomorrow, if that's what you want.'

'I don't know.'

'Do you want her to come to the funeral?'

'I don't know about that either.'

'She came to Charlie's.'

'It was on her mind for a long time. And I don't want her to see the bomb damage to the Lord Nelson. The utter destruction of everything she knew would give her nightmares.'

'You think it would be better if she didn't know too much about it?'

'In some ways.'

Nancy didn't sleep well that night. The next morning, Gavin took her to see Jago at the factory. He took her into his arms and tried to say comforting things about her father, and he too reminded her that Miles had been very ill.

'What am I to do about Caro?'

'You haven't told her yet?'

'No, I just couldn't think about it last night.'

'Leave it for a few days. If she sees you so upset, she will be too. She's feeling better about losing her father though, isn't she?'

'Yes, I think so. She's accepted it. She was terrified in the raids and she hated going down to the cellar to sleep, but I think she's forgotten about that now. She's happy and settled at her new school.'

'Then leave it for a week or so until you're feeling stronger yourself. Better, I think, if she doesn't come to the funeral. They're very sad affairs for a little girl. You and I could go together one weekend, take her out of school for a walk round the walls of Chester and have tea in the city.'

'I feel too torn up to be rational now.'

'Of course you do. When you're back on an even keel, we can both talk to her. To do it that way would give us time to concentrate on her and explain gently about her grandpops.'

'Thank you. I'd be glad if you'd come with me.'

Jago organised a cup of coffee for them and then said, 'I know how awful it is to lose one's home. I'm glad Gavin was with you when you heard about it. It's on my conscience now that I let Henrietta put you out of the Rosemead cottage.'

'I've nowhere to live. I don't know where . . .'

'Toby says there's a room you can have in Keeper's Cottage, where the land girls are housed. In times gone by, the gamekeeper used to live there and it has three bedrooms. Toby's asked the two girls to take their things out of the spare room and make the bed up for you. It isn't much, just a room, but it will give you a base for the time being. Do you know where it is?'

She shook her head. 'I'm not sure.'

'It's on the edge of his land. You know Hawthorn Farm?'

'Yes, Rita's place.'

'You can see Keeper's Cottage from there, a hundred yards further down the road.' He gave her the key. 'I'll be able to pick you up in the mornings and bring you to work.'

'Thank you, Jago. You've sorted me out again.'

'I hope this will only be a stopgap. And there's another thing. You'll have lost all your clothes and I know what that means. You'll have nothing but what you packed for a walking holiday in the Lake District.'

She smiled. 'I took a couple of decent dresses for the hotel dining room.'

'Because I was bombed out, I've been allowed enough clothing coupons to re-outfit myself, but I haven't used them yet. I want you to take them. Toby has clothed me.'

'I don't know how to thank you,' she said. 'You really look after me. When I get mine, I'll pay you back.'

'Don't worry about that.'

'I won't be too badly off for clothes, Jago. I left a few things at the back of the wardrobe at Rosemead when I made space for Henrietta's things. I'm very glad I did now, but they're mostly winter things I won't need for a while.'

'Buy yourself another white outfit for your father's funeral,' he said. 'Like the one you had for Charlie. That really suited you.'

'I will.' Nancy made an effort to pull herself together. 'Gavin, will you take me to have a look at that room now, while we're this side of the river?'

'Of course. I'm glad you'll have a roof over your head. I was worried about having to find somewhere for you.'

'We'll find you somewhere better as soon as we can,' Jago told her. 'By the way, Kevin says there wasn't a lot he could salvage from the pub, but he's got a few bits and pieces in the boot of the car. Why don't you check through it and take what you want with you?'

Biting her lip, Nancy did so. Kevin looked at it ruefully. 'It looks worse in the morning light, I'm afraid,' he said.

She asked him to ditch some of it but took three pairs of shoes and a picture of Highland cattle that had hung in her father's living room.

As Gavin drove past Rosemead Cottages Nancy

pointed out number four to him. 'But don't stop,' she said. 'We haven't time now.'

They had no trouble finding Keeper's Cottage. Once inside, Nancy said, 'How will I know which room is to be mine?'

Gavin helped her carry her bits and pieces up the steep narrow staircase. Up on the tiny landing, two doors were closed but the third stood open. The bed had been freshly made up with a white candlewick bedspread, and everything looked neat and bare.

'This'll be it,' Gavin said. 'Quite a good-sized room.'

'A pretty little cottage. I'll be all right here.' But she'd have to share it with two other girls. It wasn't like having a home of her own.

After that Gavin drove her back to Birkenhead to see Mr Hetherington, the vicar at the church Miles had attended, to arrange his funeral.

'I was sorry to hear of his death,' he told Nancy. 'Mr Milton was a great help to me in my work and I counted him a friend.'

Gavin asked if the funeral could take place as soon as possible because he wanted to be there to support Nancy.

'It's a sad time. We're very busy with funerals after these heavy raids, as you can imagine. But Mr Milton did so much for me, and for other people too, that no favour is too great to ask.' It was all arranged for ten in the morning two days hence.

'You can be proud of your dad,' Gavin said when they were back in the car. 'Everybody speaks well of him.'

'I am.' But Nancy had to keep her mind on the things she had to do. Apart from the usual tasks when a relative died, she had to apply urgently for a replacement ration book. By mid-afternoon they were heading back to the Southport shops so she could choose a new white outfit.

She was disappointed to find that only austerity clothes were available, which meant two or three basic styles that were skimpily cut to be economical on cloth. They were available in all sizes and several colours, but not white. She could have had black but she didn't want that. Gavin picked out a two-piece costume in light blue as being the best on offer.

They had to get up early on the morning of the funeral, but it promised to be a hot day. Nancy decided to wear one of the dresses she'd taken to wear at hotel meals because it would be cooler than the two-piece. It was one Charlie had chosen for her, a fairly formal style in a floral print on a peach silk background. Dad had told her he liked her in it. She had no hat, so went hatless.

When they reached the church, Nancy saw many faces she recognised. Toby and Jago were there, as well as Kevin and his brother, the barmaids, and many customers of the Lord Nelson. She felt surrounded by friends.

It was a traditional service that would have pleased her father. His favourite hymns were sung and the vicar extolled at length his work for the church. Afterwards, in his gentle manner, Mr Hetherington told her he'd arranged for Alma's funeral to follow. Nancy decided she'd like to stay for that, as did most of the other mourners.

Gavin gripped her hand and stood stalwartly beside her throughout. If she'd needed confirmation that he loved her, the way he was trying to help and support her provided it.

'We've still got five days' holiday,' Gavin said. 'Would you like to go away again?'

Nancy told herself she must try to put the horror of the last few days out of her mind and help Gavin enjoy what was left of the time they could spend together. It was a very precious interlude because she didn't know how long it would be before she saw him again – if she ever did.

'The Lake District was lovely, but it'll stay in my memory as the place where I heard Dad had been killed,' she said.

'What about the Peak District, then? We don't have all that much time left and it isn't as far. We can still have long walks and enjoy the little towns.'

So they resumed their holiday, but for Nancy the fun had gone out of it. Gavin too had lost the joy he'd had in the earlier days. She was living in dread of parting from him. As the days ticked away she found herself counting the hours. On the last day, he drove her back to Keeper's

Cottage to drop her suitcase, then took the MG to the sausage factory car park from where Kevin was going to take it to Toby's barn. He said he'd put it up on blocks for the duration.

Gavin had changed into his uniform to travel back by train to Hawkinge. Nancy felt terrible as she went with him to the station. They'd been saying their goodbyes since the previous day and neither had much more to say. She studied him, knowing she'd want to remember him over the coming months, a tall slim figure standing with his shoulders back in his air force blue, his dark eyes showing the same agony of parting she was feeling herself.

She'd found love again, but this time there was a sense of finality about having to say goodbye to him like this. She might never see him again. He, like so many others, could be killed.

He was catching the London train and the station was thronged with service personnel in uniform saying goodbye to their loved ones. The guard blew his whistle, a last hasty kiss, a slamming of train doors and the train shunted away. Gavin hung out of the window and waved until the train turned a corner. Then there was nothing but the deep void he'd left.

CHAPTER THIRTY-ONE

NANCY TOLD HERSELF she'd settled in at the cottage she shared with the land girls, Mabel and Connie. She found them friendly and welcoming, but they were always talking about clothes or boyfriends and were out and about almost every night. They asked Nancy to go with them to dances or the pictures in Southport, but she wouldn't. She felt a lot older than they were. She wasn't looking for entertainment and more men friends, she just wanted Gavin.

It meant she often had the cottage to herself in the evenings, but she was also often woken in the middle of the night when they came home. The girls were expected to start work in Toby's market garden at eight thirty in the mornings and Nancy found they were all getting up together, which meant they were competing to wash in the kitchen sink at the same time. She solved her problem by taking a bowl of water upstairs to her room each night.

Usually the land girls were setting off on their bikes

when Jago and Kevin came to pick Nancy up for work. One day Kevin was a little later than usual and he was alone.

'Do you feel all right, Nancy?' he asked as she got into the passenger seat of the company Ford. 'Jago was taken ill last night. We sent for the doctor and he came out to see him about ten o'clock.'

'Heavens. How is he?'

'I'm worried about him. He has pneumonia and is confined to bed. He's on M and B sulphonamides and has been told not to go back to work for at least two weeks. The doctor thinks he went back too soon after having flu.'

Nancy was concerned. 'He looked ill then. I knew he should have stayed at home.'

'He says he'll ring you at the office. He wants you to keep him in touch with what's going on there.'

'I will, but that means he isn't going to rest now.'

'He can't rest if he doesn't know what's going on. He imagines the worst, and that's not the only problem. Toby isn't well either; he's caught Jago's flu. I'm to do any urgent driving for the transport manager but liaise with you and take you back to check on Henrietta by mid-afternoon at the latest.'

'Oh Lord, this flu must be very infectious.'

'It's caught us at a bad time. We're all feeling low, aren't we? What with the blitz and the war in general.'

Nancy sighed. She was still too close to her father's

death not to get emotional about it; that and the dreadful wasteful loss of the Lord Nelson and of Carrington Place. She was feeling lower than low herself. 'Are you all right, Kev?'

He groaned. 'I'm not sure. I've got a bit of a sore throat but I have lots of those. It might be nothing.'

Nancy was afraid they were all sinking. That morning at work, several staff were off sick. She and Jill Jones opened and sorted the post, and found a letter from Miss Farthing regretting that she'd be unable to return to work because finding another house or flat was proving impossible.

'It's as well you're here,' Jill told Nancy.

By the time Jago rang, Nancy was able to bring him up to date. He dictated a few letters over the phone, but he sounded weary and a bit breathless.

'Put stamps on the envelopes and give them to Kevin so I can sign them,' he said. 'Toby and Colin have put together another box of food for Henrietta but neither of them is well. Colin has given it to the land girls. I'll have to ask you to deliver it and see if there's anything else she needs. Would you mind?'

Nancy shivered. She wanted to stay as far away from Henrietta as she could, but if Jago and Toby were ill there was nobody else they could ask.

'Of course not,' she said, forcing herself to sound more willing than she felt. She had to do what she could to help Jago.

She ate her lunch with Jill and picked up a packet of sausages to provide an evening meal for herself and the land girls. By four o'clock, Kevin was parking the car outside number four Rosemead Cottages. The curtains were drawn downstairs and the front door was shut.

'Is something up?' Kevin asked. 'They've always had the curtains open before.'

Twice Nancy knocked firmly with no response. 'I haven't brought my key. I didn't think I'd need to.'

Kevin grimaced at her, moved to the window and rapped hard on the glass.

The two elderly spinsters next door came out on their step. Emma Lucas said, 'We've not had sight nor sound of them all day. We hope they're all right.'

Their concern sent another cold shiver down Nancy's spine. 'Gertie,' she called, 'are you there?'

Eventually she heard Gertie's carpet-slippered feet shuffling towards the door. She fumbled with the catch, and as she opened it the Misses Lucas retreated and clicked their front door shut. Gertie was yawning on the step, looking quite shaky.

'Are you all right?' Nancy asked. She expected to hear she'd caught the flu too. 'You don't look yourself.'

Gertie was whispering. 'It's not me, it's Mrs Seymour. I'm so glad you've come. She's been very strange these last few days. I don't know what to do.'

Nancy couldn't believe the mess her cottage was in. Used crockery, food and clothing littered every surface. It looked squalid. The fire had gone out, leaving the grate full of ashes.

'I'd better get the fire going again, Gertie,' Kevin said. 'You'll need it tonight to cook.'

'Where's Henrietta?' Nancy asked, making room to unpack the box on the kitchen table. 'Toby's sent some pork chops for your dinner.'

Gertie's voice wavered. 'Mrs Seymour said the ones he sent last week were tough.'

'Oh, dear.' Kevin gave a wry laugh. 'He wouldn't like that. He's proud of the premium pork he produces.'

'We'll casserole these,' Nancy said briskly. 'That makes all meat tender.' She set about preparing the dish.

Gertie sniffed. 'I should be doing that, not you.' Listlessly she reached for a knife and some carrots.

'It needs to go into the oven soon if it's to be ready in time,' Nancy said. 'So I'm helping. Just do those few carrots and then you could make a pot of tea for us.'

'Yes, she'll be shouting for her tea in a few minutes.'

Kevin had finished clearing out the cinders and had re-laid the fire, but the first flames were just licking round the paper and sticks. 'Better if you use the Primus,' he said. 'It'll take a while before this will boil a kettle.'

'We're both scared of the Primus.' Gertie dabbed her handkerchief at her face.

Kevin filled the kettle. 'Let me show you again how it's done,' he said patiently. 'You light it like this.' Then he turned it out, and made her strike a match and do it under his supervision. He praised her effusively when she managed it.

'The Primus is a good standby,' Nancy told her. 'Without it, if you let the fire go out you can't even have a hot drink.'

'I know.' Gertie's eyes were wet with tears.

Nancy called upstairs. 'Hello, Mother-in-law. Are you all right? We've brought some food and I've got two letters for you.'

She listened, but there was no response. She had to make sure Henrietta was all right before she could leave. When the tea was ready she poured a cup and took it upstairs, where she knocked on the bedroom door and opened it.

Henrietta was indignant. 'If you don't mind, I'm just getting up.' She was sitting on the bed pulling her cardigan on. 'I haven't been sleeping well at night and it makes me nod off during the day.'

'I've brought you a cup of tea and two letters,' Nancy said.

'You know I don't drink that stuff. We've run out of Earl Grey.'

'Oh, dear.' She was already getting on Nancy's nerves. 'Did you let Jago know?'

'Of course I did. Hasn't he sent me some more?'

'Not today. I've just unpacked everything.' Nancy went on to tell her that Jago was ill.

'I don't know if I can get this awful tea down. We've had practically nothing to eat all day. Jago will have to take me out to dinner tonight.'

'Mother-in-law, that's impossible. Jago has pneumonia. I've just explained that Kevin called the doctor out to him at ten o'clock last night.'

'Then Toby . . .'

Nancy sighed; the woman was impossible. 'Toby's gone down with flu too.'

Henrietta had been lying on her bed upstairs and had heard Nancy and Kevin hammering on the door. She tried to listen to what they were saying, but she was too far away to catch much of it. She did wonder whether she should go hurtling downstairs to confront them, but there was no hurry. Better if she let Gertie wring her hands and weep.

She could hear the woman's whining voice now and guessed she was telling them a tale so full of woe it was totally unbelievable. She wanted them to think Gertie was losing her marbles.

Henrietta had been struggling to work out a plan to kill Nancy, but it was proving much harder than for her two earlier victims, because with them she'd had plenty of opportunities to put her plans into action, and nobody knew she had a motive to kill them.

Nancy was different. Henrietta had been too upset with the stupid barmaid to keep a guard on her tongue.

Nancy had done plenty to upset her. First, she'd wormed her way into the family by enticing Charlie to marry her. Then she'd tried to keep Caroline away from her and prevented her from taking the child on holiday. She'd been exceedingly rude and given her mouthfuls of verbal abuse, and finally she'd talked Jago into making her financially independent.

Henrietta had poured out her distress about that on Jago's shoulder, so he knew how she felt about Nancy. He'd made them kiss and make up but that had fooled nobody but the naive barmaid. The other problem was that Nancy had decided not to live here in the cottage with them. She hardly ever came near and when she did she usually brought Jago's lover for support.

Henrietta wasn't prepared to hang for Nancy. Her plans had to have a good chance of success. No, they had to have every chance of success. Her plans must be perfect.

She felt she couldn't improve on the method she'd used for Joseph Digby. A slash at the side of the neck to catch the main artery to the brain so she'd bleed to death before it was possible for anybody to stop it.

Henrietta had kept the knife she'd used on Digby, but unfortunately, when she was bombed out of Carrington Place, it had been lost with everything else. The first thing she'd need was a sharp knife. She'd inspected the contents of the kitchen knife box here, and there were several that might do if they were sharpened up. There were several tools to sharpen them too, but Henrietta had never sharpened anything and didn't know how.

Gertie was really getting on her nerves now. Her plan to deal with her couldn't be simpler. She'd literally drive her mad. It was happening anyway, almost without her doing anything. Gertie had neither physical nor mental strength, and little hold on reality since she'd lost her friend Mrs Trott. She was just a bag of fears and raw nerves that could be twisted so they gnawed away at her reason. Sooner or later she'd be carted off to some asylum or geriatric home. But would that result in Jago's finding another maid to come and look after her? Or would Nancy come back here to live and occupy Gertie's bed? If the latter, she'd have the opportunity to deal with her then.

In the meantime, she needed Gertie to draw Nancy in. Nancy was concerned about her and would tell everybody about Gertie's declining mental state, so they wouldn't be surprised when it happened.

Henrietta felt she was making good progress towards Gertie's demise. There was only one way in or out of the garden and that was through the back door. This morning, when Gertie had gone down to that disgusting place they called the 'little house', she'd locked the back door behind her so she couldn't come back indoors.

It had amused Henrietta to watch her from her bedroom window. Gertie had gone out in her slippers and without a coat. She'd come back and pushed at the door and fumbled with the latch for ages. It had taken her quite a time to realise the door was actually locked.

It had started to rain and Gertie had tried to take shelter in the lavatory, but it was almost impossible to breathe in there for the stink. Henrietta had watched her try the old pig sty alongside it. The air was probably fresher because no pigs had been kept there for decades, but it wasn't possible to stand up inside and there was nothing to sit on. Henrietta knew because she'd had a good look round.

Gertie had come back to thump on the back door and shout to her. She'd put up such a racket, Henrietta had had to let her in. She knew old Mr Wickham on one side was too deaf to hear, but the two old cats on the other side might. She didn't want any stories about what she was doing going back to Jago.

She'd told Gertie the key must have turned in the lock when she'd banged the door going out. Like the fool she was, she'd accepted it.

But her plan for Gertie had its downside. The woman was no longer capable of doing any work; she just writhed in her chair crying all the time. She was dishing up meals that were either burned or half raw and giving Henrietta indigestion. She needed to hurry things along, and her next step was to get some knives sharpened up in readiness.

She'd heard Nancy coming upstairs with her tea and

letters. She'd put them on her bedside table and expected her to be grateful for the service. Now she was turning silently on her heel to go back downstairs.

'Where've you been these last few weeks?' she demanded. At the moment, the only weapon she could use against Nancy was to be nasty to her and try her patience to the limit. It was achieving little, but it went some way towards making Henrietta feel she was getting her own back. 'Gertie and I could both be dead before anyone came to see how we were.'

'I've been away on holiday.'

'Jago told me that, but he also said he was busy in his office. I can see no reason why you should suddenly be given two weeks to swan off with that new boyfriend you've picked up.'

Nancy gave her a dirty look, so she knew that had struck home. The next moment her heels were clattering on the stairs. Henrietta picked up her tea and followed her. She found Kevin grinning at her.

'I didn't think you'd want to see me,' he said. 'We sent Alf twice a week with your food parcels and to run you round the shops.'

'Less of your cheek,' she told him. 'I don't even want to speak to you.' She felt frustrated and bad-tempered. With Nancy away, her plans had made no progress.

Henrietta found the biscuit box and was heading for her favourite armchair when Kevin said, 'Would you prefer cake? Jago's sent one down for you.'

'What is it?' She came back to look. 'Cherry cake? Yes, that looks nice. Cut me a large slice, Gertie.'

Gertie was nearest the cake. She picked up the knife and did as she was asked. Her nerves and shaking hand meant that she crumbled the piece she cut.

'This knife's blunt,' she said, trying to excuse herself.

Henrietta almost laughed out loud. It was so easy to get Gertie to say the right thing. Recently, every time Gertie had tried to cut anything and failed, Henrietta had commiserated with her and told her the knife was blunt and needed to be sharpened.

This time she said, 'Don't be ridiculous. Any knife will cut cake.'

Gertie looked at her in surprise. 'This one's very blunt and needs sharpening.' She wasn't far from tears again.

Kevin was dividing that slice between his plate and Nancy's. He cut another, neater piece for Henrietta.

'It's blunt. It wouldn't cut the carrots for tonight's dinner, would it, Nancy?'

'I'll sharpen it for you,' Kevin said.

Gertie was rattling the knives about in the cutlery drawer. 'They're all blunt. There's another here that's particularly blunt.'

Suddenly Henrietta had another good idea. She'd pretend to be scared of Gertie. She pulled herself up to her full height, waited until Kevin was already grinding away, then bellowed melodramatically, 'Don't sharpen anything.'

When everybody looked at her in surprise, she made her voice a stage whisper. 'Gertie's going to knife me with that when you've gone.' She was backing fearfully to her armchair.

Nancy took her cake over to her. 'No, Mother-in-law,' she said. 'She wouldn't do that.'

'She would. She wants to kill me.' Henrietta clutched at Nancy's hand and did her best to look frightened.

Nancy shivered. 'Has she said so?'

'No, but I know she does. I can see it on her face. I don't feel safe with her. She hates me.'

That pulled Nancy up sharply. It was exactly how she felt about Henrietta. Gertie's round eyes were staring at them in disbelief.

'No, no, never,' she sobbed. 'She knows I couldn't.' She folded her arms on the table and dropped her head on them.

Kevin ground on. When he'd finished sharpening the knives he gave them to Henrietta. To humour her, he said, 'Hide them all from Gertie. Just give her one when she needs to use it. That way you'll feel safe.'

Henrietta took them straight upstairs. She could feel a smile of triumph pulling at her lips and she didn't want Nancy to see it. It was all she could do not to laugh out loud. It had been almost too easy to hoodwink her and Kevin.

What she'd like now was for Kevin to take her out for a run in the car. She shook with silent mirth; she knew

440

very well how to arrange that. When she could assume and hold a reliable look of fear on her face, she went back downstairs. 'I've hidden them. Gertie won't get me now.'

CHAPTER THIRTY-TWO

'THEY AREN'T COPING here,' Kevin whispered to Nancy. They were tidying up at the far end of the living room. 'Too busy fighting each other. Things have come to a sorry pass between these two.'

'They ought to be separated, but what can we do about it?' Nancy replied under her breath.

She knew Henrietta had overheard them when she said, 'You could take me out for dinner. To get away for a while would help settle my nerves.'

'No,' Nancy said firmly. 'We've put a good dinner in the oven for you. It'll be ready on time and the meat won't be tough.'

'I need Kevin to run me into Southport.'

'No,' Nancy told her. 'Kevin finishes work at half past five.' She knew he wanted to get back to Jago.

'I have to get to a chemist. I've run out of my sleeping tablets and I won't be able to sleep tonight unless I get some more. I really need to, Nancy, I'm at the end of my tether here.'

Gertie was clattering the teacups in the sink and pretending to take no notice.

Nancy said quietly to Kevin, 'I'm worried about them. They're both acting strangely. What about it, Kev? Would you mind working on for an extra hour? I'll come with you.'

'For God's sake,' Henrietta exploded. 'Why ask him? It's what he's paid to do. He'll do what he's told.'

'OK,' Kevin said. 'To a chemist's shop. There's one in Formby.'

'I always go to the chemist's in Southport. I need to get something to read, too. I've finished my book. Half an hour in the shops.'

Nancy would have liked Gertie to come too, but what the pair seemed to need most was a break from each other. She'd ring Jago from Southport and, pneumonia or not, unload her worries on him.

Kevin made the fire up while Henrietta got ready. Just as they were leaving, Nancy saw Rita pulling up outside the next door cottage in the farm truck, and shot out to have a word with her.

'Rita, could I ask a favour of you?'

She laughed. 'Depends what it is, doesn't it?'

'The two ladies in my place are at each other's throats. We're taking Henrietta out to give her a break, but poor Gertie . . .'

'I'll ask her in to have a cup of tea with me and Dad,' Rita said. 'Would that help?'

'Oh, yes. A chat with somebody different should make her feel better. Thank you. We won't be long.' She could see Henrietta settling herself on the back seat and hurried to join her.

As they drew into Southport, the late afternoon sun was still bright but Lord Street was no longer busy. Kevin knew where the chemist's was, and pulled up at the shop door.

Nancy got out with Henrietta because there were other big shops near by and she didn't trust her to come straight back to the car. In a few minutes Henrietta came mincing out of the shop on her high heels.

'Home,' Nancy said, holding the car door open for her.

'I can't possibly, not straight away.'

'W. H. Smith's is locking up. You're too late to buy books, Mother-in-law.'

'You don't understand. I'll have to find a ladies' powder room before we go back. I should never have had that second cup of tea before coming out.'

'For heaven's sake,' Kevin said. 'I'll drive like the clappers and get you home in twenty minutes.'

'I couldn't stand all that bouncing around. And then I'd have to go down the garden to that terrible hut. D'you know what Gertie did to me this morning?'

Neither answered.

'I went down the garden and she locked the door and wouldn't let me back in the house for ages, not even when it started raining. I'm scared to go now, in case she does it again, but of course I have to.'

'Take the key out of the lock,' Kevin advised.

'What good would that do?' Henrietta demanded. 'When there are bolts top and bottom on the back door.'

'They're very stiff,' Nancy said. 'I couldn't shift them. I only ever used the key.'

Kevin sighed. 'Where d'you want me to take you?'

'A nice hotel,' Henrietta said.

'There's a car park behind the Scarisbrick,' Nancy said. 'That's the nearest.'

During the three-minute journey Henrietta didn't stop complaining about Gertie. 'She's as mad as a hatter.' She was getting angry. 'You don't seem to understand. That place and that woman will drive me out of my mind too. I've got to get away from there.'

Nancy was beginning to think she was right.

As soon as Kevin pulled up in the car park, Henrietta leapt out of the car and strode rapidly to the back entrance. She was gone in an instant. Nancy ran after her and caught her up at the reception desk in the main lobby.

'At what time d'you start serving dinner?' Henrietta was enquiring.

'At seven o'clock, madam. Do you wish to book a table?'

445

'No, thank you,' Nancy said firmly. 'We can't stay here until seven.'

'Perhaps a glass of sherry in the bar, before we go? Ten more minutes won't make any difference, will it?'

'Yes, it will.' What had got into Henrietta? At that moment, Nancy had an idea. 'Look, there's the ladies' powder room over there. I'll wait here for you.'

As Henrietta minced off, she turned to the reception clerk. 'Do you have guests who stay here permanently?'

'Yes, one or two.'

'Could I have a list of your charges for that?'

A sheet of paper came across the counter. 'These are the charges for full board by the week or by the month. For periods of longer than three months there are special terms, but you'll need to ask the manager about that.'

'Thank you. Do you have a room for tonight?'

'Yes.'

Nancy tried to think. She'd have to ring Jago. She couldn't make decisions like that for Henrietta, but she'd surely prefer to live here rather than at the cottage. At least here she'd have shops and theatres close at hand and there was a bit of life about the place.

She'd need to tell Jago both women were acting strangely and ask if she should book Henrietta in here this evening. But at the same time she wondered if Henrietta would be all right by herself in a strange place. Her behaviour no longer seemed normal.

Nancy gave Jago's telephone number to the clerk

and was waved towards the instrument at the far end of the counter. But as she heard the phone being lifted at Hattongrove, she saw Henrietta was already coming back.

'Hello, Jago, it's Nancy. We're in Southport; Henrietta insisted we bring her here. She's—'

The next moment a strong hand was twisting the receiver out of her grasp and Nancy felt herself being elbowed aside.

'This is Henrietta, Jago.' Her voice was loud, and her cut-glass enunciation meant she could be clearly heard across the reception area. 'I want you to come to the Scarisbrick Hotel immediately. What's that? Yes, Nancy said you were sick. I cannot stay at that cottage any longer. Gertie is trying to kill me.'

Nancy could see other guests turning to look at her. 'She's insane. She's going to knife me. She's got Kevin to sharpen the knives to do it. She's bent on it, I tell you.'

Nancy closed her eyes. They weren't going to welcome Henrietta as a guest here if she didn't stop this. It took superhuman strength to wrench the receiver away from her.

'Jago, things are getting fraught at the cottage. Henrietta's fallen out with Gertie.'

'How dare you?' Henrietta bellowed. 'I was talking to my husband.' In trying to retrieve the receiver she cut Jago off. 'Get him back, I haven't finished.'

'No,' Nancy whispered, urging her away. 'It's too public here. Everybody can hear what you say.'

'Nosy parkers.' Henrietta was indignant. 'Listening to what I was saying.'

'They could hardly avoid hearing you, Mother-in-law.' She led her to a small sofa. 'I've had an idea. How would you like to live here? Permanently, in this hotel?'

Henrietta's face was brightening up. 'Permanently? Is that possible?'

'Yes.' Nancy pushed the list of charges into her hand. 'I wanted to ask Jago if it was all right.'

'Of course it's all right if I want it. I wonder if they have a room for tonight? One with a sea view, or better still a small suite. I'd need a sitting room too, wouldn't I?' Henrietta leapt to her feet and headed back to the reception desk, eagerness in every step. The clerk was attending to someone else and she had to wait.

Suddenly, she turned back to Nancy and gripped her arm. 'No,' she said, 'not tonight. It wouldn't be fair to Gertie to leave her in that place alone, would it?'

Nancy's first feeling was of bewilderment. 'I thought you wanted to get away from her. I thought you were afraid she'd knife you.'

Colour was running up Henrietta's neck and into her cheeks. 'I . . . I feel sorry for her.'

Nancy couldn't believe that. 'Mother-in-law, why don't you ring Jago and tell him you'd like to stay here instead of going back to the cottage? If he's happy for you to do that, it could be—'

'It's not a question of whether Jago is happy. Gertie needs help. She couldn't manage there on her own.'

Nancy saw such a look of malevolence in Henrietta's eyes that she shuddered. Henrietta must be up to something. Nancy pulled herself together and said, 'If you were kinder to Gertie, or even just left her alone to get on with her work, I'm sure things would settle down. Not only that, but Gertie would get your meals to the table in her own time.'

Henrietta remained silent, but she was pursing her lips. Nancy thought she'd been too kind to her. Some plain speaking might help. 'I get the feeling you hassle Gertie, rush her. It bothers her, confuses her, and then . . .'

She saw Henrietta didn't like that. She drew herself up to her full height and said, 'I can assure you, Nancy, I'm doing my best to be patient with Gertie. You don't realise how trying she can be. Ever since we were bombed out . . .' Her eyes were watery and her voice shook. 'It was a terrible shock to us all, but poor Gertie . . .' She took out a lace handkerchief to dab at her eyes. 'Since then she doesn't seem to know what she's doing. She's been quite vindictive and goes out of the way to cause trouble for me. It's as though she blames me because I survived and her friend Mrs Trott did not.'

*

Henrietta sank back on the car seat and closed her eyes. She'd just made a big mistake and it was no good hoping Nancy hadn't noticed, because she'd made it clear that she had.

Of course she'd wanted to stay in Southport. Who wouldn't? The suggestion had taken her by surprise and she'd leapt at it. But of course it didn't fit in with her plan to kill Nancy.

She wiped another tear from her eyes. She'd wanted her plan to be absolutely perfect so that no one would suspect her. She'd done it twice and there was no reason to think she couldn't do it again, but now Nancy was suspicious. She must know she'd much prefer to stay in the hotel.

Henrietta felt she had to speed things up, act now before Nancy had a chance to share her suspicions with anybody else. Either that, or move into the hotel and forget all her plans.

No, she couldn't forget Nancy. It would give her great satisfaction to give her what she deserved. But even if she were at risk of being hanged for it?

She would never let them get her to the gallows. Henrietta knew well enough how she could avoid that.

They returned to the cottage to find Gertie dozing in Henrietta's favourite chair in front of the fire. She vacated it hurriedly and pointed out that she'd washed the new potatoes and shelled the peas Nancy had brought with her.

Nancy checked the casserole. 'It'll be cooked to a turn by seven o'clock,' she assured Henrietta. 'It smells lovely. It's making me feel hungry.'

'I suppose I should be grateful to have anything,' Henrietta retorted.

Gertie was wringing her hands. 'Shall I make us another cup of tea?'

'No, there's no decent tea here. I'll have a glass of sherry.'

While Nancy poured sherry for Henrietta and filled the kettle for Gertie, Kevin made up the fire. Then, feeling she could do no more tonight, Nancy wished them good night and steered Kevin to the front door.

She flopped on to the passenger seat. 'What a day! Those two are exhausting. And I don't understand Henrietta. Why did she suddenly decide to come back to Rosemead? Her face lit up when I first suggested she stay at the Scarisbrick. She was all for it for a few moments, then she seemed to have second thoughts and wanted us to bring her back to the cottage. She's always said she hates being there.'

'I was just glad she came without a fuss.'

'There's another thing. How many times did she tell us she was scared of Gertie? Afraid she'd knife her?'

'Countless.'

'Gertie wouldn't hurt a fly. She's meek and mild and barely weighs seven stone. Henrietta could lift her up by the scruff of her neck if she wanted to. She's twice

Gertie's size. Yet she gave us that story about Gertie locking her out when she went to the loo.'

'She wouldn't dare do such a thing.'

'No. Henrietta's been giving her the runaround for the last forty years. She's always had the upper hand where Gertie's concerned. I get the feeling she despises her because she can order her to do anything.'

'Henrietta is certainly the driving force in that cottage. It doesn't make sense to say she's afraid of Gertie.'

'So why is she doing it? That frightens me. Is she up to some ruse?'

'She just likes to make a fuss, try our patience and be an absolute pain in the neck. She's like that with Jago too. It's her attitude to everyone.'

'Her demands are outrageous, but I think it's more than that. I think she's up to something.' Nancy groaned, 'I'm shattered, Kev. Aren't you?'

'Worse. I don't feel well,' Kevin felt for his handkerchief. 'I reckon I'm in for a dose of that flu.'

'Oh no! Oh, glory be.'

'Looks like you're going to be the last man standing.'

When Nancy reached her lodgings, she found the land girls already home and thinking about their supper. She produced the sausages and Mabel offered to cook them. They'd brought home some of the same new potatoes and peas that she'd delivered to Henrietta.

Nancy felt hot and sticky as well as tired, and took a

bowl of hot water up to her room to have a wash before putting on clean clothes. She felt better when she went down to eat.

'Everybody's ill up at the big house,' the girls told her. 'Colin gave us some sort of fancy tea for Mrs Seymour. He's ill too and doesn't want to go himself, in case he gives her the flu. He said you'd take it.'

'I've just spent half the afternoon with her.'

'She's all right? Not caught it yet?'

'No, she's going strong.'

'There are some peaches from the greenhouse for her as well. He gave us one each to taste and they were absolutely gorgeous.'

The girls were going out. Mabel's boyfriend came to pick them up with a motor bike and sidecar. Nancy slowly cleared up the kitchen and washed up, thinking about the last few days. Her father dead and buried, Gavin on his way abroad to a new war zone, and her colleagues, family and friends decimated by illness. Kevin had been right when he'd said she was the last man standing. There was nobody else to see to Henrietta's needs.

And Henrietta was no longer acting like a normal person. She had access to everything possible in war time; nobody could be kinder or more generous than Jago, but Nancy had never met anybody so discontented. Perhaps Jago had been too generous because he couldn't be a real husband to her and wanted to make it up to her in other ways.

One thing Nancy had learned: providing Henrietta with servants to wait on her hand and foot had turned her into a woman who could do nothing for herself. She was helpless without her staff and made a terrible fuss when things were not to her liking. She was a burden to her family and many were scared of her. Nancy had to admit she was frightened of Henrietta too. She was sure she hadn't given up the idea of prising Caro away from her and bringing her up herself. She had seen bitter animosity on her face and there was something threatening about her. But now she'd have to take care of her until Jago, Toby and Kevin recovered.

She felt edgy and restless and couldn't settle to anything. It was a lovely evening and a pleasure to be outdoors. She decided she might as well cycle back to Rosemead Cottages with Henrietta's Earl Grey tea. If she went now, she needn't go tomorrow. She could just ask Alf to take Henrietta shopping.

Nancy remembered how hard she and Kevin had had to knock to make Gertie hear this afternoon, and slid the cottage key in her pocket in case she needed it. She felt better once she was spinning down the lane. As she neared Hawthorn Farm she could see Rita weeding in the front garden, and Rita had seen her. She waved a greeting and ambled down to the gate.

Nancy dismounted. 'Did you persuade Gertie to have a cup of tea with you and your father?' she asked.

Rita laughed. 'She didn't want to, but I insisted and

marched her into Dad's place. She's a bag of nerves and hardly said a word. Neither did Dad; I had to keep up a monologue. She only stayed ten minutes, and after drinking half a cup she got up and walked off. I don't think it did her much good, Nancy. She's quite strange.'

'She's a poor old soul.' Nancy related her history: how she'd always worked for Henrietta and had no home of her own and her one friend had been killed in the blitz. 'Now she's the only servant Henrietta has and she can't cope with her demands, or life in a country cottage.'

'It's time she retired,' Rita said.

'It is, but it's difficult to know how she'll survive, unless it's in an old people's home.' If Henrietta went to live in a hotel that might be the best course. Nancy knew Jago wouldn't quibble at the cost. 'I'm just going up with some Earl Grey for Henrietta. She's very fussy about everything.'

'Would you drop some soap in for Dad?' Rita asked. 'I forgot to take it when I went.'

'Of course,' Nancy waited for Rita to run and get it from the house; then she got back on her bike. As she freewheeled down the hill and Rosemead Cottages came in view, the last of the evening sun was full on them; most of the doors and windows were open. Mr Wickham was spreadeagled on the bench in front of his cottage smoking his pipe and Miss Jane Lucas was dead-heading the roses growing round her front door.

Nancy leaned her bike against the wall of number

four, where the living-room curtains were tightly drawn again, though she'd opened them on her earlier visit. It seemed strange on this warm evening but at least the window was still open to let in a little air. She took the soap from the basket on her handlebars and sank down on the bench beside Mr Wickham.

'Thank you, love.' The old man seemed pleased to have it. 'Our Rita's got a memory like a sieve. How's your little girl?'

'Caro's fine. She's settled down well and enjoys her new school.'

He was shaking his head. 'It's a very strange custom sending a child away from her mother like that. I wish you were both still living next door.'

Nancy smiled and felt in her pocket for the key to the cottage. She'd heard all this before.

'That's a rum pair we've got living there now, lass,' he said, tamping down his pipe. 'We can't make head nor tail of them.'

At that moment Nancy heard a muffled crash, followed by a scream from inside the cottage.

'They're at it again.' There was horror on Mr Wickham's face. Nancy's mouth went dry as she leapt to her feet and shot the key into the lock. The screaming was going on. She knew it was Gertie.

It was quite dark inside. The fire had burned to a dull glow, and after the bright sun Nancy's eyes took a few moments to adjust.

Henrietta had her back to her and hadn't heard her come in. She was brandishing a knife in each hand. Gertie was huddled against the back door, sobbing and screaming. Steam was rising from the tiled kitchen floor and there were little white balls all over it.

Henrietta advanced towards Gertie. 'You blithering idiot,' she ground out. 'Go on, stab me, I dare you.'

Only then did Nancy notice that Gertie also had a knife in each hand, but she wasn't brandishing them. 'No, let me be. Please, Mrs Seymour, I . . .'

'Go on, I'm telling you to do it.'

'I'd hurt you.'

'I want you to.'

'I can't. You know I can't.'

'Yes you can. Go ahead, cut my arm for me. Make me bleed.'

Nancy's heart lurched, and thudded faster.

Gertie moaned. 'No, Mrs Seymour. Please don't taunt me.'

'Do as you're told, Gertie. Just a light scratch or two.'

Nancy quaked. Why had she come alone with nobody to help her? She'd feared there might be open aggression between them but not with knives, not like this. But she should have guessed. She should have got Alf to drive her here tomorrow.

She swallowed hard. There was a lump the size of a golf ball in her throat. Tomorrow would be too late. This was happening now. When she noticed blood trickling down Gertie's arm she gasped aloud in horror.

Henrietta heard, and turned to see who it was. Nancy was shaking with panic and trying not to let it show. She had to break this up before something dreadful happened. Fear gave her voice a commanding firmness.

'Mother-in-law, stop baiting Gertie. What are you trying to do? Convince us that a frail slip of a woman like her is likely to harm you? It's all a charade, isn't it? Some sort of game?'

Henrietta was bent over with shock, her dark eyes wild with hate. Nancy stared straight into them and forced herself to move towards her. 'Give me those knives. You mustn't bully Gertie like this.'

She stepped on one of the white balls and felt it collapse beneath her foot. She couldn't stop a yelp of surprise, but how silly! She could see now it was a cooked potato. Gertie had somehow tipped the pan over and spilled the contents over the floor.

'What is she trying to do to me?' Gertie's voice was a terrified whisper. 'Is she out of her mind?'

Nancy felt the hairs on the back of her neck lift in horror.

CHAPTER THIRTY-THREE

'THE KNIVES, PLEASE.' Nancy took another step forward.

Henrietta started to laugh, wild shrieks of mad laughter that went on and on. She stepped back into a small puddle of steaming potato water that had gathered on the uneven floor and the laughter changed abruptly to a howl of pain. She was wearing pink satin bedroom mules.

Nancy stepped forward to snatch her slipper off.

'Stay away from me!' Henrietta screamed, backing off and waving the knives at her viciously. Nancy knew she had to take them from her before she did real damage.

'Give them to me,' she insisted. 'The knives, please.'

Henrietta stared venomously, then, suddenly, with a war-like whoop she leapt at her, slashing out with the larger knife.

Nancy heard it swish through the air close to her ear and had time to spring back out of the way. The knife caught her on the arm, cutting the sleeve of her cardigan. It hurt, and she let out a yelp of alarm.

'I'll give you something to howl about,' Henrietta ground out between her teeth, glowering at her again. 'You've asked for all you get, you stupid bitch.'

Gertie's mouth had dropped open, her screaming dying back to an occasional whimper. For a terrified instant, Nancy met her watery gaze. Gertie was looking to her for protection, but what could she do? She'd never been able to cope with Henrietta. She felt an over-whelming urge to turn and run while she still could. It took real effort to stand still and say, 'Henrietta, don't do anything silly. Give me those knives.'

With a manic scream Henrietta shouted, 'Here you are, have them.'

She hurled the knives at Nancy, who had been clutching the back of an armchair for support. One stabbed into the back of her left hand, the other burying itself in the seat.

She couldn't suppress the scream that rose in her throat. It was only partly caused by pain. She couldn't believe her eyes. Gertie had thrown herself at Henrietta and knocked her to the wet floor.

'Don't you hurt Nancy,' Gertie screamed. 'She's doing her best to help you.'

Rigid with shock, Nancy watched her stabbing at Henrietta's prone body with all her frail might, again and again. It took her an age to choke out the words, 'No, Gertie, stop. Stop that!'

Gertie's eyes, wide with terror, stared at Nancy, then she collapsed against her in a torrent of tears.

Nancy felt sick. The knife had not penetrated deeply enough into her hand to stay firmly upright. It was excruciatingly painful each time she moved. She took a deep breath and with a shudder pulled at the knife. One last searing pain and it was out. She tried to tell herself it was only a small cut but tears of pain and terror were clouding her sight. She could see her own blood seeping out. She snatched at a none too clean tea towel and wrapped it round her hand to stem the bleeding.

'Gertie,' she said, trying to keep her voice calm. 'Get out of here now. Go on, this minute. Go next door to Mr Wickham.'

'I'm here,' a wavering male voice said behind her, and for the first time she realised he'd followed her inside. 'Come here, Gertie,' he said. The maid almost fell into his arms and he half dragged her outside.

Nancy saw then that both the Misses Lucas had come in too, and the elderly couple from the end cottage were craning at the door. Henrietta was rolling on the floor and making noises like an animal in pain. Her dress was soaking up the spilled water but it was cooler now.

Nancy's head was swimming. Gertie had dropped the knives she'd used within reach of Henrietta, who now controlled all four of them. Nancy was afraid she'd come on the attack again and wanted to get them away from her.

She went closer. 'Has Gertie really hurt you, Mother-in-law? Can you get up?'

Henrietta's face was distorted with pain and fury; she was breathing heavily. She sounded hysterical. 'Who let this crowd of people in here? Busybodies all of you. Nosy parkers. Get out.'

A shocked Dora Lucas took a step forward. 'You aren't yourself, Mrs Seymour. Let me make you comfortable, dress those cuts . . .'

'Get out, I said. Why are you all watching me? I won't have it.'

Nancy could see several slits in the back of her dress, which was stained with blood, but she wasn't losing too much.

Dora Lucas tried again. 'Mrs Seymour, let me help you.'

Seeing her mother-in-law's attention was deflected, Nancy reached for the knives, but Henrietta saw her and shot out an arm to scoop them closer. Gripped with terror, Nancy stepped back and sensed that the neighbours had too.

'It's not a peep show,' Henrietta bellowed at them. 'Get out, all of you.'

Nancy knew she was losing control. She took a deep breath and made one last desperate effort. 'I've brought you some more Earl Grey tea, Mother-in-law. Would you like me to make you a cup? It would help you calm down.'

'Calm down! Don't you talk to me about calming down!' Henrietta brandished one of the knives at her. 'Get out, Nancy, I don't want your tea and I don't want you here. You're the last person I'd ever want.'

Nancy gave up and headed for the door, pushing everybody out in front of her. If they all got out now nobody else would be hurt. She was about to pull the front door shut when she heard a strange gurgle from Henrietta, followed by a soft moan that sounded like the wind blowing through wintry trees.

She didn't see her do it, but now there was a deep slash on the side of Henrietta's neck and blood was pumping out all over her.

Nancy felt paralysed but she heard Emma Lucas's swift intake of breath.

'Oh, my God!' It was Dora Lucas who rushed forward to do what she could for the patient. 'Nancy, have you got any towels?'

All the neighbours were gathered outside. Nancy was shocked to see Gertie lying flat at the side of the road.

'She fainted, but she's coming round now.' Mr and Mrs Walsh were both talking at once. Towels and bandages were being brought out of every cottage.

Nancy leaned against the front railings, unable to think, unable to do anything to help. Gertie was moving.

They lifted her on to Mr Wickham's bench, where she slumped back in tears.

'I've killed Mrs Seymour,' she sobbed. 'I can't stay with her any more. She won't have me after this. What'll I do? I've nowhere to go.'

'You haven't killed her,' Miss Dickens protested.

'You haven't.'

'Not you,' they chorused.

'No, Gertie,' Nancy said. 'This isn't your fault. I'll see you have somewhere to live. Don't worry about that.'

'Mrs Seymour's gone mad,' Mr Wickham said, and they all nodded. 'Gone crazy. She attacked Nancy, as well as you. We all saw her do it.'

That brought Nancy back to her senses. 'I need to get a doctor to her,' she said. 'I'm going to cycle to Rita's so I can phone for one. And I'll have to let Jago know what's happened.'

'You've got to get yourself and Gertie to a doctor,' Mr Wickham told her.

As Nancy wobbled up the lane the tea towel round her arm came loose. She tried to catch it and push it into the basket on her handlebars on top of the tea and peaches. It seemed another life when she'd only had those to worry about. The cloth fluttered away into the hedge; blood was dripping down her arm and on to her leg. Her hand throbbed, but the wind in her hair cleared her head.

She was feeling weak at the knees by the time she

reached Hawthorn Farm. She almost fell off her bike at the gate. Rita was still weeding in the front garden and came hurrying over. Nancy could hardly get the words out to tell her what had taken place.

'Good gracious. Mrs Seymour stabbed you?' Rita rushed her indoors to the sink; the gush of cold water took away the pain in her hand.

'That's better. I thought she'd cut half your hand off, but it might need stitches. Heavens, Nancy! Your arm too! I'll run you to the hospital.'

'Gertie too, but first phone for an ambulance for Henrietta,' Nancy gasped. 'And I've got to let them know at Hattongrove.'

'What's happened at Rosemead?'

'Henrietta . . . It was awful,' Nancy was doing her best to sound coherent.

What had Henrietta done? Had she deliberately tried to kill herself? Blood had been spurting out everywhere, all over her and all over the floor. She couldn't believe anybody would be able to stem bleeding like that. Certainly not Dora Lucas, even if she had once been a nurse.

Nancy and Rita were waiting for the doctors to finish stitching Gertie's arm when Colin caught up with them in the hospital's casualty department. Nancy had been given painkillers and had her wounds stitched and dressed. Her hand had needed five stitches and her arm three. She was glad to see Colin.

'I'm more or less over the flu now,' he told her. 'I seemed to have a pretty mild dose. Toby's come with me. He's waiting in the car, but he didn't want to come in here in case he's still infectious. He told me to send you home, Rita. Your dad might need you. They're all very churned up at Rosemead Cottages.'

Nancy could hardly bring herself to ask, 'How is Henrietta?' When Rita had driven her back to pick up Gertie the neighbours had been saying that Dora Lucas didn't think she'd make it.

Colin looked grim. 'It seems she turned the knife on herself and slashed the main artery to her brain. Miss Lucas said it would have been impossible for anyone to save her. She bled to death.'

'Oh, Lord!' Nancy felt sick again. 'Why did she do that? It was so unnecessary.'

'Better she killed herself than you and Gertie.' Colin's lips were in a hard straight line. 'It's this war, it's driven her out of her mind.'

The doctor came out to speak to Nancy. 'We're going to admit Miss Bell for observation,' he told her. 'She's confused and unsteady on her feet. We need to make sure she has no other problems.'

'For how long?'

'It depends how she goes on. A few days, say. A little rest will do her no harm.'

'Right,' Colin said. 'Come on, Nancy, I'll drive you home. Do you feel unsteady too? Hang on to me if you do.'

Toby got out of the car when he saw them walking across the car park.

'Jago says I must thank you, Nancy. Everybody says you were very brave.' He took her in his arms and gave her a comforting hug.

'How is he?'

'Still running a temperature. I wouldn't hear of him coming here. He's very upset and worried about what's happened. We all are. We had no idea things were so bad at the cottage.'

They dropped Nancy back to Keeper's Cottage, but even when she lay down in bed in the dark her head whirled with terrifying images and her heart continued to race. It took her a long time to get to sleep.

The next morning, Nancy rang Jago on Rita's phone. 'How are you?' he asked.

'I feel as though I've been in a fight. My arm aches and my hand is sore, but I'm all right. How about you? Toby said you were running a temperature last night.'

'It goes up a bit in the evenings, but I'm feeling better. I think I'm on the mend. We all are except Kevin, and he says he's not too bad. I'm glad you haven't gone to work. I want you to take a few days' rest. You must be in need it. I feel awful having left all the responsibility of looking after Henrietta to you.'

Nancy sighed. 'I should have been able to stop her killing herself. I'm so sorry . . .'

'Nancy, I know just how difficult she could be. Everybody's saying you were marvellous.'

'I could have done better.'

'You mustn't blame yourself. Henrietta was a law unto herself. Nothing you could have done would have stopped her.'

'I did try to take the knives from her, but when she wouldn't part with them I gave up. I'd no idea she'd use them on herself.'

'Nancy, you didn't give up. You were very brave. Will you be all right by yourself today?'

'Yes, of course. But I'm not alone, I'm ringing from Rita's place. If I want more company I can always cycle down to Rosemead and talk to the neighbours. Jago, I'd like to move back into the cottage if that's all right.'

'Of course it's all right, if that's what you want. Aren't you happy at Keeper's Cottage?'

'Yes, I'm happy enough. The girls are very kind – they brought me tea and toast in bed this morning before they went to work. But I'd rather have a cottage to myself and Rosemead feels like home. Then there's Gertie and Caro to think of; there'd be no room for them here.'

'You're right about that, but do you want to have Gertie living with you? I thought perhaps an old people's home for her.'

'I'm sure she'd do her best to fit in with what I want. She's a poor old thing. Since Mrs Trott died, she's been clinging to me. She might have saved my life, Jago. She stopped Henrietta. Threw herself at her when she hurled the knives at me.'

'What? I didn't realise it was that bad!'

'It was awful. She scared the living daylights out of me.'

'Nancy, I should never have put either of you in that position.'

'You didn't know, Jago. None of us did. Look, this has taken a lot out of Gertie. I don't think she'll want to try anything new just yet. I might pop into the hospital today and ask her what she wants to do. Give her the choice.'

'Leave it till tomorrow, Nancy, and I'll send you a car. You can't be fit enough to chase about on your bike now. I'll ring Jill Jones and get her to arrange for a couple of our cleaners to do a few hours' overtime in the cottage. It was looking messy last time I saw it.'

'Thank you. It's looking even worse now.'

The following day, Nancy visited Gertie in hospital. She looked old, frightened and ill. It made Nancy feel even more sorry for her.

'I'm going to move back into the Rosemead cottage,' she told her. 'Do you want to come back and live with me there?'

'Will you – have me?'

'Of course I will. We rub along together all right, don't we? But if you prefer, Jago says he'll look for a nice retirement home for you and pay for it.'

'Everybody's being so kind and generous.'

'You worked for him for thirty years, Gertie. Which is it to be? Do you want time to think about it?'

'No. I'd rather stay with you. You wouldn't have to look after me, and anyway I wouldn't let you. Once I'm on my feet, I'll make myself useful. I'll be able to do housework.'

'Right, then that's what we'll do.'

'But what about the school holidays? When Caro comes home she'll want her bed back, won't she?'

'I'll have the big bedroom and the double bed. She can bunk in with me.'

'But she won't like that. It wouldn't be right.'

'Caro won't mind.'

'If you're sure . . .'

'I am. I'll be back in Rosemead in a day or two. When they say you're well enough to come out, I'll fetch you.'

Nancy cycled straight round to see the cottage and found two cleaners from the factory busy scrubbing it out. She set about clearing out Henrietta's belongings. She had a big collection of jewellery and expensive knick-knacks, like silver clocks, fountain pens and cut-glass powder bowls. Nancy parcelled them up so she could give them to Jago.

Sorting out Henrietta's clothes wasn't so easy. She kept a few things for Gertie that she thought she might find useful, mostly handbags, footwear and hats. Henrietta was so much larger than either herself or Gertie that she

470

was about to give the rest away to the cleaning women, who were nearer Henrietta's build, when she had second thoughts. Henrietta's clothes were in good condition and of expensive materials. In the present time of rationing and shortages, a dressmaker could cut them down to fit others. She boxed the best things away with that in mind. The cleaning women were over the moon when she offered them the corsets and underwear.

'We've never had anything as good as this before,' they said. 'They must have cost a fortune. And there's nothing but utility available now anyway.'

The following morning, Kevin brought the milk down and said Jago had sent him to help her move her things back from Keeper's Cottage and settle in. To her it felt like going home, and she received a great welcome back from the neighbours.

That day she had a letter from Gavin for the first time since he'd gone abroad. It cheered her to be in touch with him again. He wasn't allowed to say where he was stationed and any hints would be blocked out by the censor, so she still didn't know exactly where he was. But he gave her the Forces' Middle East postal address and she guessed he must be supporting the Eighth Army in the desert.

Gertie recovered from her cuts quite quickly, and was soon able to join Nancy, but it took her a long time to regain her strength and peace of mind. She did her best to help with the housework. She'd been in service all her life and knew what was needed to keep the cottage clean and tidy. Now that she had got the hang of the oven, she could put a meal on the table for when Nancy came home from work.

Nancy knew she had some more difficult occasions to face. She'd been dreading Henrietta's inquest, though Jago said it would be no more than a formality. He was right, and she found it easier than she'd expected. The verdict given was suicide while the balance of Henrietta's mind was disturbed.

Because she had committed suicide, Jago had been afraid the vicar at Grindley would not want to bury her in consecrated ground, but nobody had ever refused Henrietta Carrington Seymour anything. Certainly not when she'd been born at Grindley Manor, and had let it be known she wanted to be laid to rest in her family vault.

It rained heavily on the day of the funeral and there were few mourners. Nancy went there with the whole family from Hattongrove. She had been to the country churchyard before, to see Charlie buried in the same grave; she felt she'd taken in very little on that occasion. Today, Charlie was in the forefront of her mind, not Henrietta.

Until, that was, Jago said he'd booked a table for lunch at Grindley Manor, which was now a hotel. Nancy looked round the lovely old Georgian house that had once been Henrietta's home and said to Kevin, 'Very grand, but I think it would have been better for her ego if she'd had a more humble beginning.'

Kevin grinned at her. 'You can say that again.'

Once Jago came back to work Nancy felt things were back to normal. Or as normal as they could be while the war continued. The sausage factory was working overtime but she enjoyed the company and the work. Jago and Toby took her out for a restaurant meal quite often. Kevin and Colin were sometimes included.

Gertie gathered strength and did more about the house. Jago arranged for her to have a car and driver on one afternoon a week to go shopping, otherwise she wouldn't have been able to go out. Gertie thought she was in clover and settled in contentedly.

Caro came home on holiday and was quite happy to spend a good bit of her time with Gertie. She was growing up and enjoying life at school.

Nancy continued to receive letters from Gavin. They confirmed her guess as to where he'd been posted. A few months later, he wrote that he was enjoying a spot of local leave and she reckoned he was in Cairo.

When Monty chased the Germans out of North Africa and the army landed in Italy, Gavin's address changed to a Forces' APO Box in Europe. During the months and years that followed, Nancy listened carefully to wireless reports of the army's advance into Germany, knowing Gavin must be providing them with air support.

The war dragged on in much the same way except that after the heavy May blitz in 1941 air raids tailed off all over the country, and no more bombs were dropped on Merseyside.

Nancy felt all they had to do was keep going and eventually they'd survive this long drawn out war. Then Gavin would come home and they could be together.

CHAPTER THIRTY-FOUR

1945–1947

BERLIN HAD FALLEN and it was more than a week since Hitler's death. Nancy kept hearing the words 'The fighting's over. The war must be won' going round the office. Everybody listened avidly to the wireless but there was no official announcement of the end of hostilities.

'Is it over or isn't it?' they asked each other.

'What I'm looking forward to,' Jill Jones said, 'is being able to buy as many clothes as I can afford. Really fashionable dresses and warm wool coats.'

Zachary McEllery said, 'I'm going to stuff myself with cream cakes. I can't wait to see the shops bulging with real food.'

'You might have quite a wait,' Jago told him. 'After the last war it took a year or so to get back to normal.'

The official announcement came at last, designating Tuesday 8 May as the day the war ended and announcing two days of celebrations. Then came the outpourings of relief, the smiles and the joyous sound of church bells ringing out a message of peace.

They were all war-weary, and had been looking forward to the end of it for so long that many people were saying it was hard to believe. Even Jago did; for Nancy things felt a little flat.

But only until she received a letter from Gavin telling her about the celebrations they'd had in their mess. He was excited and full of hope for the future. Only then did her almost permanent dread that he'd be shot down lift. Gavin had survived the war. They both had.

She imagined he'd be coming home almost immediately, and wrote back asking him when she could expect him. He couldn't give her a date, but said he understood that those who'd served abroad longest would be sent home first.

Will you want to stay in the air force? she asked. The news bulletins were now full of how keen service personnel were to be demobbed. But Gavin belonged to the peacetime service. He'd signed on for sixteen years and his term would not be up until 1947. Then he'd have the option of coming out or signing on for another term.

I haven't quite decided yet, he wrote. But he thought he might try to get a job with a civilian airline.

It wasn't long before Nancy saw signs of dissatisfaction at the factory. It was taking too long for their loved ones to be released from the services. On the home front nothing changed. There was nothing much in the shops and queues built up for every little thing there was. Rations were lower than they'd ever been, and bread was rationed for the first time.

Gertie had kept reasonably well through the later war years, and had seemed happy to potter round the house cleaning and cooking simple meals. Nancy told her she felt lucky to have her help. At weekends she took over the cooking and occasionally put on a buffet lunch on a Sunday for those at Hattongrove.

In 1945, in the early summer, Gertie began to fail. She had less energy and couldn't do as much as she had. Caro came home for her long summer holiday. She was thirteen now and seemed almost grown up. She took over a lot of the chores that Gertie had done. For her last week, Nancy took Caro to Windermere for a holiday. They were golden days, walking in the hills, boating on the lake and having tea in the little cafés.

Caro went back to school and the days grew autumnal. Nancy came home from work one evening to be met by Dora Lucas saying Gertie was not at all well. During that night she ran a temperature and told Nancy she had a pain in her chest when she coughed. She couldn't eat her breakfast porridge. Miss Lucas advised calling out the doctor and said she and Emma would pop in and make her hot drinks and something for lunch. Nancy went to work and telephoned the doctor.

When she returned home that evening, she heard that

the doctor had diagnosed pneumonia. Miss Dickens had cycled into Formby to get the prescribed M&B tablets and a tin of antiphlogistine poultice. Dora Lucas had dosed Gertie with the medicine and applied the poultice to her back. Gertie seemed a little brighter and ate some of the vegetable broth the ladies brought round in a jam jar.

At two o'clock in the morning Nancy had to get up to her and thought she was delirious. Dora had told Nancy to wake her if she was worried, so she ran next door. Dora helped her sponge Gertie down to cool her and make her more comfortable.

At work the next morning, Jago said, 'Sounds like you're working day and night. You can't come to the office and look after Gertie if she's that ill. She'd be better off in hospital.' He telephoned the doctor and made the arrangements.

At lunchtime, Kevin drove Nancy home and they dressed Gertie in Henrietta's cut-down dressing gown and slippers, and packed a bag of nightgowns and bedjackets from the same source. They helped her out to the car, wrapped her in rugs and took her to the cottage hospital.

The next day, Nancy went to see her and take her the magazines the women at Rosemead had collected for her, but she was past being able to read. Nancy sat holding her hand for half an hour.

Gertie recognised her and murmured, 'I'm very

grateful. The last years – happy with you. Thank Dora and Emma – very kind.' She smiled and squeezed her hand, but could say no more.

Two days later she was dead. Nancy learned for the first time that she was eighty-one. Jago told her she'd done a lot to make Gertie's last days happy and he was grateful to her too. The neighbours at Rosemead were quite upset and all of them turned out for her funeral.

Nancy packed up Gertie's belongings and started to clear out her bedroom so it would be ready for Caro to use when she came home at half term. It was hard work taking the rugs downstairs and beating them over the clothes line. As she often did when doing housework, she daydreamed about Gavin. He wrote several times a week and in every letter that came she expected to have news that he was on his way home.

One Saturday morning in October, she was hauling both rugs back upstairs when she heard his letter fall through the door. She rushed down eagerly to get it. Gavin's writing seemed to bounce off the paper with excitement.

I've been given twenty-eight days' leave from the day I land. I can't remember ever having so much time off at once and they want me down at Cherry Hinton when it's over. Will it be long enough for us to get married? I feel we've waited long enough.

Nancy was overwhelmed with joy and had to sink down at her table to get her breath back. She was thrilled, and wanted to write back and tell him so, but there was no time for that. She read on.

I'll be flying into Lyneham and will get the train up to Liverpool. I'll try to phone or send a telegram or something to let you know what time it will get in. Meet me if you can. If you can't don't worry, I know where to find you.

After waiting all this time, Nancy was determined to meet him even if his train arrived in the middle of the night. She wished she'd had time to let him know they'd have her cottage to themselves for the first two weeks of his leave, but after that she was expecting Caro home for her week's half-term break.

She went to work on Monday but was almost too excited to work. Jago immediately rang Toby to ask him to get the MG out of storage so they could use it. 'I'll ask Kevin to charge up its battery and put it in. If he can get the car to start, he can bring it in to the factory workshop for a service.'

At mid-morning Nancy picked up the phone and heard Gavin's voice. She was almost incoherent with excitement. Gavin said he'd landed and was about to set off to the railway station to catch the train to Liverpool. He'd be with her that afternoon. She skipped into Jago's office to tell him.

'I'll arrange for you to have a car and driver so you can get him home in comfort.'

The train was late, as many were these days, and Nancy was nervous. They hadn't seen each other for over four years and she couldn't help wondering if they'd feel the same way about each other. The war must have changed them both.

At last the train chugged in and the compartment doors flew open. Within moments the platform was swarming with service personnel. She was afraid she wouldn't be able to pick him out, but he came bounding up to her, dropped his luggage at her feet and pulled her into his arms.

He was suntanned but thinner. Nancy's heart lurched. Nothing had changed for her. He crushed her to him and his body felt lean and firm.

'Nancy love. It's great to be with you again.' His dark eyes searched her face. 'You look marvellous.'

She led him out to the car, glad that the driver was new and didn't know either of them. Kevin would have welcomed Gavin home with plenty to say. He'd have joined in, when she wanted Gavin to herself. Perhaps Jago had known that.

Once they were home in the cottage, they seemed to take up where they'd left off. Within an hour it was almost as though they'd never been separated.

'I never stopped thinking about you all the time I was away,' Gavin said. 'Let's get married as soon as we can.'

'Yes.' Nancy caught his excitement. 'I'd like to do it while Caro is with us. She thinks it's romantic that I've fallen in love with you.'

Gavin applied for a special licence and he and Nancy spent the first two days deciding what they wanted and making their plans. She wanted to get married in St Bede's in Birkenhead. She'd gone to Sunday school there as a child; the Reverend Desmond Hetherington had married her and Charlie, christened Caro and buried her father. To Nancy it seemed very fitting that he should marry her and Gavin.

She rang him up. He was delighted to hear from her and said he'd be very happy to officiate during the week Caro would be home from school. But at such short notice his only slot would be a weekday morning. Nancy booked it eagerly and said they'd be happy with a simple ceremony with no music and no fuss.

Kevin delivered the MG to the cottage that evening, so he was the first to hear their news. The next morning, Nancy took Gavin into the office to tell Jago.

'You're getting married straight away?' Jago was all smiles. 'That's marvellous news.' He put out a hand to Gavin. 'Congratulations. Nancy will make you a cracking good wife.'

'You've been a wonderful father-in-law to me,' she said. 'You provided help and support when I needed it. We're getting married in church. Will you give me away?'

'Nancy, I'd count it an honour.'

'Lovely, that's settled then. It's going to be a very quiet wedding, just family and a few friends.'

'What about your family?' he asked Gavin.

Gavin smiled. 'I'm looking for a family to join. I have only Nancy and Caro. I did have an aunt in London but she was killed by a flying bomb.'

'Right,' Jago said. 'As your closest relative, Nancy, I'll book a private room at the Adelphi for the reception. You won't have time to arrange everything yourself.'

'Do they still cater for parties?' Gavin asked.

'I can come to some arrangement with them,' Jago laughed. 'Failing all else, I could provide the sausages for sausage and mash.'

Nancy laughed too. 'That would be fine by me.'

'Just tell me how many you're going to invite.'

'I'd like to ask everybody at Rosemead Cottages. They've been so kind to me. Rita and the land girls too.'

'And Jill Jones? You've always been friendly with her.'

'Yes, please.'

The following day, Gavin drove Nancy to Caro's school and they arranged to take her out to tea. She came to the headmistress's office to meet them wearing her plain grey dress, which was kept for Sunday best and part of her school uniform.

'Uncle Gav,' she whooped as soon as she saw him.

Gavin got to his feet and gave her a hug. 'Goodness, how you've grown, Caro. And what lovely plaits.'

Two thick ropes hung nearly to her waist. Her hair, though still blonde, had darkened a little and was now much the same shade as her mother's.

Caro came to kiss her. 'Lovely to see you, Mum.' Her blue eyes danced with excitement but she had no more to say until they left the headmistress's office. Getting Caro into the MG with them was a tight squash. Nancy found her a heavy weight on her knee.

'What d'you expect?' Caro laughed. 'I'm fourteen now and almost grown up.' Fortunately, it was only a mile into town.

'She's doing well at school,' Nancy told Gavin. 'We're all pleased with her.'

'I love St Monica's. I'm form swimming captain this year.'

'Are you still fond of drawing?'

'Yes. I hope to go to art school when I leave.'

Nancy waited until they were sitting at a table in the café before she said, 'You knew Gavin and I were engaged? Well, we've decided not to wait any longer to get married. We've arranged it during your half term, and I want you to be my bridesmaid.'

Halfway through her scream of delight, Caro covered her mouth to cut it off. She beamed at them. 'Uncle Gav, I'm so pleased.'

With mock solemnity he said, 'I'm afraid it means

there'll have to be less of the Uncle Gav. I'll be your stepfather.'

'I'm to call you Dad?'

'If you want to, but plain Gavin will do.' He smiled at her. 'I always envied Charlie his little family and this will make you both my family.'

'There's something else, Caro,' Nancy prompted.

'Yes,' Gavin went on. 'I'd like to adopt you legally. Your mum and I think it would be a good idea. What d'you think, Caro? Would you like me to do that?'

'Oh, yes please, Uncle Gav – Dad, I mean. That would make you my real father, wouldn't it?'

'Well, Charlie Seymour will always be your biological father, nothing can alter that. But he can't look after you now, so I'm going to do it for him.'

She smiled. 'It'll be great to have a father again.'

After they'd taken Caro back to school, Gavin drove Nancy home to Rosemead Cottages. 'You're very quiet,' he said. 'Did I say the right things to Caro?'

'You hit exactly the right note,' she told him. 'No one could have done it better, but there's one more thing.'

'What's that?'

'Well, we're both snuggling down in the same bed, aren't we?'

'And very nice it is.' He smiled at her. 'You wouldn't believe how much I was looking forward to that.'

'Oh, I would. But as Caro's father, you'd want to teach

her that it's wrong to anticipate marriage in that way, wouldn't you?'

'Yes.'

'I want us to set her a good example. She'll be here for two nights before we're married. I want her to sleep with me and you can have her bed.'

'I'm glad it's only for two nights.' He had a wide smile. 'But you're right. I've got to take on the responsibilities of fatherhood. What about afterwards?'

She laughed. 'That'll be fine. Are we going to have a honeymoon? A few days away?'

'What about Caro? We'd have to take her with us, wouldn't we?'

'Why not? Four nights and then we'll be taking her back to school.'

'What about North Wales? If the weather's good we can sit on the beaches or go walking in the hills.'

'She'll think it's hysterical, coming with us on our honeymoon.'

'I'm sure she will. So that's everything arranged?'

'We'll have the real honeymoon first, Gavin. Two whole weeks by ourselves, with nothing to think about but each other.' Nancy sighed with contentment.

A moment later, she said, 'Hang on a minute, I've nothing to wear. There's Caro to think of too. I've spent all my clothing coupons on her school uniform. You saw the dress she has for Sunday afternoons, but that's a bit plain and ordinary if she's going to be my bridesmaid.'

'Oh, dear!' Gavin said. 'My dress uniform will do me, but I'd better have it dry-cleaned.'

'Easy for you,' Nancy said. 'I was thinking about it last night. I have several boxes full of Henrietta's clothes, top quality stuff. I couldn't bear to throw out such beautiful material.'

'Her clothes won't fit you, Nancy.'

'No, but Miss Dickens who lives in the end cottage could make them fit. She's a retired dressmaker. Well, she did retire, but wartime shortages mean she's busier than ever. She made a lovely coat for Miss Lucas from a car rug that an ex-patient gave her. A swing back with a fringed scarf instead of a collar.'

'Is it practical? To make a wedding outfit from . . .'

'Of course it is.'

Once back at the cottage, Nancy led the way upstairs and dragged out some large cardboard boxes from under her bed.

'I remember salvaging these from the ruins of Carrington Place,' she said. 'But I never did look to see what was inside them.'

A dark red velvet cocktail suit caught her eye. 'Look, there's a little velvet cap to match.' She tried it on. It had red feathers that came down the side of her face.

'That really suits you,' Gavin told her. 'Try the suit on.'

The jacket swamped Nancy; she had to hold the skirt up because the waist was larger than her hips and the hem flapped about her ankles.

She gathered the yardage of red velvet round her and hobbled along the row of cottages to see Miss Dickens. Her front door was open and Nancy could hear her treadling hard on her sewing machine before she reached it.

'Of course I can make it fit you,' she said, when Nancy explained what she wanted. 'The material is beautiful quality.' She stroked it. 'You wouldn't be able to buy anything like this now.'

'I'm getting married in a fortnight and I must have a smart outfit.' Nancy was all smiles. 'Can you do it in time?'

'Yes, for you.' She took out her tape measure and ran it over her.

'Come home with me,' Nancy said, 'and see what else I've got. There's Caro to dress too; she's to be my bridesmaid.' Soon they had much of Henrietta's wardrobe spread round the room.

'Caro's outfit will need to tone with yours.' Miss Dickens pushed her iron-grey hair back from her forehead before pulling out a red velvet evening dress.

'Henrietta was fond of red velvet.'

'It's almost the same colour.' Miss Dickens laid them side by side. 'Would that be a good idea?'

'Yes. It's a much thinner and finer material.'

'Silk velvet, too light for a suit.' Miss Dickens held the dress up. It was backless and narrow across the thighs, but fanned out into a wide fishtail at floor length.

'Plenty of material for a full skirt and a plain bodice for Caro. Have you got an old dress of hers that still fits her? I'll need to get the size.'

'The school outfitter measured her and wrote all her measurements down. Would that do?'

'That would be excellent.'

The neighbours at Rosemead were all thrilled to hear that Nancy and Gavin were getting married.

'We're inviting you all to the wedding and to the Adelphi afterwards,' Nancy told them. 'Rita too,' she told Mr Wickham. They all made a fuss of the happy pair, wanting to hear every detail about how they'd met and where Gavin had served in the war.

That evening, Jago called in to say that the Adelphi would be able to do much better than sausage and mash, and Toby was going to provide the flowers both for the church and for the bride's bouquet. He needed to know what colour outfit she'd be wearing.

'Dark red,' Nancy said.

'I hope you aren't planning to take Nancy away once she's your wife,' he said to Gavin. 'I've come to rely on her. I'd be hard pressed to keep on top of the work at the factory without her.'

'I've been trying not to think about what will happen afterwards. I'm to report back to Cherry Hinton, but I've been told to expect a posting elsewhere before long. That makes it difficult to set up home with Nancy.'

Jago looked pleased. 'I'm selfish enough to say I'm

glad to hear that,' he said. 'Are you planning to stay on in the RAF now the war's over?'

'I don't know. The trouble is, flying is all I know and all I've done for years.'

'You were thinking of getting a job with a civilian airline, weren't you, Gavin?' Nancy said.

'I was, but the trouble is, lots of men were called up and trained as pilots. Now they're being demobbed as fast as can be managed. Most are going to want that sort of work, and though the airlines will be expanding I reckon all the jobs will be gone by the time I'm released.' He smiled. 'Already some are deciding to emigrate to Australia. There are lots of opportunities for pilots there.'

Jago pulled a face. 'Would you want to go to Australia?'

'The only thing I really want is to be with Nancy,' Gavin said. 'I don't even want to be flying off on trips to the other side of the world. I'd like a more settled existence now.'

Jago asked, 'What do you want, Nancy?'

'I want to be with Gavin, but I want to stay here too. I've grown roots.'

'If it's a job you want, Gavin, I'd be delighted to offer you one in the sausage factory. I'm thinking of retiring and Nancy will need help. It seemed almost too much to hope you'd want to do that.'

'I'd be very grateful.' A smile was spreading across Gavin's face. 'I quite fancy having a complete change of job when I come out, but I thought it unlikely anybody would give me the chance.'

'That would suit me down to the ground,' Nancy said. 'I want to stay here and bring Caro up near you and Toby. You're our family, Jago.'

'Well, that settles something else. Would you like Lexington Avenue as a wedding present? I've been wondering what to do with it for some time. I think it would suit you and Gavin.'

Nancy was thrilled and almost lost for words. 'Would we like it? Jago, we'd love it. That's more than generous of you.'

'Well, as you know, there's no house on it right now, but it's a good building plot. It's been cleared, and when it's possible to build again we can draw up plans together and I'll put a house on it for you.'

'I don't know how to thank you,' Gavin said. 'That's a wedding present out of this world.'

Nancy hesitated. 'Won't you want to live there again?' she asked.

'No, I'll stay at Hattongrove with Toby. We're happier together.'

'Thank you,' Nancy reached up and kissed his cheek. 'Thank you so much.'

CHAPTER THIRTY-FIVE

NANCY STIRRED IN her sleep. It took her a moment to realise an excited Caro was prodding her.

'Mum, wake up, it's your wedding day. I'm going to make your breakfast.' She was already throwing off the bedclothes. 'Boiled eggs. I'll bring yours up here, you must have it in bed today.'

Nancy clutched at Caro's nightdress. 'No,' she said, 'I'm going to get up as usual. You can boil the eggs but we'll have a leisurely breakfast together downstairs and then we'll get dressed in our finery so we're ready when Kevin comes to pick us up.'

'Mother! Uncle Gav shouldn't see you in your wedding outfit. Not till you're coming down the aisle on Grandpa's arm.'

Nancy threw her arms round her daughter and pulled her back against her pillows. 'It's not going to be that sort of a wedding, love, and anyway, Gavin's already seen my outfit.'

'But not on.'

'Yes, on.'

She could hear approaching footsteps then a rap on the door. 'Are you ladies decent?' Gavin asked. A pause, and he came in bringing a tray. 'Morning tea for us all today.'

'Mum says you've already seen her in her wedding outfit.' Caro was indignant. 'You know you shouldn't have.'

'Oh, dear, I've seen it several times. First when it fitted your grandmother. Then I saw your mum wearing it inside out while Miss Dickens pinned it together to make it fit. And I've seen it since it's been finished.'

'Uncle Gav, that's supposed to bring you bad luck.'

'Not any more, Caro. The war changed all that.'

'Nowadays we have to make our own luck,' Nancy said between sips of tea.

'I've had marvellous luck all my life. Yes, I have, Caro. Think how many pilots were killed in the war, but I survived. And I've been lucky enough to persuade your mother to marry me, and lucky enough to get you as a daughter. That gives me a ready-made family.'

She pulled a face. 'Aren't you afraid your luck will run out on you?'

'It might have done. I wanted us to be married in style. Give your mum a big traditional wedding with all the trimmings,' Gavin said. 'A white gown and all that.'

Nancy knew he was half teasing her. 'My first wedding

to your father was without frills,' she explained. 'We didn't have much time or much money. Gavin wanted to do better than that.'

He laughed. 'We're doing it in a hurry the second time round, and although the war's over the shortages are still with us, so again we can't have the frills.'

'But we will be married,' Nancy said. 'And really that's what matters.'

After breakfast they all got dressed in plenty of time. 'Miss Dickens has done a wonderful job,' Gavin said.

Nancy smiled. 'She said she unpicked the suit, pressed the pieces and cut them smaller. She's kept all the style details.'

'You look absolutely ravishing.'

The little blouson jacket had a stand-up collar and ornamental frogging down the front. It now hugged her slender frame. The narrow skirt came just to her knee where Nancy liked it, and the little hat set the outfit off to perfection.

Caro's dress had turned out well too. Miss Dickens had been able to turn the fishtail, with all its fancy ornamental seaming, into the body of the dress. She'd given it elbow-length sleeves and a Peter Pan collar. Caro did a twirl and the skirt flared out. 'I love this,' she said. 'Grandma always had lovely clothes.'

Miss Dickens had made her a matching headband and she wore her long hair loose.

The cars Jago had organised were arriving in front of

the cottages to take their neighbours across the river. Caro and Gavin went outside too, while Nancy gave her nose a last flick of her powder puff before going out to join them. Mrs Walsh from number six gave Caro a silver horseshoe to carry.

'Left over from my son's wedding,' she told her.

As they waved the cars off, their friends were shouting their best wishes to the bride and groom. Almost immediately, Kevin arrived to drive them to the church, bringing a posy of pink roses for Nancy, a pink rose spray for Caro's dress and a buttonhole for Gavin. Kevin himself was wearing a smart grey lounge suit, not his driver's uniform. He was going to be the best man, because Gavin knew nobody in this part of the country he could ask.

Jago met them outside the church. Nancy thought he looked particularly smart and said so. 'I hope you'll forgive me, but this is the same suit I wore for your first wedding. Like me, it's survived the blitz.' That made Caro giggle.

Jago had told Nancy a few days ago that the vicar's wife, who was the usual organist and had also been Nancy's Sunday school teacher, was trying to get in touch with her, so she'd rung her.

'I was so pleased to hear you were marrying again, Nancy, and we wish you every happiness,' she said. 'I know Desmond had to fit you into a morning session, but I'd like to play the organ for you. I always think music makes a wedding a very special occasion.'

Nancy had stammered her thanks.

'Your father was a good friend to me and my husband and a pillar of the church. He did a lot for us and we owe him a great deal. He'd like you to have music at your wedding. Do you have any favourite pieces?'

Nancy thanked her and they agreed on Mendelssohn's Wedding March from *A Midsummer Night's Dream*, as well as all the traditional wedding hymns.

So now Nancy could hear the organ softly playing a Bach cantata as they reached the church door. In the porch, Jago threaded Nancy's arm through his.

'What do I do now?' Caro demanded. 'All the books said hold the bride's train.'

'Just walk behind us and smile,' her grandfather told her.

The music faded, there was a moment of expectant silence and then, as the first deep-throated organ notes rang out, Nancy felt Jago leading her up the aisle. The congregation was larger than she'd expected, swollen by friends from her Lord Nelson days. Then she saw Gavin turn to steal a glance at her and from that moment on she saw only him.

'That was a magnificent wedding,' Caro told them on the first night of their honeymoon in their Anglesey hotel. 'You thought it would be another no frills wedding, but it was lovely. The organ music lifting the roof and the ladies from Rosemead wiping their eyes and wishing it was them getting married.'

'Everybody wants to put on the best show possible for Nancy,' Gavin smiled.

'And the reception at the Adelphi was out of this world, everybody said so. I tasted champagne, and that was lovely too. I'd like a wedding just like that,' Caro said happily. 'Except I'd like a long white dress and a veil. And a wedding cake.'

'I'll see you have all that,' Gavin told her. 'But for us, in the aftermath of the war, we had the best possible.'

Later, when they were alone in their own room, Gavin said, 'I'm glad we're married, I feel more settled already.'

'So do I. Everything would be absolutely perfect if only you didn't have to go away. I wish I was coming with you.'

'Nancy, you're staying here to secure our future,' Gavin said. 'Two more years, then we'll be together for the rest of our lives.'

To Nancy, it seemed no time at all before Gavin's leave was over, their wedding just a happy memory, and she was all alone in the Rosemead Cottage. She missed him and Caro very much and and spent a goodly amount of her spare time writing letters to them.

In the office, everybody agreed that post-war Britain was a drab place. 'Austerity Britain' they called it, where make do and mend was the order of the day. Even Jill

Jones moaned about the continued shortages. To Nancy it all felt a little flat and she wondered if she'd made a mistake in not going down to Cherry Hinton with Gavin.

It was Jago who took her in hand. One morning in his office, when he'd finished dictating letters and she stood up clutching her shorthand pad and pencil, he said, 'Hang on a moment, Nancy. I want to thank you for shaming Toby and me and making us put a stop to the black market trading. Life has been a lot simpler for us since and it's a weight off our consciences.'

'I'm just glad you gave up before anybody found out.'

'So are we. You've been good for us Seymours, Nancy. In fact, there's another thing: I want to thank you for not deserting me now.'

'Oh, Jago, you don't have to. This is where I want to be.'

'I know times are hard now. Particularly for you, having to wait two more years for married life to begin. But you have a new husband and a new life to build.'

'But I can't start building anything until we're together.'

'Yes you can. You need to think about it, plan carefully for it. If you make the most of this time, you'll find it well worth while.'

'The whole country needs rebuilding, and so do most people's lives.'

Jago smiled. 'Even my life needs replanning. I'll be sixty-five next year and I'd like to retire, but I'm going to do it very gradually over the next few years until you and Gavin can run this factory without me. Caro is my main heir and I know you'll want to do your best for her.'

'Of course. Oh gosh, yes.'

'Not that there's any problem: the sausages are still very much in demand. You understand how the office runs and I'm going to push more and more work on your shoulders. I want you to learn how to run the factory too.'

'I feel lethargic. I need to wake up and get on with things, don't I?'

'Yes, we all feel like that. We're worn down by the war. There's so much you need to do. I'd like to see you learn to drive and get a small car. That'll make you independent and save you no end of time.'

'But a petrol ration . . .'

'Eventually rationing will end, but in the meantime you'll be doing valuable work here and be entitled to a ration. Britain has to be fed.'

Nancy already felt more alive. 'I've always regretted that I didn't get Charlie to teach me.'

'Good. Kevin could teach you now, but you'd learn more quickly from a professional instructor. What if I arrange for you to have driving lessons? You've got a birthday coming soon, haven't you? How old will that make you?'

'Thirty-three. That would be marvellous, Jago. Thank you.'

'Right. Then, if you're to have a house ready when Gavin comes out of the RAF, it's time we started thinking about it.'

'Goodness!' Nancy felt as though he was pumping new life into her.

'The country desperately needs more housing, and it's a government priority, but there's still a shortage of bricks and almost everything else that's needed. A smallish house,' Jago decided for her. 'Three bedrooms should give you enough space to start.'

'Any house will seem roomy after the Rosemead cottage.'

'We'll get an architect to draw up plans in such a way that when things are easier the original building can be made the nucleus of a larger house. Think about what you want, Nancy, and what would suit that site.'

'Jago, I'm overwhelmed. You're almost too generous.'

'The war's over. It's time we got on with our lives.'

Nancy went back to her desk feeling motivated to do exactly that. Silly of her to mope because she couldn't have everything she wanted right away.

Within a few weeks, she heard that Gavin had been posted to Valley in Anglesey, which meant he wasn't all that far away. As he now had the MG again, he could drive to Rosemead Cottages whenever he had time off. Nancy was able to see more of him than she'd expected.

She passed her driving test at the first attempt and

asked Kevin to look out for another second-hand MG Midget. He found her one but it wasn't green. She persuaded Gavin to swop so that she could drive the car that had been Charlie's. Once she had that, she could go to Anglesey at weekends to see him.

She had a great time working out first with Gavin and then with Caro exactly the sort of house they wanted, and she was thrilled to see it being built and gradually taking shape. Then they shared the added joy of finding furniture for it. It was completed the week before Gavin was due to be released from the RAF and come home for good.

Nancy had been kept so busy that she'd hardly had time to miss her husband and daughter, and the two years had flown past. She was simmering with excitement when Kevin helped her move her own and Caro's belongings from the cottage to number eight Lexington Avenue.

On the day she expected Gavin to arrive, she filled their new sitting room with the roses that had continued to flourish in the garden. Tingling with anticipation, she waited and watched at the window. When she saw him pull up on the drive, her heart began to race. She had the front door open before he reached it.

'Welcome home,' she sang out as he swept her into his arms. She pulled him inside, and he pushed the door shut behind him with his foot.

'It was worth waiting for this,' she murmured. 'A

dream house and a loving husband. Our married life starts here.'

She lifted her lips to his. He hugged her tight and his lips clung to hers as though they were drinking life itself.

All That Glistens

Anne Baker

When Hilda Thorpe arrives at Edwin Jardine's jewellery shop in the heart of 1970s Liverpool, he is happy to offer the attractive widow employment. A widower himself, Edwin understands that Hilda needs to work in order to support her teenage daughter Kitty.

Edwin becomes romantically involved with Hilda, but his daughter Jane suspects that Hilda is not all that she seems. As Jane's doubts grow, she and her new fiancé Nick gradually unravel the truth about the past Hilda has created for herself. But Jane fears Edwin will dismiss her revelations as jealous gossip and take a step he may live to regret bitterly.

Kitty is delighted that her mother has found some-one to take care of her and is gleefully enjoying her new-found freedom. But Kitty is in love and wilfully determined to go her own way – and the consequences could be fatal . . .

Praise for Anne Baker's touching Merseyside sagas:

'A stirring tale of romance and passion, poverty and ambition' *Liverpool Echo*

'A heart-warming saga' *Woman's Weekly*

978 0 7553 4079 8

headline

The Best of Fathers

Anne Baker

Mary and Jonty have battled against the odds to be together. Forced to run away when Mary's father disapproved of their relationship, they've managed to build a life for themselves. And their happiness would be complete if they were blessed with a child. Tragically, it seems that's not to be.

Then one night a yacht is shipwrecked near their home. Mary and Jonty rush to the rescue and, amid terrible carnage, they save a baby. Although they know it is wrong, they keep the child. Despite feeling guilty they cherish the little girl they name Charlotte.

Charlotte grows up to be an attractive young woman, devoted to her parents. But fate is to intervene when she decides to train as a nurse in Liverpool. For Liverpool is where her 'real' family lives, and it seems that secrets and lies are to be uncovered – with shocking consequences.

'[A]n immensely enjoyable read' *Coventry Telegraph*

978 0 7553 4077 4

headline

Echoes Across the Mersey

Anne Baker

It's August 1914 and the threat of war is weighing heavily on the people of Liverpool, but not on Sarah Hoxton. For Toby Percival, the dashing son of the owner of the factory where she and her mother work, has told her he loves her. Her mother is afraid they will both lose their jobs but Sarah is prepared to risk everything for Toby's love.

Maurice Percival is furious when he discovers his son is involved with a factory girl and they become locked in a fierce battle. Fired with the fever of patriotism and determined to defy his father, Toby volunteers to fight in the trenches. Sarah is left facing what seem to be insurmountable obstacles but with the help of her friends, family and a strength she never knew she possessed she struggles on while the escalating tragedy of the Great War unfolds. It's not until the fighting is over that she finds peace, and even then it's not where she expected it.

Don't miss Anne Baker's previous Merseyside sagas:

'A heartwarming saga' *Woman's Weekly*

'A delightful tale of love and family' *Woman's Realm*

'Another nostalgic story oozing with atmosphere and charm' *Liverpool Echo*

'Truly compelling . . . rich in language and descriptive prose' *Newcastle Upon Tyne Evening Chronicle*

978 0 7472 6437 8

headline